PARATIME!
COLLECTED PARATIME STORIES

PARATIME!
COLLECTED PARATIME STORIES

H. BEAM PIPER

WILDSIDE PRESS

CONTENTS

HE WALKED AROUND THE HORSES

**(From Baron Eugen von Krutz, Minister of Police, to
His Excellency the Count von Berchtenwald, Chancellor
to His Majesty Friedrich Wilhelm III of Prussia.)**

25 November, 1809

Your Excellency:

A circumstance has come to the notice of this Ministry, the significance of which I am at a loss to define, but, since it appears to involve
matters of State, both here and abroad, I am convinced that it is of suffi-
cient importance to be brought to your personal attention. Frankly, I am
unwilling to take any further action in the matter without your advice.

Briefly, the situation is this: We are holding, here at the Ministry of
Police, a person giving his name as Benjamin Bathurst, who claims to
be a British diplomat. This person was taken into custody by the police
at Perleburg yesterday, as a result of a disturbance at an inn there; he
is being detained on technical charges of causing disorder in a public
place, and of being a suspicious person. When arrested, he had in his
possession a dispatch case, containing a number of papers; these are of
such an extraordinary nature that the local authorities declined to assume any responsibility beyond having the man sent here to Berlin.

After interviewing this person and examining his papers, I am, I must
confess, in much the same position. This is not, I am convinced, any
ordinary police matter; there is something very strange and disturbing
here. The man's statements, taken alone, are so incredible as to justify
the assumption that he is mad. I cannot, however, adopt this theory,
in view of his demeanor, which is that of a man of perfect rationality,
and because of the existence of these papers. The whole thing is mad;
incomprehensible!

The papers in question accompany, along with copies of the various
statements taken at Perleburg, a personal letter to me from my nephew,
Lieutenant Rudolf von Tarlburg. This last is deserving of your particular
attention; Lieutenant von Tarlburg is a very level-headed young officer,
not at all inclined to be fanciful or imaginative. It would take a good
deal to affect him as he describes.

The man calling himself Benjamin Bathurst is now lodged in an apartment here at the Ministry; he is being treated with every consideration, and, except for freedom of movement, accorded every privilege.

I am, most anxiously awaiting your advice, et cetera, et cetera,

Krutz

**(Report of Traugott Zeller, Oberwachtmeister,
Staatspolizei, made at Perleburg, 25 November, 1809.)**

At about ten minutes past two of the afternoon of Saturday, 25 November, while I was at the police station, there entered a man known to me as Franz Bauer, an inn servant employed by Christian Hauck, at the sign of the Sword & Scepter, here in Perleburg. This man Franz Bauer made complaint to *Staatspolizeikapitan* Ernst Hartenstein, saying that there was a madman making trouble at the inn where he, Franz Bauer, worked. I was, therefore, directed, by *Staatspolizeikapitan* Hartenstein, to go to the Sword & Scepter Inn, there to act at discretion to maintain the peace.

Arriving at the inn in company with the said Franz Bauer, I found a considerable crowd of people in the common room, and, in the midst of them, the innkeeper, Christian Hauck, in altercation with a stranger. This stranger was a gentlemanly-appearing person, dressed in traveling clothes, who had under his arm a small leather dispatch case. As I entered, I could hear him, speaking in German with a strong English accent, abusing the innkeeper, the said Christian Hauck, and accusing him of having drugged his, the stranger's, wine, and of having stolen his, the stranger's, coach-and-four, and of having abducted his, the stranger's, secretary and servants. This the said Christian Hauck was loudly denying, and the other people in the inn were taking the innkeeper's part, and mocking the stranger for a madman.

On entering, I commanded everyone to be silent, in the king's name, and then, as he appeared to be the complaining party of the dispute, I required the foreign gentleman to state to me what was the trouble. He then repeated his accusations against the innkeeper, Hauck, saying that Hauck, or, rather, another man who resembled Hauck and who had claimed to be the innkeeper, had drugged his wine and stolen his coach and made off with his secretary and his servants. At this point, the innkeeper and the bystanders all began shouting denials and contradictions, so that I had to pound on a table with my truncheon to command silence.

I then required the innkeeper, Christian Hauck, to answer the charges which the stranger had made; this he did with a complete denial of all of them, saying that the stranger had had no wine in his inn, and that he had not been inside the inn until a few minutes before, when he had burst in shouting accusations, and that there had been no secretary, and no valet, and no coachman, and no coach-and-four, at the inn, and that the gentleman was raving mad. To all this, he called the people who were in the common room to witness.

I then required the stranger to account for himself. He said that his name was Benjamin Bathurst, and that he was a British diplomat, returning to England from Vienna. To prove this, he produced from his dispatch case sundry papers. One of these was a letter of safe-conduct, issued by the Prussian Chancellery, in which he was named and described as Benjamin Bathurst. The other papers were English, all bearing seals, and appearing to be official documents.

Accordingly, I requested him to accompany me to the police station, and also the innkeeper, and three men whom the innkeeper wanted to bring as witnesses.

Traugott Zeller
Oberwachtmeister

Report approved,

Ernst Hartenstein
Staatspolizeikapitan

**(Statement of the self-so-called Benjamin Bathurst, taken
at the police station at Perleburg, 25 November, 1809.)**

My name is Benjamin Bathurst, and I am Envoy Extraordinary and Minister Plenipotentiary of the government of His Britannic Majesty to the court of His Majesty Franz I, Emperor of Austria, or, at least, I was until the events following the Austrian surrender made necessary my return to London. I left Vienna on the morning of Monday, the 20th, to go to Hamburg to take ship home; I was traveling in my own coach-and-four, with my secretary, Mr. Bertram Jardine, and my valet, William Small, both British subjects, and a coachman, Josef Bidek, an Austrian subject, whom I had hired for the trip. Because of the presence of French troops, whom I was anxious to avoid, I was forced to make a detour west as far as Salzburg before turning north toward Magdeburg, where I crossed the Elbe. I was unable to get a change of horses for my coach after leaving Gera, until I reached Perleburg, where I stopped at the Sword & Scepter Inn.

Arriving there, I left my coach in the inn yard, and I and my secretary, Mr. Jardine, went into the inn. A man, not this fellow here, but another rogue, with more beard and less paunch, and more shabbily dressed, but as like him as though he were his brother, represented himself as the innkeeper, and I dealt with him for a change of horses, and ordered a bottle of wine for myself and my secretary, and also a pot of beer apiece for my valet and the coachman, to be taken outside to them. Then Jardine and I sat down to our wine, at a table in the common room, until the man who claimed to be the innkeeper came back and told us that the fresh horses were harnessed to the coach and ready to go. Then we went outside again.

I looked at the two horses on the off side, and then walked around in front of the team to look at the two nigh-side horses, and as I did I felt giddy, as though I were about to fall, and everything went black before my eyes. I thought I was having a fainting spell, something I am not at all subject to, and I put out my hand to grasp the hitching bar, but could not find it. I am sure, now, that I was unconscious for some time, because when my head cleared, the coach and horses were gone, and in their place was a big farm wagon, jacked up in front, with the right front wheel off, and two peasants were greasing the detached wheel.

I looked at them for a moment, unable to credit my eyes, and then I spoke to them in German, saying, "Where the devil's my coach-and-four?"

They both straightened, startled: the one who was holding the wheel almost dropped it.

"Pardon, excellency," he said, "there's been no coach-and-four here, all the time we've been here."

"Yes," said his mate, "and we've been here since just after noon."

I did not attempt to argue with them. It occurred to me—and it is still my opinion—that I was the victim of some plot; that my wine had been drugged, that I had been unconscious for some time, during which my coach had been removed and this wagon substituted for it, and that these peasants had been put to work on it and instructed what to say if questioned. If my arrival at the inn had been anticipated, and everything put in readiness, the whole business would not have taken ten minutes.

I therefore entered the inn, determined to have it out with this rascally innkeeper, but when I returned to the common room, he was nowhere to be seen, and this other fellow, who has given his name as Christian Hauck, claimed to be the innkeeper and denied knowledge of any of the things I have just stated. Furthermore, there were four cavalrymen, Uhlans, drinking beer and playing cards at the table where Jardine and I had had our wine, and they claimed to have been there for several hours.

I have no idea why such an elaborate prank, involving the participation of many people, should be played on me, except at the instigation of the French. In that case, I cannot understand why Prussian soldiers should lend themselves to it.

Benjamin Bathurst

(Statement of Christian Hauck, innkeeper, taken at the police station at Perleburg, 25 November, 1809.)

May it please your honor, my name is Christian Hauck, and I keep an inn at the sign of the Sword & Scepter, and have these past fifteen years, and my father, and his father, before me, for the past fifty years, and never has there been a complaint like this against my inn. Your honor, it is a hard thing for a man who keeps a decent house, and pays his taxes, and obeys the laws, to be accused of crimes of this sort.

I know nothing of this gentleman, nor of his coach, nor his secretary, nor his servants; I never set eyes on him before he came bursting into the inn from the yard, shouting and raving like a madman, and crying out, "Where the devil's that rogue of an innkeeper?"

I said to him, "I am the innkeeper; what cause have you to call me a rogue, sir?"

The stranger replied:

"You're not the innkeeper I did business with a few minutes ago, and he's the rascal I want to see. I want to know what the devil's been done with my coach, and what's happened to my secretary and my servants."

I tried to tell him that I knew nothing of what he was talking about, but he would not listen, and gave me the lie, saying that he had been drugged and robbed, and his people kidnaped. He even had the impudence to claim that he and his secretary had been sitting at a table in that room, drinking wine, not fifteen minutes before, when there had been four noncommissioned officers of the Third Uhlans at that table since noon. Everybody in the room spoke up for me, but he would not listen, and was shouting that we were all robbers, and kidnapers, and French spies, and I don't know what all, when the police came.

Your honor, the man is mad. What I have told you about this is the truth, and all that I know about this business, so help me God.

Christian Hauck

(Statement of Franz Bauer, inn servant, taken at the police station at Perleburg, 25 November, 1809.)

May it please your honor, my name is Franz Bauer, and I am a servant at the Sword & Scepter Inn, kept by Christian Hauck.

This afternoon, when I went into the inn yard to empty a bucket of slops on the dung heap by the stables, I heard voices and turned around, to see this gentleman speaking to Wilhelm Beick and Fritz Herzer, who were greasing their wagon in the yard. He had not been in the yard when I had turned away to empty the bucket, and I thought that he must have come in from the street. This gentleman was asking Beick and Herzer where was his coach, and when they told him they didn't know, he turned and ran into the inn.

Of my own knowledge, the man had not been inside the inn before then, nor had there been any coach, or any of the people he spoke of, at the inn, and none of the things he spoke of happened there, for otherwise I would know, since I was at the inn all day.

When I went back inside, I found him in the common room shouting at my master, and claiming that he had been drugged and robbed. I saw that he was mad and was afraid that he would do some mischief, so I went for the police.

Franz Bauer
his (x) mark

(Statements of Wilhelm Beick and Fritz Herzer, peasants, taken at the police station at Perleburg, 25 November, 1809.)

May it please your honor, my name is Wilhelm Beick, and I am a tenant on the estate of the Baron von Hentig. On this day, I and Fritz Herzer were sent into Perleburg with a load of potatoes and cabbages which the innkeeper at the Sword & Scepter had bought from the estate superintendent. After we had unloaded them, we decided to grease our wagon, which was very dry, before going back, so we unhitched and began working on it. We took about two hours, starting just after we had eaten lunch, and in all that time, there was no coach-and-four in the inn yard. We were just finishing when this gentleman spoke to us, demanding to know where his coach was. We told him that there had been no coach in the yard all the time we had been there, so he turned around and ran into the inn. At the time, I thought that he had come out of the inn before speaking to us, for I know that he could not have come in from the street. Now I do not know where he came from, but I know that I never saw him before that moment.

Wilhelm Beick
his (x) mark

I have heard the above testimony, and it is true to my own knowledge, and I have nothing to add to it.

Fritz Herzer
his (x) mark

(From *Staatspolizeikapitan* Ernst Hartenstein, to His Excellency, the Baron von Krutz, Minister of Police.)

25 November, 1809

Your Excellency:

The accompanying copies of statements taken this day will explain how the prisoner, the self-so-called Benjamin Bathurst, came into my custody. I have charged him with causing disorder and being a suspicious person, to hold him until more can be learned about him. However, as he represents himself to be a British diplomat, I am unwilling to assume any further responsibility, and am having him sent to your excellency, in Berlin.

In the first place, your excellency, I have the strongest doubts of the man's story. The statement which he made before me, and signed, is bad enough, with a coach-and-four turning into a farm wagon, like Cinderella's coach into a pumpkin, and three people vanishing as though swallowed by the earth. But all this is perfectly reasonable and credible, beside the things he said to me, of which no record was made.

Your excellency will have noticed, in his statement, certain allusions to the Austrian surrender, and to French troops in Austria. After his statement had been taken down, I noticed these allusions, and I inquired, what surrender, and what were French troops doing in Austria. The man looked at me in a pitying manner, and said:

"News seems to travel slowly, hereabouts; peace was concluded at Vienna on the 14th of last month. And as for what French troops are doing in Austria, they're doing the same things Bonaparte's brigands are doing everywhere in Europe."

"And who is Bonaparte?" I asked.

He stared at me as though I had asked him, "Who is the Lord Jehovah?" Then, after a moment, a look of comprehension came into his face.

"So, you Prussians concede him the title of Emperor, and refer to him as Napoleon," he said. "Well, I can assure you that His Britannic Majesty's government haven't done so, and never will; not so long as one Englishman has a finger left to pull a trigger. General Bonaparte is a usurper; His Britannic Majesty's government do not recognize any sovereignty in France except the House of Bourbon." This he said very sternly, as though rebuking me.

It took me a moment or so to digest that, and to appreciate all its implications. Why, this fellow evidently believed, as a matter of fact, that the French Monarchy had been overthrown by some military adventurer named Bonaparte, who was calling himself the Emperor Napoleon, and who had made war on Austria and forced a surrender. I made no attempt to argue with him—one wastes time arguing with madmen—but if this man could believe that, the transformation of a coach-and-four into a cabbage wagon was a small matter indeed. So, to humor him, I asked him if he thought General Bonaparte's agents were responsible for his trouble at the inn.

"Certainly," he replied. "The chances are they didn't know me to see me, and took Jardine for the minister, and me for the secretary, so they made off with poor Jardine. I wonder, though, that they left me my dispatch case. And that reminds me; I'll want that back. Diplomatic papers, you know."

I told him, very seriously, that we would have to check his credentials. I promised him I would make every effort to locate his secretary and his servants and his coach, took a complete description of all of them, and persuaded him to go into an upstairs room, where I kept him under guard. I did start inquiries, calling in all my informers and spies, but, as I expected, I could learn nothing. I could not find anybody, even, who had seen him anywhere in Perleburg before he appeared at the Sword & Scepter, and that rather surprised me, as somebody should have seen him enter the town, or walk along the street.

In this connection, let me remind your excellency of the discrepancy in the statements of the servant, Franz Bauer, and of the two peasants. The former is certain the man entered the inn yard from the street; the latter are just as positive that he did not. Your excellency, I do not like such puzzles, for I am sure that all three were telling the truth to the best of their knowledge. They are ignorant common folk, I admit, but they should know what they did or did not see.

After I got the prisoner into safekeeping, I fell to examining his papers, and I can assure your excellency that they gave me a shock. I had paid little heed to his ravings about the King of France being dethroned, or about this General Bonaparte who called himself the Emperor Napoleon, but I found all these things mentioned in his papers and dispatches, which had every appearance of being official documents. There was repeated mention of the taking, by the French, of Vienna, last May, and of the capitulation of the Austrian Emperor to this General Bonaparte, and of battles being fought all over Europe, and I don't know what other fantastic things. Your excellency, I have heard of all sorts of madmen—one believing himself to be the Archangel Gabriel, or Mohammed, or a werewolf, and another convinced that his bones are made of glass, or that he is pursued and tormented by devils—but so help me God, this is the first time I have heard of a madman who had documentary proof for his delusions! Does your excellency wonder, then, that I want no part of this business?

But the matter of his credentials was even worse. He had papers, sealed with the seal of the British Foreign Office, and to every appearance genuine—but they were signed, as Foreign Minister, by one George Canning, and all the world knows that Lord Castlereagh has been Foreign Minister these last five years. And to cap it all, he had a safe-conduct, sealed with the seal of the Prussian Chancellery—the very seal, for I compared it, under a strong magnifying glass, with one that I knew to be genuine, and they were identical!—and yet, this letter was signed, as Chancellor, not by Count von Berchtenwald, but by Baron Stein, the Minister of Agriculture, and the signature, as far as I could see, appeared to be genuine! This is too much for me, your excellency; I must ask to be excused from dealing with this matter, before I become as mad as my prisoner!

I made arrangements, accordingly, with Colonel Keitel, of the Third Uhlans, to furnish an officer to escort this man into Berlin. The coach in which they come belongs to this police station, and the driver is one of my men. He should be furnished expense money to get back to Perleburg. The guard is a corporal of Uhlans, the orderly of the officer. He will stay with the *Herr Oberleutnant*, and both of them will return here at their own convenience and expense.

I have the honor, your excellency, to be, et cetera, et cetera.

Ernst Hartenstein
Staatspolizeikapitan

**(From *Oberleutnant* Rudolf von Tarlburg,
to Baron Eugen von Krutz.)**

26 November, 1809

Dear Uncle Eugen;

This is in no sense a formal report; I made that at the Ministry, when I turned the Englishman and his papers over to one of your officers—a fellow with red hair and a face like a bulldog. But there are a few things which you should be told, which wouldn't look well in an official report, to let you know just what sort of a rare fish has got into your net.

I had just come in from drilling my platoon, yesterday, when Colonel Keitel's orderly told me that the colonel wanted to see me in his quarters. I found the old fellow in undress in his sitting room, smoking his big pipe.

"Come in, lieutenant; come in and sit down, my boy!" he greeted me, in that bluff, hearty manner which he always adopts with his junior officers when he has some particularly nasty job to be done. "How would you like to take a little trip in to Berlin? I have an errand, which won't take half an hour, and you can stay as long as you like, just so you're back by Thursday, when your turn comes up for road patrol."

Well, I thought, this is the bait. I waited to see what the hook would look like, saying that it was entirely agreeable with me, and asking what his errand was.

"Well, it isn't for myself, Tarlburg," he said. "It's for this fellow Hartenstein, the *Staatspolizeikapitan* here. He has something he wants done at the Ministry of Police, and I thought of you because I've heard you're related to the Baron von Krutz. You are, aren't you?" he asked, just as though he didn't know all about who all his officers are related to.

"That's right, colonel; the baron is my uncle," I said. "What does Hartenstein want done?"

"Why, he has a prisoner whom he wants taken to Berlin and turned over at the Ministry. All you have to do is to take him in, in a coach, and see he doesn't escape on the way, and get a receipt for him, and for some papers. This is a very important prisoner; I don't think Hartenstein has anybody he can trust to handle him. The prisoner claims to be some sort of a British diplomat, and for all Hartenstein knows, maybe he is. Also, he is a madman."

"A madman?" I echoed.

"Yes, just so. At least, that's what Hartenstein told me. I wanted to know what sort of a madman—there are various kinds of madmen, all of whom must be handled differently—but all Hartenstein would tell me was that he had unrealistic beliefs about the state of affairs in Europe."

"Ha! What diplomat hasn't?" I asked.

Old Keitel gave a laugh, somewhere between the bark of a dog and the croaking of a raven.

"Yes, exactly! The unrealistic beliefs of diplomats are what soldiers die of," he said. "I said as much to Hartenstein, but he wouldn't tell me anything more. He seemed to regret having said even that much. He looked like a man who's seen a particularly terrifying ghost." The old man puffed hard at his famous pipe for a while, blowing smoke through his mustache. "Rudi, Hartenstein has pulled a hot potato out of the ashes, this time, and he wants to toss it to your uncle, before he burns his fingers. I think that's one reason why he got me to furnish an escort for his Englishman. Now, look; you must take this unrealistic diplomat, or this undiplomatic madman, or whatever in blazes he is, in to Berlin. And understand this." He pointed his pipe at me as though it were a pistol. "Your orders are to take him there and turn him over at the Ministry of Police. Nothing has been said about whether you turn him over alive, or dead, or half one and half the other. I know nothing about this business, and want to know nothing; if Hartenstein wants us to play goal warders for him, then he must be satisfied with our way of doing it!"

Well, to cut short the story, I looked at the coach Hartenstein had placed at my disposal, and I decided to chain the left door shut on the outside, so that it couldn't be opened from within. Then, I would put my prisoner on my left, so that the only way out would be past me. I decided not to carry any weapons which he might be able to snatch from me, so I took off my saber and locked it in the seat box, along with the dispatch case containing the Englishman's papers. It was cold enough to wear a greatcoat in comfort, so I wore mine, and in the right side pocket, where my prisoner couldn't reach, I put a little leaded bludgeon, and also a brace of pocket pistols. Hartenstein was going to furnish me a guard as well as a driver, but I said that I would take a servant, who could act as guard. The servant, of course, was my orderly, old Johann; I gave him my double hunting gun to carry, with a big charge of boar shot in one barrel and an ounce ball in the other.

In addition, I armed myself with a big bottle of cognac. I thought that if I could shoot my prisoner often enough with that, he would give me no trouble.

As it happened, he didn't, and none of my precautions—except the cognac—were needed. The man didn't look like a lunatic to me. He was a rather stout gentleman, of past middle age, with a ruddy complexion and an intelligent face. The only unusual thing about him was his hat, which was a peculiar contraption, looking like a pot. I put him in the carriage, and then offered him a drink out of my bottle, taking one about half as big myself. He smacked his lips over it and said, "Well, that's real brandy; whatever we think of their detestable politics, we can't criticize the French for their liquor." Then, he said, "I'm glad they're sending me in the custody of a military gentleman, instead of a confounded gendarme. Tell me the truth, lieutenant; am I under arrest for anything?"

"Why," I said, "Captain Hartenstein should have told you about that. All I know is that I have orders to take you to the Ministry of Police, in Berlin, and not to let you escape on the way. These orders I will carry out; I hope you don't hold that against me."

He assured me that he did not, and we had another drink on it—I made sure, again, that he got twice as much as I did—and then the coachman cracked his whip and we were off for Berlin.

Now, I thought, I am going to see just what sort of a madman this is, and why Hartenstein is making a State affair out of a squabble at an inn. So I decided to explore his unrealistic beliefs about the state of affairs in Europe.

After guiding the conversation to where I wanted it, I asked him:

"What, *Herr* Bathurst, in your belief, is the real, underlying cause of the present tragic situation in Europe?"

That, I thought, was safe enough. Name me one year, since the days of Julius Caesar, when the situation in Europe hasn't been tragic! And it worked, to perfection.

"In my belief," says this Englishman, "the whole mess is the result of the victory of the rebellious colonists in North America, and their blasted republic."

Well, you can imagine, that gave me a start. All the world knows that the American Patriots lost their war for independence from England; that their army was shattered, that their leaders were either killed or driven into exile. How many times, when I was a little boy, did I not sit up long past my bedtime, when old Baron von Steuben was a guest at Tarlburg-Schloss, listening open-mouthed and wide-eyed to his stories of that gallant lost struggle! How I used to shiver at his tales of the terrible winter camp, or thrill at the battles, or weep as he told how he held the dying Washington in his arms, and listened to his noble last words, at the Battle of Doylestown! And here, this man was telling me that the Patriots had really won, and set up the republic for which they had fought! I had been prepared for some of what Hartenstein had called unrealistic beliefs, but nothing as fantastic as this.

"I can cut it even finer than that," Bathurst continued. "It was the defeat of Burgoyne at Saratoga. We made a good bargain when we got Benedict Arnold to turn his coat, but we didn't do it soon enough. If he hadn't been on the field that day, Burgoyne would have gone through Gates' army like a hot knife through butter."

But Arnold hadn't been at Saratoga. I know; I have read much of the American War. Arnold was shot dead on New Year's Day of 1776, during the storming of Quebec. And Burgoyne had done just as Bathurst had said; he had gone through Gates like a knife, and down the Hudson to join Howe.

"But, *Herr* Bathurst," I asked, "how could that affect the situation in Europe? America is thousands of miles away, across the ocean."

"Ideas can cross oceans quicker than armies. When Louis XVI decided to come to the aid of the Americans, he doomed himself and his regime. A successful resistance to royal authority in America was all the French Republicans needed to inspire them. Of course, we have Louis's own weakness to blame, too. If he'd given those rascals a whiff of grapeshot, when the mob tried to storm Versailles in 1790, there'd have been no French Revolution."

But he had. When Louis XVI ordered the howitzers turned on the mob at Versailles, and then sent the dragoons to ride down the survivors, the Republican movement had been broken. That had been when Cardinal Talleyrand, who was then merely Bishop of Autun, had came to the fore and become the power that he is today in France; the greatest King's Minister since Richelieu.

"And, after that, Louis's death followed as surely as night after day," Bathurst was saying. "And because the French had no experience in self-government, their republic was foredoomed. If Bonaparte hadn't seized power, somebody else would have; when the French murdered their king, they delivered themselves to dictatorship. And a dictator, unsupported by the prestige of royalty, has no choice but to lead his people into foreign war, to keep them from turning upon him."

It was like that all the way to Berlin. All these things seem foolish, by daylight, but as I sat in the darkness of that swaying coach, I was almost convinced of the reality of what he told me. I tell you, Uncle Eugen, it was frightening, as though he were giving me a view of Hell. *Gott im Himmel*, the things that man talked of! Armies swarming over Europe; sack and massacre, and cities burning; blockades, and starvation; kings deposed, and thrones tumbling like tenpins; battles in which the soldiers of every nation fought, and in which tens of thousands were mowed down like ripe grain; and, over all, the Satanic figure of a little man in a gray coat, who dictated peace to the Austrian Emperor in Schoenbrunn, and carried the Pope away a prisoner to Savona.

Madman, eh? Unrealistic beliefs, says Hartenstein? Well, give me madmen who drool spittle, and foam at the mouth, and shriek obscene blasphemies. But not this pleasant-seeming gentleman who sat beside me and talked of horrors in a quiet, cultured voice, while he drank my cognac.

But not all my cognac! If your man at the Ministry—the one with red hair and the bulldog face—tells you that I was drunk when I brought in that Englishman, you had better believe him!

Rudi.

(From Count von Berchtenwald, to the British Minister.)

28 November, 1809

Honored Sir:

The accompanying dossier will acquaint you with the problem confronting this Chancellery, without needless repetition on my part. Please to understand that it is not, and never was, any part of the intentions of the government of His Majesty Friedrich Wilhelm III to offer any injury or indignity to the government of His Britannic Majesty George III. We would never contemplate holding in arrest the person, or tampering with the papers, of an accredited envoy of your government. However, we have the gravest doubt, to make a considerable understatement, that this person who calls himself Benjamin Bathurst is any such envoy, and we do not think that it would be any service to the government of His Britannic Majesty to allow an impostor to travel about Europe in the guise of a British diplomatic representative. We certainly should not thank the government of His Britannic Majesty for failing to take steps to deal with some person who, in England, might falsely represent himself to be a Prussian diplomat.

This affair touches us as closely as it does your own government; this man had in his possession a letter of safe-conduct, which you will find in the accompanying dispatch case. It is of the regular form, as issued by this Chancellery, and is sealed with the Chancellery seal, or with a very exact counterfeit of it. However, it has been signed, as Chancellor of Prussia, with a signature indistinguishable from that of the Baron Stein, who is the present Prussian Minister of Agriculture. Baron Stein was shown the signature, with the rest of the letter covered, and without hesitation acknowledged it for his own writing. However, when the letter was uncovered and shown to him, his surprise and horror were such as would require the pen of a Goethe or a Schiller to describe, and he denied categorically ever having seen the document before.

I have no choice but to believe him. It is impossible to think that a man of Baron Stein's honorable and serious character would be party to the fabrication of a paper of this sort. Even aside from this, I am in the thing as deeply as he; if it is signed with his signature, it is also sealed with my seal, which has not been out of my personal keeping in the ten years that I have been Chancellor here. In fact, the word "impossible" can be used to describe the entire business. It was impossible for the man Benjamin Bathurst to have entered the inn yard—yet he did. It was impossible that he should carry papers of the sort found in his dispatch case, or that such papers should exist—yet I am sending them to you with this letter. It is impossible that Baron von Stein should sign a paper of the sort he did, or that it should be sealed by the Chancellery—yet it bears both Stein's signature and my seal.

You will also find in the dispatch case other credentials, ostensibly originating with the British Foreign Office, of the same character, being signed by persons having no connection with the Foreign Office, or even with the government, but being sealed with apparently authentic seals. If you send these papers to London, I fancy you will find that they will there create the same situation as that caused here by this letter of safe-conduct.

I am also sending you a charcoal sketch of the person who calls himself Benjamin Bathurst. This portrait was taken without its subject's knowledge. Baron von Krutz's nephew, Lieutenant von Tarlburg, who is the son of our mutual friend Count von Tarlburg, has a little friend, a very clever young lady who is, as you will see, an expert at this sort of work: she was introduced into a room at the Ministry of Police and placed behind a screen, where she could sketch our prisoner's face. If you should send this picture to London, I think that there is a good chance that it might be recognized. I can vouch that it is an excellent likeness.

To tell the truth, we are at our wits' end about this affair. I cannot understand how such excellent imitations of these various seals could be made, and the signature of the Baron von Stein is the most expert forgery that I have ever seen, in thirty years' experience as a statesman. This would indicate careful and painstaking work on the part of somebody; how, then, do we reconcile this with such clumsy mistakes, recognizable as such by any schoolboy, as signing the name of Baron Stein as Prussian Chancellor, or Mr. George Canning, who is a member of the opposition party and not connected with your government, as British Foreign secretary.

These are mistakes which only a madman would make. There are those who think our prisoner is mad, because of his apparent delusions about the great conqueror, General Bonaparte, alias the Emperor Napoleon. Madmen have been known to fabricate evidence to support their delusions, it is true, but I shudder to think of a madman having at his disposal the resources to manufacture the papers you will find in this dispatch case. Moreover, some of our foremost medical men, who have specialized in the disorders of the mind, have interviewed this man Bathurst and say that, save for his fixed belief in a nonexistent situation, he is perfectly sane.

Personally, I believe that the whole thing is a gigantic hoax, perpetrated for some hidden and sinister purpose, possibly to create confusion, and to undermine the confidence existing between your government and mine, and to set against one another various persons connected with both governments, or else as a mask for some other conspiratorial activity. Only a few months ago, you will recall, there was a Jacobin plot unmasked at Köln.

But, whatever this business may portend, I do not like it. I want to get to the bottom of it as soon as possible, and I will thank you, my dear sir, and your government, for any assistance you may find possible.

I have the honor, sir, to be, et cetera, et cetera, et cetera,

Berchtenwald

FROM BARON VON KRUTZ, TO THE COUNT VON BERCHTENWALD. MOST URGENT; MOST IMPORTANT. TO BE DELIVERED IMMEDIATELY AND IN PERSON REGARDLESS OF CIRCUMSTANCES.

28 November, 1809

Count von Berchtenwald:

Within the past half hour, that is, at about eleven o'clock tonight, the man calling himself Benjamin Bathurst was shot and killed by a sentry at the Ministry of Police, while attempting to escape from custody.

A sentry on duty in the rear courtyard of the Ministry observed a man attempting to leave the building in a suspicious and furtive manner. This sentry, who was under the strictest orders to allow no one to enter or leave without written authorization, challenged him; when he attempted to run, the sentry fired his musket at him, bringing him down. At the shot, the Sergeant of the Guard rushed into the courtyard with his detail, and the man whom the sentry had shot was found to be the Englishman, Benjamin Bathurst. He had been hit in the chest with an ounce ball, and died before the doctor could arrive, and without recovering consciousness.

An investigation revealed that the prisoner, who was confined on the third floor of the building, had fashioned a rope from his bedding, his bed cord, and the leather strap of his bell pull. This rope was only long enough to reach to the window of the office on the second floor, directly below, but he managed to enter this by kicking the glass out of the window. I am trying to find out how he could do this without being heard. I can assure you that somebody is going to smart for this night's work. As for the sentry, he acted within his orders; I have commended him for doing his duty, and for good shooting, and I assume full responsibility for the death of the prisoner at his hands.

I have no idea why the self-so-called Benjamin Bathurst, who, until now, was well-behaved and seemed to take his confinement philosophically, should suddenly make this rash and fatal attempt, unless it was because of those infernal dunderheads of madhouse doctors who have been bothering him. Only this afternoon they deliberately handed him a bundle of newspapers—Prussian, Austrian, French, and English—all dated within the last month. They wanted they said, to see how he would react. Well, God pardon them, they've found out!

What do you think should be done about giving the body burial?

Krutz

(From the British Minister, to the Count von Berchtenwald.)

December 20th, 1809

My dear Count von Berchtenwald:

Reply from London to my letter of the 28th, which accompanied the dispatch case and the other papers, has finally come to hand. The papers which you wanted returned—the copies of the statements taken at Perleburg, the letter to the Baron von Krutz from the police captain,

Hartenstein, and the personal letter of Krutz's nephew, Lieutenant von Tarlburg, and the letter of safe-conduct found in the dispatch case—accompany herewith. I don't know what the people at Whitehall did with the other papers; tossed them into the nearest fire, for my guess. Were I in your place, that's where the papers I am returning would go.

I have heard nothing, yet, from my dispatch of the 29th concerning the death of the man who called himself Benjamin Bathurst, but I doubt very much if any official notice will ever be taken of it. Your government had a perfect right to detain the fellow, and, that being the case, he attempted to escape at his own risk. After all, sentries are not required to carry loaded muskets in order to discourage them from putting their hands in their pockets.

To hazard a purely unofficial opinion, I should not imagine that London is very much dissatisfied with this dénouement. His Majesty's government are a hard-headed and matter-of-fact set of gentry who do not relish mysteries, least of all mysteries whose solution may be more disturbing than the original problem.

This is entirely confidential, but those papers which were in that dispatch case kicked up the devil's own row in London, with half the government bigwigs protesting their innocence to high Heaven, and the rest accusing one another of complicity in the hoax. If that was somebody's intention, it was literally a howling success. For a while, it was even feared that there would be questions in Parliament, but eventually, the whole vexatious business was hushed.

You may tell Count Tarlburg's son that his little friend is a most talented young lady; her sketch was highly commended by no less an authority than Sir Thomas Lawrence, and here comes the most bedeviling part of a thoroughly bedeviled business. The picture was instantly recognized. It is a very fair likeness of Benjamin Bathurst, or, I should say, Sir Benjamin Bathurst, who is King's lieutenant governor for the Crown Colony of Georgia. As Sir Thomas Lawrence did his portrait a few years back, he is in an excellent position to criticize the work of Lieutenant von Tarlburg's young lady. However, Sir Benjamin Bathurst was known to have been in Savannah, attending to the duties of his office, and in the public eye, all the while that his double was in Prussia. Sir Benjamin does not have a twin brother. It has been suggested that this fellow might be a half-brother, but, as far as I know, there is no justification for this theory.

The General Bonaparte, alias the Emperor Napoleon, who is given so much mention in the dispatches, seems also to have a counterpart in actual life; there is, in the French army, a Colonel of Artillery by that name, a Corsican who Gallicized his original name of Napolione Buonaparte. He is a most brilliant military theoretician; I am sure some of your own officers, like General Scharnhorst, could tell you about him. His loyalty to the French monarchy has never been questioned.

This same correspondence to fact seems to crop up everywhere in that amazing collection of pseudo-dispatches and pseudo-State papers. The United States of America, you will recall, was the style by which the rebellious colonies referred to themselves, in the Declaration of Philadelphia. The James Madison who is mentioned as the current President of the United States is now living, in exile, in Switzerland. His alleged predecessor in office, Thomas Jefferson, was the author of the rebel Declaration; after the defeat of the rebels, he escaped to Havana, and died, several years ago, in the Principality of Lichtenstein.

I was quite amused to find our old friend Cardinal Talleyrand—without the ecclesiastical title—cast in the role of chief adviser to the usurper, Bonaparte. His Eminence, I have always thought, is the sort of fellow who would land on his feet on top of any heap, and who would as little scruple to be Prime Minister to His Satanic Majesty as to His Most Christian Majesty.

I was baffled, however, by one name, frequently mentioned in those fantastic papers. This was the English general, Wellington. I haven't the least idea who this person might be.

I have the honor, your excellency, et cetera, et cetera, et cetera,

Sir Arthur Wellesley

POLICE OPERATION

"... there may be something in the nature of an occult police force, which operates to divert human suspicions, and to supply explanations that are good enough for whatever, somewhat in the nature of minds, human beings have—or that, if there be occult mischief makers and occult ravagers, they may be of a world also of other beings that are acting to check them, and to explain them, not benevolently, but to divert suspicion from themselves, because they, too, may be exploiting life upon this earth, but in ways more subtle, and in orderly, or organised, fashion."

Charles Fort: "LO!"

John Strawmyer stood, an irate figure in faded overalls and sweat-whitened black shirt, apart from the others, his back to the weathered farm-buildings and the line of yellowing woods and the cirrus-streaked blue October sky. He thrust out a work-gnarled hand accusingly.

"That there heifer was worth two hund'rd, two hund'rd an' fifty dollars!" he clamored. "An' that there dog was just like one uh the fam'ly; An' now look at'm! I don't like t' use profane language, but you'ns gotta *do* some'n about this!"

Steve Parker, the district game protector, aimed his Leica at the carcass of the dog and snapped the shutter. "We're doing something about it," he said shortly. Then he stepped ten feet to the left and edged around the mangled heifer, choosing an angle for his camera shot.

The two men in the gray whipcords of the State police, seeing that Parker was through with the dog, moved in and squatted to examine it. The one with the triple chevrons on his sleeves took it by both forefeet and flipped it over on its back. It had been a big brute, of nondescript breed, with a rough black-and-brown coat. Something had clawed it deeply about the head, its throat was slashed transversely several times, and it had been disemboweled by a single slash that had opened its belly from breastbone to tail. They looked at it carefully, and then went to stand beside Parker while he photographed the dead heifer. Like the dog, it had been talon-raked on either side of the head, and its throat had been slashed deeply several times. In addition, flesh had been torn from one flank in great strips.

"I can't kill a bear outa season, no!" Strawmyer continued his plaint. "But a bear comes an' kills my stock an' my dog; that there's all right! That's the kinda deal a farmer always gits, in this state! I don't like t' use profane language—"

"Then don't!" Parker barked at him, impatiently. "Don't use any kind of language. Just put in your claim and shut up!" He turned to the men in whipcords and gray Stetsons. "You boys seen everything?" he asked. "Then let's go."

* * * *

They walked briskly back to the barnyard, Strawmyer following them, still vociferating about the wrongs of the farmer at the hands of a cynical and corrupt State government. They climbed into the State police car, the sergeant and the private in front and Parker into the rear, laying his camera on the seat beside a Winchester carbine.

"Weren't you pretty short with that fellow, back there, Steve?" the sergeant asked as the private started the car.

"Not too short. 'I don't like t' use profane language'," Parker mimicked the bereaved heifer owner, and then he went on to specify: "I'm morally certain that he's shot at least four illegal deer in the last year. When and if I ever get anything on him, he's going to be sorrier for himself then he is now."

"They're the characters that always beef their heads off," the sergeant agreed. "You think that whatever did this was the same as the others?"

"Yes. The dog must have jumped it while it was eating at the heifer. Same superficial scratches about the head, and deep cuts on the throat or belly. The bigger the animal, the farther front the big slashes occur. Evidently something grabs them by the head with front claws, and slashes with hind claws; that's why I think it's a bobcat."

"You know," the private said, "I saw a lot of wounds like that during the war. My outfit landed on Mindanao, where the guerrillas had been active. And this looks like bolo-work to me."

"The surplus-stores are full of machetes and jungle knives," the sergeant considered. "I think I'll call up Doc Winters, at the County Hospital, and see if all his squirrel-fodder is present and accounted for."

"But most of the livestock was eaten at, like the heifer," Parker objected.

"By definition, nuts have abnormal tastes," the sergeant replied. "Or the eating might have been done later, by foxes."

"I hope so; that'd let me out," Parker said.

"Ha, listen to the man!" the private howled, stopping the car at the end of the lane. "He thinks a nut with a machete and a Tarzan complex is just good clean fun. Which way, now?"

"Well, let's see." The sergeant had unfolded a quadrangle sheet; the game protector leaned forward to look at it over his shoulder. The sergeant ran a finger from one to another of a series of variously colored crosses which had been marked on the map.

"Monday night, over here on Copperhead Mountain, that cow was killed," he said. "The next night, about ten o'clock, that sheepflock was hit, on this side of Copperhead, right about here. Early Wednesday night, that mule got slashed up in the woods back of the Weston farm. It was only slightly injured; must have kicked the whatzit and got away, but the whatzit wasn't too badly hurt, because a few hours later, it hit that turkey-flock on the Rhymer farm. And last night, it did that." He jerked a thumb over his shoulder at the Strawmyer farm. "See, following the ridges, working toward the southeast, avoiding open ground, killing only at night. Could be a bobcat, at that."

"Or Jink's maniac with the machete," Parker agreed. "Let's go up by Hindman's gap and see if we can see anything."

* * * *

They turned, after a while, into a rutted dirt road, which deteriorated steadily into a grass-grown track through the woods. Finally, they stopped, and the private backed off the road. The three men got out; Parker with his Winchester, the sergeant checking the drum of a Thompson, and the private pumping a buckshot shell into the chamber of a riot gun. For half an hour, they followed the brush-grown trail beside the little stream; once, they passed a dark gray commercial-model jeep, backed to one side. Then they came to the head of the gap.

A man, wearing a tweed coat, tan field boots, and khaki breeches, was sitting on a log, smoking a pipe; he had a bolt-action rifle across his knees, and a pair of binoculars hung from his neck. He seemed about thirty years old, and any bobby-soxer's idol of the screen would have envied him the handsome regularity of his strangely immobile features.

As Parker and the two State policemen approached, he rose, slinging his rifle, and greeted them.

"Sergeant Haines, isn't it?" he asked pleasantly. "Are you gentlemen out hunting the critter, too?"

"Good afternoon, Mr. Lee. I thought that was your jeep I saw, down the road a little." The sergeant turned to the others. "Mr. Richard Lee; staying at the old Kinchwalter place, the other side of Rutter's Fort. This is Mr. Parker, the district game protector. And Private Zinkowski." He glanced at the rifle. "Are you out hunting for it, too?"

"Yes, I thought I might find something, up here. What do you think it is?"

"I don't know," the sergeant admitted. "It could be a bobcat. Canada lynx. Jink, here, has a theory that it's some escapee from the paper-doll factory, with a machete. Me, I hope not, but I'm not ignoring the possibility."

The man with the matinee-idol's face nodded. "It could be a lynx. I understand they're not unknown, in this section."

"We paid bounties on two in this county, in the last year," Parker said. "Odd rifle you have, there; mind if I look at it?"

"Not at all." The man who had been introduced as Richard Lee unslung and handed it over. "The chamber's loaded," he cautioned.

"I never saw one like this," Parker said. "Foreign?"

"I think so. I don't know anything about it; it belongs to a friend of mine, who loaned it to me. I think the action's German, or Czech; the rest of it's a custom job, by some West Coast gunmaker. It's chambered for some ultra-velocity wildcat load."

The rifle passed from hand to hand; the three men examined it in turn, commenting admiringly.

"You find anything, Mr. Lee?" the sergeant asked, handing it back.

"Not a trace." The man called Lee slung the rifle and began to dump the ashes from his pipe. "I was along the top of this ridge for about a mile on either side of the gap, and down the other side as far as Hindman's Run; I didn't find any tracks, or any indication of where it had made a kill."

The game protector nodded, turning to Sergeant Haines.

"There's no use us going any farther," he said. "Ten to one, it followed that line of woods back of Strawmyer's, and crossed over to the other ridge. I think our best bet would be the hollow at the head of Lowrie's Run. What do you think?"

The sergeant agreed. The man called Richard Lee began to refill his pipe methodically.

"I think I shall stay here for a while, but I believe you're right. Lowrie's Run, or across Lowrie's Gap into Coon Valley," he said.

* * * *

After Parker and the State policemen had gone, the man whom they had addressed as Richard Lee returned to his log and sat smoking, his rifle across his knees. From time to time, he glanced at his wrist watch and raised his head to listen. At length, faint in the distance, he heard the sound of a motor starting.

Instantly, he was on his feet. From the end of the hollow log on which he had been sitting, he produced a canvas musette-bag. Walking briskly to a patch of damp ground beside the little stream, he leaned the rifle against a tree and opened the bag. First, he took out a pair of gloves of some greenish, rubberlike substance, and put them on, drawing the long gauntlets up over his coat sleeves. Then he produced a bottle and unscrewed the cap. Being careful to avoid splashing his clothes, he went about, pouring a clear liquid upon the ground in several places. Where he poured, white vapors rose, and twigs and grass grumbled into brownish dust. After he had replaced the cap and returned the bottle to the bag, he waited for a few minutes, then took a spatula from the musette and dug where he had poured the fluid, prying loose four black, irregular-shaped lumps of matter, which he carried to the running water and washed carefully, before wrapping them and putting them in the bag, along with the gloves. Then he slung bag and rifle and started down the trail to where he had parked the jeep.

Half an hour later, after driving through the little farming village of Rutter's Fort, he pulled into the barnyard of a rundown farm and backed through the open doors of the barn. He closed the double doors behind him, and barred them from within. Then he went to the rear wall of the barn, which was much closer the front than the outside dimensions of the barn would have indicated.

He took from his pocket a black object like an automatic pencil. Hunting over the rough plank wall, he found a small hole and inserted the pointed end of the pseudo-pencil, pressing on the other end. For an instant, nothing happened. Then a ten-foot-square section of the wall receded two feet and slid noiselessly to one side. The section which had slid inward had been built of three-inch steel, masked by a thin covering of boards; the wall around it was two-foot concrete, similarly camouflaged. He stepped quickly inside.

Fumbling at the right side of the opening, he found a switch and flicked it. Instantly, the massive steel plate slid back into place with a soft, oily click. As it did, lights came on within the hidden room, disclosing a great semiglobe of some fine metallic mesh, thirty feet in diameter and fifteen in height. There was a sliding door at one side of this; the man called Richard Lee opened and entered through it, closing it behind him. Then he turned to the center of the hollow dome, where an armchair was placed in front of a small desk below a large instrument panel. The gauges and dials on the panel, and the levers and switches and buttons on the desk control board, were all lettered and numbered with characters not of the Roman alphabet or the Arabic notation, and, within instant reach of the occupant of the chair, a pistollike weapon lay on the desk. It had a conventional index-finger trigger and a hand-fit grip, but, instead of a tubular barrel, two slender parallel metal rods extended about four inches forward of the receiver, joined together at what would correspond to the muzzle by a streamlined knob of some light blue ceramic or plastic substance.

The man with the handsome immobile face deposited his rifle and musette on the floor beside the chair and sat down. First, he picked up the pistollike weapon and checked it, and then he examined the many instruments on the panel in front of him. Finally, he flicked a switch on the control board.

At once, a small humming began, from some point overhead. It wavered and shrilled and mounted in intensity, and then fell to a steady monotone. The dome about him flickered with a queer, cold iridescence, and slowly vanished. The hidden room vanished, and he was looking into the shadowy interior of a deserted barn. The barn vanished; blue sky appeared above, streaked with wisps of high cirrus cloud. The autumn landscape flickered unreally. Buildings appeared and vanished, and other buildings came and went in a twinkling. All around him, half-seen shapes moved briefly and disappeared.

Once, the figure of a man appeared, inside the circle of the dome. He had an angry, brutal face, and he wore a black tunic piped with silver, and black breeches, and polished black boots, and there was an insignia, composed of a cross and thunderbolt, on his cap. He held an automatic pistol in his hand.

Instantly, the man at the desk snatched up his own weapon and thumbed off the safety, but before he could lift and aim it, the intruder stumbled and passed outside the force-field which surrounded the chair and instruments.

For a while, there were fires raging outside, and for a while, the man at the desk was surrounded by a great hall, with a high, vaulted ceiling, through which figures flitted and vanished. For a while, there were vistas of deep forests, always set in the same background of mountains and always under the same blue cirrus-laced sky. There was an interval of flickering blue-white light, of unbearable intensity. Then the man at the desk was surrounded by the interior of vast industrial works. The moving figures around him slowed, and became more distinct. For an instant, the man in the chair grinned as he found himself looking into a big washroom, where a tall blond girl was taking a shower bath, and a pert little redhead was vigorously drying herself with a towel. The dome grew visible, coruscating with many-colored lights and then the humming died and the dome became a cold and inert mesh of fine white metal. A green light above flashed on and off slowly.

He stabbed a button and flipped a switch, then got to his feet, picking up his rifle and musette and fumbling under his shirt for a small mesh bag, from which he took an inch-wide disk of blue plastic. Unlocking a container on the instrument panel, he removed a small roll of solidograph-film, which he stowed in his bag. Then he slid open the door and emerged into his own dimension of space-time.

Outside was a wide hallway, with a pale green floor, paler green walls, and a ceiling of greenish off-white. A big hole had been cut to accommodate the dome, and across the hallway a desk had been set up, and at it sat a clerk in a pale blue tunic, who was just taking the audio-plugs of a music-box out of his ears. A couple of policemen in green uniforms, with ultrasonic paralyzers dangling by thongs from their left wrists and bolstered sigma-ray needlers like the one on the desk inside the dome, were kidding with some girls in vivid orange and scarlet and green smocks. One of these, in bright green, was a duplicate of the one he had seen rubbing herself down with a towel.

"Here comes your boss-man," one of the girls told the cops, as he approached. They both turned and saluted casually. The man who had lately been using the name of Richard Lee responded to their greeting and went to the desk. The policemen grasped their paralyzers, drew their needlers, and hurried into the dome.

Taking the disk of blue plastic from his packet, he handed it to the clerk at the desk, who dropped it into a slot in the voder in front of him. Instantly, a mechanical voice responded:

"Verkan Vall, blue-seal noble, hereditary Mavrad of Nerros. Special Chief's Assistant, Paratime Police, special assignment. Subject to no orders below those of Tortha Karf, Chief of Paratime Police. To be given all courtesies and co-operation within the Paratime Transposition Code and the Police Powers Code. Further particulars?"

The clerk pressed the "no"-button. The blue sigil fell out the release-slot and was handed back to its bearer, who was drawing up his left sleeve.

"You'll want to be sure I'm *your* Verkan Vall, I suppose?" he said, extending his arm.

"Yes, quite, sir."

The clerk touched his arm with a small instrument which swabbed it with antiseptic, drew a minute blood-sample, and medicated the needle prick, all in one almost painless operation. He put the blood-drop on a slide and inserted it at one side of a comparison microscope, nodding. It showed the same distinctive permanent colloid pattern as the sample he had ready for comparison; the colloid pattern given in infancy by injection to the man in front of him, to set him apart from all the myriad other Verkan Valls on every other probability-line of paratime.

"Right, sir," the clerk nodded.

The two policemen came out of the dome, their needlers holstered and their vigilance relaxed. They were lighting cigarettes as they emerged.

"It's all right, sir," one of them said. "You didn't bring anything in with you, this trip."

The other cop chuckled. "Remember that Fifth Level wild-man who came in on the freight conveyor at Jandar, last month?" he asked.

If he was hoping that some of the girls would want to know, what wild-man, it was a vain hope. With a blue-seal mavrad around, what chance did a couple of ordinary coppers have? The girls were already converging on Verkan Vall.

"When are you going to get that monstrosity out of our restroom," the little redhead in green coveralls was demanding. "If it wasn't for that thing, I'd be taking a shower, right now."

"You were just finishing one, about fifty paraseconds off, when I came through," Verkan Vall told her.

The girl looked at him in obviously feigned indignation.

"Why, you—You *parapeeper*!"

Verkan Vall chuckled and turned to the clerk. "I want a strato-rocket and pilot, for Dhergabar, right away. Call Dhergabar Paratime Police Field and give them my ETA; have an air-taxi meet me, and have the chief notified that I'm coming in. Extraordinary report. Keep a guard over the conveyor; I think I'm going to need it, again, soon." He turned to the little redhead. "Want to show me the way out of here, to the rocket field?" he asked.

Outside, on the open landing field, Verkan Vall glanced up at the sky, then looked at his watch. It had been twenty minutes since he had backed the jeep into the barn, on that distant other time-line; the same delicate lines of white cirrus were etched across the blue above. The constancy of the weather, even across two hundred thousand parayears of perpendicular time, never failed to impress him. The long curve of the mountains was the same, and they were mottled with the same autumn colors, but where the little village of Rutter's Fort stood on that other line of probability, the white towers of an apartment-city rose— the living quarters of the plant personnel.

The rocket that was to take him to headquarters was being hoisted with a crane and lowered into the firing-stand, and he walked briskly toward it, his rifle and musette slung. A boyish-looking pilot was on the platform, opening the door of the rocket; he stood aside for Verkan Vall to enter, then followed and closed it, dogging it shut while his passenger stowed his bag and rifle and strapped himself into a seat.

"Dhergabar Commercial Terminal, sir?" the pilot asked, taking the adjoining seat at the controls.

"Paratime Police Field, back of the Paratime Administration Building."

"Right, sir. Twenty seconds to blast, when you're ready."

"Ready now." Verkan Vall relaxed, counting seconds subconsciously.

The rocket trembled, and Verkan Vall felt himself being pushed gently back against the upholstery. The seats, and the pilot's instrument panel in front of them, swung on gimbals, and the finger of the indicator swept slowly over a ninety-degree arc as the rocket rose and leveled. By then, the high cirrus clouds Verkan Vall had watched from the field were far below; they were well into the stratosphere.

There would be nothing to do, now, for the three hours in which the rocket sped northward across the pole and southward to Dhergabar; the navigation was entirely in the electronic hands of the robot controls. Verkan Vall got out his pipe and lit it; the pilot lit a cigarette.

"That's an odd pipe, sir," the pilot said. "Out-time item?"

"Yes, Fourth Probability Level; typical of the whole paratime belt I was working in." Verkan Vall handed it over for inspection. "The bowl's natural brier-root; the stem's a sort of plastic made from the sap of certain tropical trees. The little white dot is the maker's trademark; it's made of elephant tusk."

"Sounds pretty crude to me, sir." The pilot handed it back. "Nice workmanship, though. Looks like good machine production."

"Yes. The sector I was on is really quite advanced, for an electro-chemical civilization. That weapon I brought back with me—that solid-missile projector—is typical of most Fourth Level culture. Moving parts machined to the closest tolerances, and interchangeable with similar parts of all similar weapons. The missile is a small bolt of cupro-alloy coated lead, propelled by expanding gases from the ignition of some nitro-cellulose compound. Most of their scientific advance occurred within the past century, and most of that in the past forty years. Of course, the life-expectancy on that level is only about seventy years."

"Humph! I'm seventy-eight, last birthday," the boyish-looking pilot snorted. "Their medical science must be mostly witchcraft!"

"Until quite recently, it was," Verkan Vall agreed. "Same story there as in everything else—rapid advancement in the past few decades, after thousands of years of cultural inertia."

"You know, sir, I don't really understand this paratime stuff," the pilot confessed. "I know that all time is totally present, and that every moment has its own past-future line of event-sequence, and that all events in space-time occur according to maximum probability, but I just don't get this alternate probability stuff, at all. If something exists, it's because it's the maximum-probability effect of prior causes; why does anything else exist on any other time-line?"

Verkan Vall blew smoke at the air-renovator. A lecture on paratime theory would nicely fill in the three-hour interval until the landing at

Dhergabar. At least, this kid was asking intelligent questions.

"Well, you know the principal of time-passage, I suppose?" he began.

"Yes, of course; Rhogom's Doctrine. The basis of most of our psychical science. We exist perpetually at all moments within our life-span; our extraphysical ego component passes from the ego existing at one moment to the ego existing at the next. During unconsciousness, the EPC is 'time-free'; it may detach, and connect at some other moment, with the ego existing at that time-point. That's how we precog. We take an autohypno and recover memories brought back from the future moment and buried in the subconscious mind."

"That's right," Verkan Vall told him. "And even without the autohypno, a lot of precognitive matter leaks out of the subconscious and into the conscious mind, usually in distorted forms, or else inspires 'instinctive' acts, the motivation for which is not brought to the level of consciousness. For instance, suppose, you're walking along North Promenade, in Dhergabar, and you come to the Martian Palace Café, and you go in for a drink, and meet same girl, and strike up an acquaintance with her. This chance acquaintance develops into a love affair, and a year later, out of jealousy, she rays you half a dozen times with a needler."

"Just about that happened to a friend of mine, not long ago," the pilot said. "Go on, sir."

"Well, in the microsecond or so before you die—or afterward, for that matter, because we know that the extraphysical component survives physical destruction—your EPC slips back a couple of years, and reconnects at some point pastward of your first meeting with this girl, and carries with it memories of everything up to the moment of detachment, all of which are indelibly recorded in your subconscious mind. So, when you re-experience the event of standing outside the Martian Palace with a thirst, you go on to the Starway, or Nhergal's, or some other bar. In both cases, on both time-lines, you follow the line of maximum probability; in the second case, your subconscious future memories are an added causal factor."

"And when I back-slip, after I've been needled, I generate a new time-line? Is that it?"

Verkan Vall made a small sound of impatience. "No such thing!" he exclaimed. "It's semantically inadmissible to talk about the total presence of time with one breath and about generating new time-lines with the next. *All* time-lines are totally present, in perpetual co-existence.

The theory is that the EPC passes from one moment, on one time-line, to the next moment on the next line, so that the true passage of the EPC from moment to moment is a two-dimensional diagonal. So, in the case we're using, the event of your going into the Martian Palace exists on one time-line, and the event of your passing along to the Starway exists on another, but both are events in real existence.

"Now, what we do, in paratime transposition, is to build up a hyper-temporal field to include the time-line we want to reach, and then shift over to it. Same point in the plenum; same point in primary time—plus primary time elapsed during mechanical and electronic lag in the relays—but a different line of secondary time."

"Then why don't we have past-future time travel on our own time-line?" the pilot wanted to know.

That was a question every paratimer has to answer, every time he talks paratime to the laity. Verkan Vall had been expecting it; he answered patiently.

"The Ghaldron-Hesthor field-generator is like every other mechanism; it can operate only in the area of primary time in which it exists. It can transpose to any other time-line, and carry with it anything inside its field, but it can't go outside its own temporal area of existence, any more than a bullet from that rifle can hit the target a week before it's fired," Verkan Vall pointed out. "Anything inside the field is supposed to be unaffected by anything outside. *Supposed to be* is the way to put it; it doesn't always work. Once in a while, something pretty nasty gets picked up in transit." He thought, briefly, of the man in the black tunic. "That's why we have armed guards at terminals."

"Suppose you pick up a blast from a nucleonic bomb," the pilot asked, "or something red-hot, or radioactive?"

"We have a monument, at Paratime Police Headquarters, in Dhergabar, bearing the names of our own personnel who didn't make it back. It's a large monument; over the past ten thousand years, it's been inscribed with quite a few names."

"You can have it; I'll stick to rockets!" the pilot replied. "Tell me another thing, though: What's all this about levels, and sectors, and belts? What's the difference?"

"Purely arbitrary terms. There are five main probability levels, derived from the five possible outcomes of the attempt to colonize this planet, seventy-five thousand years ago. We're on the First Level—

complete success, and colony fully established. The Fifth Level is the probability of complete failure—no human population established on this planet, and indigenous quasi-human life evolved indigenously. On the Fourth Level, the colonists evidently met with some disaster and lost all memory of their extraterrestrial origin, as well as all extraterrestrial culture. As far as they know, they are an indigenous race; they have a long pre-history of stone-age savagery.

"Sectors are areas of paratime on any level in which the prevalent culture has a common origin and common characteristics. They are divided more or less arbitrarily into sub-sectors. Belts are areas within sub-sectors where conditions are the result of recent alternate probabilities. For instance, I've just come from the Europo-American Sector of the Fourth Level, an area of about ten thousand parayears in depth, in which the dominant civilization developed on the North-West Continent of the Major Land Mass, and spread from there to the Minor Land Mass. The line on which I was operating is also part of a sub-sector of about three thousand parayears' depth, and a belt developing from one of several probable outcomes of a war concluded about three elapsed years ago. On that time-line, the field at the Hagraban Synthetics Works, where we took off, is part of an abandoned farm; on the site of Hagraban City is a little farming village. Those things are there, right now, both in primary time and in the plenum. They are about two hundred and fifty thousand parayears perpendicular to each other, and each is of the same general order of reality."

The red light overhead flashed on. The pilot looked into his visor and put his hands to the manual controls, in case of failure of the robot controls. The rocket landed smoothly, however; there was a slight jar as it was grappled by the crane and hoisted upright, the seats turning in their gimbals. Pilot and passenger unstrapped themselves and hurried through the refrigerated outlet and away from the glowing-hot rocket.

* * * *

An air-taxi, emblazoned with the device of the Paratime Police, was waiting. Verkan Vall said good-by to the rocket-pilot and took his seat beside the pilot of the aircab; the latter lifted his vehicle above the building level and then set it down on the landing-stage of the Paratime Police Building in a long, side-swooping glide. An express elevator took

Verkan Vall down to one of the middle stages, where he showed his sigil to the guard outside the door of Tortha Karf's office and was admitted at once.

The Paratime Police chief rose from behind his semicircular desk, with its array of keyboards and viewing-screens and communicators. He was a big man, well past his two hundredth year; his hair was iron-gray and thinning in front, he had begun to grow thick at the waist, and his calm features bore the lines of middle age. He wore the dark-green uniform of the Paratime Police.

"Well, Vall," he greeted. "Everything secure?"

"Not exactly, sir." Verkan Vall came around the desk, deposited his rifle and bag on the floor, and sat down in one of the spare chairs. "I'll have to go back again."

"So?" His chief lit a cigarette and waited.

"I traced Gavran Sarn." Verkan Vall got out his pipe and began to fill it. "But that's only the beginning. I have to trace something else. Gavran Sarn exceeded his Paratime permit, and took one of his pets along. A Venusian nighthound."

Tortha Karf's expression did not alter; it merely grew more intense. He used one of the short, semantically ugly terms which serve, in place of profanity, as the emotional release of a race that has forgotten all the taboos and terminologies of supernaturalistic religion and sex-inhibition.

"You're sure of this, of course." It was less a question than a statement.

Verkan Vall bent and took cloth-wrapped objects from his bag, unwrapping them and laying them on the desk. They were casts, in hard black plastic, of the footprints of some large three-toed animal.

"What do these look like, sir?" he asked.

Tortha Karf fingered them and nodded. Then he became as visibly angry as a man of his civilization and culture-level ever permitted himself.

"What does that fool think we have a Paratime Code for?" he demanded. "It's entirely illegal to transpose any extraterrestrial animal or object to any time-line on which space-travel is unknown. I don't care if he is a green-seal thavrad; he'll face charges, when he gets back, for this!"

"He *was* a green-seal thavrad," Verkan Vall corrected. "And he won't be coming back."

"I hope you didn't have to deal summarily with him," Tortha Karf said. "With his title, and social position, and his family's political importance, that might make difficulties. Not that it wouldn't be all right with me, of course, but we never seem to be able to make either the Management or the public realize the extremities to which we are forced, at times." He sighed. "We probably never shall."

Verkan Vall smiled faintly. "Oh, no, sir; nothing like that. He was dead before I transposed to that time-line. He was killed when he wrecked a self-propelled vehicle he was using. One of those Fourth Level automobiles. I posed as a relative and tried to claim his body for the burial-ceremony observed on that cultural level, but was told that it had been completely destroyed by fire when the fuel tank of this automobile burned. I was given certain of his effects which had passed through the fire; I found his sigil concealed inside what appeared to be a cigarette case." He took a green disk from the bag and laid it on the desk. "There's no question; Gavran Sarn died in the wreck of that automobile."

"And the nighthound?"

"It was in the car with him, but it escaped. You know how fast those things are. I found that track"—he indicated one of the black casts—"in some dried mud near the scene of the wreck. As you see, the cast is slightly defective. The others were fresh this morning, when I made them."

"And what have you done so far?"

"I rented an old farm near the scene of the wreck, and installed my field-generator there. It runs through to the Hagraban Synthetics Works, about a hundred miles east of Thalna-Jarvizar. I have my this-line terminal in the girls' rest room at the durable plastics factory; handled that on a local police-power writ. Since then, I've been hunting for the nighthound. I think I can find it, but I'll need some special equipment, and a hypno-mech indoctrination. That's why I came back."

"Has it been attracting any attention?" Tortha Karf asked anxiously.

"Killing cattle in the locality; causing considerable excitement. Fortunately, it's a locality of forested mountains and valley farms, rather than a built-up industrial district. Local police and wild-game protection officers are concerned; all the farmers excited, and going armed. The theory is that it's either a wildcat of some sort, or a maniac armed with a cutlass. Either theory would conform, more or less, to the nature of its depredations. Nobody has actually seen it."

"That's good!" Tortha Karf was relieved. "Well, you'll have to go and bring it out, or kill it and obliterate the body. You know why, as well as I do."

"Certainly, sir," Verkan Vall replied. "In a primitive culture, things like this would be assigned supernatural explanations, and imbedded in the locally accepted religion. But this culture, while nominally religious, is highly rationalistic in practice. Typical lag-effect, characteristic of all expanding cultures. And this Europo-American Sector really has an expanding culture. A hundred and fifty years ago, the inhabitants of this particular time-line didn't even know how to apply steam power; now they've begun to release nuclear energy, in a few crude forms."

Tortha Karf whistled, softly. "That's quite a jump. There's a sector that'll be in for trouble, in the next few centuries."

"That is realized, locally, sir." Verkan Vall concentrated on relighting his pipe, for a moment, then continued: "I would predict space-travel on that sector within the next century. Maybe the next half-century, at least to the Moon. And the art of taxidermy is very highly developed. Now, suppose some farmer shoots that thing; what would he do with it, sir?"

Tortha Karf grunted. "Nice logic, Vall. On a most uncomfortable possibility. He'd have it mounted, and it'd be put in a museum, somewhere. And as soon as the first spaceship reaches Venus, and they find those things in a wild state, they'll have the mounted specimen identified."

"Exactly. And then, instead of beating their brains about *where* their specimen came from, they'll begin asking *when* it came from. They're quite capable of such reasoning, even now."

"A hundred years isn't a particularly long time," Tortha Karf considered. "I'll be retired, then, but you'll have my job, and it'll be your headache. You'd better get this cleaned up, now, while it can be handled. What are you going to do?"

"I'm not sure, now, sir. I want a hypno-mech indoctrination, first." Verkan Vall gestured toward the communicator on the desk. "May I?" he asked.

"Certainly." Tortha Karf slid the instrument across the desk. "Anything you want."

"Thank you, sir." Verkan Vall snapped on the code-index, found the symbol he wanted, and then punched it on the keyboard. "Special Chief's Assistant Verkan Vall," he identified himself. "Speaking from office of Tortha Karf, Chief Paratime Police. I want a complete hypno-mech on Venusian nighthounds, emphasis on wild state, special emphasis domesticated nighthounds reverted to wild state in terrestrial surroundings, extra-special emphasis hunting techniques applicable to same. The word 'nighthound' will do for trigger-symbol." He turned to Tortha Karf. "Can I take it here?"

Tortha Karf nodded, pointing to a row of booths along the far wall of the office.

"Make set-up for wired transmission; I'll take it here."

"Very well, sir; in fifteen minutes," a voice replied out of the communicator.

Verkan Vall slid the communicator back. "By the way, sir; I had a hitchhiker, on the way back. Carried him about a hundred or so para-years; picked him up about three hundred parayears after leaving my other-line terminal. Nasty-looking fellow, in a black uniform; looked like one of these private-army storm troopers you find all through that sector. Armed, and hostile. I thought I'd have to ray him, but he blundered outside the field almost at once. I have a record, if you'd care to see it."

"Yes, put it on," Tortha Karf gestured toward the solidograph-projector. "It's set for miniature reproduction here on the desk; that be all right?"

Verkan Vall nodded, getting out the film and loading it into the projector. When he pressed a button, a dome of radiance appeared on the desk top; two feet in width and a foot in height. In the middle of this appeared a small solidograph image of the interior of the conveyor, showing the desk, and the control board, and the figure of Verkan Vall seated at it. The little figure of the storm trooper appeared, pistol in hand. The little Verkan Vall snatched up his tiny needler; the storm trooper moved into one side of the dome and vanished.

Verkan Vall flipped a switch and cut out the image.

"Yes. I don't know what causes that, but it happens, now and then," Tortha Karf said. "Usually at the beginning of a transposition. I remember, when I was just a kid, about a hundred and fifty years ago—a hundred and thirty-nine, to be exact—I picked up a fellow on the Fourth Level, just about where you're operating, and dragged him a couple of hundred parayears. I went back to find him and return him to his own time-line, but before I could locate him, he'd been arrested by the local authorities as a suspicious character, and got himself shot trying to escape. I felt badly about that, but—" Tortha Karf shrugged. "Anything else happen on the trip?"

"I ran through a belt of intermittent nucleonic bombing on the Second Level." Verkan Vall mentioned an approximate paratime location.

"Aaagh! That Khiftan civilization—by courtesy so called!" Tortha Karf pulled a wry face. "I suppose the intra-family enmities of the Hvadka Dynasty have reached critical mass again. They'll fool around till they blast themselves back to the stone age."

"Intellectually, they're about there, now. I had to operate in that sector, once—Oh, yes, another thing, sir. This rifle." Verkan Vall picked it up, emptied the magazine, and handed it to his superior. "The supplies office slipped up on this; it's not appropriate to my line of operation. It's a lovely rifle, but it's about two hundred percent in advance of existing arms design on my line. It excited the curiosity of a couple of police officers and a game-protector, who should be familiar with the weapons of their own time-line. I evaded by disclaiming ownership or intimate knowledge, and they seemed satisfied, but it worried me."

"Yes. That was made in our duplicating shops, here in Dhergabar." Tortha Karf carried it to a photographic bench, behind his desk. "I'll have it checked, while you're taking your hypno-mech. Want to exchange it for something authentic?"

"Why, no, sir. It's been identified to me, and I'd excite less suspicion with it than I would if I abandoned it and mysteriously acquired another rifle. I just wanted a check, and Supplies warned to be more careful in future."

Tortha Karf nodded approvingly. The young Mavrad of Nerros was thinking as a paratimer should.

"What's the designation of your line, again?"

Verkan Vall told him. It was a short numerical term of six places, but it expressed a number of the order of ten to the fortieth power, exact to the last digit. Tortha Karf repeated it into his stenomemograph, with explanatory comment.

"There seems to be quite a few things going wrong, in that area," he said. "Let's see, now."

He punched the designation on a keyboard; instantly, it appeared on a translucent screen in front of him. He punched another combination, and, at the top of the screen, under the number, there appeared:

EVENTS, PAST ELAPSED FIVE YEARS.

He punched again; below this line appeared the sub-heading:

EVENTS INVOLVING PARATIME TRANSPOSITION.

Another code-combination added a third line:

(ATTRACTING PUBLIC NOTICE AMONG INHABITANTS.)

He pressed the "start"-button; the headings vanished, to be replaced by page after page of print, succeeding one another on the screen as the two men read. They told strange and apparently disconnected stories— of unexplained fires and explosions; of people vanishing without trace; of unaccountable disasters to aircraft. There were many stories of an epidemic of mysterious disk-shaped objects seen in the sky, singly or in numbers. To each account was appended one or more reference-numbers. Sometimes Tortha Karf or Verkan Vall would punch one of these, and read, on an adjoining screen, the explanatory matter referred to.

Finally Tortha Karf leaned back and lit a fresh cigarette.

"Yes, indeed, Vall; very definitely we will have to take action in the matter of the runaway nighthound of the late Gavran Sarn," he said. "I'd forgotten that that was the time-line onto which the *Ardrath* expedition launched those antigrav disks. If this extraterrestrial monstrosity turns up, on the heels of that 'Flying Saucer' business, everybody above the order of intelligence of a cretin will suspect some connection."

"What really happened, in the *Ardrath* matter?" Verkan Vall inquired. "I was on the Third Level, on that Luvarian Empire operation, at the time."

"That's right; you missed that. Well, it was one of these joint-operation things. The Paratime Commission and the Space Patrol were experimenting with a new technique for throwing a spaceship into paratime. They used the cruiser *Ardrath*, Kalzarn Jann commanding. Went into space about halfway to the Moon and took up orbit, keeping on the sunlit side of the planet to avoid being observed. That was all right. But then, Captain Kalzarn ordered away a flight of antigrav disks, fully manned, to take pictures, and finally authorized a landing in the western mountain range, Northern Continent, Minor Land-Mass. That's when the trouble started."

He flipped the run-back switch, till he had recovered the page he wanted. Verkan Vall read of a Fourth Level aviator, in his little airscrew-drive craft, sighting nine high-flying saucerlike objects.

"That was how it began," Tortha Karf told him. "Before long, as other incidents of the same sort occurred, our people on that line began sending back to know what was going on. Naturally, from the different descriptions of these 'saucers', they recognized the objects as antigrav landing-disks from a spaceship. So I went to the Commission and raised atomic blazes about it, and the *Ardrath* was ordered to confine operations to the lower areas of the Fifth Level. Then our people on that time-line went to work with corrective action. Here."

He wiped the screen and then began punching combinations. Page after page appeared, bearing accounts of people who had claimed to have seen the mysterious disks, and each report was more fantastic than the last.

"The standard smother-out technique," Verkan Vall grinned. "I only heard a little talk about the 'Flying Saucers', and all of that was in joke. In that order of culture, you can always discredit one true story by set-ting up ten others, palpably false, parallel to it—Wasn't that the time-line the Tharmax Trading Corporation almost lost their paratime license on?"

"That's right; it was! They bought up all the cigarettes, and caused a conspicuous shortage, after Fourth Level cigarettes had been introduced on this line and had become popular. They should have spread their purchases over a number of lines, and kept them within the local supply-demand frame. And they also got into trouble with the local government for selling unrationed petrol and automobile tires. We had to send in a special-operations group, and they came closer to having to engage in out-time local politics than I care to think of." Tortha Karf quoted a line from a currently popular song about the sorrows of a policeman's life. "We're jugglers, Vall; trying to keep our traders and sociological observers and tourists and plain idiots like the late Gavran Sarn out of trouble; trying to prevent panics and disturbances and dislocations of lo-cal economy as a result of our operations; trying to keep out of out-time politics—and, at all times, at all costs and hazards, by all means, guard-ing the secret of paratime transposition. Sometimes I wish Ghaldron Karf and Hesthor Ghrom had strangled in their cradles!"

Verkan Vall shook his head. "No, chief," he said. "You don't mean that; not really," he said. "We've been paratiming for the past ten thousand years. When the Ghaldron-Hesthor trans-temporal field was discovered, our ancestors had pretty well exhausted the resources of this planet. We had a world population of half a billion, and it was all they could do to keep alive. After we began paratime transposition, our population climbed to ten billion, and there it stayed for the last eight thousand years. Just enough of us to enjoy our planet and the other planets of the system to the fullest; enough of everything for everybody that nobody needs fight anybody for anything. We've tapped the resources of those other worlds on other time-lines, a little here, a little there, and not enough to really hurt anybody. We've left our mark in a few places—the Dakota Badlands, and the Gobi, on the Fourth Level, for instance—but we've done no great damage to any of them."

"Except the time they blew up half the Southern Island Continent, over about five hundred parayears on the Third Level," Tortha Karf mentioned.

"Regrettable accident, to be sure," Verkan Vall conceded. "And look how much we've learned from the experiences of those other time-lines. During the Crisis, after the Fourth Interplanetary War, we might have adopted Palnar Sarn's 'Dictatorship of the Chosen' scheme, if we hadn't seen what an exactly similar scheme had done to the Jak-Hakka Civilization, on the Second Level. When Palnar Sarn was told about that, he went into paratime to see for himself, and when he returned, he renounced his proposal in horror."

Tortha Karf nodded. He wouldn't be making any mistake in turning his post over to the Mavrad of Nerros on his retirement.

"Yes, Vall; I know," he said. "But when you've been at this desk as long as I have, you'll have a sour moment or two, now and then, too."

* * * *

A blue light flashed over one of the booths across the room. Verkan Vall got to his feet, removing his coat and hanging it on the back of his chair, and crossed the room, rolling up his left shirt sleeve. There was a relaxer-chair in the booth, with a blue plastic helmet above it. He glanced at the indicator-screen to make sure he was getting the indoctrination he called for, and then sat down in the chair and lowered the helmet over his head, inserting the ear plugs and fastening the chin strap. Then he touched his left arm with an injector which was lying on the arm of the chair, and at the same time flipped the starter switch.

Soft, slow music began to chant out of the earphones. The insidious fingers of the drug blocked off his senses, one by one. The music diminished, and the words of the hypnotic formula lulled him to sleep.

He woke, hearing the lively strains of dance music. For a while, he lay relaxed. Then he snapped off the switch, took out the ear plugs, removed the helmet and rose to his feet. Deep in his subconscious mind was the entire body of knowledge about the Venusian nighthound. He mentally pronounced the word, and at once it began flooding into his conscious mind. He knew the animal's evolutionary history, its anatomy, its characteristics, its dietary and reproductive habits, how it hunted, how it fought its enemies, how it eluded pursuit, and how best it could be tracked down and killed. He nodded. Already, a plan for dealing with Gavran Sarn's renegade pet was taking shape in his mind.

He picked a plastic cup from the dispenser, filled it from a cooler-tap with amber-colored spiced wine, and drank, tossing the cup into the disposal-bin. He placed a fresh injector on the arm of the chair, ready for the next user of the booth. Then he emerged, glancing at his Fourth Level wrist watch and mentally translating to the First Level time-scale. Three hours had passed; there had been more to learn about his quarry than he had expected.

Tortha Karf was sitting behind his desk, smoking a cigarette. It seemed as though he had not moved since Verkan Vall had left him, though the special agent knew that he had dined, attended several conferences, and done many other things.

"I checked up on your hitchhiker, Vall," the chief said. "We won't bother about him. He's a member of something called the Christian Avengers—one of those typical Europo-American race-and-religious hate groups. He belongs in a belt that is the outcome of the Hitler victory of 1940, whatever that was. Something unpleasant, I daresay. We don't owe him anything; people of that sort should be stepped on, like cockroaches. And he won't make any more trouble on the line where you dropped him than they have there already. It's in a belt of complete social and political anarchy; somebody probably shot him as soon as he emerged, because he wasn't wearing the right sort of a uniform. Nineteen-forty what, by the way?"

"Elapsed years since the birth of some religious leader," Verkan Vall explained. "And did you find out about my rifle?"

"Oh, yes. It's reproduction of something that's called a Sharp's Model '37 .235 Ultraspeed-Express. Made on an adjoining paratime belt by a company that went out of business sixty-seven years ago, elapsed time, on your line of operation. What made the difference was the Second War Between The States. I don't know what that was, either—I'm not too well up on Fourth Level history—but whatever, your line of operation didn't have it. Probably just as well for them, though they very likely had something else, as bad or worse. I put in a complaint to Supplies about it, and got you some more ammunition and reloading tools. Now, tell me what you're going to do about this nighthound business."

Tortha Karf was silent for a while, after Verkan Vall had finished.

"You're taking some awful chances, Vall," he said, at length. "The way you plan doing it, the advantages will all be with the nighthound. Those things can see as well at night as you can in daylight. I suppose you know that, though; you're the nighthound specialist, now."

"Yes. But they're accustomed to the Venus hotland marshes; it's been dry weather for the last two weeks, all over the northeastern section of the Northern Continent. I'll be able to hear it, long before it gets close to me. And I'll be wearing an electric headlamp. When I snap that on, it'll be dazzled, for a moment."

"Well, as I said, you're the nighthound specialist. There's the communicator; order anything you need." He lit a fresh cigarette from the end of the old one before crushing it out. "But be careful, Vall. It took me close to forty years to make a paratimer out of you; I don't want to have to repeat the process with somebody else before I can retire."

* * * *

The grass was wet as Verkan Vall—who reminded himself that here he was called Richard Lee—crossed the yard from the farmhouse to the ramshackle barn, in the early autumn darkness. It had been raining that morning when the strato-rocket from Dhergabar had landed him at the Hagraban Synthetics Works, on the First Level; unaffected by the probabilities of human history, the same rain had been coming down on the old Kinchwalter farm, near Rutter's Fort, on the Fourth Level. And it had persisted all day, in a slow, deliberate drizzle.

He didn't like that. The woods would be wet, muffling his quarry's footsteps, and canceling his only advantage over the night-prowler he hunted. He had no idea, however, of postponing the hunt. If anything, the rain had made it all the more imperative that the nighthound be killed at once. At this season, a falling temperature would speedily follow. The nighthound, a creature of the hot Venus marshes, would suffer from the cold, and, taught by years of domestication to find warmth among human habitations, it would invade some isolated farmhouse, or, worse, one of the little valley villages. If it were not killed tonight, the incident he had come to prevent would certainly occur.

Going to the barn, he spread an old horse blanket on the seat of the jeep, laid his rifle on it, and then backed the jeep outside. Then he took off his coat, removing his pipe and tobacco from the pockets, and spread it on the wet grass. He unwrapped a package and took out a small plastic spray-gun he had brought with him from the First Level, aiming it at the coat and pressing the trigger until it blew itself empty. A sickening, rancid fetor tainted the air—the scent of the giant poison-roach of Venus, the one creature for which the nighthound bore an inborn, implacable hatred. It was because of this compulsive urge to attack and kill the deadly poison-roach that the first human settlers on Venus, long millennia ago, had domesticated the ugly and savage nighthound. He remembered that the Gavran family derived their title from their vast Venus hotlands estates; that Gavran Sarn, the man who had brought this thing to the Fourth Level, had been born on the inner planet. When Verkan Vall donned that coat, he would become his own living bait for the murderous fury of the creature he sought. At the moment, mastering his queasiness and putting on the coat, he objected less to that danger than to the hideous stench of the scent, to obtain which a valuable specimen had been sacrificed at the Dhergabar Museum of Extraterrestrial Zoology, the evening before.

Carrying the wrapper and the spray-gun to an outside fireplace, he snapped his lighter to them and tossed them in. They were highly inflammable, blazing up and vanishing in a moment. He tested the electric headlamp on the front of his cap; checked his rifle; drew the heavy revolver, an authentic product of his line of operation, and flipped the cylinder out and in again. Then he got into the jeep and drove away.

For half an hour, he drove quickly along the valley roads. Now and then, he passed farmhouses, and dogs, puzzled and angered by the alien scent his coat bore, barked furiously. At length, he turned into a back road, and from this to the barely discernible trace of an old log road. The rain had stopped, and, in order to be ready to fire in any direction at any time, he had removed the top of the jeep. Now he had to crouch below the windshield to avoid overhanging branches. Once three deer—a buck and two does—stopped in front of him and stared for a moment, then bounded away with a flutter of white tails.

He was driving slowly, now; laying behind him a reeking trail of scent. There had been another stock-killing, the night before, while he had been on the First Level. The locality of this latest depredation had confirmed his estimate of the beast's probable movements, and indicated where it might be prowling, tonight. He was certain that it was somewhere near; sooner or later, it would pick up the scent.

Finally, he stopped, snapping out his lights. He had chosen this spot carefully, while studying the Geological Survey map, that afternoon; he was on the grade of an old railroad line, now abandoned and its track long removed, which had served the logging operations of fifty years ago. On one side, the mountain slanted sharply upward; on the other, it fell away sharply. If the nighthound were below him, it would have to climb that forty-five degree slope, and could not avoid dislodging loose stones, or otherwise making a noise. He would get out on that side; if the nighthound were above him, the jeep would protect him when it charged. He got to the ground, thumbing off the safety of his rifle, and an instant later he knew that he had made a mistake which could easily cost him his life; a mistake from which neither his comprehensive logic nor his hypnotically acquired knowledge of the beast's habits had saved him.

As he stepped to the ground, facing toward the front of the jeep, he heard a low, whining cry behind him, and a rush of padded feet. He whirled, snapping on the headlamp with his left hand and thrusting out his rifle pistol-wise in his right. For a split second, he saw the charging animal, its long, lizardlike head split in a toothy grin, its talon-tipped fore-paws extended.

He fired, and the bullet went wild. The next instant, the rifle was knocked from his hand. Instinctively, he flung up his left arm to shield his eyes. Claws raked his left arm and shoulder, something struck him heavily along the left side, and his cap-light went out as he dropped and rolled under the jeep, drawing in his legs and fumbling under his coat for the revolver.

In that instant, he knew what had gone wrong. His plan had been entirely too much of a success. The nighthound had winded him as he had driven up the old railroad-grade, and had followed. Its best running speed had been just good enough to keep it a hundred or so feet behind the jeep, and the motor-noise had covered the padding of its feet. In the few moments between stopping the little car and getting out, the nighthound had been able to close the distance and spring upon him.

It was characteristic of First-Level mentality that Verkan Vall wasted no moments on self-reproach or panic. While he was still rolling under his jeep, his mind had been busy with plans to retrieve the situation. Something touched the heel of one boot, and he froze his leg into immobility, at the same time trying to get the big Smith & Wesson free. The shoulder-holster, he found, was badly torn, though made of the heaviest skirting-leather, and the spring which retained the weapon in place had been wrenched and bent until he needed both hands to draw. The eight-inch slashing-claw of the nighthound's right intermediary limb had raked him; only the instinctive motion of throwing up his arm, and the fact that he wore the revolver in a shoulder-holster, had saved his life.

The nighthound was prowling around the jeep, whining frantically. It was badly confused. It could see quite well, even in the close darkness of the starless night; its eyes were of a nature capable of perceiving infrared radiations as light. There were plenty of these; the jeep's engine, lately running on four-wheel drive, was quite hot. Had he been standing alone, especially on this raw, chilly night, Verkan Vall's own body-heat would have lighted him up like a jack-o'-lantern. Now, however, the hot engine above him masked his own radiations. Moreover, the poison-roach scent on his coat was coming up through the floor board and mingling with the scent on the seat, yet the nighthound couldn't find the two-and-a-half foot insectlike thing that should have been producing it. Verkan Vall lay motionless, wondering how long the next move would be in coming. Then he heard a thud above him, followed by a furious tearing as the nighthound ripped the blanket and began rending at the seat cushion.

"Hope it gets a paw-full of seat-springs," Verkan Vall commented mentally. He had already found a stone about the size of his two fists, and another slightly smaller, and had put one in each of the side pockets of the coat. Now he slipped his revolver into his waist-belt and writhed out of the coat, shedding the ruined shoulder-holster at the same time. Wriggling on the flat of his back, he squirmed between the rear wheels, until he was able to sit up, behind the jeep. Then, swinging the weighted coat, he flung it forward, over the nighthound and the jeep itself, at the same time drawing his revolver.

Immediately, the nighthound, lured by the sudden movement of the principal source of the scent, jumped out of the jeep and bounded after the coat, and there was considerable noise in the brush on the lower side of the railroad grade. At once, Verkan Vall swarmed into the jeep and snapped on the lights.

His stratagem had succeeded beautifully. The stinking coat had landed on the top of a small bush, about ten feet in front of the jeep and ten feet from the ground. The nighthound, erect on its haunches, was reaching out with its front paws to drag it down, and slashing angrily at it with its single-clawed intermediary limbs. Its back was to Verkan Vall.

His sights clearly defined by the lights in front of him, the paratimer centered them on the base of the creature's spine, just above its secondary shoulders, and carefully squeezed the trigger. The big .357 Magnum bucked in his hand and belched flame and sound—if only these Fourth Level weapons weren't so confoundedly boisterous!—and the nighthound screamed and fell. Recocking the revolver, Verkan Vall waited for an instant, then nodded in satisfaction. The beast's spine had been smashed, and its hind quarters, and even its intermediary fighting limbs had been paralyzed. He aimed carefully for a second shot and fired into the base of the thing's skull. It quivered and died.

* * * *

Getting a flashlight, he found his rifle, sticking muzzle-down in the mud a little behind and to the right of the jeep, and swore briefly in the local Fourth Level idiom, for Verkan Vall was a man who loved good weapons, be they sigma-ray needlers, neutron-disruption blasters, or the solid-missile projectors of the lower levels. By this time, he was feeling considerable pain from the claw-wounds he had received. He peeled off his shirt and tossed it over the hood of the jeep.

Tortha Karf had advised him to carry a needler, or a blaster, or a neurostat-gun, but Verkan Vall had been unwilling to take such arms onto the Fourth Level. In event of mishap to himself, it would be all too easy for such a weapon to fall into the hands of someone able to deduce from it scientific principles too far in advance of the general Fourth

Level culture. But there had been one First Level item which he had permitted himself, mainly because, suitably packaged, it was not readily identifiable as such. Digging a respectable Fourth-Level leatherette case from under the seat, he opened it and took out a pint bottle with a red poison-label, and a towel. Saturating the towel with the contents of the bottle, he rubbed every inch of his torso with it, so as not to miss even the smallest break made in his skin by the septic claws of the nighthound. Whenever the lotion-soaked towel touched raw skin, a pain like the burn of a hot iron shot through him; before he was through, he was in agony. Satisfied that he had disinfected every wound, he dropped the towel and clung weakly to the side of the jeep. He grunted out a string of English oaths, and capped them with an obscene Spanish blasphemy he had picked up among the Fourth Level inhabitants of his island home of Nerros, to the south, and a thundering curse in the name of Mogga, Fire-God of Dool, in a Third-Level tongue. He mentioned Fasif, Great God of Khift, in a manner which would have got him an acid-bath if the Khiftan priests had heard him. He alluded to the baroque amatory practices of the Third-Level Illyalla people, and soothed himself, in the classical Dar-Halma tongue, with one of those rambling genealogical insults favored in the Indo-Turanian Sector of the Fourth Level.

By this time, the pain had subsided to an over-all smarting itch. He'd have to bear with that until his work was finished and he could enjoy a hot bath. He got another bottle out of the first-aid kit—a flat pint, labeled "Old Overholt," containing a locally-manufactured specific for inward and subjective wounds—and medicated himself copiously from it, corking it and slipping it into his hip pocket against future need. He gathered up the ruined shoulder-holster and threw it under the back seat. He put on his shirt. Then he went and dragged the dead nighthound onto the grade by its stumpy tail.

It was an ugly thing, weighing close to two hundred pounds, with powerfully muscled hind legs which furnished the bulk of its motive-power, and sturdy three-clawed front legs. Its secondary limbs, about a third of the way back from its front shoulders, were long and slender; normally, they were carried folded closely against the body, and each was armed with a single curving claw. The revolver-bullet had gone in at the base of the skull and emerged under the jaw; the head was relatively undamaged. Verkan Vall was glad of that; he wanted that head for the trophy-room of his home on Nerros. Grunting and straining, he got the thing into the back of the jeep, and flung his almost shredded tweed coat over it.

A last look around assured him that he had left nothing unaccountable or suspicious. The brush was broken where the nighthound had been tearing at the coat; a bear might have done that. There were splashes of the viscid stuff the thing had used for blood, but they wouldn't be there long. Terrestrial rodents liked nighthound blood, and the woods were full of mice. He climbed in under the wheel, backed, turned, and drove away.

* * * *

Inside the paratime-transposition dome, Verkan Vall turned from the body of the nighthound, which he had just dragged in, and considered the inert form of another animal—a stump-tailed, tuft-eared, tawny Canada lynx. That particular animal had already made two paratime transpositions; captured in the vast wilderness of Fifth-Level North America, it had been taken to the First Level and placed in the Dhergabar Zoological Gardens, and then, requisitioned on the authority of Tortha Karf, it had been brought to the Fourth Level by Verkan Vall. It was almost at the end of all its travels.

Verkan Vall prodded the supine animal with the toe of his boot; it twitched slightly. Its feet were cross-bound with straps, but when he saw that the narcotic was wearing off, Verkan Vall snatched a syringe, parted the fur at the base of its neck, and gave it an injection. After a moment, he picked it up in his arms and carried it out to the jeep.

"All right, pussy cat," he said, placing it under the rear seat, "this is the one-way ride. The way you're doped up, it won't hurt a bit."

He went back and rummaged in the debris of the long-deserted barn. He picked up a hoe, and discarded it as too light. An old plowshare was too unhandy. He considered a grate-bar from a heating furnace, and then he found the poleax, lying among a pile of wormeaten boards. Its handle had been shortened, at some time, to about twelve inches, converting it into a heavy hatchet. He weighed it, and tried it on a block of wood, and then, making sure that the secret door was closed, he went out again and drove off.

An hour later, he returned. Opening the secret door, he carried the ruined shoulder holster, and the straps that had bound the bobcat's feet, and the ax, now splotched with blood and tawny cat-hairs, into the dome. Then he closed the secret room, and took a long drink from the bottle on his hip.

The job was done. He would take a hot bath, and sleep in the farmhouse till noon, and then he would return to the First Level. Maybe Tortha Karf would want him to come back here for a while. The situation on this time-line was far from satisfactory, even if the crisis threatened by Gavran Sarn's renegade pet had been averted. The presence of a chief's assistant might be desirable.

At least, he had a right to expect a short vacation. He thought of the little redhead at the Hagraban Synthetics Works. What was her name? Something Kara—Morvan Kara; that was it. She'd be coming off shift about the time he'd make First Level, tomorrow afternoon.

The claw-wounds were still smarting vexatiously. A hot bath, and a night's sleep—He took another drink, lit his pipe, picked up his rifle and started across the yard to the house.

* * * *

Private Zinkowski cradled the telephone and got up from the desk, stretching. He left the orderly-room and walked across the hall to the recreation room, where the rest of the boys were loafing. Sergeant Haines, in a languid gin-rummy game with Corporal Conner, a sheriff's deputy, and a mechanic from the service station down the road, looked up.

"Well, Sarge, I think we can write off those stock-killings," the private said.

"Yeah?" The sergeant's interest quickened.

"Yeah. I think the whatzit's had it. I just got a buzz from the railroad cops at Logansport. It seems a track-walker found a dead bobcat on the Logan River branch, about a mile or so below MMY signal tower. Looks like it tangled with that night freight up-river, and came off second best. It was near chopped to hamburger."

"MMY signal tower; that's right below Yoder's Crossing," the sergeant considered. "The Strawmyer farm night-before-last, the Amrine farm last night—Yeah, that would be about right."

"That'll suit Steve Parker; bobcats aren't protected, so it's not his trouble. And they're not a violation of state law, so it's none of our worry," Conner said. "Your deal, isn't it, Sarge?"

"Yeah. Wait a minute." The sergeant got to his feet. "I promised Sam Kane, the AP man at Logansport, that I'd let him in on anything new." He got up and started for the phone. "Phantom Killer!" He blew an impolite noise.

"Well, it was a lot of excitement, while it lasted," the deputy sheriff said. "Just like that Flying Saucer thing."

LAST ENEMY

Along the U-shaped table, the subdued clatter of dinnerware and the buzz of conversation was dying out; the soft music that drifted down from the overhead sound outlets seemed louder as the competing noises diminished. The feast was drawing to a close, and Dallona of Hadron fidgeted nervously with the stem of her wineglass as last-moment doubts assailed her.

The old man at whose right she sat noticed, and reached out to lay his hand on hers.

"My dear, you're worried," he said softly. "You, of all people, shouldn't be, you know."

"The theory isn't complete," she replied. "And I could wish for more positive verification. I'd hate to think I'd got you into this—"

Garnon of Roxor laughed. "No, no!" he assured her. "I'd decided upon this long before you announced the results of your experiments. Ask Girzon; he'll bear me out."

"That's true," the young man who sat at Garnon's left said, leaning forward. "Father has meant to take this step for a long time. He was waiting until after the election, and then he decided to do it now, to give you an opportunity to make experimental use of it."

The man on Dallona's right added his voice. Like the others at the table, he was of medium stature, brown-skinned and dark-eyed, with a wide mouth, prominent cheekbones and a short, square jaw. Unlike the others, he was armed, with a knife and pistol on his belt, and on the breast of his black tunic he wore a scarlet oval patch on which a pair of black wings, with a tapering silver object between them had been superimposed.

"Yes, Lady Dallona; the Lord Garnon and I discussed this, oh, two years ago at the least. Really, I'm surprised that you seem to shrink from it, now. Of course, you're Venus-born, and customs there may be different, but with your scientific knowledge—"

"That may be the trouble, Dirzed," Dallona told him. "A scientist gets in the way of doubting, and one doubts one's own theories most of all."

"That's the scientific attitude, I'm told," Dirzed replied, smiling. "But somehow, I cannot think of you as a scientist." His eyes traveled over her in a way that would have made most women, scientists or other-wise, blush. It gave Dallona of Hadron a feeling of pleasure. Men often looked at her that way, especially here at Darsh. Novelty had something to do with it—her skin was considerably lighter than usual, and there was a pleasing oddness about the structure of her face. Her alleged Ve-nusian origin was probably accepted as the explanation of that, as of so many other things.

As she was about to reply, a man in dark gray, one of the upper-servants who were accepted as social equals by the Akor-Neb nobles, approached the table. He nodded respectfully to Garnon of Roxor.

"I hate to seem to hurry things, sir, but the boy's ready. He's in a trance-state now," he reported, pointing to the pair of visiplates at the end of the room.

Both of the ten-foot-square plates were activated. One was a solid luminous white; on the other was the image of a boy of twelve or four-teen, seated at a big writing machine. Even allowing for the fact that the boy was in a hypnotic trance, there was an expression of idiocy on his loose-lipped, slack-jawed face, a pervading dullness.

"One of our best sensitives," a man with a beard, several places down the table on Dallona's right, said. "You remember him, Dallona; he produced that communication from the discarnate Assassin, Sirzim. Normally, he's a low-grade imbecile, but in trance-state he's wonderful. And there can be no argument that the communications he produces originates in his own mind; he doesn't have mind enough, of his own, to operate that machine."

Garnon of Roxor rose to his feet, the others rising with him. He un-fastened a jewel from the front of his tunic and handed it to Dallona.

"Here, my dear Lady Dallona; I want you to have this," he said. "It's been in the family of Roxor for six generations, but I know that you will appreciate and cherish it." He twisted a heavy ring from his left hand and gave it to his son. He unstrapped his wrist watch and passed it across the table to the gray-clad upper-servant. He gave a pocket case, containing writing tools, slide rule and magnifier, to the bearded man on the other side of Dallona. "Something you can use, Dr. Harnosh," he said. Then he took a belt, with a knife and holstered pistol, from a servant who had brought it to him, and gave it to the man with the red badge. "And something for you, Dirzed. The pistol's by Farnor of Yand, and the knife was forged and tempered on Luna."

The man with the winged-bullet badge took the weapons, exclaiming in appreciation. Then he removed his own belt and buckled on the gift.

"The pistol's fully loaded," Garnon told him.

Dirzed drew it and checked—a man of his craft took no statement about weapons without verification—then slipped it back into the holster.

"Shall I use it?" he asked.

"By all means; I'd had that in mind when I selected it for you."

Another man, to the left of Girzon, received a cigarette case and lighter. He and Garnon hooked fingers and clapped shoulders.

"Our views haven't been the same, Garnon," he said, "but I've always valued your friendship. I'm sorry you're doing this, now; I believe you'll be disappointed."

Garnon chuckled. "Would you care to make a small wager on that, Nirzav?" he asked. "You know what I'm putting up. If I'm proven right, will you accept the Volitionalist theory as verified?"

Nirzav chewed his mustache for a moment. "Yes, Garnon, I will." He pointed toward the blankly white screen. "If we get anything conclusive on that, I'll have no other choice."

"All right, friends," Garnon said to those around him. "Will you walk with me to the end of the room?"

Servants removed a section from the table in front of him, to allow him and a few others to pass through; the rest of the guests remained standing at the table, facing toward the inside of the room. Garnon's son, Girzon, and the gray-mustached Nirzav of Shonna, walked on his left; Dallona of Hadron and Dr. Harnosh of Hosh on his right. The gray-clad upper-servant, and two or three ladies, and a nobleman with a small chin-beard, and several others, joined them; of those who had sat close to Garnon, only the man in the black tunic with the scarlet badge hung back. He stood still, by the break in the table, watching Garnon of Roxor walk away from him. Then Dirzed the Assassin drew the pistol he had lately received as a gift, hefted it in his hand, thumbed off the safety, and aimed at the back of Garnon's head.

They had nearly reached the end of the room when the pistol cracked. Dallona of Hadron started, almost as though the bullet had crashed into her own body, then caught herself and kept on walking. She closed her eyes and laid a hand on Dr. Harnosh's arm for guidance, concentrating her mind upon a single question. The others went on as though Garnon of Roxor were still walking among them.

"Look!" Harnosh of Hosh cried, pointing to the image in the visiplate ahead. "He's under control!"

They all stopped short, and Dirzed, holstering his pistol, hurried forward to join them. Behind, a couple of servants had approached with a stretcher and were gathering up the crumpled figure that had, a moment ago, been Garnon.

A change had come over the boy at the writing machine. His eyes were still glazed with the stupor of the hypnotic trance, but the slack jaw had stiffened, and the loose mouth was compressed in a purposeful line. As they watched, his hands went out to the keyboard in front of him and began to move over it, and as they did, letters appeared on the white screen on the left.

Garnon of Roxor, discarnate, communicating, they read. The machine stopped for a moment, then began again. To Dallona of Hadron: The question you asked, after I discarnated, was: What was the last book I read, before the feast? While waiting for my valet to prepare my bath, I read the first ten verses of the fourth Canto of "Splendor of Space," by Larnov of Horka, in my bedroom. When the bath was ready, I marked the page with a strip of message tape, containing a message from the bailiff of my estate on the Shevva River, concerning a breakdown at the power plant, and laid the book on the ivory-inlaid table beside the big red chair.

Harnosh of Hosh looked at Dallona inquiringly; she nodded.

"I rejected the question I had in my mind, and substituted that one, after the shot," she said.

He turned quickly to the upper-servant. "Check on that, right away, Kirzon," he directed.

As the upper-servant hurried out, the writing machine started again.

And to my son, Girzon: I will not use your son, Garnon, as a reincarnation-vehicle; I will remain discarnate until he is grown and has a son of his own; if he has no male child, I will reincarnate in the first available male child of the family of Roxor, or of some family allied to us by marriage. In any case, I will communicate before reincarnating.

To Nirzav of Shonna: Ten days ago, when I dined at your home, I took a small knife and cut three notches, two close together and one a little apart from the others, on the under side of the table. As I remember, I sat two places down on the left. If you find them, you will know that I have won that wager that I spoke of a few minutes ago.

"I'll have my butler check on that, right away," Nirzav said. His eyes were wide with amazement, and he had begun to sweat; a man does not casually watch the beliefs of a lifetime invalidated in a few moments.

To Dirzed the Assassin: the machine continued. You have served me faithfully, in the last ten years, never more so than with the last shot you fired in my service. After you fired, the thought was in your mind that you would like to take service with the Lady Dallona of Hadron, whom you believe will need the protection of a member of the Society of Assassins. I advise you to do so, and I advise her to accept your offer. Her work, since she has come to Darsh, has not made her popular in some quarters. No doubt Nirzav of Shonna can bear me out on that.

"I won't betray things told me in confidence, or said at the Councils of the Statisticalists, but he's right," Nirzav said. "You need a good Assassin, and there are few better than Dirzed."

I see that this sensitive is growing weary, the letters on the screen spelled out. His body is not strong enough for prolonged communication. I bid you all farewell, for the time; I will communicate again. Good evening, my friends, and I thank you for your presence at the feast.

The boy, on the other screen, slumped back in his chair, his face relaxing into its customary expression of vacancy.

"Will you accept my offer of service, Lady Dallona?" Dirzed asked. "It's as Garnon said; you've made enemies."

Dallona smiled at him. "I've not been too deep in my work to know that. I'm glad to accept your offer, Dirzed."

* * * *

Nirzav of Shonna had already turned away from the group and was hurrying from the room, to call his home for confirmation on the notches made on the underside of his dining table. As he went out the door, he almost collided with the upper-servant, who was rushing in with a book in his hand.

"Here it is," the latter exclaimed, holding up the book. "Larnov's 'Splendor of Space,' just where he said it would be. I had a couple of servants with me as witnesses; I can call them in now, if you wish." He handed the book to Harnosh of Hosh. "See, a strip of message tape in it, at the tenth verse of the Fourth Canto."

Nirzav of Shonna re-entered the room; he was chewing his mustache and muttering to himself. As he rejoined the group in front of the now dark visiplates, he raised his voice, addressing them all generally.

"My butler found the notches, just as the communication described," he said. "This settles it! Garnon, if you're where you can hear me, you've won. I can't believe in the Statisticalist doctrines after this, or in the political program based upon them. I'll announce my change of attitude at the next meeting of the Executive Council, and resign my seat. I was elected by Statisticalist votes, and I cannot hold office as a Volitionalist."

"You'll need a couple of Assassins, too," the nobleman with the chin-beard told him. "Your former colleagues and fellow-party-members are regrettably given to the forcible discarnation of those who differ with them."

"I've never employed personal Assassins before," Nirzav replied, "but I think you're right. As soon as I get home, I'll call Assassins' Hall and make the necessary arrangements."

"Better do it now," Girzon of Roxor told him, lowering his voice. "There are over a hundred guests here, and I can't vouch for all of them. The Statisticalists would be sure to have a spy planted among them. My father was one of their most dangerous opponents, when he was on the Council; they've always been afraid he'd come out of retirement and stand for re-election. They'd want to make sure he was really discarnate. And if that's the case, you can be sure your change of attitude is known to old Mirzark of Bashad by this time. He won't dare allow you to make a public renunciation of Statisticalism." He turned to the other nobleman. "Prince Jirzyn, why don't you call the Volitionist headquarters and have a couple of our Assassins sent here to escort Lord Nirzav home?"

"I'll do that immediately," Jirzyn of Starpha said. "It's as Lord Girzon says; we can be pretty sure there was a spy among the guests, and now that you've come over to our way of thinking, we're responsible for your safety."

He left the room to make the necessary visiphone call. Dallona, accompanied by Dirzed, returned to her place at the table, where she was joined by Harnosh of Hosh and some of the others.

"There's no question about the results," Harnosh was exulting. "I'll grant that the boy might have picked up some of that stuff telepathically from the carnate minds present here; even from the mind of Garnon, before he was discarnated. But he could not have picked up enough data, in that way, to make a connected and coherent communication. It takes a sensitive with a powerful mind of his own to practice telesthesia, and that boy's almost an idiot." He turned to Dallona. "You asked a question, mentally, after Garnon was discarnate, and got an answer that could have been contained only in Garnon's mind. I think it's conclusive proof that the discarnate Garnon was fully conscious and communicating."

"Dirzed also asked a question, mentally, after the discarnation, and got an answer. Dr. Harnosh, we can state positively that the surviving individuality is fully conscious in the discarnate state, is telepathically sensitive, and is capable of telepathic communication with other minds," Dallona agreed. "And in view of our earlier work with memory-recalls, we're justified in stating positively that the individual is capable of exercising choice in reincarnation vehicles."

"My father had been considering voluntary discarnation for a long time," Girzon of Roxor said. "Ever since the discarnation of my mother. He deferred that step because he was unwilling to deprive the Volitionalist Party of his support. Now it would seem that he has done more to combat Statisticalism by discarnating than he ever did in his carnate existence."

"I don't know, Girzon," Jirzyn of Starpha said, as he joined the group. "The Statisticalists will denounce the whole thing as a prearranged fraud. And if they can discarnate the Lady Dallona before she can record her testimony under truth hypnosis or on a lie detector, we're no better off than we were before. Dirzed, you have a great responsibility in guarding the Lady Dallona; some extraordinary security precautions will be needed."

* * * *

In his office, in the First Level city of Dhergabar, Tortha Karf, Chief of Paratime Police, leaned forward in his chair to hold his lighter for his special assistant, Verkan Vall, then lit his own cigarette. He was a man of middle age—his three hundredth birthday was only a decade or so off—and he had begun to acquire a double chin and a bulge at his waistline. His hair, once black, had turned a uniform iron-gray and was beginning to thin in front.

"What do you know about the Second Level Akor-Neb Sector, Vall?" he inquired. "Ever work in that paratime-area?"

Verkan Vall's handsome features became even more immobile than usual as he mentally pronounced the verbal trigger symbols which should bring hypnotically-acquired knowledge into his conscious mind. Then he shook his head.

"Must be a singularly well-behaved sector, sir," he said. "Or else we've been lucky, so far. I never was on an Akor-Neb operation; don't even have a hypno-mech for that sector. All I know is from general reading.

"Like all the Second Level, its time-lines descend from the probability of one or more shiploads of colonists having come to Terra from Mars about seventy-five to a hundred thousand years ago, and then having been cut off from the home planet and forced to develop a civilization of their own here. The Akor-Neb civilization is of a fairly high culture-order, even for Second Level. An atomic-power, interplanetary culture; gravity-counteraction, direct conversion of nuclear energy to electrical power, that sort of thing. We buy fine synthetic plastics and fabrics from them." He fingered the material of his smartly-cut green police uniform. "I think this cloth is Akor-Neb. We sell a lot of Venusian *zerfa*-leaf; they smoke it, straight and mixed with tobacco. They have a single System-wide government, a single race, and a universal language. They're a dark-brown race, which evolved in its present form about fifty thousand years ago; the present civilization is about ten thousand years old, developed out of the wreckage of several earlier civilizations which decayed or fell through wars, exhaustion of resources, et cetera. They have legends, maybe historical records, of their extraterrestrial origin."

Tortha Karf nodded. "Pretty good, for consciously acquired knowledge," he commented. "Well, our luck's run out, on that sector; we have troubles there, now. I want you to go iron them out. I know, you've been going pretty hard, lately—that nighthound business, on the Fourth Level Europo-American Sector, wasn't any picnic. But the fact is that a lot of my ordinary and deputy assistants have a little too much regard for the alleged sanctity of human life, and this is something that may need some pretty drastic action."

"Some of our people getting out of line?" Verkan Vall asked.

"Well, the data isn't too complete, but one of our people has run into trouble on that sector, and needs rescuing—a psychic-science research-er, a young lady named Hadron Dalla. I believe you know her, don't you?" Tortha Karf asked innocently.

"Slightly," Verkan Vall deadpanned. "I enjoyed a brief but rather hec-tic companionate-marriage with her, about twenty years ago. What sort of a jam's little Dalla got herself into, now?"

"Well, frankly, we don't know. I hope she's still alive, but I'm not unduly optimistic. It seems that about a year ago, Dr. Hadron transposed to the Second Level, to study alleged proof of reincarnation which the Akor-Neb people were reported to possess. She went to Gindrabar, on Venus, and transposed to the Second Paratime Level, to a station main-tained by Outtime Import & Export Trading Corporation—a *zerfa* plan-tation just east of the High Ridge country. There she assumed an identity as the daughter of a planter, and took the name of Dallona of Hadron. Parenthetically, all Akor-Neb family-names are prepositional; family-names were originally place names. I believe that ancient Akor-Neb marital relations were too complicated to permit exact establishment of paternity. And all Akor-Neb men's personal names have *-irz-* or *-arn-* inserted in the middle, and women's names end in *-itra-* or *-ona*. You could call yourself Virzal of Verkan, for instance.

"Anyhow, she made the Second Level Venus-Terra trip on a regu-lar passenger liner, and landed at the Akor-Neb city of Ghamma, on the upper Nile. There she established contact with the Outtime Trading Corporation representative, Zortan Brend, locally known as Brarnend of Zorda. He couldn't call himself Brarnend of Zortan—in the Akor-Neb language, *zortan* is a particularly nasty dirty-word. Hadron Dalla spent a few weeks at his residence, briefing herself on local conditions. Then she went to the capital city, Darsh, in eastern Europe, and enrolled as a student at something called the Independent Institute for Reincarnation Research, having secured a letter of introduction to its director, a Dr. Harnosh of Hosh.

"Almost at once, she began sending in reports to her home orga-nization, the Rhogom Memorial Foundation of Psychic Science, here at Dhergabar, through Zortan Brend. The people there were wildly enthusiastic. I don't have more than the average intelligent—I hope—layman's knowledge of psychics, but Dr. Volzar Darv, the director of Rhogom Foundation, tells me that even in the present incomplete form, her reports have opened whole new horizons in the science. It seems that these Akor-Neb people have actually demonstrated, as a scientific fact, that the human individuality reincarnates after physical death—that your personality, and mine, have existed, as such, for ages, and will exist for ages to come. More, they have means of recovering, from almost anybody, memories of past reincarnations.

"Well, after about a month, the people at this Reincarnation Institute realized that this Dallona of Hadron wasn't any ordinary student. She probably had trouble keeping down to the local level of psychic knowledge. So, as soon as she'd learned their techniques, she was allowed to undertake experimental work of her own. I imagine she let herself out on that; as soon as she'd mastered the standard Akor-Neb methods of recovering memories of past reincarnations, she began refining and developing them more than the local yokels had been able to do in the past thousand years. I can't tell you just what she did, because I don't know the subject, but she must have lit things up properly. She got quite a lot of local publicity; not only scientific journals, but general newscasts.

"Then, four days ago, she disappeared, and her disappearance seems to have been coincident with an unsuccessful attempt on her life. We don't know as much about this as we should; all we have is Zortan Brend's account.

"It seems that on the evening of her disappearance, she had been attending the voluntary discarnation feast—suicide party—of a prominent nobleman named Garnon of Roxor. Evidently when the Akor-Neb people get tired of their current reincarnation they invite in their friends, throw a big party, and then do themselves in in an atmosphere of general conviviality. Frequently they take poison or inhale lethal gas; this fellow had his personal trigger man shoot him through the head. Dalla was one of the guests of honor, along with this Harnosh of Hosh. They'd made rather elaborate preparations, and after the shooting they got a detailed and apparently authentic spirit-communication from the late Garnon. The voluntary discarnation was just a routine social event, it seems, but the communication caused quite an uproar, and rated top place on the System-wide newscasts, and started a storm of controversy.

"After the shooting and the communication, Dalla took the officiating gun artist, one Dirzed, into her own service. This Dirzed was spoken of as a generally respected member of something called the Society of Assassins, and that'll give you an idea of what things are like on that sector, and why I don't want to send anybody who might develop trigger-finger cramp at the wrong moment. She and Dirzed left the home of the gentleman who had just had himself discarnated, presumably for Dalla's apartment, about a hundred miles away. That's the last that's been heard of either of them.

"This attempt on Dalla's life occurred while the pre-mortem revels were still going on. She lived in a six-room apartment, with three servants, on one of the upper floors of a three-thousand-foot tower— Akor-Neb cities are built vertically, with considerable interval between units—and while she was at this feast, a package was delivered at the apartment, ostensibly from the Reincarnation Institute and made up to look as though it contained record tapes. One of the servants accepted it from a service employee of the apartments. The next morning, a little before noon, Dr. Harnosh of Hosh called her on the visiphone and got no answer; he then called the apartment manager, who entered the apartment. He found all three of the servants dead, from a lethal-gas bomb which had exploded when one of them had opened this package. However, Hadron Dalla had never returned to the apartment, the night before."

* * * *

Verkan Vall was sitting motionless, his face expressionless as he ran Tortha Karf's narrative through the intricate semantic and psychological processes of the First Level mentality. The fact that Hadron Dalla had been a former wife of his had been relegated to one corner of his consciousness and contained there; it was not a fact that would, at the moment, contribute to the problem or to his treatment of it.

"The package was delivered while she was at this suicide party," he considered. "It must, therefore, have been sent by somebody who either did not know she would be out of the apartment, or who did not expect it to function until after her return. On the other hand, if her disappearance was due to hostile action, it was the work of somebody who knew she was at the feast and did not want her to reach her apartment again. This would seem to exclude the sender of the package bomb."

Tortha Karf nodded. He had reached that conclusion, himself.

"Thus," Verkan Vall continued, "if her disappearance was the work of an enemy, she must have two enemies, each working in ignorance of the other's plans."

"What do you think she did to provoke such enmity?"

"Well, of course, it just might be that Dalla's normally complicated love-life had got a little more complicated than usual and short-circuited on her," Verkan Vall said, out of the fullness of personal knowledge, "but I doubt that, at the moment. I would think that this affair has political implications."

"So?" Tortha Karf had not thought of politics as an explanation. He waited for Verkan Vall to elaborate.

"Don't you see, chief?" the special assistant asked. "We find a belief in reincarnation on many time-lines, as a religious doctrine, but these people accept it as a scientific fact. Such acceptance would carry much more conviction; it would influence a people's entire thinking. We see it reflected in their disregard for death—suicide as a social function, this Society of Assassins, and the like. It would naturally color their political thinking, because politics is nothing but common action to secure more favorable living conditions, and to these people, the term 'living conditions' includes not only the present life, but also an indefinite number of future lives as well. I find this title, 'Independent' Institute, suggestive. Independent of what? Possibly of partisan affiliation."

"But wouldn't these people be grateful to her for her new discoveries, which would enable them to plan their future reincarnations more intelligently?" Tortha Karf asked.

"Oh, chief!" Verkan Vall reproached. "You know better than that! How many times have our people got in trouble on other time-lines because they divulged some useful scientific fact that conflicted with the locally revered nonsense? You show me ten men who cherish some religious doctrine or political ideology, and I'll show you nine men whose minds are utterly impervious to any factual evidence which contradicts their beliefs, and who regard the producer of such evidence as a criminal who ought to be suppressed. For instance, on the Fourth Level Europo-American Sector, where I was just working, there is a political sect, the Communists, who, in the territory under their control, forbid the teaching of certain well-established facts of genetics and heredity, because those facts do not fit the world-picture demanded by their political doctrines. And on the same sector, a religious sect recently tried, in some sections successfully, to outlaw the teaching of evolution by natural selection."

Tortha Karf nodded. "I remember some stories my grandfather told me, about his narrow escapes from an organization called the Holy Inquisition, when he was a paratime trader on the Fourth Level, about four hundred years ago. I believe that thing's still operating, on the Europo-American Sector, under the name of the NKVD. So you think Dalla may have proven something that conflicted with local reincarnation theories, and somebody who had a vested interest in maintaining those theories is trying to stop her?"

"You spoke of a controversy over the communication alleged to have originated with this voluntarily discarnated nobleman. That would suggest a difference of opinion on the manner of nature of reincarnation or the discarnate state. This difference may mark the dividing line between the different political parties. Now, to get to this Darsh place, do I have to go to Venus, as Dalla did?"

"No. The Outtime Trading Corporation has transposition facilities at Ravvanan, on the Nile, which is spatially co-existent with the city of Ghamma on the Akor-Neb Sector, where Zortan Brend is. You transpose through there, and Zortan Brend will furnish you transportation to Darsh. It'll take you about two days, here, getting your hypno-mech indoctrinations and having your skin pigmented, and your hair turned black. I'll notify Zortan Brend at once that you're coming through. Is there anything special you'll want?"

"Why, I'll want an abstract of the reports Dalla sent back to Rhogom Foundation. It's likely that there is some clue among them as to whom her discoveries may have antagonized. I'm going to be a Venusian *zerfa*-planter, a friend of her father's; I'll want full hypno-mech indoctrination to enable me to play that part. And I'll want to familiarize myself with Akor-Neb weapons and combat techniques. I think that will be all, chief."

* * * *

The last of the tall city-units of Ghamma were sliding out of sight as the ship passed over them—shaft-like buildings that rose two or three thousand feet above the ground in clumps of three or four or six, one at each corner of the landing stages set in series between them. Each of these units stood in the middle of a wooded park some five miles square; no unit was much more or less than twenty miles from its nearest neighbor, and the land between was the uniform golden-brown of ripening grain, crisscrossed with the threads of irrigation canals and dotted here and there with sturdy farm-village buildings and tall, stacklike granaries. There were a few other ships in the air at the fifty-thousand-foot level, and below, swarms of small airboats darted back and forth on different levels, depending upon speed and direction. Far ahead, to the northeast, was the shimmer of the Red Sea and the hazy bulk of Asia Minor beyond.

Verkan Vall—the Lord Virzal of Verkan, temporarily—stood at the glass front of the observation deck, looking down. He was a different Verkan Vall from the man who had talked with Tortha Karf in the latter's office, two days before. The First Level cosmeticists had worked miracles upon him with their art. His skin was a soft chocolate-brown, now; his hair was jet-black, and so were his eyes. And in his subconscious mind, instantly available to consciousness, was a vast body of knowledge about conditions on the Akor-Neb sector, as well as a complete command of the local language, all hypnotically acquired.

He knew that he was looking down upon one of the minor provincial cities of a very respectably advanced civilization. A civilization which built its cities vertically, since it had learned to counteract gravitation. A civilization which still depended upon natural cereals for food, but one which had learned to make the most efficient use of its soil. The network of dams and irrigation canals which he saw was as good as anything on his own paratime level. The wide dispersal of buildings, he knew, was a heritage of a series of disastrous atomic wars of several thousand years before; the Akor-Neb people had come to love the wide inter-vistas of open country and forest, and had continued to scatter their buildings, even after the necessity had passed. But the slim, towering buildings could only have been reared by a people who had banished nationalism and, with it, the threat of total war. He contrasted them with the ground-hugging dome cities of the Khiftan civilization, only a few thousand parayears distant.

Three men came out of the lounge behind him and joined him. One was, like himself, a disguised paratimer from the First Level—the Out-time Export and Import man, Zortan Brend, here known as Brarnend of Zorda. The other two were Akor-Neb people, and both wore the black tunics and the winged-bullet badges of the Society of Assassins. Unlike Verkan Vall and Zortan Brend, who wore shoulder holsters under their short tunics, the Assassins openly displayed pistols and knives on their belts.

"We heard that you were coming two days ago, Lord Virzal," Zortan Brend said. "We delayed the take-off of this ship, so that you could travel to Darsh as inconspicuously as possible. I also booked a suite for you at the Solar Hotel, at Darsh. And these are your Assassins—Olirzon, and Marnik."

Verkan Vall hooked fingers and clapped shoulders with them.

"Virzal of Verkan," he identified himself. "I am satisfied to intrust myself to you."

"We'll do our best for you, Lord Virzal," the older of the pair, Olirzon, said. He hesitated for a moment, then continued: "Understand, Lord Virzal, I only ask for information useful in serving and protecting you. But is this of the Lady Dallona a political matter?"

"Not from our side," Verkan Vall told him. "The Lady Dallona is a scientist, entirely nonpolitical. The Honorable Brarnend is a business man; he doesn't meddle with politics as long as the politicians leave him alone. And I'm a planter on Venus; I have enough troubles, with the natives, and the weather, and blue-rot in the *zerfa* plants, and poison roaches, and javelin bugs, without getting into politics. But psychic science is inextricably mixed with politics, and the Lady Dallona's work had evidently tended to discredit the theory of Statistical Reincarnation."

"Do you often make understatements like that, Lord Virzal?" Olirzon grinned. "In the last six months, she's knocked Statistical Reincarnation to splinters."

"Well, I'm not a psychic scientist, and as I said, I don't know much about Terran politics," Verkan Vall replied. "I know that the Statisticalists favor complete socialization and political control of the whole economy, because they want everybody to have the same opportunities in every reincarnation. And the Volitionalists believe that everybody reincarnates as he pleases, and so they favor continuance of the present system of private ownership of wealth and private profit under a system of free competition. And that's about all I do know. Naturally, as a landowner and the holder of a title of nobility, I'm a Volitionalist in politics, but the socialization issue isn't important on Venus. There is still too much unseated land there, and too many personal opportunities, to make socialism attractive to anybody."

"Well, that's about it," Zortan Brend told him. "I'm not enough of a psychicist to know what the Lady Dallona's been doing, but she's knocked the theoretical basis from under Statistical Reincarnation, and that's the basis, in turn, of Statistical Socialism. I think we'll find that the Statisticalist Party is responsible for whatever happened to her."

Marnik, the younger of the two Assassins, hesitated for a moment, then addressed Verkan Vall:

"Lord Virzal, I know none of the personalities involved in this matter, and I speak without wishing to give offense, but is it not possible that the Lady Dallona and the Assassin Dirzed may have gone somewhere together voluntarily? I have met Dirzed, and he has many qualities which women find attractive, and he is by no means indifferent to the opposite sex. You understand, Lord Virzal—"

"I understand all too perfectly, Marnik," Verkan Vall replied, out of the fullness of experience. "The Lady Dallona has had affairs with a number of men, myself among them. But under the circumstances, I find that explanation unthinkable."

Marnik looked at him in open skepticism. Evidently, in his book, where an attractive man and a beautiful woman were concerned, that explanation was never unthinkable.

"The Lady Dallona is a scientist," Verkan Vall elaborated. "She is not above diverting herself with love affairs, but that's all they are—a not too important form of diversion. And, if you recall, she had just participated in a most significant experiment: you can be sure that she had other things on her mind at the time than pleasure jaunts with good-looking Assassins."

* * * *

The ship was passing around the Caucasus Mountains, with the Caspian Sea in sight ahead, when several of the crew appeared on the observation deck and began preparing the shielding to protect the deck from gunfire. Zortan Brend inquired of the petty officer in charge of the work as to the necessity.

"We've been getting reports of trouble at Darsh, sir," the man said. "Newscast bulletins every couple of minutes: rioting in different parts of the city. Started yesterday afternoon, when a couple of Statisticalist members of the Executive Council resigned and went over to the Volitionalists. Lord Nirzav of Shonna, the only nobleman of any importance in the Statisticalist Party, was one of them; he was shot immediately afterward, while leaving the Council Chambers, along with a couple of Assassins who were with him. Some people in an airboat sprayed them with a machine rifle as they came out onto the landing stage."

The two Assassins exclaimed in horrified anger over this.

"That wasn't the work of members of the Society of Assassins!" Olirzon declared. "Even after he'd resigned, the Lord Nirzav was still immune till he left the Government Building. There's too blasted much illegal assassination going on!"

"What happened next?" Verkan Vall wanted to know.

"About what you'd expect, sir. The Volitionalists weren't going to take that quietly. In the past eighteen hours, four prominent Statistical-ists were forcibly discarnated, and there was even a fight in Mirzark of Bashad's house, when Volitionalist Assassins broke in; three of them and four of Mirzark's Assassins were discarnated."

"You know, something is going to have to be done about that, too," Olirzon said to Marnik. "It's getting to a point where these political faction fights are being carried on entirely between members of the Society. In Ghamma alone, last year, thirty or forty of our members were discarnated that way."

"Plug in a newscast visiplate, Karnil," Zortan Brend told the petty officer. "Let's see what's going on in Darsh now."

In Darsh, it seemed, an uneasy peace was being established. Verkan Vall watched heavily-armed airboats and light combat ships patrolling among the high towers of the city. He saw a couple of minor riots be-ing broken up by the blue-uniformed Constabulary, with considerable shooting and a ruthless disregard for who might get shot. It wasn't ex-actly the sort of policing that would have been tolerated in the First Level Civil Order Section, but it seemed to suit Akor-Neb conditions. And he listened to a series of angry recriminations and contradictory statements by different politicians, all of whom blamed the disorders on their opponents. The Volitionalists spoke of the Statisticalists as "insane criminals" and "underminers of social stability," and the Statisticalists called the Volitionalists "reactionary criminals" and "enemies of social progress." Politicians, he had observed, differed little in their vocabular-ies from one time-line to another.

This kept up all the while the ship was passing over the Caspian Sea; as they were turning up the Volga valley, one of the ship's officers came down from the control deck, above.

"We're coming into Darsh, now," he said, and as Verkan Vall turned from the visiplate to the forward windows, he could see the white and pastel-tinted towers of the city rising above the hardwood forests that covered the whole Volga basin on this sector. "Your luggage has been put into the airboat, Lord Virzal and Honorable Assassins, and it's ready for launching whenever you are." The officer glanced at his watch. "We dock at Commercial Center in twenty minutes; we'll be passing the Solar Hotel in ten."

They all rose, and Verkan Vall hooked fingers and clapped shoulders with Zortan Brend.

"Good luck, Lord Virzal," the latter said. "I hope you find the Lady Dallona safe and carnate. If you need help, I'll be at Mercantile House for the next day or so; if you get back to Ghamma before I do, you know who to ask for there."

* * * *

A number of assassins loitered in the hallways and offices of the Independent Institute of Reincarnation Research when Verkan Vall, accompanied by Marnik, called there that afternoon. Some of them carried submachine-guns or sleep-gas projectors, and they were stopping people and questioning them. Marnik needed only to give them a quick gesture and the words, "Assassins' Truce," and he and his client were allowed to pass. They entered a lifter tube and floated up to the office of Dr. Harnosh of Hosh, with whom Verkan Vall had made an appointment.

"I'm sorry, Lord Virzal," the director of the Institute told him, "but I have no idea what has befallen the Lady Dallona, or even if she is still carnate. I am quite worried; I admired her extremely, both as an individual and as a scientist. I do hope she hasn't been discarnated; that would be a serious blow to science. It is fortunate that she accomplished as much as she did, while she was with us."

"You think she is no longer carnate, then?"

"I'm afraid so. The political effects of her discoveries—" Harnosh of Hosh shrugged sadly. "She was devoted, to a rare degree, to her work. I am sure that nothing but her discarnation could have taken her away from us, at this time, with so many important experiments still uncompleted."

Marnik nodded to Verkan Vall, as much as to say: "You were right."

"Well, I intend acting upon the assumption that she is still carnate and in need of help, until I am positive to the contrary," Verkan Vall said. "And in the latter case, I intend finding out who discarnated her, and send him to apologize for it in person. People don't forcibly discarnate my friends with impunity."

"Sound attitude," Dr. Harnosh commented. "There's certainly no positive evidence that she isn't still carnate. I'll gladly give you all the assistance I can, if you'll only tell me what you want."

"Well, in the first place," Verkan Vall began, "just what sort of work was she doing?" He already knew the answer to that, from the reports she had sent back to the First Level, but he wanted to hear Dr. Harnosh's version. "And what, exactly, are the political effects you mentioned? Understand, Dr. Harnosh, I am really quite ignorant of any scientific subject unrelated to *zerfa* culture, and equally so of Terran politics. Politics, on Venus, is mainly a question of who gets how much graft out of what."

Dr. Harnosh smiled; evidently he had heard about Venusian politics. "Ah, yes, of course. But you are familiar with the main differences between Statistical and Volitional reincarnation theories?"

"In a general way. The Volitionalists hold that the discarnate individuality is fully conscious, and is capable of something analogous to sense-perception, and is also capable of exercising choice in the matter of reincarnation vehicles, and can reincarnate or remain in the discarnate state as it chooses. They also believe that discarnate individualities can communicate with one another, and with at least some carnate individualities, by telepathy," he said. "The Statisticalists deny all this; their opinion is that the discarnate individuality is in a more or less somnambulistic state, that it is drawn by a process akin to tropism to the nearest available reincarnation vehicle, and that it must reincarnate in and only in that vehicle. They are labeled Statisticalists because they believe that the process of reincarnation is purely at random, or governed by unknown and uncontrollable causes, and is unpredictable except as to aggregates."

"That's a fairly good generalized summary," Dr. Harnosh of Hosh grudged, unwilling to give a mere layman too much credit. He dipped a spoon into a tobacco humidor, dusted the tobacco lightly with dried *zerfa*, and rammed it into his pipe. "You must understand that our modern Statisticalists are the intellectual heirs of those ancient materialistic thinkers who denied the possibility of any discarnate existence, or of any extraphysical mind, or even of extrasensory perception. Since all these things have been demonstrated to be facts, the materialistic dogma has been broadened to include them, but always strictly within the frame of materialism.

"We have proven, for instance, that the human individuality can exist in a discarnate state, and that it reincarnates into the body of an infant, shortly after birth. But the Statisticalists cannot accept the idea of discarnate consciousness, since they conceive of consciousness purely as a function of the physical brain. So they postulate an unconscious discarnate personality, or, as you put it, one in a somnambulistic state. They have to concede memory to this discarnate personality, since it was by recovery of memories of previous reincarnations that discarnate existence and reincarnation were proven to be facts. So they picture the discarnate individuality as a material object, or physical event, of negligible but actual mass, in which an indefinite number of memories can be stored as electronic charges. And they picture it as being drawn irresistibly to the body of the nearest non-incarnated infant. Curiously enough, the reincarnation vehicle chosen is almost always of the same sex as the vehicle of the previous reincarnation, the exceptions being cases of persons who had a previous history of psychological sex-inversion."

Dr. Harnosh remembered the unlighted pipe in his hand, thrust it into his mouth, and lit it. For a moment, he sat with it jutting out of his black beard, until it was drawing to his satisfaction. "This belief in immediate reincarnation leads the Statisticalists, when they fight duels or perform voluntary discarnation, to do so in the neighborhood of maternity hospitals," he added. "I know, personally, of one reincarnation memory-recall, in which the subject, a Statisticalist, voluntarily discarnated by lethal-gas inhaler in a private room at one of our local maternity hospitals, and reincarnated twenty years later in the city of Jeddul, three thousand miles away." The square black beard jiggled as the scientist laughed.

"Now, as to the political implications of these contradictory theories: Since the Statisticalists believe that they will reincarnate entirely at random, their aim is to create an utterly classless social and economic order, in which, theoretically, each individuality will reincarnate into a condition of equality with everybody else. Their political program, therefore, is one of complete socialization of all means of production and distribution, abolition of hereditary titles and inherited wealth—eventually, all private wealth—and total government control of all economic, social and cultural activities. Of course," Dr. Harnosh apologized, "politics isn't my subject; I wouldn't presume to judge how that would function in practice."

"I would," Verkan Vall said shortly, thinking of all the different time-lines on which he had seen systems like that in operation. "You wouldn't like it, doctor. And the Volitionalists?"

"Well, since they believe that they are able to choose the circumstances of their next reincarnations for themselves, they are the party of the *status quo*. Naturally, almost all the nobles, almost all the wealthy trading and manufacturing families, and almost all professional people, are Volitionalists; most of the workers and peasants are Statisticalists. Or, at least, they were, for the most part, before we began announcing the results of the Lady Dallona's experimental work."

"Ah; now we come to it," Verkan Vall said as the story clarified.

"Yes. In somewhat oversimplified form, the situation is rather like this," Dr. Harnosh of Hosh said. "The Lady Dallona introduced a number of refinements and some outright innovations into our technique of recovering memories of past reincarnations. Previously, it was necessary to keep the subject in an hypnotic trance, during which he or she would narrate what was remembered of past reincarnations, and this would be recorded. On emerging from the trance, the subject would remember nothing; the tape-recording would be all that would be left. But the Lady Dallona devised a technique by which these memories would remain in what might be called the fore part of the subject's subconscious mind, so that they could be brought to the level of consciousness at will. More, she was able to recover memories of past discarnate existences, something we had never been able to do heretofore." Dr. Harnosh shook his head. "And to think, when I first met her, I thought that she was just another sensation-seeking young lady of wealth, and was almost about to refuse her enrollment!"

He wasn't the only one whom little Dalla had surprised, Verkan Vall thought. At least, he had been pleasantly surprised.

"You see, this entirely disproves the Statistical Theory of Reincarnation. For example, we got a fine set of memory-recalls from one subject, for four previous reincarnations and four intercarnations. In the first of these, the subject had been a peasant on the estate of a wealthy noble. Unlike most of his fellows, who reincarnated into other peasant families almost immediately after discarnation, this man waited for fifty years in the discarnate state for an opportunity to reincarnate as the son of an over-servant. In his next reincarnation, he was the son of a technician, and received a technical education; he became a physics researcher. For his next reincarnation, he chose the son of a nobleman by a concubine as his vehicle; in his present reincarnation, he is a member of a wealthy manufacturing family, and married into a family of the nobility. In five reincarnations, he has climbed from the lowest to the next-to-highest rung of the social ladder. Few individuals of the class from whence he began this ascent possess so much persistence or determination. Then, of course, there was the case of Lord Garnon of Roxor."

He went on to describe the last experiment in which Hadron Dalla had participated.

"Well, that all sounds pretty conclusive," Verkan Vall commented. "I take it the leaders of the Volitionalist Party here are pleased with the result of the Lady Dallona's work?"

"Pleased? My dear Lord Virzal, they're fairly bursting with glee over it!" Harnosh of Hosh declared. "As I pointed out, the Statisticalist program of socialization is based entirely on the proposition that no one can choose the circumstances of his next reincarnation, and that's been demonstrated to be utter nonsense. Until the Lady Dallona's discoveries were announced, they were the dominant party, controlling a majority of the seats in Parliament and on the Executive Council. Only the Constitution kept them from enacting their entire socialization program long ago, and they were about to legislate constitutional changes which would remove that barrier. They had expected to be able to do so after the forthcoming general elections. But now, social inequality has become desirable: it gives people something to look forward to in the next reincarnation. Instead of wanting to abolish wealth and privilege and nobility, the proletariat want to reincarnate into them." Harnosh of Hosh laughed happily. "So you can see how furious the Statisticalist Party organization is!"

"There's a catch to this, somewhere," Marnik the Assassin, speaking for the first time, declared. "They can't all reincarnate as princes, there aren't enough vacancies to go 'round. And no noble is going to reincarnate as a tractor driver to make room for a tractor driver who wants to reincarnate as a noble."

"That's correct," Dr. Harnosh replied. "There is a catch to it; a catch most people would never admit, even to themselves. Very few individuals possess the will power, the intelligence or the capacity for mental effort displayed by the subject of the case I just quoted. The average man's interests are almost entirely on the physical side; he actually finds mental effort painful, and makes as little of it as possible. And that is the only sort of effort a discarnate individuality can exert. So, unable to endure the fifty or so years needed to make a really good reincarnation, he reincarnates in a year or so, out of pure boredom, into the first vehicle he can find, usually one nobody else wants." Dr. Harnosh dug out the heel of his pipe and blew through the stem. "But nobody will admit his own mental inferiority, even to himself. Now, every machine operator and field hand on the planet thinks he can reincarnate as a prince or a millionaire. Politics isn't my subject, but I'm willing to bet that since Statistical Reincarnation is an exploded psychic theory, Statisticalist Socialism has been caught in the blast area and destroyed along with it."

* * * *

Olirzon was in the drawing room of the hotel suite when they returned, sitting on the middle of his spinal column in a reclining chair, smoking a pipe, dressing the edge of his knife with a pocket-hone, and gazing lecherously at a young woman in the visiplate. She was an extremely well-designed young woman, in a rather fragmentary costume, and she was heaving her bosom at the invisible audience in anger, sorrow, scorn, entreaty, and numerous other emotions.

"... this revolting crime," she was declaiming, in a husky contralto, as Verkan Vall and Marnik entered, "foul even for the criminal beasts who conceived and perpetrated it!" She pointed an accusing finger. "This murder of the beautiful Lady Dallona of Hadron!"

Verkan Vall stopped short, considering the possibility of something having been discovered lately of which he was ignorant. Olirzon must have guessed his thought; he grinned reassuringly.

"Think nothing of it, Lord Virzal," he said, waving his knife at the visiplate. "Just political propaganda; strictly for the sparrows. Nice propagandist, though."

"And now," the woman with the magnificent natural resources lowered her voice reverently, "we bring you the last image of the Lady Dallona, and of Dirzed, her faithful Assassin, taken just before they vanished, never to be seen again."

The plate darkened, and there were strains of slow, dirgelike music; then it lighted again, presenting a view of a broad hallway, thronged with men and women in bright varicolored costumes. In the foreground, wearing a tight skirt of deep blue and a short red jacket, was Hadron Dalla, just as she had looked in the solidographs taken in Dhergabar after her alteration by the First Level cosmeticians to conform to the appearance of the Malayoid Akor-Neb people. She was holding the arm of a man who wore the black tunic and red badge of an Assassin, a handsome specimen of the Akor-Neb race. Trust little Dalla for that, Verkan Vall thought. The figures were moving with exaggerated slowness, as though a very fleeting picture were being stretched out as far as possible. Having already memorized his former wife's changed appearance, Verkan Vall concentrated on the man beside her until the picture faded.

"All right, Olirzon; what did you get?" he asked.

"Well, first of all, at Assassins' Hall," Olirzon said, rolling up his left sleeve, holding his bare forearm to the light, and shaving a few fine hairs from it to test the edge of his knife. "Of course, they never tell one Assassin anything about the client of another Assassin; that's standard practice. But I was in the Lodge Secretary's office, where nobody but Assassins are ever admitted. They have a big panel in there, with the names of all the Lodge members on it in light-letters; that's standard in all Lodges. If an Assassin is unattached and free to accept a client, his name's in white light. If he has a client, the light's changed to blue, and the name of the client goes up under his. If his whereabouts are unknown, the light's changed to amber. If he is discarnated, his name's removed entirely, unless the circumstances of his discarnation are such as to constitute an injury to the Society. In that case, the name's in red light until he's been properly avenged, or, as we say, till his blood's been mopped up. Well, the name of Dirzed is up in blue light, with the name of Dallona of Hadron under it. I found out that the light had been amber for two days after the disappearance, and then had been changed back to blue. Get it, Lord Virzal?"

Verkan Vall nodded. "I think so. I'd been considering that as a possibility from the first. Then what?"

"Then I was about and around for a couple of hours, buying drinks for people—unattached Assassins, Constabulary detectives, political workers, newscast people. You owe me fifteen System Monetary Units for that, Lord Virzal. What I got, when it's all sorted out—I taped it in detail, as soon as I got back—reduces to this: The Volitionalists are moving mountains to find out who was the spy at Garnon of Roxor's discarnation feast, but are doing nothing but nothing at all to find the Lady Dallona or Dirzed. The Statisticalists are making all sorts of secret efforts to find out what happened to her. The Constabulary blame the Statistos for the package-bomb: they're interested in that because of the discarnation of the three servants by an illegal weapon of indiscriminate effect. They claim that the disappearance of Dirzed and the Lady Dallona was a publicity hoax. The Volitionalists are preparing a line of publicity to deny this."

Verkan Vall nodded. "That ties in with what you learned at Assassins' Hall," he said. "They're hiding out somewhere. Is there any chance of reaching Dirzed through the Society of Assassins?"

Olirzon shook his head. "If you're right—and that's the way it looks to me, too—he's probably just called in and notified the Society that he's still carnate and so is the Lady Dallona, and called off any search the Society might be making for him."

"And I've got to find the Lady Dallona as soon as I can. Well, if I can't reach her, maybe I can get her to send word to me," Verkan Vall said. "That's going to take some doing, too."

"What did you find out, Lord Virzal?" Olirzon asked. He had a piece of soft leather, now, and was polishing his blade lovingly.

"The Reincarnation Research people don't know anything," Verkan Vall replied. "Dr. Harnosh of Hosh thinks she's discarnate. I did find out that the experimental work she's done, so far, has absolutely disproved the theory of Statistical Reincarnation. The Volitionalists' theory is solidly established."

"Yes, what do you think, Olirzon?" Marnik added. "They have a case on record of a man who worked up from field hand to millionaire in five reincarnations. Deliberately, that is." He went on to repeat what Harnosh of Hosh had said; he must have possessed an almost eidetic memory, for he gave the bearded psychicist's words verbatim, and threw in the gestures and voice-inflections.

Olirzon grinned. "You know, there's a chance for the easy-money boys," he considered. "'You, too, can Reincarnate as a millionaire! Let

Dr. Nirzutz of Futzbutz Help You! Only 49.98 System Monetary Units for the Secret, Infallible, Autosuggestive Formula.' And would it sell!" He put away the hone and the bit of leather and slipped his knife back into its sheath. "If I weren't a respectable Assassin, I'd give it a try, myself."

Verkan Vall looked at his watch. "We'd better get something to eat," he said. "We'll go down to the main dining room; the Martian Room, I think they call it. I've got to think of some way to let the Lady Dallona know I'm looking for her."

* * * *

The Martian Room, fifteen stories down, was a big place, occupying almost half of the floor space of one corner tower. It had been fitted to resemble one of the ruined buildings of the ancient and vanished race of Mars who were the ancestors of Terran humanity. One whole side of the room was a gigantic cine-solidograph screen, on which the gullied desolation of a Martian landscape was projected; in the course of about two hours, the scene changed from sunrise through daylight and night to sunrise again.

It was high noon when they entered and found a table; by the time they had finished their dinner, the night was ending and the first glow of dawn was tinting the distant hills. They sat for a while, watching the light grow stronger, then got up and left the table.

There were five men at a table near them; they had come in before the stars had grown dim, and the waiters were just bringing their first dishes. Two were Assassins, and the other three were of a breed Verkan Vall had learned to recognize on any time-line—the arrogant, cocksure, ambitious, leftist politician, who knows what is best for everybody better than anybody else does, and who is convinced that he is inescapably right and that whoever differs with him is not only an ignoramus but a venal scoundrel as well. One was a beefy man in a gold-laced cream-colored dress tunic; he had thick lips and a too-ready laugh. Another was a rather monkish-looking young man who spoke earnestly and rolled his eyes upward, as though at some celestial vision. The third had the faint powdering of gray in his black hair which was, among the Akor-Neb people, almost the only indication of advanced age.

"Of course it is; the whole thing is a fraud," the monkish young man was saying angrily. "But we can't prove it."

"Oh, Sirzob, here, can prove anything, if you give him time," the beefy one laughed. "The trouble is, there isn't too much time. We know that that communication was a fake, prearranged by the Volitionalists, with Dr. Harnosh and this Dallona of Hadron as their tools. They fed the whole thing to that idiot boy hypnotically, in advance, and then, on a signal, he began typing out this spurious communication. And then, of course, Dallona and this Assassin of hers ran off somewhere together, so that we'd be blamed with discarnating or abducting them, and so that they wouldn't be made to testify about the communication on a lie detector."

A sudden happy smile touched Verkan Vall's eyes. He caught each of his Assassins by an arm.

"Marnik, cover my back," he ordered. "Olirzon, cover everybody at the table. Come on!"

Then he stepped forward, halting between the chairs of the young man and the man with the gray hair and facing the beefy man in the light tunic.

"You!" he barked. "I mean YOU."

The beefy man stopped laughing and stared at him; then sprang to his feet. His hand, streaking toward his left armpit, stopped and dropped to his side as Olirzon aimed a pistol at him. The others sat motionless.

"You," Verkan Vall continued, "are a complete, deliberate, malicious, and unmitigated liar. The Lady Dallona of Hadron is a scientist of integrity, incapable of falsifying her experimental work. What's more, her father is one of my best friends; in his name, and in hers, I demand a full retraction of the slanderous statements you have just made."

"Do you know who I am?" the beefy one shouted.

"I know *what* you are," Verkan Vall shouted back. Like most ancient languages, the Akor-Neb speech included an elaborate, delicately-shaded, and utterly vile vocabulary of abuse; Verkan Vall culled from it judiciously and at length. "And if I don't make myself understood verbally, we'll go down to the object level," he added, snatching a bowl of soup from in front of the monkish-looking young man and throwing it across the table.

The soup was a dark brown, almost black. It contained bits of meat, and mushrooms, and slices of hard-boiled egg, and yellow Martian rock lichen. It produced, on the light tunic, a most spectacular effect.

For a moment, Verkan Vall was afraid the fellow would have an apo-plectic stroke, or an epileptic fit. Mastering himself, however, he bowed jerkily.

"Marnark of Bashad," he identified himself. "When and where can my friends consult yours?"

"Lord Virzal of Verkan," the paratimer bowed back. "Your friends can negotiate with mine here and now. I am represented by these Gen-tlemen-Assassins."

"I won't submit my friends to the indignity of negotiating with them," Marnark retorted. "I insist that you be represented by persons of your own quality and mine."

"Oh, you do?" Olirzon broke in. "Well, is your objection personal to me, or to Assassins as a class? In the first case, I'll remember to make a private project of you, as soon as I'm through with my present employ-ment; if it's the latter, I'll report your attitude to the Society. I'll see what Klarnood, our President-General, thinks of your views."

A crowd had begun to accumulate around the table. Some of them were persons in evening dress, some were Assassins on the hotel pay-roll, and some were unattached Assassins.

"Well, you won't have far to look for him," one of the latter said, pushing through the crowd to the table.

He was a man of middle age, inclined to stoutness; he made Verkan Vall think of a chocolate figure of Tortha Karf. The red badge on his breast was surrounded with gold lace, and, instead of black wings and a silver bullet, it bore silver wings and a golden dagger. He bowed con-temptuously at Marnark of Bashad.

"Klarnood, President-General of the Society of Assassins," he an-nounced. "Marnark of Bashad, did I hear you say that you considered members of the Society as unworthy to negotiate an affair of honor with your friends, on behalf of this nobleman who has been courteous enough to accept your challenge?" he demanded.

Marnark of Bashad's arrogance suffered considerable evaporation-loss. His tone became almost servile.

"Not at all, Honorable Assassin-President," he protested. "But as I was going to ask these gentlemen to represent me, I thought it would be more fitting for the other gentleman to be represented by personal friends, also. In that way—"

"Sorry, Marnark," the gray-haired man at the table said. "I can't second you; I have a quarrel with the Lord Virzal, too." He rose and bowed. "Sirzob of Abo. Inasmuch as the Honorable Marnark is a guest at my table, an affront to him is an affront to me. In my quality as his host, I must demand satisfaction from you, Lord Virzal."

"Why, gladly, Honorable Sirzob," Verkan Vall replied. This was getting better and better every moment. "Of course, your friend, the Honorable Marnark, enjoys priority of challenge; I'll take care of you as soon as I have, shall we say, satisfied, him."

The earnest and rather consecrated-looking young man rose also, bowing to Verkan Vall.

"Yirzol of Narva. I, too, have a quarrel with you, Lord Virzal; I cannot submit to the indignity of having my food snatched from in front of me, as you just did. I also demand satisfaction."

"And quite rightly, Honorable Yirzol," Verkan Vall approved. "It looks like such good soup, too," he sorrowed, inspecting the front of Marnark's tunic. "My seconds will negotiate with yours immediately; your satisfaction, of course, must come after that of Honorable Sirzob."

"If I may intrude," Klarnood put in smoothly, "may I suggest that as the Lord Virzal is represented by his Assassins, yours can represent all three of you at the same time. I will gladly offer my own good offices as impartial supervisor."

Verkan Vall turned and bowed as to royalty. "An honor, Assassin-President: I am sure no one could act in that capacity more satisfactorily."

"Well, when would it be most convenient to arrange the details?" Klarnood inquired. "I am completely at your disposal, gentlemen."

"Why, here and now, while we're all together," Verkan Vall replied.

"I object to that!" Marnark of Bashad vociferated. "We can't make arrangements here; why, all these hotel people, from the manager down, are nothing but tipsters for the newscast services!"

"Well, what's wrong with that?" Verkan Vall demanded. "You knew that when you slandered the Lady Dallona in their hearing."

"The Lord Virzal of Verkan is correct," Klarnood ruled. "And the offenses for which you have challenged him were also committed in public. By all means, let's discuss the arrangements now." He turned to Verkan Vall. "As the challenged party, you have the choice of weapons; your opponents, then, have the right to name the conditions under which they are to be used."

Marnark of Bashad raised another outcry over that. The assault upon him by the Lord Virzal of Verkan was deliberately provocative, and therefore tantamount to a challenge; he, himself, had the right to name the weapons. Klarnood upheld him.

"Do the other gentlemen make the same claim?" Verkan Vall wanted to know.

"If they do, I won't allow it," Klarnood replied. "You deliberately provoked Honorable Marnark, but the offenses of provoking him at Honorable Sirzob's table, and of throwing Honorable Yirzol's soup at him, were not given with intent to provoke. These gentlemen have a right to challenge, but not to consider themselves provoked."

"Well, I choose knives, then," Marnark hastened to say.

Verkan Vall smiled thinly. He had learned knife-play among the greatest masters of that art in all paratime, the Third Level Khanga pirates of the Caribbean Islands.

"And we fight barefoot, stripped to the waist, and without any parrying weapon in the left hand," Verkan Vall stipulated.

The beefy Marnark fairly licked his chops in anticipation. He outweighed Verkan Vall by forty pounds; he saw an easy victory ahead. Verkan Vall's own confidence increased at these signs of his opponent's assurance.

"And as for Honorable Sirzob and Honorable Yirzol, I chose pistols," he added.

Sirzob and Yirzol held a hasty whispered conference.

"Speaking both for Honorable Yirzol and for myself," Sirzob announced, "we stipulate that the distance shall be twenty meters, that the pistols shall be fully loaded, and that fire shall be at will after the command."

"Twenty rounds, fire at will, at twenty meters!" Olirzon hooted. "You must think our principal's as bad a shot as you are!"

The four Assassins stepped aside and held a long discussion about something, with considerable argument and gesticulation. Klarnood, observing Verkan Vall's impatience, leaned close to him and whispered:

"This is highly irregular; we must pretend ignorance and be patient. They're laying bets on the outcome. You must do your best, Lord Virzal; you don't want your supporters to lose money."

He said it quite seriously, as though the outcome were otherwise a matter of indifference to Verkan Vall.

Marnark wanted to discuss time and place, and proposed that all three duels be fought at dawn, on the fourth landing stage of Darsh Central Hospital; that was closest to the maternity wards, and statistics showed that most births occurred just before that hour.

"Certainly not," Verkan Vall vetoed. "We'll fight here and now; I don't propose going a couple of hundred miles to meet you at any such unholy hour. We'll fight in the nearest hallway that provides twenty meters' shooting distance."

Marnark, Sirzob and Yirzol all clamored in protest. Verkan Vall shouted them down, drawing on his hypnotically acquired knowledge of Akor-Neb duelling customs. "The code explicitly states that satisfaction shall be rendered as promptly as possible, and I insist on a literal interpretation. I'm not going to inconvenience myself and Assassin-President Klarnood and these four Gentlemen-Assassins just to humor Statisticalist superstitions."

The manager of the hotel, drawn to the Martian Room by the uproar, offered a hallway connecting the kitchens with the refrigerator rooms; it was fifty meters long by five in width, was well-lighted and soundproof, and had a bay in which the seconds and other could stand during the firing.

They repaired thither in a body, Klarnood gathering up several hotel servants on the way through the kitchen. Verkan Vall stripped to the waist, pulled off his ankle boots, and examined Olirzon's knife. Its tapering eight-inch blade was double-edged at the point, and its handle was covered with black velvet to afford a good grip, and wound with gold wire. He nodded approvingly, gripped it with his index finger crooked around the cross-guard, and advanced to meet Marnark of Bashad.

As he had expected, the burly politician was depending upon his greater brawn to overpower his antagonist. He advanced with a sidling, spread-legged gait, his knife hand against his right hip and his left hand extended in front. Verkan Vall nodded with pleased satisfaction; a wrist-grabber. Then he blinked. Why, the fellow was actually holding his knife reversed, his little finger to the guard and his thumb on the pommel!

Verkan Vall went briskly to meet him, made a feint at his knife hand with his own left, and then side-stepped quickly to the right. As Marnark's left hand grabbed at his right wrist, his left hand brushed against it and closed into a fist, with Marnark's left thumb inside of it, He gave a quick downward twist with his wrist, pulling Marnark off balance.

Caught by surprise, Marnark stumbled, his knife flailing wildly away from Verkan Vall. As he stumbled forward, Verkan Vall pivoted on his left heel and drove the point of his knife into the back of Marnark's neck, twisting it as he jerked it free. At the same time, he released Marnark's thumb. The politician continued his stumble and fell forward on his face, blood spurting from his neck. He gave a twitch or so, and was still.

Verkan Vall stooped and wiped the knife on the dead man's clothes—another Khanga pirate gesture—and then returned it to Olirzon.

"Nice weapon, Olirzon," he said. "It fitted my hand as though I'd been born holding it."

"You used it as though you had, Lord Virzal," the Assassin replied. "Only eight seconds from the time you closed with him."

The function of the hotel servants whom Klarnood had gathered up now became apparent; they advanced, took the body of Marnark by the heels, and dragged it out of the way. The others watched this removal with mixed emotions. The two remaining principals were impassive and frozen-faced. Their two Assassins, who had probably bet heavily on Marnark, were chagrined. And Klarnood was looking at Verkan Vall with a considerable accretion of respect. Verkan Vall pulled on his boots and resumed his clothing.

There followed some argument about the pistols; it was finally decided that each combatant should use his own shoulder-holster weapon. All three were nearly enough alike—small weapons, rather heavier than they looked, firing a tiny ten-grain bullet at ten thousand foot-seconds. On impact, such a bullet would almost disintegrate; a man hit anywhere in the body with one would be killed instantly, his nervous system paralyzed and his heart stopped by internal pressure. Each of the pistols carried twenty rounds in the magazine.

Verkan Vall and Sirzob of Abo took their places, their pistols lowered at their sides, facing each other across a measured twenty meters.

"Are you ready, gentlemen?" Klarnood asked. "You will not raise your pistols until the command to fire; you may fire at will after it. Ready. *Fire!*"

Both pistols swung up to level. Verkan Vall found Sirzob's head in his sights and squeezed; the pistol kicked back in his hand, and he saw a lance of blue flame jump from the muzzle of Sirzob's. Both weapons barked together, and with the double report came the whip-cracking sound of Sirzob's bullet passing Verkan Vall's head. Then Sirzob's face altered its appearance unpleasantly, and he pitched forward. Verkan Vall thumbed on his safety and stood motionless, while the servants advanced, took Sirzob's body by the heels, and dragged it over beside Marnark's.

"All right; Honorable Yirzol, you're next," Verkan Vall called out.

"The Lord Virzal has fired one shot," one of the opposing seconds objected, "and Honorable Yirzol has a full magazine. The Lord Virzal should put in another magazine."

"I grant him the advantage; let's get on with it," Verkan Vall said.

Yirzol of Narva advanced to the firing point. He was not afraid of death—none of the Akor-Neb people were; their language contained no word to express the concept of total and final extinction—and discarnation by gunshot was almost entirely painless. But he was beginning to suspect that he had made a fool of himself by getting into this affair, he had work in his present reincarnation which he wanted to finish, and his political party would suffer loss, both of his services and of prestige.

"Are you ready, gentlemen?" Klarnood intoned ritualistically. "You will not raise your pistols until the command to fire; you may fire at will after it. Ready, *Fire!*"

Verkan Vall shot Yirzol of Narva through the head before the latter had his pistol half raised. Yirzol fell forward on the splash of blood Sirzob had made, and the servants came forward and dragged his body over with the others. It reminded Verkan Vail of some sort of industrial assembly-line operation. He replaced the two expended rounds in his magazine with fresh ones and slid the pistol back into its holster. The two Assassins whose principals had been so expeditiously massacred were beginning to count up their losses and pay off the winners.

Klarnood, the President-General of the Society of Assassins, came over, hooking fingers and clapping shoulders with Verkan Vall.

"Lord Virzal, I've seen quite a few duels, but nothing quite like that," he said. "You should have been an Assassin!"

That was a considerable compliment. Verkan Vall thanked him modestly.

"I'd like to talk to you privately," the Assassin-President continued. "I think it'll be worth your while if we have a few words together."

Verkan Vall nodded. "My suite is on the fifteenth floor above; will that be all right?" He waited until the losers had finished settling their bets, then motioned to his own pair of Assassins.

* * * *

As they emerged into the Martian Room again, the manager was waiting; he looked as though he were about to demand that Verkan Vall vacate his suite. However, when he saw the arm of the President-General of the Society of Assassins draped amicably over his guest's shoulder, he came forward bowing and smiling.

"Larnorm, I want you to put five of your best Assassins to guarding the approaches to the Lord Virzal's suite," Klarnood told him. "I'll send five more from Assassins' Hall to replace them at their ordinary duties. And I'll hold you responsible with your carnate existence for the Lord Virzal's safety in this hotel. Understand?"

"Oh, yes, Honorable Assassin-President; you may trust me. The Lord Virzal will be perfectly safe."

In Verkan Vall's suite, above, Klarnood sat down and got out his pipe, filling it with tobacco lightly mixed with *zerfa*. To his surprise, he saw his host light a plain tobacco cigarette.

"Don't you use *zerfa*?" he asked.

"Very little," Verkan Vall replied. "I grow it. If you'd see the bums who hang around our drying sheds, on Venus, cadging rejected leaves and smoking themselves into a stupor, you'd be frugal in using it, too."

Klarnood nodded. "You know, most men would want a pipe of fifty percent, or a straight *zerfa* cigarette, after what you've been through," he said.

"I'd need something like that, to deaden my conscience, if I had one to deaden," Verkan Vall said. "As it is, I feel like a murderer of babes. That overgrown fool, Marnark, handled his knife like a cow-butcher. The young fellow couldn't handle a pistol at all. I suppose the old fellow, Sirzob, was a fair shot, but dropping him wasn't any great feat of arms, either."

Klarnood looked at him curiously for a moment. "You know," he said, at length, "I believe you actually mean that. Well, until he met you, Marnark of Bashad was rated as the best knife-fighter in Darsh. Sirzob had ten dueling victories to his credit, and young Yirzol four." He puffed slowly on his pipe. "I like you, Lord Virzal; a great Assassin was lost when you decided to reincarnate as a Venusian land-owner. I'd hate to see you discarnated without proper warning. I take it you're ignorant of the intricacies of Terran politics?"

"To a large extent, yes."

"Well, do you know who those three men were?" When Verkan Vall shook his head, Klarnood continued: "Marnark was the son and right-hand associate of old Mirzark of Bashad, the Statisticalist Party leader. Sirzob of Abo was their propaganda director. And Yirzol of Narva was their leading socio-economic theorist, and their candidate for Executive Chairman. In six minutes, with one knife thrust and two shots, you did the Statisticalist Party an injury second only to that done them by the young lady in whose name you were fighting. In two weeks, there will be a planet-wide general election. As it stands, the Statisticalists have a majority of the seats in Parliament and on the Executive Council. As a result of your work and the Lady Dallona's, they'll lose that majority, and more, when the votes are tallied."

"Is that another reason why you like me?" Verkan Vall asked.

"Unofficially, yes. As President-General of the Society of Assassins, I must be nonpolitical. The Society is rigidly so; if we let ourselves become involved, as an organization, in politics, we could control the System Government inside of five years, and we'd be wiped out of existence in fifty years by the very forces we sought to control," Klarnood said. "But personally, I would like to see the Statisticalist Party destroyed. If they succeed in their program of socialization, the Society would be finished. A socialist state is, in its final development, an absolute, total, state; no total state can tolerate extra-legal and para-governmental organizations. So we have adopted the policy of giving a little inconspicuous aid, here and there, to people who are dangerous to the Statisticalists. The Lady Dallona of Hadron, and Dr. Harnosh of Hosh, are such persons. You appear to be another. That's why I ordered that fellow, Larnorm, to make sure you were safe in his hotel."

"Where is the Lady Dallona?" Verkan Vall asked. "From your use of the present tense, I assume you believe her to be still carnate."

Klarnood looked at Verkan Vall keenly. "That's a pretty blunt question, Lord Virzal," he said. "I wish I knew a little more about you. When you and your Assassins started inquiring about the Lady Dallona, I tried to check up on you. I found out that you had come to Darsh from Ghamma on a ship of the family of Zorda, accompanied by Brarnend of Zorda himself. And that's all I could find out. You claim to be a Venusian planter, and you might be. Any Terran who can handle weapons as you can would have come to my notice long ago. But you have no more ascertainable history than if you'd stepped out of another dimension."

That was getting uncomfortably close to the truth. In fact, it *was* the truth. Verkan Vall laughed.

"Well, confidentially," he said, "I'm from the Arcturus System. I followed the Lady Dallona here from our home planet, and when I have rescued her from among you Solarians, I shall, according to our customs, receive her hand in marriage. As she is the daughter of the Emperor of Arcturus, that'll be quite a good thing for me."

Klarnood chuckled. "You know, you'd only have to tell me that about three or four times and I'd start believing it," he said. "And Dr. Harnosh of Hosh would believe it the first time; he's been talking to himself ever since the Lady Dallona started her experimental work here. Lord Virzal, I'm going to take a chance on you. The Lady Dallona is still carnate, or was four days ago, and the same for Dirzed. They both went into hiding after the discarnation feast of Garnon of Roxor, to escape the enmity of the Statisticalists. Two days after they disappeared, Dirzed called Assassins' Hall and reported this, but told us nothing more. I suppose, in about three or four days, I could re-establish contact with him. We want the public to think that the Statisticalists made away with the Lady Dallona, at least until the election's over."

Verkan Vall nodded. "I was pretty sure that was the situation," he said. "It may be that they will get in touch with me; if they don't, I'll need your help in reaching them."

"Why do you think the Lady Dallona will try to reach you?"

"She needs all the help she can get. She knows she can get plenty from me. Why do you think I interrupted my search for her, and risked my carnate existence, to fight those people over a matter of verbalisms and political propaganda?" Verkan Vall went to the newscast visiplate and snapped it on. "We'll see if I'm getting results, yet."

The plate lighted, and a handsome young man in a gold-laced green suit was speaking out of it:

"... where he is heavily guarded by Assassins. However, in an exclusive interview with representatives of this service, the Assassin Hirzif, one of the two who seconded the men the Lord Virzal fought, said that in his opinion all of the three were so outclassed as to have had no chance whatever, and that he had already refused an offer of ten thousand System Monetary Units to discarnate the Lord Virzal for the Statisticalist Party. 'When I want to discarnate,' Hirzif the Assassin said, 'I'll invite in my friends and do it properly; until I do, I wouldn't go up against the Lord Virzal of Verkan for ten million S.M.U.'"

Verkan Vall snapped off the visiplate. "See what I mean?" he asked. "I fought those politicians just for the advertising. If Dallona and Dirzed are anywhere near a visiplate, they'll know how to reach me."

"Hirzif shouldn't have talked about refusing that retainer," Klarnood frowned. "That isn't good Assassin ethics. Why, yes, Lord Virzal; that was cleverly planned. It ought to get results. But I wish you'd get the Lady Dallona out of Darsh, and preferably off Terra, as soon as you can. We've benefited by this, so far, but I shouldn't like to see things go much further. A real civil war could develop out of this situation, and I don't want that. Call on me for help; I'll give you a code word to use at Assassins' Hall."

* * * *

A real civil war was developing even as Klarnood spoke; by mid-morning of the next day, the fighting that had been partially suppressed by the Constabulary had broken out anew. The Assassins employed by the Solar Hotel—heavily re-enforced during the night—had fought a pitched battle with Statisticalist partisans on the landing-stage above Verkan Vall's suite, and now several Constabulary airboats were patrolling around the building. The rule on Constabulary interference seemed to be that while individuals had an unquestionable right to shoot out their differences among themselves, any fighting likely to endanger nonparticipants was taboo.

Just how successful in enforcing this rule the Constabulary were was open to some doubt. Ever since arising, Verkan Vall had heard the crash of small arms and the hammering of automatic weapons in other parts of the towering city-unit. There hadn't been a civil war on the Akor-Neb Sector for over five centuries, he knew, but then, Hadron Dalla, Doctor of Psychic Science, and intertemporal trouble-carrier extraordinary, had only been on this sector for a little under a year. If anything, he was surprised that the explosion had taken so long to occur.

One of the servants furnished to him by the hotel management approached him in the drawing room, holding a four-inch-square wafer of white plastic.

"Lord Virzal, there is a masked Assassin in the hallway who brought this under Assassins' Truce," he said.

Verkan Vall took the wafer and pared off three of the four edges, which showed black where they had been fused. Unfolding it, he found, as he had expected, that the pyrographed message within was in the alphabet and language of the First Paratime Level:

Vall, darling:
    Am I glad you got here; this time I really *am* in the middle, but good! The Assassin, Dirzed, who brings this, is in my service. You can trust him implicitly; he's about the only person in Darsh you can trust. He'll bring you to where I am.

Dalla

P.S. I hope you're not still angry about that musician. I told you, at the time, that he was just helping me with an experiment in telepathy.

D.

Verkan Vall grinned at the postscript. That had been twenty years ago, when he'd been eighty and she'd been seventy. He supposed she'd expect him to take up his old relationship with her again. It probably wouldn't last any longer than it had, the other time; he recalled a Fourth Level proverb about the leopard and his spots. It certainly wouldn't be boring, though.

"Tell the Assassin to come in," he directed. Then he tossed the message down on a table. Outside of himself, nobody in Darsh could read it but the woman who had sent it; if, as he thought highly probable, the Statisticalists had spies among the hotel staff, it might serve to reduce some cryptanalyst to gibbering insanity.

The Assassin entered, drawing off a cowllike mask. He was the man whose arm Dalla had been holding in the visiplate picture; Verkan Vall even recognized the extremely ornate pistol and knife on his belt.

"Dirzed the Assassin," he named himself. "If you wish, we can visiphone Assassins' Hall for verification of my identity."

"Lord Virzal of Verkan. And my Assassins, Marnik and Olirzon." They all hooked fingers and clapped shoulders with the newcomer. "That won't be needed," Verkan Vall told Dirzed. "I know you from seeing you with the Lady Dallona, on the visiplate; you're 'Dirzed, her faithful Assassin.'"

Dirzed's face, normally the color of a good walnut gunstock, turned almost black. He used shockingly bad language.

"And that's why I have to wear this abomination," he finished, displaying the mask. "The Lady Dallona and I can't show our faces anywhere; if we did, every Statisticalist and his six-year-old brat would know us, and we'd be fighting off an army of them in five minutes."

"Where's the Lady Dallona, now?"

"In hiding, Lord Virzal, at a private dwelling dome in the forest; she's most anxious to see you. I'm to take you to her, and I would strongly advise that you bring your Assassins along. There are other people at this dome, and they are not personally loyal to the Lady Dallona. I've no reason to suspect them of secret enmity, but their friendship is based entirely on political expediency."

"And political expediency is subject to change without notice," Verkan Vall finished for him. "Have you an airboat?"

"On the landing stage below. Shall we go now, Lord Virzal?"

"Yes." Verkan Vall made a two-handed gesture to his Assassins, as though gripping a submachine-gun; they nodded, went into another room, and returned carrying light automatic weapons in their hands and pouches of spare drums slung over their shoulders. "And may I suggest, Dirzed, that one of my Assassins drives the airboat? I want you on the back seat with me, to explain the situation as we go."

Dirzed's teeth flashed white against his brown skin as he gave Verkan Vall a quick smile.

"By all means, Lord Virzal; I would much rather be distrusted than to find that my client's friends were not discreet."

There were a couple of hotel Assassins guarding Dirzed's airboat, on the landing stage. Marnik climbed in under the controls, with Olirzon beside him; Verkan Vall and Dirzed entered the rear seat. Dirzed gave Marnik the co-ordinate reference for their destination.

"Now, what sort of a place is this, where we're going?" Verkan Vall asked. "And who's there whom we may or may not trust?"

"Well, it's a dome house belonging to the family of Starpha; they own a five-mile radius around it, oak and beech forest and underbrush, stocked with deer and boar. A hunting lodge. Prince Jirzyn of Starpha, Lord Girzon of Roxor, and a few other top-level Volitionalists, know that the Lady Dallona's hiding there. They're keeping her out of sight till after the election, for propaganda purposes. We've been hiding there since immediately after the discarnation feast of the Lord Garnon of Roxor."

"What happened, after the feast?" Verkan Vall wanted to know.

"Well, you know how the Lady Dallona and Dr. Harnosh of Hosh had this telepathic-sensitive there, in a trance and drugged with a *zerfa*-derivative alkaloid the Lady Dallona had developed. I was Lord Garnon's Assassin; I discarnated him, myself. Why, I hadn't even put my pistol away before he was in control of this sensitive, in a room five stories above the banquet hall; he began communicating at once. We had visiplates to show us what was going on.

"Right away, Nirzav of Shonna, one of the Statisticalist leaders who was a personal friend of Lord Garnon's in spite of his politics, renounced Statisticalism and went over to the Volitionalists, on the strength of this communication. Prince Jirzyn, and Lord Girzon, the new family-head of Roxor, decided that there would be trouble in the next few days, so they advised the Lady Dallona to come to this hunting lodge for safety. She and I came here in her airboat, directly from the feast. A good thing we did, too; if we'd gone to her apartment, we'd have walked in before that lethal gas had time to clear.

"There are four Assassins of the family of Starpha, and six menservants, and an upper-servant named Tarnod, the gamekeeper. The Starpha Assassins and I have been keeping the rest under observation. I left one of the Starpha Assassins guarding the Lady Dallona when I came for you, under brotherly oath to protect her in my name till I returned."

The airboat was skimming rapidly above the treetops, toward the northern part of the city.

"What's known about that package bomb?" Verkan Vall asked. "Who sent it?"

Dirzed shrugged. "The Statisticalists, of course. The wrapper was stolen from the Reincarnation Research Institute; so was the case. The Constabulary are working on it." Dirzed shrugged again.

The dome, about a hundred and fifty feet in width and some fifty in height, stood among the trees ahead. It was almost invisible from any distance; the concrete dome was of mottled green and gray concrete, trees grew so close as to brush it with their branches, and the little pavilion on the flattened top was roofed with translucent green plastic. As the airboat came in, a couple of men in Assassins' garb emerged from the pavilion to meet them.

"Marnik, stay at the controls," Verkan Vall directed. "I'll send Olirzon up for you if I want you. If there's any trouble, take off for Assassins' Hall and give the code word, then come back with twice as many men as you think you'll need."

Dirzed raised his eyebrows over this. "I hadn't known the Assassin-President had given you a code word, Lord Virzal," he commented. "That doesn't happen very often."

"The Assassin-President has honored me with his friendship," Verkan Vall replied noncommittally, as he, Dirzed and Olirzon climbed out of the airboat. Marnik was holding it an unobtrusive inch or so above the flat top of the dome, away from the edge of the pavilion roof.

The two Assassins greeted him, and a man in upper-servants' garb and wearing a hunting knife and a long hunting pistol approached.

"Lord Virzal of Verkan? Welcome to Starpha Dome. The Lady Dallona awaits you below."

Verkan Vall had never been in an Akor-Neb dwelling dome, but a description of such structures had been included in his hypno-mech indoctrination. Originally, they had been the standard structure for all purposes; about two thousand elapsed years ago, when nationalism had still existed on the Akor-Neb Sector, the cities had been almost entirely under ground, as protection from air attack. Even now, the design had been retained by those who wished to live apart from the towering city units, to preserve the natural appearance of the landscape. The Starpha hunting lodge was typical of such domes. Under it was a circular well, eighty feet in depth and fifty in width, with a fountain and a shallow circular pool at the bottom. The storerooms, kitchens and servants' quarters were at the top, the living quarters at the bottom, in segments of a wide circle around the well, back of balconies.

"Tarnod, the gamekeeper," Dirzed performed the introductions. "And Erarno and Kirzol, Assassins."

Verkan Vall hooked fingers and clapped shoulders with them. Tarnod accompanied them to the lifter tubes—two percent positive gravitation for descent and two percent negative for ascent—and they all floated down the former, like air-filled balloons, to the bottom level.

"The Lady Dallona is in the gun room," Tarnod informed Verkan Vall, making as though to guide him.

"Thanks, Tarnod; we know the way," Dirzed told him shortly, turning his back on the upper-servant and walking toward a closed door on the other side of the fountain. Verkan Vall and Olirzon followed; for a moment, Tarnod stood looking after them, then he followed the other two Assassins into the ascent tube.

"I don't relish that fellow," Dirzed explained. "The family of Starpha use him for work they couldn't hire an Assassin to do at any price. I've been here often, when I was with the Lord Garnon; I've always thought he had something on Prince Jirzyn."

He knocked sharply on the closed door with the butt of his pistol. In a moment, it slid open, and a young Assassin with a narrow mustache and a tuft of chin beard looked out.

"Ah, Dirzed." He stepped outside. "The Lady Dallona is within; I return her to your care."

Verkan Vall entered, followed by Dirzed and Olirzon. The big room was fitted with reclining chairs and couches and low tables; its walls were hung with the heads of deer and boar and wolves, and with racks holding rifles and hunting pistols and fowling pieces. It was filled with the soft glow of indirect cold light. At the far side of the room, a young woman was seated at a desk, speaking softly into a sound transcriber. As they entered, she snapped it off and rose.

Hadron Dalla wore the same costume Verkan Vall had seen on the visiplate: he recognized her instantly. It took her a second or two to perceive Verkan Vall under the brown skin and black hair of the Lord Virzal of Verkan. Then her face lighted with a happy smile.

"Why, Va-a-a-ll!" she whooped, running across the room and tossing herself into his not particularly reluctant arms. After all, it had been twenty years—"I didn't know you, at first!"

"You mean, in these clothes?" he asked, seeing that she had forgotten, for the moment, the presence of the two Assassins. She had even called him by his First Level name, but that was unimportant—the Akor-Neb affectionate diminutive was formed by omitting the *-irz-* or *-arn-*. "Well, they're not exactly what I generally wear on the plantation." He kissed her again, then turned to his companions. "Your pardon, Gentlemen-Assassins; it's been something over a year since we've seen each other."

Olirzon was smiling at the affectionate reunion; Dirzed wore a look of amused resignation, as though he might have expected something like this to happen. Verkan Vall and Dalla sat down on a couch near the desk.

"That was really sweet of you, Vall, fighting those men for talking about me," she began. "You took an awful chance, though. But if you hadn't, I'd never have known you were in Darsh—Oh-oh! That was why you did it, wasn't it?"

"Well, I had to do something. Everybody either didn't know or weren't saying where you were. I assumed, from the circumstances, that you were hiding somewhere. Tell me, Dalla; do you really have scientific proof of reincarnation? I mean, as an established fact?"

"Oh, yes; these people on this sector have had that for over ten centuries. They have hypnotic techniques for getting back into a part of the subconscious mind that we've never been able to reach. And after I found out how they did it, I was able to adapt some of our hypno-epistemological techniques to it, and—"

"All right; that's what I wanted to know," he cut her off. "We're getting out of here, right away."

"But where?"

"Ghamma, in an airboat I have outside, and then back to the First Level. Unless there's a paratime-transposition conveyor somewhere nearer."

"But why, Vall? I'm not ready to go back; I have a lot of work to do here, yet. They're getting ready to set up a series of control-experiments at the Institute, and then, I'm in the middle of an experiment, a two-hundred-subject memory-recall experiment. See, I distributed two hundred sets of equipment for my new technique—injection-ampoules of this *zerfa*-derivative drug, and sound records of the hypnotic suggestion formula, which can be played on an ordinary reproducer. It's just a crude variant of our hypno-mech process, except that instead of implanting information in the subconscious mind, to be brought at will to the level of consciousness, it works the other way, and draws into conscious knowledge information already in the subconscious mind. The way these people have always done has been to put the subject in an hypnotic trance and then record verbal statements made in the trance state; when the subject comes out of the trance, the record is all there is, because the memories of past reincarnations have never been in the conscious mind. But with my process, the subject can consciously remember everything about his last reincarnation, and as many reincarnations before that as he wishes to. I haven't heard from any of the people who received these auto-recall kits, and I really must—"

"Dalla, I don't want to have to pull Paratime Police authority on you, but, so help me, if you don't come back voluntarily with me, I will. Security of the secret of paratime transposition."

"Oh, my eye!" Dalla exclaimed. "Don't give me that, Vall!"

"Look, Dalla. Suppose you get discarnated here," Verkan Vall said. "You say reincarnation is a scientific fact. Well, you'd reincarnate on this sector, and then you'd take a memory-recall, under hypnosis. And when you did, the paratime secret wouldn't be a secret any more."

"Oh!" Dalla's hand went to her mouth in consternation. Like every paratimer, she was conditioned to shrink with all her being from the mere thought of revealing to any out-time dweller the secret ability of her race to pass to other time-lines, or even the existence of alternate lines of probability. "And if I took one of the old-fashioned trance-recalls, I'd blat out everything; I wouldn't be able to keep a thing back. And I even know the principles of transposition!" She looked at him, aghast.

"When I get back, I'm going to put a recommendation through department channels that this whole sector be declared out of bounds for all paratime-transposition, until you people at Rhogom Foundation work out the problem of discarnate return to the First Level," he told her. "Now, have you any notes or anything you want to take back with you?"

She rose. "Yes; just what's on the desk. Find me something to put the tape spools and notebooks in, while I'm getting them in order."

He secured a large game bag from under a rack of fowling pieces, and held it while she sorted the material rapidly, stuffing spools of record tape and notebooks into it. They had barely begun when the door slid open and Olirzon, who had gone outside, sprang into the room, his pistol drawn, swearing vilely.

"They've double-crossed us!" he cried. "The servants of Starpha have turned on us." He holstered his pistol and snatched up his submachine-gun, taking cover behind the edge of the door and letting go with a burst in the direction of the lifter tubes. "Got that one!" he grunted.

"What happened, Olirzon?" Verkan Vall asked, dropping the game bag on the table and hurrying across the room.

"I went up to see how Marnik was making out. As I came out of the lifter tube, one of the obscenities took a shot at me with a hunting pistol. He missed me; I didn't miss him. Then a couple more of them were coming up, with fowling pieces; I shot one of them before they could fire, and jumped into the descent tube and came down heels over ears. I don't know what's happened to Marnik." He fired another burst, and swore. "Missed him!"

"Assassins' Truce! Assassins' Truce!" a voice howled out of the descent tube. "Hold your fire, we want to parley."

"Who is it?" Dirzed shouted, over Olirzon's shoulder. "You, Sarnax? Come on out; we won't shoot."

The young Assassin with the mustache and chin beard emerged from the descent tube, his weapons sheathed and his clasped hands extended in front of him in a peculiarly ecclesiastical-looking manner. Dirzed and Olirzon stepped out of the gun room, followed by Verkan Vall and Hadron Dalla. Olirzon had left his submachine-gun behind. They met the other Assassin by the rim of the fountain pool.

"Lady Dallona of Hadron," the Starpha Assassin began. "I and my colleagues, in the employ of the family of Starpha, have received orders from our clients to withdraw our protection from you, and to discarnate you, and all with you who undertake to protect or support you." That much sounded like a recitation of some established formula; then his voice became more conversational. "I and my colleagues, Erarno and Kirzol and Harnif, offer our apologies for the barbarity of the servants of the family of Starpha, in attacking without declaration of cessation of friendship. Was anybody hurt or discarnated?"

"None of us," Olirzon said. "How about Marnik?"

"He was warned before hostilities were begun against him," Sarnax replied. "We will allow five minutes until—"

Olirzon, who had been looking up the well, suddenly sprang at Dalla, knocking her flat, and at the same time jerking out his pistol. Before he could raise it, a shot banged from above and he fell on his face. Dirzed, Verkan Vall, and Sarnax, all drew their pistols, but whoever had fired the shot had vanished. There was an outburst of shouting above.

"Get to cover," Sarnax told the others. "We'll let you know when we're ready to attack; we'll have to deal with whoever fired that shot, first." He looked at the dead body on the floor, exclaimed angrily, and hurried to the ascent tube, springing upward.

Verkan Vall replaced the small pistol in his shoulder holster and took Olirzon's belt, with his knife and heavier pistol.

"Well, there you see," Dirzed said, as they went back to the gun room. "So much for political expediency."

"I think I understand why your picture and the Lady Dallona's were exhibited so widely," Verkan Vall said. "Now, anybody would recognize your bodies, and blame the Statisticalists for discarnating you."

"That thought had occurred to me, Lord Virzal," Dirzed said. "I suppose our bodies will be atrociously but not unidentifiably mutilated, to further enrage the public," he added placidly. "If I get out of this carnate, I'm going to pay somebody off for it."

After a few minutes, there was more shouting of: "Assassins' Truce!" from the descent tube. The two Assassins, Erarno and Kirzol, emerged, dragging the gamekeeper, Tarnod, between them. The upper-servant's face was bloody, and his jaw seemed to be broken. Sarnax followed, carrying a long hunting pistol in his hand.

"Here he is!" he announced. "He fired during Assassins' Truce; he's subject to Assassins' Justice!"

He nodded to the others. They threw the gamekeeper forward on the floor, and Sarnax shot him through the head, then tossed the pistol down beside him. "Any more of these people who violate the decencies will be treated similarly," he promised.

"Thank you, Sarnax," Dirzed spoke up. "But we lost an Assassin: discarnating this lackey won't equalize that. We think you should retire one of your number."

"That at least, Dirzed; wait a moment."

The three Assassins conferred at some length. Then Sarnax hooked fingers and clapped shoulders with his companions.

"See you in the next reincarnation, brothers," he told them, walking toward the gun-room door, where Verkan Vall, Dalla and Dirzed stood. "I'm joining you people. You had two Assassins when the parley began, you'll have two when the shooting starts."

Verkan Vall looked at Dirzed in some surprise. Hadron Dalla's Assassin nodded.

"He's entitled to do that, Lord Virzal; the Assassins' code provides for such changes of allegiance."

"Welcome, Sarnax," Verkan Vall said, hooking fingers with him. "I hope we'll all be together when this is over."

"We will be," Sarnax assured him cheerfully. "Discarnate. We won't get out of this in the body, Lord Virzal."

A submachine-gun hammered from above, the bullets lashing the fountain pool; the water actually steamed, so great was their velocity.

"All right!" a voice called down. "Assassins' Truce is over!"

Another burst of automatic fire smashed out the lights at the bottom of the ascent tube. Dirzed and Dalla struggled across the room, pushing a heavy steel cabinet between them; Verkan Vall, who was holding Olirzon's submachine-gun, moved aside to allow them to drop it on edge in the open doorway, then wedged the door half-shut against it. Sarnax came over, bringing rifles, hunting pistols, and ammunition.

"What's the situation, up there?" Verkan Vall asked him. "What force have they, and why did they turn against us?"

"Lord Virzal!" Dirzed objected, scandalized. "You have no right to ask Sarnax to betray confidences!"

Sarnax spat against the door. "In the face of Jirzyn of Starpha!" he said. "And in the face of his *zortan* mother, and of his father, whoever he was! Dirzed, do not talk foolishly; one does not speak of betraying betrayers." He turned to Verkan Vall. "They have three menservants of the family of Starpha; your Assassin, Olirzon, discarnated the other three. There is one of Prince Jirzyn's poor relations, named Girzad. There are three other men, Volitionalist precinct workers, who came with Girzad, and four Assassins, the three who were here, and one who came with Girzad. Eleven, against the three of us."

"The four of us, Sarnax," Dalla corrected. She had buckled on a hunting pistol, and had a light deer rifle under her arm.

Something moved at the bottom of the descent tube. Verkan Vall gave it a short burst, though it was probably only a dummy, dropped to draw fire.

"The four of us, Lady Dallona," Sarnax agreed. "As to your other Assassin, the one who stayed in the airboat, I don't know how he fared. You see, about twenty minutes ago, this Girzad arrived in an airboat, with an Assassin and these three Volitionalist workers. Erarno and I were at the top of the dome when he came in. He told us that he had orders from Prince Jirzyn to discarnate the Lady Dallona and Dirzed at once. Tarnod, the gamekeeper"—Sarnax spat ceremoniously against the door again—"told him you were here, and that Marnik was one of your men. He was going to shoot Marnik at once, but Erarno and I and his Assassin stopped him. We warned Marnik about the change in the situation, according to the code, expecting Marnik to go down here and join you. Instead, he lifted the airboat, zoomed over Girzad's boat, and let go a rocket blast, setting Girzad's boat on fire. Well, that was a hostile act, so we all fired after him. We must have hit something, because the boat went down, trailing smoke, about ten miles away. Girzad got another airboat out of the hangar and he and his Assassin started after your man. About that time, your Assassin, Olirzon—happy reincarnation to him—came up, and the Starpha servants fired at him, and he fired back and discarnated two of them, and then jumped down the descent tube. One of the servants jumped after him; I found his body at the bottom when I came down to warn you formally. You know what happened after that."

"But why did Prince Jirzyn order our discarnation?" Dalla wanted to know. "Was it to blame the Statisticalists with it?"

Sarnax, about to answer, broke off suddenly and began firing at the opening of the ascent tube with a hunting pistol.

"I got him," he said, in a pleased tone. "That was Erarno; he was always playing tricks with the tubes, climbing down against negative gravity and up against positive gravity. His body will float up to the top—Why, Lady Dallona, that was only part of it. You didn't hear about the big scandal, on the newscast, then?"

"We didn't have it on. What scandal?"

Sarnax laughed. "Oh, the very father and family-head of all scandals! You ought to know about it, because you started it; that's why Prince Jirzyn wants you out of the body—You devised a process by which people could give themselves memory-recalls of previous reincarnations, didn't you? And distributed apparatus to do it with? And gave one set to young Tarnov, the son of Lord Tirzov of Fastor?"

Dalla nodded. Sarnax continued:

"Well, last evening, Tarnox of Fastor used his recall outfit, and what do you think? It seems that thirty years ago, in his last reincarnation, he was Jirzid of Starpha, Jirzyn's older brother. Jirzid was betrothed to the Lady Annitra of Zabna. Well, his younger brother was carrying on a clandestine affair with the Lady Annitra, and he also wanted the title of Prince and family-head of Starpha. So he bribed this fellow Tarnod, whom I had the pleasure of discarnating, and who was an underservant here at the hunting lodge. Between them, they shot Jirzid during a boar hunt. An accident, of course. So Jirzyn married the Lady Annitra, and when old Prince Jarnid, his father, discarnated a year later, he succeeded to the title. And immediately, Tarnod was made head gamekeeper here."

"What did I tell you, Lord Virzal? I knew that son of a *zortan* had something on Jirzyn of Starpha!" Dirzed exclaimed. "A nice family, this of Starpha!"

"Well, that's not the end of it," Sarnax continued. "This morning, Tarnov of Fastor, late Jirzid of Starpha, went before the High Court of Estates and entered suit to change his name to Jirzid of Starpha and laid claim to the title of Starpha family-head. The case has just been entered, so there's been no hearing, but there's the blazes of an argument among all the nobles about it—some are claiming that the individuality doesn't change from one reincarnation to the next, and others claiming that property and titles should pass along the line of physical descent, no matter what individuality has reincarnated into what body. They're the ones who want the Lady Dallona discarnated and her discoveries suppressed. And there's talk about revising the entire system of estate-ownership and estate-inheritance. Oh, it's an utter obscenity of a business!"

"This," Verkan Vall told Dalla, "is something we will not emphasize when we get home." That was as close as he dared come to it, but she caught his meaning. The working of major changes in out-time social structures was not viewed with approval by the Paratime Commission on the First Level. "*If* we get home," he added. Then an idea occurred to him.

"Dirzed, Sarnax; this place must have been used by the leaders of the Volitionalists for top-level conferences. Is there a secret passage anywhere?"

Sarnax shook his head. "Not from here. There is one, on the floor above, but they control it. And even if there were one down here, they would be guarding the outlet."

"That's what I was counting on. I'd hoped to simulate an escape that way, and then make a rush up the regular tubes." Verkan Vall shrugged. "I suppose Marnik's our only chance. I hope he got away safely."

"He was going for help? I was surprised that an Assassin would desert his client; I should have thought of that," Sarnax said. "Well, even if he got down carnate, and if Girzad didn't catch him, he'd still be afoot ten miles from the nearest city unit. That gives us a little chance—about one in a thousand."

"Is there any way they can get at us, except by those tubes?" Dalla asked.

"They could cut a hole in the floor, or burn one through," Sarnax replied. "They have plenty of thermite. They could detonate a charge of explosives over our heads, or clear out of the dome and drop one down the well. They could use lethal gas or radiodust, but their Assassins wouldn't permit such illegal methods. Or they could shoot sleepgas down at us, and then come down and cut our throats at their leisure."

"We'll have to get out of this room, then," Verkan Vall decided. "They know we've barricaded ourselves in here; this is where they'll attack. So we'll patrol the perimeter of the well; we'll be out of danger from above if we keep close to the wall. And we'll inspect all the rooms on this floor for evidence of cutting through from above."

Sarnax nodded. "That's sense, Lord Virzal. How about the lifter tubes?"

"We'll have to barricade them. Sarnax, you and Dirzed know the layout of this place better than the Lady Dallona or I; suppose you two check the rooms, while we cover the tubes and the well," Verkan Vall directed. "Come on, now."

* * * *

They pushed the door wide-open and went out past the cabinet. Hugging the wall, they began a slow circuit of the well, Verkan Vall in the lead with the submachine-gun, then Sarnax and Dirzed, the former with a heavy boar-rifle and the latter with a hunting pistol in each hand, and Hadron Dalla brought up in the rear with her rifle. It was she who noticed a movement along the rim of the balcony above and snapped a shot at it; there was a crash above, and a shower of glass and plastic and metal fragments rattled on the pavement of the court. Somebody had been trying to lower a scanner or a visiplate-pickup, or something of the sort; the exact nature of the instrument was not evident from the wreckage Dalla's bullet had made of it.

The rooms Dirzed and Sarnax entered were all quiet; nobody seemed to be attempting to cut through the ceiling, fifteen feet above. They dragged furniture from a couple of rooms, blocking the openings of the lifter tubes, and continued around the well until they had reached the gun room again.

Dirzed suggested that they move some of the weapons and ammunition stored there to Prince Jirzyn's private apartment, halfway around to the lifter tubes, so that another place of refuge would be stocked with munitions in event of their being driven from the gun room.

Leaving him on guard outside, Verkan Vall, Dalla and Sarnax entered the gun room and began gathering weapons and boxes of ammunition. Dalla finished packing her game bag with the recorded data and notes of her experiments. Verkan Vall selected four more of the heavy hunting pistols, more accurate than his shoulder-holster weapon or the dead Olirzon's belt arm, and capable of either full or semi-automatic fire. Sarnax chose a couple more boar rifles. Dalla slung her bag of recorded notes, and another bag of ammunition, and secured another deer rifle. They carried this accumulation of munitions to the private apartments of Prince Jirzyn, dumping everything in the middle of the drawing room, except the bag of notes, from which Dalla refused to separate herself.

"Maybe we'd better put some stuff over in one of the rooms on the other side of the well," Dirzed suggested. "They haven't really begun to come after us; when they do, we'll probably be attacked from two or three directions at once."

They returned to the gun room, casting anxious glances at the edge of the balcony above and at the barricade they had erected across the openings to the lifter tubes. Verkan Vall was not satisfied with this last; it looked to him as though they had provided a breastwork for somebody to fire on them from, more than anything else.

He was about to step around the cabinet which partially blocked the gun-room door when he glanced up, and saw a six-foot circle on the ceiling turning slowly brown. There was a smell of scorched plastic. He grabbed Sarnax by the arm and pointed.

"Thermite," the Assassin whispered. "The ceiling's got six inches of spaceship-insulation between it and the floor above; it'll take them a few minutes to burn through it." He stooped and pushed on the barricade, shoving it into the room. "Keep back; they'll probably drop a grenade or so through, first, before they jump down. If we're quick, we can get a couple of them."

Dirzed and Sarnax crouched, one at either side of the door, with weapons ready. Verkan Vall and Dalla had been ordered, rather peremptorily, to stay behind them; in a place of danger, an Assassin was obliged to shield his client. Verkan Vall, unable to see what was going on inside the room, kept his eyes and his gun muzzle on the barricade across the openings to the lifter tubes, the erection of which he was now regretting as a major tactical error.

Inside the gun room, there was a sudden crash, as the circle of thermite burned through and a section of ceiling dropped out and hit the floor. Instantly, Dirzed flung himself back against Verkan Vall, and there was a tremendous explosion inside, followed by another and another. A second or so passed, then Dirzed, leaning around the corner of the door, began firing rapidly into the room. From the other side of the door, Sarnax began blazing away with his rifle. Verkan Vall kept his position, covering the lifter tubes.

Suddenly, from behind the barricade, a blue-white gun flash leaped into being, and a pistol banged. He sprayed the opening between a couch and a section of bookcase from whence it had come, releasing his trigger as the gun rose with the recoil, squeezing and releasing and squeezing again. Then he jumped to his feet.

"Come on, the other place; hurry!" he ordered.

Sarnax swore in exasperation. "Help me with her, Dirzed!" he implored.

Verkan Vall turned his head, to see the two Assassins drag Dalla to her feet and hustle her away from the gun room; she was quite senseless, and they had to drag her between them. Verkan Vall gave a quick glance into the gun room; two of the Starpha servants and a man in rather flashy civil dress were lying on the floor, where they had been shot as they had jumped down from above. He saw a movement at the edge of the irregular, smoking, hole in the ceiling, and gave it a short burst, then fired another at the exit from the descent tube. Then he took to his heels and followed the Assassins and Hadron Dalla into Prince Jirzyn's apartment.

As he ran through the open door, the Assassins were letting Dalla down into a chair; they instantly threw themselves into the work of barricading the doorway so as to provide cover and at the same time allow them to fire out into the central well.

For an instant, as he bent over her, he thought Dalla had been killed, an assumption justified by his knowledge of the deadliness of Akor-Neb bullets. Then he saw her eye-lids flicker. A moment later, he had the explanation of her escape. The bullet had hit the game bag at her side; it was full of spools of metal tape, in metal cases, and notes in written form, pyrographed upon sheets of plastic ring fastened into metal binders. Because of their extreme velocity, Akor-Neb bullets were sure killers when they struck animal tissue, but for the same reason, they had very poor penetration on hard objects. The alloy-steel tape, and the steel spools and spool cases, and the notebook binders, had been enough to shatter the little bullet into splinters of magnesium-nickel alloy, and the stout leather back of the game bag had stopped all of these. But the impact, even distributed as it had been through the contents of the bag, had been enough to knock the girl unconscious.

He found a bottle of some sort of brandy and a glass on a serving table nearby and poured her a drink, holding it to her lips. She spluttered over the first mouthful, then took the glass from him and sipped the rest.

"What happened?" she asked. "I thought those bullets were sure death."

"Your notes. The bullet hit the bag. Are you all right, now?"

She finished the brandy. "I think so." She put a hand into the game bag and brought out a snarled and tangled mess of steel tape. "Oh, *blast*! That stuff was important; all the records on the preliminary auto-recall experiments." She shrugged. "Well, it wouldn't have been worth much more if I'd stopped that bullet, myself." She slipped the strap over her shoulder and started to rise.

As she did, a bedlam of firing broke out, both from the two Assassins at the door and from outside. They both hit the floor and crawled out of line of the partly-open door; Verkan Vall recovered his submachine-gun, which he had set down beside Dalla's chair. Sarnax was firing with his rifle at some target in the direction of the lifter tubes; Dirzed lay slumped over the barricade, and one glance at his crumpled figure was enough to tell Verkan Vall that he was dead.

"You fill magazines for us," he told Dalla, then crawled to Dirzed's place at the door. "What happened, Sarnax?"

"They shoved over the barricade at the lifter tubes and came out into the well. I got a couple, they got Dirzed, and now they're holed up in rooms all around the circle. They—Aah!" He fired three shots, quickly, around the edge of the door. "That stopped that." The Assassin crouched to insert a fresh magazine into his rifle.

Verkan Vall risked one eye around the corner of the doorway, and as he did, there was a red flash and a dull roar, unlike the blue flashes and sharp cracking reports of the pistols and rifles, from the doorway of the gun room. He wondered, for a split second, if it might be one of the fowling pieces he had seen there, and then something whizzed past his head and exploded with a soft *plop* behind him. Turning, he saw a pool of gray vapor beginning to spread in the middle of the room. Dalla must have got a breath of it, for she was slumped over the chair from which she had just risen.

Dropping the submachine-gun and gulping a lungful of fresh air from outside, Verkan Vall rushed to her, caught her by the heels, and dragged her into Prince Jirzyn's bedroom, beyond. Leaving her in the middle of the floor, he took another deep breath and returned to the drawing room, where Sarnax was already overcome by the sleep-gas.

He saw the serving table from which he had got the brandy, and dragged it over to the bedroom door, overturning it and laying it across the doorway, its legs in the air. Like most Akor-Neb serving tables, it had a gravity-counteraction unit under it; he set this for double minus-gravitation and snapped it on. As it was now above the inverted table, the table did not rise, but a tendril, of sleep-gas, curling toward it, bent upward and drifted away from the doorway. Satisfied that he had made a temporary barrier against the sleep-gas, Verkan Vall secured Dalla's hunting pistol and spare magazines and lay down at the bedroom door.

For some time, there was silence outside. Then the besiegers evidently decided that the sleep-gas attack had been a success. An Assassin, wearing a gas mask and carrying a submachine-gun, appeared in the doorway, and behind him came a tall man in a tan tunic, similarly masked. They stepped into the room and looked around.

Knowing that he would be shooting over a two hundred percent negative gravitation-field, Verkan Vall aimed for the Assassin's belt-buckle and squeezed. The bullet caught him in the throat. Evidently the bullet had not only been lifted in the negative gravitation, but lifted point-first and deflected upward. He held his front sight just above the other man's knee, and hit him in the chest.

As he fired, he saw a wisp of gas come sliding around the edge of the inverted table. There was silence outside, and for an instant, he was tempted to abandon his post and go to the bathroom, back of the bedroom, for wet towels to improvise a mask. Then, when he tried to crawl backward, he could not. There was an impression of distant shouting which turned to a roaring sound in his head. He tried to lift his pistol, but it slipped from his fingers.

* * * *

When consciousness returned, he was lying on his back, and something cold and rubbery was pressing into his face. He raised his arms to fight off whatever it was, and opened his eyes, to find that he was staring directly at the red oval and winged bullet of the Society of Assassins. A hand caught his wrist as he reached for the small pistol under his arm. The pressure on his face eased.

"It's all right, Lord Virzal," a voice came to him. "Assassins' Truce!"

He nodded stupidly and repeated the words. "Assassins' Truce; I won't shoot. What happened?"

Then he sat up and looked around. Prince Jirzyn's bedchamber was full of Assassins. Dalla, recovering from her touch of sleep-gas, was sitting groggily in a chair, while five or six of them fussed around her, getting in each others' way, handing her drinks, chaffing her wrists, holding damp cloths on her brow. That was standard procedure, when any group of males thought Dalla needed any help. Another Assassin, beside the bed, was putting away an oxygen-mask outfit, and the Assassin who had prevented Verkan Vall from drawing his pistol was his own follower, Marnik. And Klarnood, the Assassin-President, was sitting on the foot of the bed, smoking one of Prince Jirzyn's monogrammed and crested cigarettes critically.

Verkan Vall looked at Marnik, and then at Klarnood, and back to Marnik.

"You got through," he said. "Good work, Marnik; I thought they'd downed you."

"They did; I had to crash-land in the woods. I went about a mile on foot, and then I found a man and woman and two children, hiding in one of these little log rain shelters. They had an airboat, a good one. It seemed that rioting had broken out in the city unit where they lived, and they'd taken to the woods till things quieted down again. I offered them Assassins' protection if they'd take me to Assassins' Hall, and they did."

"By luck, I was in when Marnik arrived," Klarnood took over. "We brought three boatloads of men, and came here at once. Just as we got here, two boatloads of Starpha dependents arrived; they tried to give us an argument, and we discarnated the lot of them. Then we came down here, crying Assassins' Truce. One of the Starpha Assassins, Kirzol, was still carnate; he told us what had been going on." The President-General's face became grim. "You know, I take a rather poor view of Prince Jirzyn's procedure in this matter, not to mention that of his underlings. I'll have to speak to him about this. Now, how about you and the Lady Dallona? What do you intend doing?"

"We're getting out of here," Verkan Vall said. "I'd like air transport and protection as far as Ghamma, to the establishment of the family of Zorda. Brarnend of Zorda has a private space yacht; he'll get us to Venus."

Klarnood gave a sigh of obvious relief. "I'll have you and the Lady Dallona airborne and off for Ghamma as soon as you wish," he promised. "I will, frankly, be delighted to see the last of both of you. The Lady Dallona has started a fire here at Darsh that won't burn out in a half-century, and who knows what it may consume." He was interrupted by a heaving shock that made the underground dome dwelling shake like a light airboat in turbulence. Even eighty feet under the ground, they could hear a continued crashing roar. It was an appreciable interval before the sound and the shock ceased.

For an instant, there was silence, and then an excited bedlam of shouting broke from the Assassins in the room: Klarnood's face was frozen in horror.

"That was a fission bomb!" he exclaimed. "The first one that has been exploded on this planet in hostility in a thousand years!" He turned to Verkan Vall. "If you feel well enough to walk, Lord Virzal, come with us. I must see what's happened."

They hurried from the room and went streaming up the ascent tube to the top of the dome. About forty miles away, to the south, Verkan Vall saw the sinister thing that he had seen on so many other time-lines, in so many other paratime sectors—a great pillar of varicolored fire-shot smoke, rising to a mushroom head fifty thousand feet above.

"Well, that's it," Klarnood said sadly. "That is civil war."

"May I make a suggestion, Assassin-President?" Verkan Vall asked. "I understand that Assassins' Truce is binding even upon non-Assassins; is that correct?"

"Well, not exactly; it's generally kept by such non-Assassins as want to remain in their present reincarnations, though."

"That's what I meant. Well, suppose you declare a general, planet-wide Assassins' Truce in this political war, and make the leaders of both parties responsible for keeping it. Publish lists of the top two or three thousand Statisticalists and Volitionalists, starting with Mirzark of Bashad and Prince Jirzyn of Starpha, and inform them that they will be assassinated, in order, if the fighting doesn't cease."

"Well!" A smile grew on Klarnood's face. "Lord Virzal, my thanks; a good suggestion. I'll try it. And furthermore, I'll withdraw all Assassin protection permanently from anybody involved in political activity, and forbid any Assassin to accept any retainer connected with political factionalism. It's about time our members stopped discarnating each other in these political squabbles." He pointed to the three airboats drawn up on the top of the dome; speedy black craft, bearing the red oval and winged bullet. "Take your choice, Lord Virzal. I'll lend you a couple of my men, and you'll be in Ghamma in three hours." He hooked fingers and clapped shoulders with Verkan Vall, bent over Dalla's hand. "I still like you, Lord Virzal, and I have seldom met a more charming lady than you, Lady Dallona. But I sincerely hope I never see either of you again."

* * * *

The ship for Dhergabar was driving north and west; at seventy thousand feet, it was still daylight, but the world below was wrapping itself in darkness. In the big visiscreens, which served in lieu of the windows which could never have withstood the pressure and friction heat of the ship's speed, the sun was sliding out of sight over the horizon to port. Verkan Vall and Dalla sat together, watching the blazing western sky— the sky of their own First Level time-line.

"I blame myself terribly, Vall," Dalla was saying. "And I didn't mean any of them the least harm. All I was interested in was learning the facts. I know, that sounds like 'I didn't know it was loaded,' but—"

"It sounds to me like those Fourth Level Europo-American Sector physicists who are giving themselves guilt-complexes because they designed an atomic bomb," Verkan Vall replied. "All you were interested in was learning the facts. Well, as a scientist, that's all you're supposed to be interested in. You don't have to worry about any social or political implications. People have to learn to live with newly-discovered facts; if they don't, they die of them."

"But, Vall; that sounds dreadfully irresponsible—"

"Does it? You're worrying about the results of your reincarnation memory-recall discoveries, the shootings and riotings and the bombing we saw." He touched the pommel of Olirzon's knife, which he still wore. "You're no more guilty of that than the man who forged this blade is guilty of the death of Marnark of Bashad; if he'd never lived, I'd have killed Marnark with some other knife somebody else made. And what's more, you can't know the results of your discoveries. All you can see is a thin film of events on the surface of an immediate situation, so you can't say whether the long-term results will be beneficial or calamitous.

"Take this Fourth Level Europo-American atomic bomb, for example. I choose that because we both know that sector, but I could think of a hundred other examples in other paratime areas. Those people, because of deforestation, bad agricultural methods and general mismanagement, are eroding away their arable soil at an alarming rate. At the same time, they are breeding like rabbits. In other words, each successive generation has less and less food to divide among more and more people, and, for inherited traditional and superstitious reasons, they refuse to adopt any rational program of birth-control and population-limitation.

"But, fortunately, they now have the atomic bomb, and they are developing radioactive poisons, weapons of mass-effect. And their racial, nationalistic and ideological conflicts are rapidly reaching the explosion point. A series of all-out atomic wars is just what that sector needs, to bring their population down to their world's carrying capacity; in a century or so, the inventors of the atomic bomb will be hailed as the saviors of their species."

"But how about my work on the Akor-Neb Sector?" Dalla asked. "It seems that my memory-recall technique is more explosive than any fission bomb. I've laid the train for a century-long reign of anarchy!"

"I doubt that; I think Klarnood will take hold, now that he has committed himself to it. You know, in spite of his sanguinary profession, he's the nearest thing to a real man of good will I've found on that sector. And here's something else you haven't considered. Our own First Level life expectancy is from four to five hundred years. That's the main reason why we've accomplished as much as we have. We have, individually, time to accomplish things. On the Akor-Neb Sector, a scientist or artist or scholar or statesman will grow senile and die before he's as old as either of us. But now, a young student of twenty or so can take one of your auto-recall treatments and immediately have available all the knowledge and experience gained in four or five previous lives. He can start where he left off in his last reincarnation. In other words, you've made those people time-binders, individually as well as racially. Isn't that worth the temporary discarnation of a lot of ward-heelers and plug-uglies, or even a few decent types like Dirzed and Olirzon? If it isn't, I don't know what scales of values you're using."

"Vall!" Dalla's eyes glowed with enthusiasm. "I never thought of that! And you said, 'temporary discarnation.' That's just what it is. Dirzed and Olirzon and the others aren't dead; they're just waiting, discarnate, between physical lives. You know, in the sacred writings of one of the Fourth Level peoples it is stated: 'Death is the last enemy.' By proving that death is just a cyclic condition of continued individual existence, these people have conquered their last enemy."

"Last enemy but one," Verkan Vall corrected. "They still have one enemy to go, an enemy within themselves. Call it semantic confusion, or illogic, or incomprehension, or just plain stupidity. Like Klarnood, stymied by verbal objections to something labeled 'political intervention.' He'd never have consented to use the power of his Society if he hadn't been shocked out of his inhibitions by that nuclear bomb. Or the Statisticalists, trying to create a classless order of society through a political program which would only result in universal servitude to an omnipotent government. Or the Volitionalist nobles, trying to preserve their hereditary feudal privileges, and now they can't even agree on a definition of the term 'hereditary.' Might they not recover all the silly prejudices of their past lives, along with the knowledge and wisdom?"

"But ... I thought you said—" Dalla was puzzled, a little hurt.

Verkan Vall's arm squeezed around her waist, and he laughed comfortingly.

"You see? Any sort of result is possible, good or bad. So don't blame yourself in advance for something you can't possibly estimate." An idea occurred to him, and he straightened in the seat. "Tell you what; if you people at Rhogom Foundation get the problem of discarnate paratime transposition licked by then, let's you and I go back to the Akor-Neb Sector in about a hundred years and see what sort of a mess those people have made of things."

"A hundred years: that would be Year Twenty-Two of the next millennium. It's a date, Vall; we'll do it."

They bent to light their cigarettes together at his lighter. When they raised their heads again and got the flame glare out of their eyes, the sky was purple-black, dusted with stars, and dead ahead, spilling up over the horizon, was a golden glow—the lights of Dhergabar and home.

TEMPLE TROUBLE

Through a haze of incense and altar smoke, Yat-Zar looked down from his golden throne at the end of the dusky, many-pillared temple. Yat-Zar was an idol, of gigantic size and extraordinarily good workmanship; he had three eyes, made of turquoises as big as doorknobs, and six arms. In his three right hands, from top to bottom, he held a sword with a flame-shaped blade, a jeweled object of vaguely phallic appearance, and, by the ears, a rabbit. In his left hands were a bronze torch with burnished copper flames, a big goblet, and a pair of scales with an egg in one pan balanced against a skull in the other. He had a long bifurcate beard made of gold wire, feet like a bird's, and other rather startling anatomical features. His throne was set upon a stone plinth about twenty feet high, into the front of which a doorway opened; behind him was a wooden screen, elaborately gilded and painted.

Directly in front of the idol, Ghullam the high priest knelt on a big blue and gold cushion. He wore a gold-fringed robe of dark blue, and a tall conical gold miter, and a bright blue false beard, forked like the idol's golden one: he was intoning a prayer, and holding up, in both hands, for divine inspection and approval, a long curved knife. Behind him, about thirty feel away, stood a square stone altar, around which four of the lesser priests, in light blue robes with less gold fringe and dark-blue false beards, were busy with the preliminaries to the sacrifice. At considerable distance, about halfway down the length of the temple, some two hundred worshipers—a few substantial citizens in gold-fringed tunics, artisans in tunics without gold fringe, soldiers in mail hauberks and plain steel caps, one officer in ornately gilded armor, a number of peasants in nondescript smocks, and women of all classes— were beginning to prostrate themselves on the stone floor.

Ghullam rose to his feet, bowing deeply to Yat-Zar and holding the knife extended in front of him, and backed away toward the altar. As he did, one of the lesser priests reached into a fringed and embroidered sack and pulled out a live rabbit, a big one, obviously of domestic breed, holding it by the ears while one of his fellows took it by the hind legs. A third priest caught up a silver pitcher, while the fourth fanned the altar fire with a sheet-silver fan. As they began chanting antiphonally, Ghullam turned and quickly whipped the edge of his knife across the rabbit's throat. The priest with the pitcher stepped in to catch the blood, and when the rabbit was bled, it was laid on the fire. Ghullam and his four assistants all shouted together, and the congregation shouted in response.

The high priest waited as long as was decently necessary and then, holding the knife in front of him, stepped around the prayer-cushion and went through the door under the idol into the Holy of Holies. A boy in novice's white robes met him and took the knife, carrying it reverently to a fountain for washing. Eight or ten under-priests, sitting at a long table, rose and bowed, then sat down again and resumed their eating and drinking. At another table, a half-dozen upper priests nodded to him in casual greeting.

Crossing the room, Ghullam went to the Triple Veil in front of the House of Yat-Zar, where only the highest of the priesthood might go, and parted the curtains, passing through, until he came to the great gilded door. Here he fumbled under his robe and produced a small object like a mechanical pencil, inserting the pointed end in a tiny hole in the door and pressing on the other end. The door opened, then swung shut behind him, and as it locked itself, the lights came on within. Ghullam removed his miter and his false beard, tossing them aside on a table, then undid his sash and peeled out of his robe. His regalia discarded, he stood for a moment in loose trousers and a soft white shirt, with a pistollike weapon in a shoulder holster under his left arm—no longer Ghullam the high priest of Yat-Zar, but now Stranor Sleth, resident agent on this time-line of the Fourth Level Proto-Aryan Sector for the Transtemporal Mining Corporation. Then he opened a door at the other side of the anteroom and went to the antigrav shaft, stepping over the edge and floating downward.

* * * *

There were temples of Yat-Zar on every time-line of the Proto-Aryan Sector, for the worship of Yat-Zar was ancient among the Hulgun people of that area of paratime, but there were only a few which had such installations as this, and all of them were owned and operated by Transtemporal Mining, which had the fissionable ores franchise for this sector. During the ten elapsed centuries since Transtemporal had begun operations on this sector, the process had become standardized. A few First Level paratimers would transpose to a selected time-line and abduct an upper-priest of Yat-Zar, preferably the high priest of the temple at Yoldav or Zurb. He would be drugged and transposed to the First Level, where he would receive hypnotic indoctrination and, while unconscious, have an operation performed on his ears which would enable him to hear sounds well above the normal audible range. He would be able to hear the shrill sonar-cries of bats, for instance, and, more important, he would be able to hear voices when the speaker used a First Level audio-frequency step-up phone. He would also receive a memory-obliteration from the moment of his abduction, and a set of pseudo-memories of a visit to the Heaven of Yat-Zar, on the other side of the sky. Then he would be returned to his own time-line and left on a mountain top far from his temple, where an unknown peasant, leading a donkey, would always find him, return him to the temple, and then vanish inexplicably.

Then the priest would begin hearing voices, usually while serving at the altar. They would warn of future events, which would always come to pass exactly as foretold. Or they might bring tidings of things happening at a distance, the news of which would not arrive by normal means for days or even weeks. Before long, the holy man who had been carried alive to the Heaven of Yat-Zar would acquire a most awesome reputation as a prophet, and would speedily rise to the very top of the priestly hierarchy.

Then he would receive two commandments from Yat-Zar. The first would ordain that all lower priests must travel about from temple to temple, never staying longer than a year at any one place. This would insure a steady influx of newcomers personally unknown to the local upper-priests, and many of them would be First Level paratimers. Then, there would be a second commandment: A house must be built for Yat-Zar, against the rear wall of each temple. Its dimensions were minutely stipulated; its walls were to be of stone, without windows, and there was to be a single door, opening into the Holy of Holies, and before the walls were finished, the door was to be barred from within. A triple veil of brocaded fabric was to be hung in front of this door. Sometimes such innovations met with opposition from the more conservative members of the hierarchy: when they did, the principal objector would be seized with a sudden and violent illness; he would recover if and when he withdrew his objections.

Very shortly after the House of Yat-Zar would be completed, strange noises would be heard from behind the thick walls. Then, after a while, one of the younger priests would announce that he had been commanded in a vision to go behind the veil and knock upon the door. Going behind the curtains, he would use his door-activator to let himself in, and return by paratime-conveyer to the First Level to enjoy a well-earned vacation. When the high priest would follow him behind the veil, after a few hours, and find that he had vanished, it would be announced as a miracle. A week later, an even greater miracle would be announced. The young priest would return from behind the Triple Veil, clad in such raiment as no man had ever seen, and bearing in his hands a strange box. He would announce that Yat-Zar had commanded him to build a new temple in the mountains, at a place to be made known by the voice of the god speaking out of the box.

This time, there would be no doubts and no objections. A procession would set out, headed by the new revelator bearing the box, and when the clicking voice of the god spoke rapidly out of it, the site would be marked and work would begin. No local labor would ever be employed on such temples; the masons and woodworkers would be strangers, come from afar and speaking a strange tongue, and when the temple was completed, they would never be seen to leave it. Men would say that they had been put to death by the priest and buried under the altar to preserve the secrets of the god. And there would always be an idol to preserve the secrets of the god. And there would always be an idol of Yat-Zar, obviously of heavenly origin, since its workmanship was beyond the powers of any local craftsman. The priests of such a temple would be exempt, by divine decree, from the rule of yearly travel.

Nobody, of course, would have the least idea that there was a uranium mine in operation under it, shipping ore to another time-line. The Hulgun people knew nothing about uranium, and neither did they as much as dream that there were other time-lines. The secret of paratime transposition belonged exclusively to the First Level civilization which had discovered it, and it was a secret that was guarded well.

* * * *

Stranor Sleth, dropping to the bottom of the antigrav shaft, cast a hasty and instinctive glance to the right, where the freight conveyers were. One was gone, taking its cargo over hundreds of thousands of para-years to the First Level. Another had just returned, empty, and a third was receiving its cargo from the robot mining machines far back under the mountain. Two young men and a girl, in First Level costumes, sat at a bank of instruments and visor-screens, handling the whole operation, and six or seven armed guards, having inspected the newly-arrived conveyer and finding that it had picked up nothing inimical en route, were relaxing and lighting cigarettes. Three of them, Stranor Sleth noticed, wore the green uniforms of the Paratime Police.

"When did those fellows get in?" he asked the people at the control desk, nodding toward the green-clad newcomers.

"About ten minutes ago, on the passenger conveyer," the girl told him. "The Big Boy's here. Brannad Klav. And a Paratime Police officer. They're in your office."

"Uh huh; I was expecting that," Stranor Sleth nodded. Then he turned down the corridor to the left.

Two men were waiting for him, in his office. One was short and stocky, with an angry, impatient face—Brannad Klav, Transtemporal's vice president in charge of operations. The other was tall and slender with handsome and entirely expressionless features; he wore a Paratime Police officer's uniform, with the blue badge of hereditary nobility on his breast, and carried a sigma-ray needler in a belt holster.

"Were you waiting long, gentlemen?" Stranor Sleth asked. "I was holding Sunset Sacrifice up in the temple."

"No, we just got here," Brannad Klav said. "This is Verkan Vall, Mavrad of Nerros, special assistant to Chief Tortha of the Paratime Police, Stranor Sleth, our resident agent here."

Stranor Sleth touched hands with Verkan Vall.

"I've heard a lot about you, sir," he said. "Everybody working in paratime has, of course. I'm sorry we have a situation here that calls for your presence, but since we have, I'm glad you're here in person. You know what our trouble is, I suppose?"

"In a general way," Verkan Vall replied. "Chief Tortha, and Brannad Klav, have given me the main outline, but I'd like to have you fill in the details."

"Well, I told you everything," Brannad Klav interrupted impatiently. "It's just that Stranor's let this blasted local king, Kurchuk, get out of control. If I—" He stopped short, catching sight of the shoulder holster under Stranor Sleth's left arm. "Were you wearing that needler up in the temple?" he demanded.

"You're blasted right I was!" Stranor Sleth retorted. "And any time I can't arm myself for my own protection on this time-line, you can have my resignation. I'm not getting into the same jam as those people at Zurb."

"Well, never mind about that," Verkan Vall intervened. "Of course Stranor Sleth has a right to arm himself; I wouldn't think of being caught without a weapon on this time-line, myself. Now, Stranor, suppose you tell me what's been happening, here, from the beginning of this trouble."

"It started, really, about five years ago, when Kurchuk, the King of Zurb, married this Chuldun princess, Darith, from the country over beyond the Black Sea, and made her his queen, over the heads of about a dozen daughters of the local nobility, whom he'd married previously. Then he brought in this Chuldun scribe, Labdurg, and made him Overseer of the Kingdom—roughly, prime minister. There was a lot of dissatisfaction about that, and for a while it looked as though he was going to have a revolution on his hands, but he brought in about five thousand Chuldun mercenaries, all archers—these Hulguns can't shoot a bow worth beans—so the dissatisfaction died down, and so did most of the leaders of the disaffected group. The story I get is that this Labdurg arranged the marriage, in the first place. It looks to me as though the Chuldun emperor is intending to take over the Hulgun kingdoms, starting with Zurb.

"Well, these Chulduns all worship a god called Muz-Azin. Muz-Azin is a crocodile with wings like a bat and a lot of knife blades in his tail. He makes this Yat-Zar look downright beautiful. So do his habits. Muz-Azin fancies human sacrifices. The victims are strung up by the ankles on a triangular frame and lashed to death with iron-barbed whips. Nasty sort of a deity, but this is a nasty time-line. The people here get a big kick out of watching these sacrifices. Much better show than our bunny-killing. The victims are usually criminals, or overage or incorrigible slaves, or prisoners of war.

"Of course, when the Chulduns began infiltrating the palace, they brought in their crocodile-god, too, and a flock of priests, and King Kurchuk let them set up a temple in the palace. Naturally, we preached against this heathen idolatry in our temples, but religious bigotry isn't one of the numerous imperfections of this sector. Everybody's deity is as good as anybody else's—indifferentism, I believe, is the theological term. Anyhow, on that basis things went along fairly well, till two years ago, when we had this run of bad luck."

"Bad luck!" Brannad Klav snorted. "That's the standing excuse of every incompetent!"

"Go on, Stranor; what sort of bad luck?" Verkan Vall asked.

"Well, first we had a drought, beginning in early summer, that burned up most of the grain crop. Then, when that broke, we got heavy rains and hailstorms and floods, and that destroyed what got through the dry spell. When they harvested what little was left, it was obvious there'd be a famine, so we brought in a lot of grain by conveyer and distributed it from the temples—miraculous gift of Yat-Zar, of course. Then the main office on First Level got scared about flooding this time-line with a lot of unaccountable grain and were afraid we'd make the people suspicious, and ordered it stopped.

"Then Kurchuk, and I might add that the kingdom of Zurb was the hardest hit by the famine, ordered his army mobilized and started an invasion of the Jumdun country, south of the Carpathians, to get grain. He got his army chopped up, and only about a quarter of them got back, with no grain. You ask me, I'd say that Labdurg framed it to happen that way. He advised Kurchuk to invade, in the first place, and I mentioned my suspicion that Chombrog, the Chuldun Emperor, is planning to move in on the Hulgun kingdoms. Well, what would be smarter than to get Kurchuk's army smashed in advance?"

"How did the defeat occur?" Verkan Vall asked. "Any suspicion of treachery?"

"Nothing you could put your finger on, except that the Jumduns seemed to have pretty good intelligence about Kurchuk's invasion route and battle plans. It could have been nothing worse than stupid tactics on Kurchuk's part. See, these Hulguns, and particularly the Zurb Hulguns, are spearmen. They fight in a fairly thin line, with heavy-armed infantry in front and light infantry with throwing-spears behind. The nobles fight in light chariots, usually at the center of the line, and that's where they were at this Battle of Jorm. Kurchuk himself was at the center, with his Chuldun archers massed around him.

"The Jumduns use a lot of cavalry, with long swords and lances, and a lot of big chariots with two javelin men and a driver. Well, instead of ramming into Kurchuk's center, where he had his archers, they hit the extreme left and folded it up, and then swung around behind and hit the right from the rear. All the Chuldun archers did was stand fast around the king and shoot anybody who came close to them: they were left pretty much alone. But the Hulgun spearmen were cut to pieces. The battle ended with Kurchuk and his nobles and his archers making a fighting retreat, while the Jumdun cavalry were chasing the spearmen every which way and cutting them down or lancing them as they ran.

"Well, whether it was Labdurg's treachery or Kurchuk's stupidity, in either case, it was natural for the archers to come off easiest and the Hulgun spearmen to pay the butcher's bill. But try and tell these knuckle-heads anything like that! Muz-Azin protected the Chulduns, and Yat-Zar let the Hulguns down, and that was all there was to it. The Zurb temple started losing worshipers, particularly the families of the men who didn't make it back from Jorm.

"If that had been all there'd been to it, though, it still wouldn't have hurt the mining operations, and we could have got by. But what really tore it was when the rabbits started to die." Stranor Sleth picked up a cigar from his desk and bit the end, spitting it out disgustedly. "Tularemia, of course," he said, touching his lighter to the tip. "When that hit, they started going over to Muz-Azin in droves, not only at Zurb but all over the Six Kingdoms. You ought to have seen the house we had for Sunset Sacrifice, this evening! About two hundred, and we used to get two thousand. It used to be all two men could do to lift the offering box at the door, afterward, and all the money we took in tonight I could put in one pocket!" The high priest used language that would have been considered unclerical even among the Hulguns.

Verkan Vall nodded. Even without the quickie hypno-mech he had taken for this sector, he knew that the rabbit was domesticated among the Proto-Aryan Hulguns and was their chief meat animal. Hulgun rabbits were even a minor import on the First Level, and could be had at all the better restaurants in cities like Dhergabar. He mentioned that.

"That's not the worst of it," Stranor Sleth told him. "See, the rabbit's sacred to Yat-Zar. Not taboo; just sacred. They have to use a specially consecrated knife to kill them—consecrating rabbit knives has always been an item of temple revenue—and they must say a special prayer before eating them. We could have got around the rest of it, even the Battle of Jorm—punishment by Yat-Zar for the sin of apostasy—but Yat-Zar just wouldn't make rabbits sick. Yat-Zar thinks too well of rabbits to do that, and it'd not been any use claiming he would. So there you are."

"Well, I take the attitude that this situation is the result of your incompetence," Brannad Klav began, in a bullyragging tone. "You're not only the high priest of this temple, you're the acknowledged head of the religion in all the Hulgun kingdoms. You should have had more hold on the people than to allow anything like this to happen."

"Hold on the people!" Stranor Sleth fairly howled, appealing to Verkan Vall. "What does he think a religion is, on this sector, anyhow? You think these savages dreamed up that six-armed monstrosity, up there, to express their yearning for higher things, or to symbolize their moral ethos, or as a philosophical escape-hatch from the dilemma of causation? They never even heard of such matters. On this sector, gods are strictly utilitarian. As long as they take care of their worshipers, they get their sacrifices: when they can't put out, they have to get out. How do you suppose these Chulduns, living in the Caucasus Mountains, got the idea of a god like a crocodile, anyhow? Why, they got it from Homran traders, people from down in the Nile Valley. They had a god, once, something basically like a billy goat, but he let them get licked in a couple of battles, so out he went. Why, all the deities on this sector have hyphenated names, because they're combinations of several deities, worshiped in one person. Do you know anything about the history of this sector?" he asked the Paratime Police officer.

"Well, it develops from an alternate probability of what we call the Nilo-Mesopotamian Basic sector-group," Verkan Vall said. "On most Nilo-Mesopotamian sectors, like the Macedonian Empire Sector, or the Alexandrian-Roman or Alexandrian-Punic or Indo-Turanian or Europo-American, there was an Aryan invasion of Eastern Europe and Asia Minor about four thousand elapsed years ago. On this sector, the ancestors of the Aryans came in about fifteen centuries earlier, as neolithic savages, about the time that the Sumerian and Egyptian civilizations were first developing, and overran all southeast Europe, Asia Minor and the Nile Valley. They developed to the bronze-age culture of the civilizations they overthrew, and then, more slowly, to an iron-age culture. About two thousand years ago, they were using hardened steel and building large stone cities, just as they do now. At that time, they reached cultural stasis. But as for their religious beliefs, you've described them quite accurately. A god is only worshiped as long as the people think him powerful enough to aid and protect them; when they lose that confidence, he is discarded and the god of some neighboring people is adopted instead." He turned to Brannad Klav. "Didn't Stranor report this situation to you when it first developed?" he asked. "I know he did; he speaks of receiving shipments of grain by conveyer for temple distribution. Then why didn't you report it to Paratime Police? That's what we have a Paratime Police Force for."

"Well, yes, of course, but I had enough confidence in Stranor Sleth to think that he could handle the situation himself. I didn't know he'd gone slack—"

"Look, I can't make weather, even if my parishioners think I can," Stranor Sleth defended himself. "And I can't make a great military genius out of a blockhead like Kurchuk. And I can't immunize all the rabbits on this time-line against tularemia, even if I'd had any reason to expect a tularemia epidemic, which I hadn't because the disease is unknown on this sector; this is the only outbreak of it anybody's ever heard of on any Proto-Aryan time-line."

"No, but I'll tell you what you could have done," Verkan Vall told him. "When this Kurchuk started to apostatize, you could have gone to him at the head of a procession of priests, all paratimers and all armed with energy-weapons, and pointed out his spiritual duty to him, and if he gave you any back talk, you could have pulled out that needler and rayed him down and then cried, 'Behold the vengeance of Yat-Zar upon the wicked king!' I'll bet any sum at any odds that his successor would have thought twice about going over to Muz-Azin, and none of these other kings would have even thought once about it."

"Ha, that's what I wanted to do!" Stranor Sleth exclaimed. "And who stopped me? I'll give you just one guess."

"Well, it seems there was slackness here, but it wasn't Stranor Sleth who was slack," Verkan Vall commented.

"Well! I must say; I never thought I'd hear an officer of the Paratime Police criticizing me for trying to operate inside the Paratime Transposition Code!" Brannad Klav exclaimed.

Verkan Vall, sitting on the edge of Stranor Sleth's desk, aimed his cigarette at Brannad Klav like a blaster.

"Now, look," he began. "There is one, and only one, inflexible law regarding outtime activities. The secret of paratime transposition must be kept inviolate, and any activity tending to endanger it is prohibited. That's why we don't allow the transposition of any object of extraterrestrial origin to any time-line on which space travel has not been developed. Such an object may be preserved, and then, after the local population begin exploring the planet from whence it came, there will be dangerous speculations and theories as to how it arrived on Terra at such an early date. I came within inches, literally, of getting myself killed, not long ago, cleaning up the result of a violation of that regulation. For the same reason, we don't allow the export, to outtime natives, of manufactured goods too far in advance of their local culture. That's why, for instance, you people have to hand-finish all those big Yat-Zar idols, to remove traces of machine work. One of those things may be around, a few thousand years from now, when these people develop a mechanical civilization. But as far as raying down this Kurchuk is concerned, these Hulguns are completely nonscientific. They wouldn't have the least idea what happened. They'd believe that Yat-Zar struck him dead, as gods on this plane of culture are supposed to do, and if any of them noticed the needler at all, they'd think it was just a holy amulet of some kind."

"But the law is the law—" Brannad Klav began.

Verkan Vall shook his head. "Brannad, as I understand, you were promoted to your present position on the retirement of Salvan Marth, about ten years ago; up to that time, you were in your company's financial department. You were accustomed to working subject to the First Level Commercial Regulation Code. Now, any law binding upon our people at home, on the First Level, is inflexible. It has to be. We found out, over fifty centuries ago, that laws have to be rigid and without discretionary powers in administration in order that people may be able to predict their effect and plan their activities accordingly. Naturally, you became conditioned to operating in such a climate of legal inflexibility.

"But in paratime, the situation is entirely different. There exist, within the range of the Ghaldron-Hesthor paratemporal-field generator, a number of time-lines of the order of ten to the hundred-thousandth power. In effect, that many different worlds. In the past ten thousand years, we have visited only the tiniest fraction of these, but we have found everything from time-lines inhabited only by subhuman ape-men to Second Level civilizations which are our own equal in every respect but knowledge of paratemporal transposition. We even know of one Second Level civilization which is approaching the discovery of an interstellar hyperspatial drive, something we've never even come close to. And in between are every degree of savagery, barbarism and civilization. Now, it's just not possible to frame any single code of laws applicable to conditions on all of these. The best we can do is prohibit certain flagrantly immoral types of activity, such as slave-trading, introduction of new types of narcotic drugs, or out-and-out piracy and brigandage. If you're in doubt as to the legality of anything you want to do outtime, go to the Judicial Section of the Paratime Commission and get an opinion on it. That's where you made your whole mistake. You didn't find out just how far it was allowable for you to go."

He turned to Stranor Sleth again. "Well, that's the background, then. Now tell me about what happened yesterday at Zurb."

"Well, a week ago, Kurchuk came out with this decree closing our temple at Zurb and ordering his subjects to perform worship and make money offerings to Muz-Azin. The Zurb temple isn't a mask for a mine: Zurb's too far south for the uranium deposits. It's just a center for propaganda and that sort of thing. But they have a House of Yat-Zar, and a conveyer, and most of the upper-priests are paratimers. Well, our man there, Tammand Drav, alias Khoram, defied the king's order, so Kurchuk sent a company of Chuldun archers to close the temple and arrest the priests. Tammand Drav got all his people who were in the temple at the time into the House of Yat-Zar and transposed them back to the First Level. He had orders"—Stranor Sleth looked meaningly at Brannad Klav—"not to resist with energy-weapons or even ultrasonic paralyzers. And while we're on the subject of letting the local yokels see too much, about fifteen of the under-priests he took to the First Level were Hulgun natives."

"Nothing wrong about that: they'll get memory-obliteration and pseudo-memory treatment," Verkan Vall said. "But he should have been allowed to needle about a dozen of those Chulduns. Teach the beggars to respect Yat-Zar in the future. Now, how about the six priests who were outside the temple at the time? All but one were paratimers. We'll have to find out about them, and get them out of Zurb."

"That'll take some doing," Stranor Sleth said. "And it'll have to be done before sunset tomorrow. They are all in the dungeon of the palace citadel, and Kurchuk is going to give them to the priests of Muz-Azin to be sacrificed tomorrow evening."

"How'd you learn that?" Verkan Vall asked.

"Oh, we have a man in Zurb, not connected with the temple," Stranor Sleth said. "Name's Crannar Jurth; calls himself Kranjur, locally. He has a swordmaker's shop, employs about a dozen native journeymen and apprentices who hammer out the common blades he sells in the open market. Then, he imports a few high-class alloy-steel blades from the First Level, that'll cut through this local low-carbon armor like cheese. Fits them with locally-made hilts and sells them at unbelievable prices to the nobility. He's Swordsmith to the King; picks up all the inside palace dope. Of course, he was among the first to accept the New Gospel and go over to Muz-Azin. He has a secret room under his shop, with his conveyer and a radio.

"What happened was this: These six priests were at a consecration ceremony at a rabbit-ranch outside the city, and they didn't know about the raid on the temple. On their way back, they were surrounded by Chuldun archers and taken prisoner. They had no weapons but their sacrificial knives." He threw another dirty look at Brannad Klav. "So they're due to go up on the triangles at sunset tomorrow."

"We'll have to get them out before then," Verkan Vall stated. "They're our people, and we can't let them down; even the native is under our protection, whether he knows it or not. And in the second place, if those priests are sacrificed to Muz-Azin," he told Brannad Klav, "you can shut down everything on this time-line, pull out or disintegrate your installations, and fill in your mine-tunnels. Yat-Zar will be through on this time-line, and you'll be through along with him. And considering that your fissionables franchise for this sector comes up for renewal next year, your company will be through in this paratime area."

"You believe that would happen?" Brannad Klav asked anxiously.

"I know it will, because I'll put through a recommendation to that effect, if those six men are tortured to death tomorrow," Verkan Vall replied. "And in the fifty years that I've been in the Police Department, I've only heard of five such recommendations being ignored by the commission. You know, Fourth Level Mineral Products Syndicate is after your franchise. Ordinarily, they wouldn't have a chance of getting it, but with this, maybe they will, even without my recommendation. This was all your fault, for ignoring Stranor Sleth's proposal and for denying those men the right to carry energy weapons."

"Well, we were only trying to stay inside the Paratime Code," Brannad Klav pleaded. "If it isn't too late, now, you can count on me for every co-operation." He fiddled with some papers on the desk. "What do you want me to do to help?"

"I'll tell you that in a minute." Verkan Vall walked to the wall and looked at the map, then returned to Stranor Sleth's desk. "How about these dungeons?" he asked. "How are they located, and how can we get in to them?"

"I'm afraid we can't," Stranor Sleth told him. "Not without fighting our way in. They're under the palace citadel, a hundred feet below ground. They're spatially co-existent with the heavy water barriers around one of our company's plutonium piles on the First Level, and below surface on any unoccupied time-line I know of, so we can't transpose in to them. This palace is really a walled city inside a city. Here, I'll show you."

Going around the desk, he sat down and, after looking in the index-screen, punched a combination on the keyboard. A picture, projected from the microfilm-bank, appeared on the view-screen. It was an air-view of the city of Zurb—taken, the high priest explained, by infrared light from an airboat over the city at night. It showed a city of an entirely pre-mechanical civilization, with narrow streets, lined on either side by low one and two story buildings. Although there would be considerable snow in winter, the roofs were usually flat, probably massive stone slabs supported by pillars within. Even in the poorer sections, this was true except for the very meanest houses and out-buildings, which were thatched. Here and there, some huge pile of masonry would rear itself above its lower neighbors, and, where the streets were wider, occasional groups of large buildings would be surrounded by battlemented walls. Stranor Sleth indicated one of the larger of these.

"Here's the palace," he said. "And here's the temple of Yat-Zar, about half a mile away." He touched a large building, occupying an entire block; between it and the palace was a block-wide park, with lawns and trees on either side of a wide roadway connecting the two.

"Now, here's a detailed view of the palace." He punched another combination; the view of the City was replaced by one, taken from directly overhead, of the walled palace area. "Here's the main gate, in front, at the end of the road from the temple," he pointed out. "Over here, on the left, are the slaves' quarters and the stables and workshops and store houses and so on. Over here, on the other side, are the nobles' quarters. And this,"—he indicated a towering structure at the rear of the walled enclosure—"is the citadel and the royal dwelling. Audience hall on this side; harem over here on this side. A wide stone platform, about fifteen feet high, runs completely across the front of the citadel, from the audience hall to the harem. Since this picture was taken, the new temple of Muz-Azin was built right about here." He indicated that it extended out from the audience hall into the central courtyard. "And out here on the platform, they've put up about a dozen of these triangles, about twelve feet high, on which the sacrificial victims are whipped to death."

"Yes. About the only way we could get down to the dungeons would be to make an airdrop onto the citadel roof and fight our way down with needlers and blasters, and I'm not willing to do that as long as there's any other way," Verkan Vall said. "We'd lose men, even with needlers against bows, and there's a chance that some of our equipment might be lost in the melee and fall into outtime hands. You say this sacrifice comes off tomorrow at sunset?"

"That would be about actual sunset plus or minus an hour; these people aren't astronomers, they don't even have good sundials, and it might be a cloudy day," Stranor Sleth said. "There will be a big idol of Muz-Azin on a cart, set about here." He pointed. "After the sacrifice, it is to be dragged down this road, outside, to the temple of Yat-Zar, and set up there. The temple is now occupied by about twenty Chuldun mercenaries and five or six priests of Muz-Azin. They haven't, of course, got into the House of Yat-Zar; the door's of impervium steel, about six inches thick, with a plating of collapsed nickel under the gilding. It would take a couple of hours to cut through it with our best atomic torch; there isn't a tool on this time-line that could even scratch it. And the insides of the walls are lined with the same thing."

"Do you think our people have been tortured, yet?" Verkan Vall asked.

"No." Stranor Sleth was positive. "They'll be fairly well treated, until the sacrifice. The idea's to make them last as long as possible on the triangles; Muz-Azin likes to see a slow killing, and so does the mob of spectators."

"That's good. Now, here's my plan. We won't try to rescue them from the dungeons. Instead, we'll transpose back to the Zurb temple from the First Level, in considerable force—say a hundred or so men—and march on the palace, to force their release. You're in constant radio communication with all the other temples on this time-line, I suppose?"

"Yes, certainly."

"All right. Pass this out to everybody, authority Paratime Police, in my name, acting for Tortha Karf. I want all paratimers who can possibly be spared to transpose to First Level immediately and rendezvous at the First Level terminal of the Zurb temple conveyer as soon as possible. Close down all mining operations, and turn over temple routine to the native under-priests. You can tell them that the upper-priests are retiring to their respective Houses of Yat-Zar to pray for the deliverance of the priests in the hands of King Kurchuk. And everybody is to bring back his priestly regalia to the First Level; that will be needed." He turned to Brannad Klav. "I suppose you keep spare regalia in stock on the First Level?"

"Yes, of course; we keep plenty of everything in stock. Robes, miters, false beards of different shades, everything."

"And these big Yat-Zar idols: they're mass-produced on the First Level? You have one available now? Good. I'll want some alterations made on one. For one thing, I'll want it plated heavily, all over, with collapsed nickel. For another, I'll want it fitted with antigrav units and some sort of propulsion-units, and a loud-speaker, and remote control.

"And, Stranor, you get in touch with this swordmaker, Crannar Jurth, and alert him to co-operate with us. Tell him to start calling Zurb temple on his radio about noon tomorrow, and keep it up till he gets an answer. Or, better, tell him to run his conveyer to his First Level terminal, and bring with him an extra suit of clothes appropriate to the role of journeyman-mechanic. I'll want to talk to him, and furnish him with special equipment. Got all that? Well, carry on with it, and bring your own paratimers, priests and mining operators, back with you as soon as you've taken care of everything. Brannad, you come with me, now. We're returning to First Level immediately. We have a lot of work to do, so let's get started."

"Anything I can do to help, just call on me for it," Brannad Klav promised earnestly. "And, Stranor, I want to apologize. I'll admit, now, that I ought to have followed your recommendations, when this situation first developed."

* * * *

By noon of the next day, Verkan Vall had at least a hundred men gathered in the big room at the First Level fissionables refinery at Jarnabar, spatially co-existent with the Fourth Level temple of Yat-Zar at Zurb. He was having a little trouble distinguishing between them, for every man wore the fringed blue robe and golden miter of an upper-priest, and had his face masked behind a blue false beard. It was, he admitted to himself, a most ludicrous-looking assemblage; one of the most ludicrous things about it was the fact that it would have inspired only pious awe in a Hulgun of the Fourth Level Proto-Aryan Sector. About half of them were priests from the Transtemporal Mining Corporation's temples; the other half were members of the Paratime Police. All of them wore, in addition to their temple knives, holstered sigma-ray needlers. Most of them carried ultrasonic paralyzers, eighteen-inch batonlike things with bulbous ends. Most of the Paratime Police and a few of the priests also carried either heat-ray pistols or neutron-disruption blasters; Verkan Vall wore one of the latter in a left-hand belt holster.

The Paratime Police were lined up separately for inspection, and Stranor Sleth, Tammand Drav of the Zurb temple, and several other high priests were checking the authenticity of their disguises. A little apart from the others, a Paratime Policeman, in high priest's robes and beard, had a square box slung in front of him; he was fiddling with knobs and buttons on it, practicing. A big idol of Yat-Zar, on antigravity, was floating slowly about the room in obedience to its remote controls, rising and lowering, turning about and pirouetting gracefully.

"Hey, Vall!" he called to his superior. "How's this?"

The idol rose about five feet, turned slowly in a half-circle, moved to the right a little, and then settled slowly toward the floor.

"Fine, fine, Horv," Verkan Vall told him, "but don't set it down on anything, or turn off the antigravity. There's enough collapsed nickel-plating on that thing to sink it a yard in soft ground."

"I don't know what the idea of that was," Brannad Klav, standing beside him, said. "Understand, I'm not criticizing. I haven't any right to, under the circumstances. But it seems to me that armoring that thing in collapsed nickel was an unnecessary precaution."

"Maybe it was," Verkan Vall agreed. "I sincerely hope so. But we can't take any chances. This operation has to be absolutely right. Ready, Tammand? All right; first detail into the conveyer."

He turned and strode toward a big dome of fine metallic mesh, thirty feet high and sixty in diameter, at the other end of the room. Tammand Drav, and his ten paratimer priests, and Brannad Klav, and ten Paratime Police, followed him in. One of the latter slid shut the door and locked it; Verkan Vall went to the control desk, at the center of the dome, and picked up a two-foot globe of the same fine metallic mesh, opening it and making some adjustments inside, then attaching an electric cord and closing it. He laid the globe on the floor near the desk and picked up the hand battery at the other end of the attached cord.

"Not taking any chances at all, are you?" Brannad Klav asked, watching this operation with interest.

"I never do, unnecessarily. There are too many necessary chances that have to be taken, in this work." Verkan Vall pressed the button on the hand battery. The globe on the floor flashed and vanished. "Yesterday, five paratimers were arrested. Any or all of them could have had door-activators with them. Stranor Sleth says they were not tortured, but that is a purely inferential statement. They may have been, and the use of the activator may have been extorted from one of them. So I want a look at the inside of that conveyer-chamber before we transpose into it."

He laid the hand battery, with the loose-dangling wire that had been left behind, on the desk, then lit a cigarette. The others gathered around, smoking and watching, careful to avoid the place from which the globe had vanished. Thirty minutes passed, and then, in a queer iridescence, the globe reappeared. Verkan Vall counted ten seconds and picked it up, taking it to the desk and opening it to remove a small square box. This he slid into a space under the desk and flipped a switch. Instantly, a viewscreen lit up and a three-dimensional picture appeared—the interior of a big room a hundred feet square and some seventy in height. There was a big desk and a radio; tables, couches, chairs and an arms-rack full of weapons, and at one end, a remarkably clean sixty-foot circle on the concrete floor, outlined in faintly luminous red.

"How about it?" Verkan Vall asked Tammand Drav. "Anything wrong?"

The Zurb high priest shook his head. "Just as we left it," he said. "Nobody's been inside since we left."

* * * *

One of the policemen took Verkan Vall's place at the control desk and threw the master switch, after checking the instruments. Immediately, the paratemporal-transposition field went on with a humming sound that mounted to a high scream, then settled to a steady drone. The mesh dome flickered with a cold iridescence and vanished, and they were looking into the interior of a great fissionables refinery plant, operated by paratimers on another First Level time-line. The structural details altered, from time-line to time-line, as they watched. Buildings appeared and vanished. Once, for a few seconds, they were inside a cool, insulated bubble in the midst of molten lead. Tammand Drav jerked a thumb at it, before it vanished.

"That always bothers me," he said. "Bad place for the field to go weak. I'm fussy as an old hen about inspection of the conveyer, on account of that."

"Don't blame you," Verkan Vall agreed. "Probably the cooling system of a breeder-pile."

They passed more swiftly, now, across the Second Level and the Third. Once they were in the midst of a huge land battle, with great tanklike vehicles spouting flame at one another. Another moment was spent in an air bombardment. On any time-line, this section of East Europe was a natural battleground. Once a great procession marched toward them, carrying red banners and huge pictures of a coarse-faced man with a black mustache—Verkan Vall recognized the environment as Fourth Level Europo-American Sector. Finally, as the transposition-rate slowed, they saw a clutter of miserable thatched huts, in the rear of a granite wall of a Fourth Level Hulgun temple of Yat-Zar—a temple not yet infiltrated by Transtemporal Mining Corporation agents. Finally, they were at their destination. The dome around them became visible, and an overhead green light flashed slowly on and off.

Verkan Vall opened the door and stepped outside, his needler drawn. The House of Yat-Zar was just as he had seen it in the picture photographed by the automatic reconnaissance-conveyer. The others crowded outside after him. One of the regular priests pulled off his miter and beard and went to the radio, putting on a headset. Verkan Vall and Tammand Drav snapped on the visiscreen, getting a view of the Holy of Holies outside.

There were six men there, seated at the upper-priests' banquet table, drinking from golden goblets. Five of them wore the black robes with green facings which marked them as priests of Muz-Azin; the sixth was an officer of the Chuldun archers, in gilded mail and helmet.

"Why, those are the sacred vessels of the temple!" Tammand Drav cried, scandalized. Then he laughed in self-ridicule. "I'm beginning to take this stuff seriously, myself; time I put in for a long vacation. I was actually shocked at the sacrilege!"

"Well, let's overtake the infidels in their sins," Verkan Vall said. "Paralyzers will be good enough."

He picked up one of the bulb-headed weapons, and unlocked the door. Tammand Drav and another of the priests of the Zurb temple following and the others crowding behind, they passed out through the veils, and burst into the Holy of Holies. Verkan Vall pointed the bulb of his paralyzer at the six seated men and pressed the button; other paralyzers came into action, and the whole sextet were knocked senseless. The officer rolled from his chair and fell to the floor in a clatter of armor. Two of the priests slumped forward on the table. The others merely sank back in their chairs, dropping their goblets.

"Give each one of them another dose, to make sure," Verkan Vall directed a couple of his own men. "Now, Tammand; any other way into the main temple beside that door?"

"Up those steps," Tammand Drav pointed. "There's a gallery along the side; we can cover the whole room from there."

"Take your men and go up there. I'll take a few through the door. There'll be about twenty archers out there, and we don't want any of them loosing any arrows before we can knock them out. Three minutes be time enough?"

"Easily. Make it two," Tammand Drav said.

* * * *

He took his priests up the stairway and vanished into the gallery of the temple. Verkan Vall waited until one minute had passed and then, followed by Brannad Klav and a couple of Paratime Policemen, he went under the plinth and peered out into the temple. Five or six archers, in steel caps and sleeveless leather jackets sewn with steel rings, were gathered around the altar, cooking something in a pot on the fire. Most of the others, like veteran soldiers, were sprawled on the floor, trying to catch a short nap, except half a dozen, who crouched in a circle, playing some game with dice—another almost universal military practice.

The two minutes were up. He aimed his paralyzer at the men around the altar and squeezed the button, swinging it from one to another and knocking them down with a bludgeon of inaudible sound. At the same time, Tammand Drav and his detail were stunning the gamblers. Stepping forward and to one side, Verkan Vall, Brannad Klav and the others took care of the sleepers on the floor. In less than thirty seconds, every Chuldun in the temple was incapacitated.

"All right, make sure none of them come out of it prematurely," Verkan Vall directed. "Get their weapons, and be sure nobody has a knife or anything hidden on him. Who has the syringe and the sleep-drug ampoules?"

Somebody had, it developed, who was still on the First Level, to come up with the second conveyer load. Verkan Vall swore. Something like this always happened, on any operation involving more than half a dozen men.

"Well, some of you stay here: patrol around, and use your paralyzers on anybody who even twitches a muscle." Ultrasonics were nice, effective, humane police weapons, but they were unreliable. The same dose that would keep one man out for an hour would paralyze another for no more than ten or fifteen minutes. "And be sure none of them are playing 'possum."

He went back through the door under the plinth, glancing up at the decorated wooden screen and wondering how much work it would take to move the new Yat-Zar in from the conveyers. The five priests and the archer-captain were still unconscious; one of the policemen was searching them.

"Here's the sort of weapons these priests carry," he said, holding up a short iron mace with a spiked head. "Carry them on their belts." He tossed it on the table, and began searching another knocked-out hierophant. "Like this—*Hey!* Look at this, will you!"

He drew his hand from under the left side of the senseless man's robe and held up a sigma-ray needler. Verkan Vall looked at it and nodded grimly.

"Had it in a regular shoulder holster," the policeman said, handing the weapon across the table. "What do you think?"

"Find anything else funny on him?"

"Wait a minute." The policeman pulled open the robe and began stripping the priest of Muz-Azin; Verkan Vall came around the table to help. There was nothing else of a suspicious nature.

"Could have got it from one of the prisoners, but I don't like the familiar way he's wearing that holster," Verkan Vall said. "Has the conveyer gone back, yet?" When the policeman nodded, he continued: "When it returns, take him to the First Level. I hope they bring up the sleep-drug with the next load. When you get him back, take him to Dhergabar by strato-rocket immediately, and make sure he gets back alive. I want him questioned under narco-hypnosis by a regular Paratime Commission psycho-technician, in the presence of Chief Tortha Karf and some responsible Commission official. This is going to be hot stuff."

Within an hour, the whole force was assembled in the temple. The wooden screen had presented no problem—it slid easily to one side—and the big idol floated on antigravity in the middle of the temple. Verkan Vall was looking anxiously at his watch.

"It's about two hours to sunset," he said, to Stranor Sleth. "But as you pointed out, these Hulguns aren't astronomers, and it's a bit cloudy. I wish Crannar Jurth would call in with something definite."

Another twenty minutes passed. Then the man at the radio came out into the temple.

"O. K.!" he called. "The man at Crannar Jurth's called in. Crannar Jurth contacted him with a midget radio he has up his sleeve; he's in the palace courtyard now. They haven't brought out the victims, yet, but Kurchuk has just been carried out on his throne to that platform in front of the citadel. Big crowd gathering in the inner courtyard; more in the streets outside. Palace gates are wide open."

"That's it!" Verkan Vall cried. "Form up; the parade's starting. Brannad, you and Tammand and Stranor and I in front; about ten men with paralyzers a little behind us. Then Yat-Zar, about ten feet off the ground, and then the others. Forward—*ho-o!*"

* * * *

They emerged from the temple and started down the broad roadway toward the palace. There was not much of a crowd, at first. Most of Zurb had flocked to the palace earlier; the lucky ones in the courtyard and the late comers outside. Those whom they did meet stared at them in open-mouthed amazement, and then some, remembering their doubts and blasphemies, began howling for forgiveness. Others—a substantial majority—realizing that it would be upon King Kurchuk that the real weight of Yat-Zar's six hands would fall, took to their heels, trying to put as much distance as possible between them and the palace before the blow fell.

As the procession approached the palace gates, the crowds were thicker, made up of those who had been unable to squeeze themselves inside. The panic was worse, here, too. A good many were trampled and hurt in the rush to escape, and it became necessary to use paralyzers to clear a way. That made it worse: everybody was sure that Yat-Zar was striking sinners dead left and right.

Fortunately, the gates were high enough to let the god through without losing altitude appreciably. Inside, the mob surged back, clearing a way across the courtyard. It was only necessary to paralyze a few here, and the levitated idol and its priestly attendants advanced toward the stone platform, where the king sat on his throne, flanked by court functionaries and black-robed priests of Muz-Azin. In front of this, a rank of Chuldun archers had been drawn up.

"Horv; move Yat-Zar forward about a hundred feet and up about fifty," Verkan Vall directed. "Quickly!"

As the six-armed anthropomorphic idol rose and moved closer toward its saurian rival, Verkan Vall drew his needler, scanning the assemblage around the throne anxiously.

"*Where is the wicked King?*" a voice thundered—the voice of Stranor Sleth, speaking into a midget radio tuned to the loud-speaker inside the idol. "*Where is the blasphemer and desecrator, Kurchuk?*"

"There's Labdurg, in the red tunic, beside the throne," Tammand Drav whispered. "And that's Ghromdur, the Muz-Azin high priest, beside him."

Verkan Vall nodded, keeping his eyes on the group on the platform. Ghromdur, the high priest of Muz-Azin, was edging backward and reaching under his robe. At the same time, an officer shouted an order, and the Chuldun archers drew arrows from their quivers and fitted them to their bowstrings. Immediately, the ultrasonic paralyzers of the advancing paratimers went into action, and the mercenaries began dropping.

"*Lay down your weapons, fools!*" the amplified voice boomed at them. "*Lay down your weapons or you shall surely die! Who are you, miserable wretches, to draw bows against Me?*"

At first a few, then all of them, the Chulduns lowered or dropped their weapons and began edging away to the sides. At the center, in front of the throne, most of them had been knocked out. Verkan Vall was still watching the Muz-Azin high priest intently; as Ghromdur raised his arm, there was a flash and a puff of smoke from the front of Yat-Zar—the paint over the collapsed nickel was burned off, but otherwise the idol was undamaged. Verkan Vall swung up his needler and rayed Ghromdur dead; as the man in the green-faced black robes fell, a blaster clattered on the stone platform.

"Is that your puny best, Muz-Azin?" the booming voice demanded. *"Where is your high priest now?"*

"Horv; face Yat-Zar toward Muz-Azin," Verkan Vall said over his shoulder, drawing his blaster with his left hand. Like all First Level people, he was ambidextrous, although, like all paratimers, he habitually concealed the fact while outtime. As the levitated idol swung slowly to look down upon its enemy on the built-up cart, Verkan Vall aimed the blaster and squeezed.

In a spot less than a millimeter in diameter on the crocodile idol's side, a certain number of neutrons in the atomic structure of the stone from which it was carved broke apart, becoming, in effect, atoms of hydrogen. With a flash and a bang, the idol burst and vanished. Yat-Zar gave a dirty laugh and turned his back on the cart, which was now burning fiercely facing King Kurchuk again.

"Get your hands up, all of you!" Verkan Vall shouted, in the First Level language, swinging the stubby muzzle of the blaster and the knob-tipped twin tubes of the needler to cover the group around the throne, "Come forward, before I start blasting!"

Labdurg raised his hands and stepped forward. So did two of the priests of Yat-Zar. They were quickly seized by Paratime Policemen who swarmed up onto the platform and disarmed. All three were carrying sigma-ray needlers, and Labdurg had a blaster as well.

King Kurchuk was clinging to the arms of his throne, a badly frightened monarch trying desperately not to show it. He was a big man, heavy-shouldered, black-bearded; under ordinary circumstances he would probably have cut an imposing figure, in his gold-washed mail and his golden crown. Now his face was a dirty gray, and he was biting nervously at his lower lip. The others on the platform were in even worse state. The Hulgun nobles were grouped together, trying to disassociate themselves from both the king and the priests of Muz-Azin. The latter were staring in a daze at the blazing cart from which their idol had just been blasted. And the dozen men who were to have done the actual work of the torture-sacrifice had all dropped their whips and were fairly gibbering in fear.

Yat-Zar, manipulated by the robed paratimer, had taken a position directly above the throne and was lowering slowly. Kurchuk stared up at the massive idol descending toward him, his knuckles white as he clung to the arms of his throne. He managed to hold out until he could feel the weight of the idol pressing on his head. Then, with a scream, he hurled himself from the throne and rolled forward almost to the edge of the platform. Yat-Zar moved to one side, swung slightly and knocked the throne toppling, and then settled down on the platform. To Kurchuk, who was rising cautiously on his hands and knees, the big idol seemed to be looking at him in contempt.

"*Where are my holy priests, Kurchuk?*" Stranor Sleth demanded in to his sleeve-hidden radio. "*Let them be brought before me, alive and unharmed, or it shall be better for you had you never been born!*"

The six priests of Yat-Zar, it seemed, were already being brought onto the platform by one of Kurchuk's nobles. This noble, whose name was Yorzuk, knew a miracle when he saw one, and believed in being on the side of the god with the heaviest artillery. As soon as he had seen Yat-Zar coming through the gate without visible means of support, he had hastened to the dungeons with half a dozen of his personal retainers and ordered the release of the six captives. He was now escorting them onto the platform, assuring them that he had always been a faithful servant of Yat-Zar and had been deeply grieved at his sovereign's apostasy.

"*Hear my word, Kurchuk,*" Stranor Sleth continued through the loudspeaker in the idol. "*You have sinned most vilely against me, and were I a cruel god, your fate would be such as no man has ever before suffered. But I am a merciful god; behold, you may gain forgiveness in my sight. For thirty days, you shall neither eat meat nor drink wine, nor shall you wear gold nor fine raiment, and each day shall you go to my temple and beseech me for my forgiveness. And on the thirty-first day, you shall set out, barefoot and clad in the garb of a slave, and journey to my temple that is in the mountains over above Yoldav, and there will I forgive you, after you have made sacrifice to me. I, Yat-Zar, have spoken!*"

The king started to rise, babbling thanks.

"*Rise not before me until I have forgiven you!*" Yat-Zar thundered. "*Creep out of my sight upon your belly, wretch!*"

* * * *

The procession back to the temple was made quietly and sedately along an empty roadway. Yat-Zar seemed to be in a kindly humor; the people of Zurb had no intention of giving him any reason to change his mood. The priests of Muz-Azin and their torturers had been flung into the dungeon. Yorzuk, appointed regent for the duration of Kurchuk's penance, had taken control and was employing Hulgun spearmen and hastily-converted Chuldun archers to restore order and, incidentally, purge a few of his personal enemies and political rivals. The priests, with the three prisoners who had been found carrying First Level weapons among them and Yat-Zar floating triumphantly in front, entered the temple. A few of the devout, who sought admission after them, were told that elaborate and secret rites were being held to cleanse the profaned altar, and sent away. Verkan Vall and Brannad Klav and Stranor Sleth were in the conveyer chamber, with the Paratime Policemen and the extra priests; along with them were the three prisoners. Verkan Vall pulled off his false beard and turned to face these. He could see that they all recognized him.

"Now," he began, "you people are in a bad jam. You've violated the Paratime Transposition Code, the Commercial Regulation Code, and the First Level Criminal Code, all together. If you know what's good for you, you'll start talking."

"I'm not saying anything till I have legal advice," the man who had been using the local alias of Labdurg replied. "And if you're through searching me, I'd like to have my cigarettes and lighter back."

"Smoke one of mine, for a change," Verkan Vall told him. "I don't know what's in yours beside tobacco." He offered his case and held a light for the prisoner before lighting his own cigarette. "I'm going to be sure you get back to the First Level alive."

The former Overseer of the Kingdom of Zurb shrugged. "I'm still not talking," he said.

"Well, we can get it all out of you by narco-hypnosis, anyhow," Verkan Vall told him. "Besides, we got that man of yours who was here at the temple when we came in. He's being given a full treatment, as a presumed outtime native found in possession of First Level weapons. If you talk now it'll go easier with you."

The prisoner dropped the cigarette on the floor and tramped it out.

"Anything you cops get out of me, you'll have to get the hard way," he said. "I have friends on the First Level who'll take care of me."

"I doubt that. They'll have their hands full taking care of themselves, after this gets out." Verkan Vall turned to the two in the black robes. "Either of you want to say anything?" When they shook their heads, he nodded to a group of his policemen; they were hustled into the conveyer. "Take them to the First Level terminal and hold them till I come in. I'll be along with the next conveyer load."

* * * *

The conveyer flashed and vanished. Brannad Klav stared for a moment at the circle of concrete floor from whence it had disappeared. Then he turned to Verkan Vall.

"I still can't believe it," he said. "Why, those fellows were First Level paratimers. So was that priest, Ghromdur: the one you rayed."

"Yes, of course. They worked for your rivals, the Fourth Level Mineral Products Syndicate; the outfit that was trying to get your Proto-Aryan Sector fissionables franchise away from you. They operate on this sector already; have the petroleum franchise for the Chuldun country, east of the Caspian Sea. They export to some of these internal-combustion-engine sectors, like Europo-American. You know, most of the wars they've been fighting, lately, on the Europo-American Sector have been, at least in part, motivated by rivalry for oil fields. But now that the Europo-Americans have begun to release nuclear energy, fissionables have become more important than oil. In less than a century, it's predicted that atomic energy will replace all other forms of power. Mineral Products Syndicate wanted to get a good source of supply for uranium, and your Proto-Aryan Sector franchise was worth grabbing.

"I had considered something like this as a possibility when Stranor, here, mentioned that tularemia was normally unknown in Eurasia on this sector. That epidemic must have been started by imported germs. And I knew that Mineral Products has agents at the court of the Chuldun emperor, Chombrog: they have to, to protect their oil wells on his eastern frontiers. I spent most of last night checking up on some stuff by video-transcription from the Paratime Commission's microfilm library at Dhergabar. I found out, for one thing, that while there is a King Kurchuk of Zurb on every time-line for a hundred para-years on either side of this one, this is the only time-line on which he married a Princess Darith of Chuldun, and it's the only time-line on which there is any trace of a Chuldun scribe named Labdurg.

"That's why I went to all the trouble of having that Yat-Zar plated with collapsed nickel. If there were disguised paratimers among the Muz-Azin party at Kurchuk's court, I expected one of them to try to blast our idol when we brought it into the palace. I was watching Ghromdur and Labdurg in particular; as soon as Ghromdur used his blaster, I needled him. After that, it was easy."

"Was that why you insisted on sending that automatic viewer on ahead?"

"Yes. There was a chance that they might have planted a bomb in the House of Yat-Zar, here. I knew they'd either do that or let the place entirely alone. I suppose they were so confident of getting away with this that they didn't want to damage the conveyer or the conveyer chamber. They expected to use them, themselves, after they took over your company's franchise."

"Well, what's going to be done about it by the Commission?" Brannad Klav wanted to know.

"Plenty. The syndicate will probably lose their paratime license; any of its officials who had guilty knowledge of this will be dealt with according to law. You know, this was a pretty nasty business."

"You're telling me!" Stranor Sleth exclaimed. "Did you get a look at those whips they were going to use on our people? Pointed iron barbs a quarter-inch long braided into them, all over the lash-ends!"

"Yes. Any punitive action you're thinking about taking on these priests of Muz-Azin—the natives, I mean—will be ignored on the First Level. And that reminds me: you'd better work out a line of policy, pretty soon."

"Well, as for the priests and the torturers, I think I'll tell Yorzuk to have them sold to the Bhunguns, to the east. They're always in the market for galley slaves," Stranor Sleth said. He turned to Brannad Klav. "And I'll want six gold crowns made up, as soon as possible. Strictly Hulgun design, with Yat-Zar religious symbolism, very rich and ornate, all slightly different. When I give Kurchuk absolution, I'll crown him at the altar in the name of Yat-Zar. Then I'll invite in the other five Hulgun kings, lecture them on their religious duties, make them confess their secret doubts, forgive them, and crown them, too. From then on, they can all style themselves as ruling by the will of Yat-Zar."

"And from then on, you'll have all of them eating out of your hand,"

Verkan Vall concluded. "You know, this will probably go down in Hulgun history as the Reformation of Ghullam the Holy. I've always wondered whether the theory of the divine right of kings was invented by the kings, to establish their authority over the people, or by the priests, to establish *their* authority over the kings. It works about as well one way as the other."

"What I can't understand is this," Brannad Klav said. "It was entirely because of my respect for the Paratime Code that I kept Stranor Sleth from using Fourth Level weapons and other techniques to control these people with a show of apparent miraculous powers. But this Fourth Level Mineral Products Syndicate was operating in violation of the Paratime Code by invading our franchise area. Why didn't they fake up a supernatural reign of terror to intimidate these natives?"

"Ha, exactly because they *were* operating illegally," Verkan Vall replied. "Suppose they had started using needlers and blasters and antigravity and nuclear-energy around here. The natives would have thought it was the power of Muz-Azin, of course, but what would you have thought? You'd have known, as soon as they tried it, that First Level paratimers were working against you, and you'd have laid the facts before the Commission, and this time-line would have been flooded with Paratime Police. They had to conceal their operations not only from the natives, as you do, but also from us. So they didn't dare make public use of First Level techniques.

"Of course, when we came marching into the palace with that idol on antigravity, they knew, at once, what was happening. I have an idea that they only tried to blast that idol to create a diversion which would permit them to escape—if they could have got out of the palace, they'd have made their way, in disguise, to the nearest Mineral Products Syndicate conveyer and transposed out of here. I realized that they could best delay us by blasting our idol, and that's why I had it plated with collapsed nickel. I think that where they made their mistake was in allowing Kurchuk to have those priests arrested, and insisting on sacrificing them to Muz-Azin. If it hadn't been for that, the Paratime Police wouldn't have been brought into this, at all.

"Well, Stranor, you'll want to get back to your temple, and Brannad and I want to get back to the First Level. I'm supposed to take my wife to a banquet in Dhergabar, tonight, and with the fastest strato-rocket, I'll just barely make it."

GENESIS

Aboard the ship, there was neither day nor night; the hours slipped gently by, as vistas of star-gemmed blackness slid across the visiscreens. For the crew, time had some meaning—one watch on duty and two off. But for the thousand-odd colonists, the men and women who were to be the spearhead of migration to a new and friendlier planet, it had none. They slept, and played, worked at such tasks as they could invent, and slept again, while the huge ship followed her plotted trajectory.

Kalvar Dard, the army officer who would lead them in their new home, had as little to do as any of his followers. The ship's officers had all the responsibility for the voyage, and, for the first time in over five years, he had none at all. He was finding the unaccustomed idleness more wearying than the hectic work of loading the ship before the blast-off from Doorsha. He went over his landing and security plans again, and found no probable emergency unprepared for. Dard wandered about the ship, talking to groups of his colonists, and found morale even better than he had hoped. He spent hours staring into the forward visiscreens, watching the disc of Tareesh, the planet of his destination, grow larger and plainer ahead.

Now, with the voyage almost over, he was in the cargo-hold just aft of the Number Seven bulkhead, with six girls to help him, checking construction material which would be needed immediately after landing. The stuff had all been checked two or three times before, but there was no harm in going over it again. It furnished an occupation to fill in the time; it gave Kalvar Dard an excuse for surrounding himself with half a dozen charming girls, and the girls seemed to enjoy being with him. There was tall blonde Olva, the electromagnetician; pert little Varnis, the machinist's helper; Kyna, the surgeon's-aide; dark-haired Analea; Dorita, the accountant; plump little Eldra, the armament technician. At the moment, they were all sitting on or around the desk in the corner of the store-room, going over the inventory when they were not just gabbling.

"Well, how about the rock-drill bitts?" Dorita was asking earnestly, trying to stick to business. "Won't we need them almost as soon as we're off?"

"Yes, we'll have to dig temporary magazines for our explosives, small-arms and artillery ammunition, and storage-pits for our fission-ables and radioactives," Kalvar Dard replied. "We'll have to have safe places for that stuff ready before it can be unloaded; and if we run into hard rock near the surface, we'll have to drill holes for blasting-shots."

"The drilling machinery goes into one of those prefabricated sheds," Eldra considered. "Will there be room in it for all the bitts, too?"

Kalvar Dard shrugged. "Maybe. If not, we'll cut poles and build racks for them outside. The bitts are nono-steel; they can be stored in the open."

"If there are poles to cut," Olva added.

"I'm not worrying about that," Kalvar Dard replied. "We have a pretty fair idea of conditions on Tareesh; our astronomers have been making telescopic observations for the past fifteen centuries. There's a pretty big Arctic ice-cap, but it's been receding slowly, with a wide belt of what's believed to be open grassland to the south of it, and a belt of what's assumed to be evergreen forest south of that. We plan to land somewhere in the northern hemisphere, about the grassland-forest line. And since Tareesh is richer in water that Doorsha, you mustn't think of grassland in terms of our wire-grass plains, or forests in terms of our brush thickets. The vegetation should be much more luxuriant."

"If there's such a large polar ice-cap, the summers ought to be fairly cool, and the winters cold," Varnis reasoned. "I'd think that would mean fur-bearing animals. Colonel, you'll have to shoot me something with a nice soft fur; I like furs."

Kalvar Dard chuckled. "Shoot you nothing, you can shoot your own furs. I've seen your carbine and pistol scores," he began.

* * * *

There was a sudden suck of air, disturbing the papers on the desk. They all turned to see one of the ship's rocket-boat bays open; a young Air Force lieutenant named Seldar Glav, who would be staying on Tareesh with them to pilot their aircraft, emerged from an open airlock.

"Don't tell me you've been to Tareesh and back in that thing," Olva greeted him.

Seldar Glav grinned at her. "I could have been, at that; we're only twenty or thirty planetary calibers away, now. We ought to be enter-ing Tareeshan atmosphere by the middle of the next watch. I was only checking the boats, to make sure they'll be ready to launch.... Colonel Kalvar, would you mind stepping over here? There's something I think you should look at, sir."

Kalvar Dard took one arm from around Analea's waist and lifted the other from Varnis' shoulder, sliding off the desk. He followed Glav into the boat-bay; as they went through the airlock, the cheerfulness left the young lieutenant's face.

"I didn't want to say anything in front of the girls, sir," he began, "but I've been checking boats to make sure we can make a quick get-away. Our meteor-security's gone out. The detectors are deader then the Fourth Dynasty, and the blasters won't synchronize.... Did you hear a big thump, about a half an hour ago, Colonel?"

"Yes, I thought the ship's labor-crew was shifting heavy equipment in the hold aft of us. What was it, a meteor-hit?"

"It was. Just aft of Number Ten bulkhead. A meteor about the size of the nose of that rocket-boat."

Kalvar Dard whistled softly. "Great Gods of Power! The detectors must be dead, to pass up anything like that.... Why wasn't a boat-stations call sent out?"

"Captain Vlazil was unwilling to risk starting a panic, sir," the Air Force officer replied. "Really, I'm exceeding my orders in mentioning it to you, but I thought you should know...."

Kalvar Dard swore. "It's a blasted pity Captain Vlazil didn't try thinking! Gold-braided quarter-wit! Maybe his crew might panic, but my people wouldn't.... I'm going to call the control-room and have it out with him. By the Ten Gods...!"

* * * *

He ran through the airlock and back into the hold, starting toward the intercom-phone beside the desk. Before he could reach it, there was another heavy jar, rocking the entire ship. He, and Seldar Glav, who had followed him out of the boat-bay, and the six girls, who had risen on hearing their commander's angry voice, were all tumbled into a heap. Dard surged to his feet, dragging Kyna up along with him; together, they helped the others to rise. The ship was suddenly filled with jangling bells, and the red danger-lights on the ceiling were flashing on and off.

"Attention! Attention!" the voice of some officer in the control-room blared out of the intercom-speaker. "The ship has just been hit by a large meteor! All compartments between bulkheads Twelve and Thirteen are sealed off. All persons between bulkheads Twelve and Thirteen, put on oxygen helmets and plug in at the nearest phone connection. Your air is leaking, and you can't get out, but if you put on oxygen equipment immediately, you'll be all right. We'll get you out as soon as we can, and in any case, we are only a few hours out of Tareeshan atmosphere. All persons in Compartment Twelve, put on...."

Kalvar Dard was swearing evilly. "That does it! That does it for good!... Anybody else in this compartment, below the living quarter level?"

"No, we're the only ones," Analea told him.

"The people above have their own boats; they can look after themselves. You girls, get in that boat, in there. Glav, you and I'll try to warn the people above...."

There was another jar, heavier than the one which had preceded it, throwing them all down again. As they rose, a new voice was shouting over the public-address system:

"*Abandon ship! Abandon ship!* The converters are backfiring, and rocket-fuel is leaking back toward the engine-rooms! An explosion is imminent! Abandon ship, all hands!"

Kalvar Dard and Seldar Glav grabbed the girls and literally threw them through the hatch, into the rocket-boat. Dard pushed Glav in ahead of him, then jumped in. Before he had picked himself up, two or three of the girls were at the hatch, dogging the cover down.

"All right, Glav, blast off!" Dard ordered. "We've got to be at least a hundred miles from this ship when she blows, or we'll blow with her!"

"Don't I know!" Seldar Glav retorted over his shoulder, racing for the controls. "Grab hold of something, everybody; I'm going to fire all jets at once!"

An instant later, while Kalvar Dard and the girls clung to stanchions and pieces of fixed furniture, the boat shot forward out of its housing. When Dard's head had cleared, it was in free flight.

"How was that?" Glav yelled. "Everybody all right?" He hesitated for a moment. "I think I blacked out for about ten seconds."

Kalvar Dard looked the girls over. Eldra was using a corner of her smock to stanch a nosebleed, and Olva had a bruise over one eye. Otherwise, everybody was in good shape.

"Wonder we didn't all black out, permanently," he said. "Well, put on the visiscreens, and let's see what's going on outside. Olva, get on the radio and try to see if anybody else got away."

"Set course for Tareesh?" Glav asked. "We haven't fuel enough to make it back to Doorsha."

"I was afraid of that," Dard nodded. "Tareesh it is; northern hemisphere, daylight side. Try to get about the edge of the temperate zone, as near water as you can...."

2

They were flung off their feet again, this time backward along the boat. As they picked themselves up, Seldar Glav was shaking his head, sadly. "That was the ship going up," he said; "the blast must have caught us dead astern."

"All right." Kalvar Dard rubbed a bruised forehead. "Set course for Tareesh, then cut out the jets till we're ready to land. And get the screens on, somebody; I want to see what's happened."

The screens glowed; then full vision came on. The planet on which they would land loomed huge before them, its north pole toward them, and its single satellite on the port side. There was no sign of any rocket-boat in either side screen, and the rear-view screen was a blur of yellow flame from the jets.

"Cut the jets, Glav," Dard repeated. "Didn't you hear me?"

"But I did, sir!" Seldar Glav indicated the firing-panel. Then he glanced at the rear-view screen. "The gods help us! It's yellow flame; the jets are burning out!"

Kalvar Dard had not boasted idly when he had said that his people would not panic. All the girls went white, and one or two gave low cries of consternation, but that was all.

"What happens next?" Analea wanted to know. "Do we blow, too?"

"Yes, as soon as the fuel-line burns up to the tanks."

"Can you land on Tareesh before then?" Dard asked.

"I can try. How about the satellite? It's closer."

"It's also airless. Look at it and see for yourself," Kalvar Dard advised. "Not enough mass to hold an atmosphere."

Glav looked at the army officer with new respect. He had always been inclined to think of the Frontier Guards as a gang of scientifically illiterate dirk-and-pistol bravos. He fiddled for a while with instruments on the panel; an automatic computer figured the distance to the planet, the boat's velocity, and the time needed for a landing.

"We have a chance, sir," he said. "I think I can set down in about thirty minutes; that should give us about ten minutes to get clear of the boat, before she blows up."

"All right; get busy, girls," Kalvar Dard said. "Grab everything we'll need. Arms and ammunition first; all of them you can find. After that, warm clothing, bedding, tools and food."

With that, he jerked open one of the lockers and began pulling out weapons. He buckled on a pistol and dagger, and handed other weapon-belts to the girls behind him. He found two of the heavy big-game rifles, and several bandoliers of ammunition for them. He tossed out carbines, and boxes of carbine and pistol cartridges. He found two bomb-bags, each containing six light anti-personnel grenades and a big demolition-bomb. Glancing, now and then, at the forward screen, he caught glimpses of blue sky and green-tinted plains below.

"All right!" the pilot yelled. "We're coming in for a landing! A couple of you stand by to get the hatch open."

There was a jolt, and all sense of movement stopped. A cloud of white smoke drifted past the screens. The girls got the hatch open; snatching up weapons and bedding-wrapped bundles they all scrambled up out of the boat.

There was fire outside. The boat had come down upon a grassy plain; now the grass was burning from the heat of the jets. One by one, they ran forward along the top of the rocket-boat, jumping down to the ground clear of the blaze. Then, with every atom of strength they possessed they ran away from the doomed boat.

* * * *

The ground was rough, and the grass high, impeding them. One of the girls tripped and fell; without pausing, two others pulled her to her feet, while another snatched up and slung the carbine she had dropped. Then, ahead, Kalvar Dard saw a deep gully, through which a little stream trickled.

They huddled together at the bottom of it, waiting, for what seemed like a long while. Then a gentle tremor ran through the ground, and swelled to a sickening, heaving shock. A roar of almost palpable sound swept over them, and a flash of blue-white light dimmed the sun above. The sound, the shock, and the searing light did not pass away at once; they continued for seconds that seemed like an eternity. Earth and stones pelted down around them; choking dust rose. Then the thunder and the earth-shock were over; above, incandescent vapors swirled, and darkened into an overhanging pall of smoke and dust.

For a while, they crouched motionless, too stunned to speak. Then shaken nerves steadied and jarred brains cleared. They all rose weakly. Trickles of earth were still coming down from the sides of the gully, and the little stream, which had been clear and sparkling, was roiled with mud. Mechanically, Kalvar Dard brushed the dust from his clothes and looked to his weapons.

"That was just the fuel-tank of a little Class-3 rocket-boat," he said. "I wonder what the explosion of the ship was like." He thought for a moment before continuing. "Glav, I think I know why our jets burned out. We were stern-on to the ship when she blew; the blast drove our flame right back through the jets."

"Do you think the explosion was observed from Doorsha?" Dorita inquired, more concerned about the practical aspects of the situation. "The ship, I mean. After all, we have no means of communication, of our own."

"Oh, I shouldn't doubt it; there were observatories all around the planet watching our ship," Kalvar Dard said. "They probably know all about it, by now. But if any of you are thinking about the chances of rescue, forget it. We're stuck here."

"That's right. There isn't another human being within fifty million miles," Seldar Glav said. "And that was the first and only space-ship ever built. It took fifty years to build her, and even allowing twenty for research that wouldn't have to be duplicated, you can figure when we can expect another one."

"The answer to that one is, never. The ship blew up in space; fifty years' effort and fifteen hundred people gone, like that." Kalvar Dard snapped his fingers. "So now, they'll try to keep Doorsha habitable for a few more thousand years by irrigation, and forget about immigrating to Tareesh."

"Well, maybe, in a hundred thousand years, our descendants will build a ship and go to Doorsha, then," Olva considered.

"Our descendants?" Eldra looked at her in surprize. "You mean, then...?"

Kyna chuckled. "Eldra, you are an awful innocent, about anything that doesn't have a breech-action or a recoil-mechanism," she said. "Why do you think the women on this expedition outnumbered the men seven to five, and why do you think there were so many obstetricians and pediatricians in the med. staff? We were sent out to put a human population on Tareesh, weren't we? Well, here we are."

"But.... Aren't we ever going to...?" Varnis began. "Won't we ever see anybody else, or do anything but just live here, like animals, without machines or ground-cars or aircraft or houses or anything?" Then she began to sob bitterly.

Analea, who had been cleaning a carbine that had gotten covered with loose earth during the explosion, laid it down and went to Varnis, putting her arm around the other girl and comforting her. Kalvar Dard picked up the carbine she had laid down.

"Now, let's see," he began. "We have two heavy rifles, six carbines, and eight pistols, and these two bags of bombs. How much ammunition, counting what's in our belts, do we have?"

They took stock of their slender resources, even Varnis joining in the task, as he had hoped she would. There were over two thousand rounds for the pistols, better than fifteen hundred for the carbines, and four hundred for the two big-game guns. They had some spare clothing, mostly space-suit undergarments, enough bed-robes, one hand-axe, two flashlights, a first-aid kit, and three atomic lighters. Each one had a combat-dagger. There was enough tinned food for about a week.

"We'll have to begin looking for game and edible plants, right away," Glav considered. "I suppose there is game, of some sort; but our ammunition won't last forever."

"We'll have to make it last as long as we can; and we'll have to begin improvising weapons," Dard told him. "Throwing-spears, and throwing-axes. If we can find metal, or any recognizable ore that we can smelt, we'll use that; if not, we'll use chipped stone. Also, we can learn to make snares and traps, after we learn the habits of the animals on this planet. By the time the ammunition's gone, we ought to have learned to do without firearms."

"Think we ought to camp here?"

Kalvar Dard shook his head. "No wood here for fuel, and the blast will have scared away all the game. We'd better go upstream; if we go down, we'll find the water roiled with mud and unfit to drink. And if the game on this planet behave like the game-herds on the wastelands of Doorsha, they'll run for high ground when frightened."

Varnis rose from where she had been sitting. Having mastered her emotions, she was making a deliberate effort to show it.

"Let's make up packs out of this stuff," she suggested. "We can use the bedding and spare clothing to bundle up the food and ammunition."

They made up packs and slung them, then climbed out of the gully. Off to the left, the grass was burning in a wide circle around the crater left by the explosion of the rocket-boat. Kalvar Dard, carrying one of the heavy rifles, took the lead. Beside and a little behind him, Analea walked, her carbine ready. Glav, with the other heavy rifle, brought up in the rear, with Olva covering for him, and between, the other girls walked, two and two.

Ahead, on the far horizon, was a distance-blue line of mountains. The little company turned their faces toward them and moved slowly away, across the empty sea of grass.

3

They had been walking, now, for five years. Kalvar Dard still led, the heavy rifle cradled in the crook of his left arm and a sack of bombs slung from his shoulder, his eyes forever shifting to right and left searching for hidden danger. The clothes in which he had jumped from the rocket-boat were patched and ragged; his shoes had been replaced by high laced buskins of smoke-tanned hide. He was bearded, now, and his hair had been roughly trimmed with the edge of his dagger.

Analea still walked beside him, but her carbine was slung, and she carried three spears with chipped flint heads; one heavy weapon, to be thrown by hand or used for stabbing, and two light javelins to be thrown with the aid of the hooked throwing-stick Glav had invented. Beside her trudged a four-year old boy, hers and Dard's, and on her back, in a fur-lined net bag, she carried their six-month-old baby.

In the rear, Glav still kept his place with the other big-game gun, and Olva walked beside him with carbine and spears; in front of them, their three-year-old daughter toddled. Between vanguard and rearguard, the rest of the party walked: Varnis, carrying her baby on her back, and Dorita, carrying a baby and leading two other children. The baby on her back had cost the life of Kyna in childbirth; one of the others had been left motherless when Eldra had been killed by the Hairy People.

* * * *

That had been two years ago, in the winter when they had used one of their two demolition-bombs to blast open a cavern in the mountains. It had been a hard winter; two children had died, then—Kyna's firstborn, and the little son of Kalvar Dard and Dorita. It had been their first encounter with the Hairy People, too.

Eldra had gone outside the cave with one of the skin water-bags, to fill it at the spring. It had been after sunset, but she had carried her pistol, and no one had thought of danger until they heard the two quick shots, and the scream. They had all rushed out, to find four shaggy, manlike things tearing at Eldra with hands and teeth, another lying dead, and a sixth huddled at one side, clutching its abdomen and whimpering. There had been a quick flurry of shots that had felled all four of the assailants, and Seldar Glav had finished the wounded creature with his dagger, but Eldra was dead. They had built a cairn of stones over her body, as they had done over the bodies of the two children killed by the cold. But, after an examination to see what sort of things they were, they had tumbled the bodies of the Hairy People over the cliff. These had been too bestial to bury as befitted human dead, but too manlike to skin and eat as game.

Since then, they had often found traces of the Hairy People, and when they met with them, they killed them without mercy. These were great shambling parodies of humanity, long-armed, short-legged, twice as heavy as men, with close-set reddish eyes and heavy bone-crushing jaws. They may have been incredibly debased humans, or perhaps beasts on the very threshold of manhood. From what he had seen of conditions on this planet, Kalvar Dard suspected the latter to be the case. In a million or so years, they might evolve into something like humanity. Already, the Hairy ones had learned the use of fire, and of chipped crude stone implements—mostly heavy triangular choppers to be used in the hand, without helves.

Twice, after that night, the Hairy People had attacked them—once while they were on the march, and once in camp. Both assaults had been beaten off without loss to themselves, but at cost of precious ammunition. Once they had caught a band of ten of them swimming a river on logs; they had picked them all off from the bank with their carbines. Once, when Kalvar Dard and Analea had been scouting alone, they had come upon a dozen of them huddled around a fire and had wiped them out with a single grenade. Once, a large band of Hairy People hunted them for two days, but only twice had they come close, and both times, a single shot had sent them all scampering. That had been after the bombing of the group around the fire. Dard was convinced that the beings possessed the rudiments of a language, enough to communicate a few simple ideas, such as the fact that this little tribe of aliens were dangerous in the extreme.

* * * *

There were Hairy People about now; for the past five days, moving northward through the forest to the open grasslands, the people of Kalvar Dard had found traces of them. Now, as they came out among the seedling growth at the edge of the open plains, everybody was on the alert.

They emerged from the big trees and stopped among the young growth, looking out into the open country. About a mile away, a herd of game was grazing slowly westward. In the distance, they looked like the little horse-like things, no higher than a man's waist and heavily maned and bearded, that had been one of their most important sources of meat. For the ten thousandth time, Dard wished, as he strained his eyes, that somebody had thought to secure a pair of binoculars when they had abandoned the rocket-boat. He studied the grazing herd for a long time.

The seedling pines extended almost to the game-herd and would offer concealment for the approach, but the animals were grazing into the wind, and their scent was much keener than their vision. This would prelude one of their favorite hunting techniques, that of lurking in the high grass ahead of the quarry. It had rained heavily in the past few days, and the undermat of dead grass was soaked, making a fire-hunt impossible. Kalvar Dard knew that he could stalk to within easy carbine-shot, but he was unwilling to use cartridges on game; and in view of the proximity of

Hairy People, he did not want to divide his band for a drive hunt.

"What's the scheme?" Analea asked him, realizing the problem as well as he did. "Do we try to take them from behind?"

"We'll take them from an angle," he decided. "We'll start from here and work in, closing on them at the rear of the herd. Unless the wind shifts on us, we ought to get within spear-cast. You and I will use the spears; Varnis can come along and cover for us with a carbine. Glav, you and Olva and Dorita stay here with the children and the packs. Keep a sharp lookout; Hairy People around, somewhere." He unslung his rifle and exchanged it for Olva's spears. "We can only eat about two of them before the meat begins to spoil, but kill all you can," he told Analea; "we need the skins."

Then he and the two girls began their slow, cautious, stalk. As long as the grassland was dotted with young trees, they walked upright, making good time, but the last five hundred yards they had to crawl, stopping often to check the wind, while the horse-herd drifted slowly by. Then they were directly behind the herd, with the wind in their faces, and they advanced more rapidly.

"Close enough?" Dard whispered to Analea.

"Yes; I'm taking the one that's lagging a little behind."

"I'm taking the one on the left of it." Kalvar Dard fitted a javelin to the hook of his throwing-stick. "Ready? Now!"

He leaped to his feet, drawing back his right arm and hurling, the throwing-stick giving added velocity to the spear. Beside him, he was conscious of Analea rising and propelling her spear. His missile caught the little bearded pony in the chest; it stumbled and fell forward to its front knees. He snatched another light spear, set it on the hook of the stick and darted it at another horse, which reared, biting at the spear with its teeth. Grabbing the heavy stabbing-spear, he ran forward, finishing it off with a heart-thrust. As he did, Varnis slung her carbine, snatched a stone-headed throwing axe from her belt, and knocked down another horse, then ran forward with her dagger to finish it.

By this time, the herd, alarmed, had stampeded and was galloping away, leaving the dead and dying behind. He and Analea had each killed two; with the one Varnis had knocked down, that made five. Using his dagger, he finished off one that was still kicking on the ground, and then began pulling out the throwing-spears. The girls, shouting in unison, were announcing the successful completion of the hunt; Glav, Olva, and

Dorita were coming forward with the children.

* * * *

It was sunset by the time they had finished the work of skinning and cutting up the horses and had carried the hide-wrapped bundles of meat to the little brook where they had intended camping. There was firewood to be gathered, and the meal to be cooked, and they were all tired.

"We can't do this very often, any more," Kalvar Dard told them, "but we might as well, tonight. Don't bother rubbing sticks for fire; I'll use the lighter."

He got it from a pouch on his belt—a small, gold-plated, atomic lighter, bearing the crest of his old regiment of the Frontier Guards. It was the last one they had, in working order. Piling a handful of dry splinters under the firewood, he held the lighter to it, pressed the activator, and watched the fire eat into the wood.

The greatest achievement of man's civilization, the mastery of the basic, cosmic, power of the atom—being used to kindle a fire of natural fuel, to cook unseasoned meat killed with stone-tipped spears. Dard looked sadly at the twinkling little gadget, then slipped it back into its pouch. Soon it would be worn out, like the other two, and then they would gain fire only by rubbing dry sticks, or hacking sparks from bits of flint or pyrites. Soon, too, the last cartridge would be fired, and then they would perforce depend for protection, as they were already doing for food, upon their spears.

And they were so helpless. Six adults, burdened with seven little children, all of them requiring momently care and watchfulness. If the cartridges could be made to last until they were old enough to fend for themselves.... If they could avoid collisions with the Hairy People.... Some day, they would be numerous enough for effective mutual protection and support; some day, the ratio of helpless children to able adults would redress itself. Until then, all that they could do would be to survive; day after day, they must follow the game-herds.

4

For twenty years, now, they had been following the game. Winters had come, with driving snow, forcing horses and deer into the woods, and the little band of humans to the protection of mountain caves. Springtime followed, with fresh grass on the plains and plenty of meat for the people of Kalvar Dard. Autumns followed summers, with fire-hunts, and the smoking and curing of meat and hides. Winters followed autumns, and springtimes came again, and thus until the twentieth year after the landing of the rocket-boat.

Kalvar Dard still walked in the lead, his hair and beard flecked with gray, but he no longer carried the heavy rifle; the last cartridge for that had been fired long ago. He carried the hand-axe, fitted with a long helve, and a spear with a steel head that had been worked painfully from the receiver of a useless carbine. He still had his pistol, with eight cartridges in the magazine, and his dagger, and the bomb-bag, containing the big demolition-bomb and one grenade. The last shred of clothing from the ship was gone, now; he was clad in a sleeveless tunic of skin and horsehide buskins.

Analea no longer walked beside him; eight years before, she had broken her back in a fall. It had been impossible to move her, and she stabbed herself with her dagger to save a cartridge. Seldar Glav had broken through the ice while crossing a river, and had lost his rifle; the next day he died of the chill he had taken. Olva had been killed by the Hairy People, the night they had attacked the camp, when Varnis' child had been killed.

They had beaten off that attack, shot or speared ten of the huge sub-men, and the next morning they buried their dead after their custom, under cairns of stone. Varnis had watched the burial of her child with blank, uncomprehending eyes, then she had turned to Kalvar Dard and said something that had horrified him more than any wild outburst of grief could have.

"Come on, Dard; what are we doing this for? You promised you'd take us to Tareesh, where we'd have good houses, and machines, and all sorts of lovely things to eat and wear. I don't like this place, Dard; I want to go to Tareesh."

From that day on, she had wandered in merciful darkness. She had not been idiotic, or raving mad; she had just escaped from a reality that she could no longer bear.

Varnis, lost in her dream-world, and Dorita, hard-faced and haggard, were the only ones left, beside Kalvar Dard, of the original eight. But the band had grown, meanwhile, to more than fifteen. In the rear, in Seldar

Glav's old place, the son of Kalvar Dard and Analea walked. Like his father, he wore a pistol, for which he had six rounds, and a dagger, and in his hand he carried a stone-headed killing-maul with a three-foot handle which he had made for himself. The woman who walked beside him and carried his spears was the daughter of Glav and Olva; in a net-bag on her back she carried their infant child. The first Tareeshan born of Tareeshan parents; Kalvar Dard often looked at his little grandchild during nights in camp and days on the trail, seeing, in that tiny fur-swaddled morsel of humanity, the meaning and purpose of all that he did. Of the older girls, one or two were already pregnant, now; this tiny threatened beachhead of humanity was expanding, gaining strength. Long after man had died out on Doorsha and the dying planet itself had become an arid waste, the progeny of this little band would continue to grow and to dominate the younger planet, nearer the sun. Some day, an even mightier civilization than the one he had left would rise here....

* * * *

All day the trail had wound upward into the mountains. Great cliffs loomed above them, and little streams spumed and dashed in rocky gorges below. All day, the Hairy People had followed, fearful to approach too close, unwilling to allow their enemies to escape. It had started when they had rushed the camp, at daybreak; they had been beaten off, at cost of almost all the ammunition, and the death of one child. No sooner had the tribe of Kalvar Dard taken the trail, however, than they had been pressing after them. Dard had determined to cross the mountains, and had led his people up a game-trail, leading toward the notch of a pass high against the skyline.

The shaggy ape-things seemed to have divined his purpose. Once or twice, he had seen hairy brown shapes dodging among the rocks and stunted trees to the left. They were trying to reach the pass ahead of him. Well, if they did.... He made a quick mental survey of his resources. His pistol, and his son's, and Dorita's, with eight, and six, and seven rounds. One grenade, and the big demolition bomb, too powerful to be thrown by hand, but which could be set for delayed explosion and dropped over a cliff or left behind to explode among pursuers. Five steel daggers, and plenty of spears and slings and axes. Himself, his son and his son's woman, Dorita, and four or five of the older boys and girls, who would make effective front-line fighters. And Varnis, who might come out of her private dream-world long enough to give account for herself, and even the tiniest of the walking children could throw stones or light spears. Yes, they could force the pass, if the Hairy People reached it ahead of them, and then seal it shut with the heavy bomb. What lay on the other side, he did not know; he wondered how much game there would be, and if there were Hairy People on that side, too.

Two shots slammed quickly behind him. He dropped his axe and took a two-hand grip on his stabbing-spear as he turned. His son was hurrying forward, his pistol drawn, glancing behind as he came.

"Hairy People. Four," he reported. "I shot two; she threw a spear and killed another. The other ran."

The daughter of Seldar Glav and Olva nodded in agreement.

"I had no time to throw again," she said, "and Bo-Bo would not shoot the one that ran."

Kalvar Dard's son, who had no other name than the one his mother had called him as a child, defended himself. "He was running away. It is the rule: *use bullets only to save life, where a spear will not serve.*"

Kalvar Dard nodded. "You did right, son," he said, taking out his own pistol and removing the magazine, from which he extracted two cartridges. "Load these into your pistol; four rounds aren't enough. Now we each have six. Go back to the rear, keep the little ones moving, and don't let Varnis get behind."

"That is right. *We must all look out for Varnis, and take care of her,*" the boy recited obediently. "That is the rule."

He dropped to the rear. Kalvar Dard holstered his pistol and picked up his axe, and the column moved forward again. They were following a ledge, now; on the left, there was a sheer drop of several hundred feet, and on the right a cliff rose above them, growing higher and steeper as the trail slanted upward. Dard was worried about the ledge; if it came to an end, they would all be trapped. No one would escape. He suddenly felt old and unutterably weary. It was a frightful weight that he bore—responsibility for an entire race.

* * * *

Suddenly, behind him, Dorita fired her pistol upward. Dard sprang forward—there was no room for him to jump aside—and drew his pistol. The boy, Bo-Bo, was trying to find a target from his position in the rear. Then Dard saw the two Hairy People; the boy fired, and the stone fell, all at once.

It was a heavy stone, half as big as a man's torso, and it almost missed Kalvar Dard. If it had hit him directly, it would have killed him instantly, mashing him to a bloody pulp; as it was, he was knocked flat, the stone pinning his legs.

At Bo-Bo's shot, a hairy body plummeted down, to hit the ledge. Bo-Bo's woman instantly ran it through with one of her spears. The other ape-thing, the one Dorita had shot, was still clinging to a rock above. Two of the children scampered up to it and speared it repeatedly, screaming like little furies. Dorita and one of the older girls got the rock off Kalvar Dard's legs and tried to help him to his feet, but he collapsed, unable to stand. Both his legs were broken.

This was it, he thought, sinking back. "Dorita, I want you to run ahead and see what the trail's like," he said. "See if the ledge is passable. And find a place, not too far ahead, where we can block the trail by exploding that demolition-bomb. It has to be close enough for a couple of you to carry or drag me and get me there in one piece."

"What are you going to do?"

"What do you think?" he retorted. "I have both legs broken. You can't carry me with you; if you try it, they'll catch us and kill us all. I'll have to stay behind; I'll block the trail behind you, and get as many of them as I can, while I'm at it. Now, run along and do as I said."

She nodded. "I'll be back as soon as I can," she agreed.

The others were crowding around Dard. Bo-Bo bent over him, perplexed and worried. "What are you going to do, father?" he asked. "You are hurt. Are you going to go away and leave us, as mother did when she was hurt?"

"Yes, son; I'll have to. You carry me on ahead a little, when Dorita gets back, and leave me where she shows you to. I'm going to stay behind and block the trail, and kill a few Hairy People. I'll use the big bomb."

"The *big* bomb? The one nobody dares throw?" The boy looked at his father in wonder.

"That's right. Now, when you leave me, take the others and get away as fast as you can. Don't stop till you're up to the pass. Take my pistol and dagger, and the axe and the big spear, and take the little bomb, too.

Take everything I have, only leave the big bomb with me. I'll need that."

Dorita rejoined them. "There's a waterfall ahead. We can get around it, and up to the pass. The way's clear and easy; if you put off the bomb just this side of it, you'll start a rock-slide that'll block everything."

"All right. Pick me up, a couple of you. Don't take hold of me below the knees. And hurry."

* * * *

A hairy shape appeared on the ledge below them; one of the older boys used his throwing-stick to drive a javelin into it. Two of the girls picked up Dard; Bo-Bo and his woman gathered up the big spear and the axe and the bomb-bag.

They hurried forward, picking their way along the top of a talus of rubble at the foot of the cliff, and came to where the stream gushed out of a narrow gorge. The air was wet with spray there, and loud with the roar of the waterfall. Kalvar Dard looked around; Dorita had chosen the spot well. Not even a sure-footed mountain-goat could make the ascent, once that gorge was blocked.

"All right; put me down here," he directed. "Bo-Bo, take my belt, and give me the big bomb. You have one light grenade; know how to use it?"

"Of course, you have often showed me. I turn the top, and then press in the little thing on the side, and hold it in till I throw. I throw it at least a spear-cast, and drop to the ground or behind something."

"That's right. And use it only in greatest danger, to save everybody. Spare your cartridges; use them only to save life. And save everything of metal, no matter how small."

"Yes. Those are the rules. I will follow them, and so will the others. And we will always take care of Varnis."

"Well, goodbye, son." He gripped the boy's hand. "Now get everybody out of here; don't stop till you're at the pass."

"You're not staying behind!" Varnis cried. "Dard, you promised us! I remember, when we were all in the ship together—you and I and Analea and Olva and Dorita and Eldra and, oh, what was that other girl's name, Kyna! And we were all having such a nice time, and you were telling us how we'd all come to Tareesh, and we were having such fun talking about it...."

"That's right, Varnis," he agreed. "And so I will. I have something to do, here, but I'll meet you on top of the mountain, after I'm through, and in the morning we'll all go to Tareesh."

She smiled—the gentle, childlike smile of the harmlessly mad—and turned away. The son of Kalvar Dard made sure that she and all the children were on the way, and then he, too, turned and followed them, leaving Dard alone.

Alone, with a bomb and a task. He'd borne that task for twenty years, now; in a few minutes, it would be ended, with an instant's searing heat. He tried not to be too glad; there were so many things he might have done, if he had tried harder. Metals, for instance. Somewhere there surely must be ores which they could have smelted, but he had never found them. And he might have tried catching some of the little horses they hunted for food, to break and train to bear burdens. And the alphabet—why hadn't he taught it to Bo-Bo and the daughter of Seldar Glav, and laid on them an obligation to teach the others? And the grass-seeds they used for making flour sometimes; they should have planted fields of the better kinds, and patches of edible roots, and returned at the proper time to harvest them. There were so many things, things that none of those young savages or their children would think of in ten thousand years....

Something was moving among the rocks, a hundred yards away. He straightened, as much as his broken legs would permit, and watched. Yes, there was one of them, and there was another, and another. One rose from behind a rock and came forward at a shambling run, making bestial sounds. Then two more lumbered into sight, and in a moment the ravine was alive with them. They were almost upon him when Kalvar Dard pressed in the thumbpiece of the bomb; they were clutching at him when he released it. He felt a slight jar....

* * * *

When they reached the pass, they all stopped as the son of Kalvar Dard turned and looked back. Dorita stood beside him, looking toward the waterfall too; she also knew what was about to happen. The others merely gaped in blank incomprehension, or grasped their weapons, thinking that the enemy was pressing close behind and that they were making a stand here. A few of the smaller boys and girls began picking up stones.

Then a tiny pin-point of brilliance winked, just below where the snow-fed stream vanished into the gorge. That was all, for an instant, and then a great fire-shot cloud swirled upward, hundreds of feet into the air; there was a crash, louder than any sound any of them except Dorita and Varnis had ever heard before.

"He did it!" Dorita said softly.

"Yes, he did it. My father was a brave man," Bo-Bo replied. "We are safe, now."

Varnis, shocked by the explosion, turned and stared at him, and then she laughed happily. "Why, there you are, Dard!" she exclaimed. "I was wondering where you'd gone. What did you do, after we left?"

"What do you mean?" The boy was puzzled, not knowing how much he looked like his father, when his father had been an officer of the Frontier Guards, twenty years before.

His puzzlement worried Varnis vaguely. "You.... You are Dard, aren't you?" she asked. "But that's silly; of course you're Dard! Who else could you be?"

"Yes. I am Dard," the boy said, remembering that it was the rule for everybody to be kind to Varnis and to pretend to agree with her. Then another thought struck him. His shoulders straightened. "Yes. I am Dard, son of Dard," he told them all. "I lead, now. Does anybody say no?"

He shifted his axe and spear to his left hand and laid his right hand on the butt of his pistol, looking sternly at Dorita. If any of them tried to dispute his claim, it would be she. But instead, she gave him the nearest thing to a real smile that had crossed her face in years.

"You are Dard," she told him; "you lead us, now."

"But of course Dard leads! Hasn't he always led us?" Varnis wanted to know. "Then what's all the argument about? And tomorrow he's going to take us to Tareesh, and we'll have houses and ground-cars and aircraft and gardens and lights, and all the lovely things we want. Aren't you, Dard?"

"Yes, Varnis; I will take you all to Tareesh, to all the wonderful things," Dard, son of Dard, promised, for such was the rule about Varnis.

Then he looked down from the pass into the country beyond. There were lower mountains, below, and foothills, and a wide blue valley, and, beyond that, distant peaks reared jaggedly against the sky. He pointed with his father's axe.

"We go down that way," he said.

* * * *

So they went, down, and on, and on, and on. The last cartridge was fired; the last sliver of Doorshan metal wore out or rusted away. By then, however, they had learned to make chipped stone, and bone, and reindeer-horn, serve their needs. Century after century, millennium after millennium, they followed the game-herds from birth to death, and birth replenished their numbers faster than death depleted. Bands grew in numbers and split; young men rebelled against the rule of the old and took their women and children elsewhere.

They hunted down the hairy Neanderthalers, and exterminated them ruthlessly, the origin of their implacable hatred lost in legend. All that they remembered, in the misty, confused, way that one remembers a dream, was that there had once been a time of happiness and plenty, and that there was a goal to which they would some day attain. They left the mountains—were they the Caucasus? The Alps? The Pamirs?—and spread outward, conquering as they went.

We find their bones, and their stone weapons, and their crude paintings, in the caves of Cro-Magnon and Grimaldi and Altimira and Mas-d'Azil; the deep layers of horse and reindeer and mammoth bones at their feasting-place at Solutre. We wonder how and whence a race so like our own came into a world of brutish sub-humans.

Just as we wonder, too, at the network of canals which radiate from the polar caps of our sister planet, and speculate on the possibility that they were the work of hands like our own. And we concoct elaborate jokes about the "Men From Mars"—*ourselves*.

TIME CRIME

Kiro Soran, the guard captain, stood in the shadow of the veranda roof, his white cloak thrown back to display the scarlet lining. He rubbed his palm reflectively on the checkered butt of his revolver and watched the four men at the table.

"And ten tens are a hundred," one of the clerks in blue jackets said, adding another stack to the pile of gold coins.

"Nineteen hundreds," one of the pair in dirty striped robes agreed, taking a stone from the box in front of him and throwing it away. Only one stone remained. "One more hundred to pay."

One of the blue-jacketed plantation clerks made a tally mark; his companion counted out coins, ten and ten and ten.

Dosu Golan, the plantation manager, tapped impatiently on his polished boot leg with a thin riding whip.

"I don't like this," he said, in another and entirely different language. "I know, chattel slavery's an established custom on this sector, and we have to conform to local usages, but it sickens me to have to haggle with these swine over the price of human beings. On the Zarkantha Sector, we used nothing but free wage-labor."

"Migratory workers," the guard captain said. "Humanitarian considerations aside, I can think of a lot better ways of meeting the labor problem on a fruit plantation than by buying slaves you need for three months a year and have to feed and quarter and clothe and doctor the whole twelve."

"Twenty hundreds of *obus*," the clerk who had been counting the money said. "That is the payment, is it not, Coru-hin-Irigod?"

"That is the payment," the slave dealer replied.

The clerk swept up the remaining coins, and his companion took them over and put them in an iron-bound chest, snapping the padlock. The two guards who had been loitering at one side slung their rifles and picked up the chest, carrying it into the plantation house. The slave dealer and his companion arose, putting their money into a leather bag; Coru-hin-Irigod turned and bowed to the two men in white cloaks.

"The slaves are yours, noble lords," he said.

Across the plantation yard, six more men in striped robes, with carbines slung across their backs, approached; with them came another man in a hooded white cloak, and two guards in blue jackets and red caps, with bayoneted rifles. The man in white and his armed attendants came toward the house; the six Calera slavers continued across the yard to where their horses were picketed.

"If I do not offend the noble lords, then," Coru-hin-Irigod said, "I beg their sufferance to depart. I and my men have far to ride if we would reach Careba by nightfall. The Lord, the Great Lord, the Lord God Safar watch between us until we meet again."

Urado Alatana, the labor foreman, came up onto the porch as the two slavers went down.

"Have a good look at them, Radd?" the guard captain asked.

"You think I'm crazy enough to let those bandits out of here with two thousand *obus*—forty thousand Paratemporal Exchange Units—of the Company's money without knowing what we're getting?" the other parried. "They're all right—nice, clean, healthy-looking lot. I did everything but take them apart and inspect the pieces while they were being unshackled at the stockade. I'd like to know where this Coru-hin-Whatshisname got them, though. They're not local stuff. Lot darker, and they're jabbering among themselves in some lingo I never heard before. A few are wearing some rags of clothing, and they have odd-looking sandals. I noticed that most of them showed marks of recent whipping. That may mean they're troublesome, or it may just mean that these Caleras are a lot of sadistic brutes."

"Poor devils!" The man called Dosu Golan was evidently hoping that he'd never catch himself talking about fellow humans like that. The guard captain turned to him.

"Coming to have a look at them, Doth?" he asked.

"You go, Kirv; I'll see them later."

"Still not able to look the Company's property in the face?" the captain asked gently. "You'll not get used to it any sooner than now."

"I suppose you're right." For a moment Dosu Golan watched Coru-hin-Irigod and his followers canter out of the yard and break into a gallop on the road beyond. Then he tucked his whip under his arm. "All right, then. Let's go see them."

The labor foreman went into the house; the manager and the guard captain went down the steps and set out across the yard. A big slat-sided wagon, drawn by four horses, driven by an old slave in a blue smock and a thing like a sunbonnet, rumbled past, loaded with newly-picked oranges. Blue woodsmoke was beginning to rise from the stoves at the open kitchen and a couple of slaves were noisily chopping wood. Then they came to the stockade of close-set pointed poles. A guard sergeant in a red-trimmed blue jacket, armed with a revolver, met them with a salute which Kiro Soran returned: he unfastened the gate and motioned four or five riflemen into positions from which they could fire in between the poles in case the slaves turned on their new owners.

There seemed little danger of that, though Kiro Soran kept his hand close to the butt of his revolver. The slaves, an even hundred of them, squatted under awnings out of the sun, or stood in line to drink at the water-butt. They furtively watched the two men who had entered among them, as though expecting blows or kicks; when none were forthcoming, they relaxed slightly. As the labor foreman had said, they were clean and looked healthy. They were all nearly naked; there were about as many women as men, but no children or old people.

"Radd's right," the captain told the new manager. "They're not local. Much darker skins, and different face-structure; faces wedge-shaped instead of oval, and differently shaped noses, and brown eyes instead of black. I've seen people like that, somewhere, but—"

He fell silent. A suspicion, utterly fantastic, had begun to form in his mind, and he stepped closer to a group of a dozen-odd, the manager following him. One or two had been unmercifully lashed, not long ago, and all bore a few lash-marks. Odd sort of marks, more like burn-blisters than welts. He'd have to have the Company doctor look at them. Then he caught their speech, and the suspicion was converted to certainty.

"These are not like the others: they wear fine garments, and walk proudly. They look stern, but not cruel. They are the real masters here; the others are but servants."

He grasped the manager's arm and drew him aside.

"You know that language?" he asked. When the man called Dosu Golan shook his head, he continued: "That's Kharanda; it's a dialect spoken by a people in the Ganges Valley, in India, on the Kholghoor Sector of the Fourth Level."

Dosu Golan blinked, and his face went blank for a moment.

"You mean they're from outtime?" he demanded. "Are you sure?"

"I did two years on Fourth Level Kholghoor with the Paratime Police, before I took this job," the man called Kiro Soran replied. "And another thing. Those lash-marks were made with some kind of an electric whip. Not these rawhide quirts the Caleras use."

It took the plantation manager all of five seconds to add that up. The answer frightened him.

"Kirv, this is going to make a simply hideous uproar, all the way up to Home Time Line main office," he said. "I don't know what I'm going to do—"

"Well, I know what I have to do." The captain raised his voice, using the local language: "Sergeant! Run to the guardhouse, and tell Sergeant Adarada to mount up twenty of his men and take off after those Caleras who sold us these slaves. They're headed down the road toward the river. Tell him to bring them all back, and especially their chief, Coruhin-Irigod, and him I want alive and able to answer questions. And then get the white-cloak lord Urado Alatena, and come back here."

"Yes, captain." The guards were all Yarana people; they disliked Caleras intensely. The sergeant threw a salute, turned, and ran.

"Next, we'll have to isolate these slaves," Kiro Soran said. "You'd better make a full report to the Company as soon as possible. I'm going to transpose to Police Terminal Time Line and make my report to the Sector-Regional Subchief. Then—"

"Now wait a moment, Kirv," Dosu Golan protested. "After all, I'm the manager, even if I am new here. It's up to me to make the decisions—"

Kiro Soran shook his head. "Sorry, Doth. Not this one," he said. "You know the terms under which I was hired by the Company. I'm still a field agent of the Paratime Police, and I'm reporting back on duty as soon as I can transpose to Police Terminal. Look; here are a hundred men and women who have been shifted from one time-line, on one paratemporal sector of probability, to another. Why, the world from which these people came doesn't even exist in this space-time continuum. There's only one way they could have gotten here, and that's the way we did—in a Ghaldron-Hesthor paratemporal transposition field. You can carry it on from there as far as you like, but the only thing it adds up to is a case for the Paratime Police. You had better include in your report mention that I've reverted to police status; my Company pay ought to be stopped as of now. And until somebody who outranks me is sent here, I'm in complete charge. Paratime Transposition Code, Section XVII, Article 238."

The plantation manager nodded. Kiro Soran knew how he must feel; he laid a hand gently on the younger man's shoulder.

"You understand how it is, Doth; this is the only thing I can do."

"I understand, Kirv. Count on me for absolutely anything." He looked at the brown-skinned slaves, and lines of horror and loathing appeared around his mouth. "To think that some of our own people would do a thing like this! I hope you can catch the devils! Are you transposing out, now?"

"In a few minutes. While I'm gone, have the doctor look at those whip-injuries. Those things could get infected. Fortunately, he's one of our own people."

"Yes, of course. And I'll have these slaves isolated, and if Adarada brings back Coru-hin-Irigod and his gang before you get back, I'll have them locked up and waiting for you. I suppose you want to narco-hypnotize and question the whole lot, slaves and slavers?"

The labor foreman, known locally as Urado Alatena, entered the stockade.

"What's wrong, Kirv?" he asked.

The Paratime Police agent told him, briefly. The labor foreman whistled, threw a quick glance at the nearest slaves, and nodded.

"I knew there was something funny about them," he said. "Doth, what a simply beastly thing to happen, two days after you take charge here!"

"Not his fault," the Paratime Police agent said. "I'm the one the Company'll be sore at, but I'd rather have them down on me rather than old Tortha Karf. Well, sit on the lid till I get back," he told both of them. "We'll need some kind of a story for the locals. Let's see—Explain to the guards, in the hearing of some of the more talkative slaves, that these slaves are from the Asian mainland, that they are of a people friendly to our people, and that they were kidnaped by pirates, our enemies. That ought to explain everything satisfactorily."

On his way back to the plantation house, he saw a clump of local slaves staring curiously at the stockade, and noticed that the guards had unslung their rifles and fixed their bayonets. None of them had any idea, of course, of what had happened, but they all seemed to know, by some sort of ESP, that something was seriously wrong. It was going to get worse, too, when strangers began arriving, apparently from nowhere, at the plantation.

* * * *

Verkan Vall waited until the small, dark-eyed woman across the circular table had helped herself from one of the bowls on the revolving disk in the middle, then rotated it to bring the platter of cold boar-ham around to himself.

"Want some of this, Dalla?" he asked, transferring a slice of ham and a spoonful of wine sauce to his plate.

"No, I'll have some of the venison," the black-haired girl beside him said. "And some of the pickled beans. We'll be getting our fill of pork, for the next month."

"I thought the Dwarma Sector people were vegetarians," Jandar Jard, the theatrical designer, said. "Most nonviolent peoples are, aren't they?"

"Well, the Dwarma people haven't any specific taboo against taking life," Bronnath Zara, the dark-eyed woman in the brightly colored gown, told him. "They're just utterly noncombative, nonaggressive. When I was on the Dwarma Sector, there was a horrible scandal at the village where I was staying. It seems that a farmer and a meat butcher fought over the price of a pig. They actually raised their voices and shouted contradictions at each other. That happened two years before, and people were still talking about it."

"I didn't think they had any money, either," Verkan Vall's wife, Hadron Dalla, said.

"They don't," Zara said. "It's all barter and trade. What are you and Vall going to use for a visible means of support, while you're there?"

"Oh, I have my mandolin, and I've learned all the traditional Dwarma songs by hypno-mech," Dalla said. "And Transtime Tours is fitting Vall out with a bag of tools; he's going to do repair work and carpentry."

"Oh, good; you'll be welcome anywhere," Zara, the sculptress, said. "They're always glad to entertain a singer, and for people who do the fine decorative work they do, they're the most incompetent practical mechanics I've ever seen or heard of. You're going to travel from village to village?"

"Yes. The cover-story is that we're lovers who have left our village in order not to make Vall's former wife unhappy by our presence," Dalla said.

"Oh, good! That's entirely in the Dwarma romantic tradition," Bronnath Zara approved. "Ordinarily, you know, they don't like to travel. They have a saying: 'Happy are the trees, they abide in their own place; sad are the winds, forever they wander.' But that'll be a fine explanation."

Thalvan Dras, the big man with the black beard and the long red coat and cloth-of-gold sash who lounged in the host's seat, laughed.

"I can just see Vall mending pots, and Dalla playing that mandolin and singing," he said. "At least, you'll be getting away from police work. I don't suppose they have anything like police on the Dwarma Sector?"

"Oh, no; they don't even have any such concept," Bronnath Zara said. "When somebody does something wrong, his neighbors all come and talk to him about it till he gets ashamed, then they all forgive him and have a feast. They're lovely people, so kind and gentle. But you'll get awfully tired of them in about a month. They have absolutely no respect for anybody's privacy. In fact, it seems slightly indecent to them for anybody to want privacy."

One of Thalvan Dras' human servants came into the room, coughed apologetically, and said:

"A visiphone-call for His Valor, the Mavrad of Nerros."

Vall went on nibbling ham and wine sauce; the servant repeated the announcement a trifle more loudly.

"Vall, you're being paged!" Thalvan Dras told him, with a touch of impatience.

Verkan Vall looked blank for an instant, then grinned. It had been so long since he had even bothered to think about that antiquated title of nobility—

"Vall's probably forgotten that he has a title," a girl across the table, wearing an almost transparent gown and nothing else, laughed.

"That's something the Mavrad of Mnirna and Thalvabar never forgets," Jandar Jard drawled, with what, in a woman, would have been cattishness.

Thalvan Dras gave him a hastily repressed look of venomous anger, then said something, more to Verkan Vall than to Jandar Jard, about titles of nobility being the marks of social position and responsibility which their bearers should never forget. That jab, Vall thought, following the servant out of the room, had been a mistake on Jard's part. A music-drama, for which he had designed the settings, was due to open here in Dhergabar in another ten days. Thalvan Dras would cherish spite, and a word from the Mavrad of Mnirna and Thalvabar would set a dozen critics to disparaging Jandar's work. On the other hand, maybe it had been smart of Jandar Jard to antagonize Thalvan Dras; for every critic who bowed slavishly to the wealthy nobleman, there were at least two more who detested him unutterably, and they would rush to Jandar Jard's defense, and in the ensuing uproar, the settings would get more publicity than the drama itself.

* * * *

In the visiphone booth, Vall found a girl in a green blouse, with the Paratime Police insigne on her shoulder, looking out of the screen. The wall behind her was pale green striped in gold and black.

"Hello, Eldra," he greeted her.

"Hello, Chief's Assistant: I'm sorry to bother you, but the Chief wants to talk to you. Just a moment, please."

The screen exploded into a kaleidoscopic flash of lights and colors, then cleared again. This time, a man looked out of it. He was well into middle age; close to his three hundredth year. His hair, a uniform iron-gray, was beginning to thin in front, and he was acquiring the beginnings of a double chin. His name was Tortha Karf, and he was Chief of Paratime Police, and Verkan Vall's superior.

"Hello, Vall. Glad I was able to locate you. When are you and Dalla leaving?"

"As soon as we can get away from this luncheon, here. Oh, say an hour. We're taking a rocket to Zarabar, and transposing from there to Passenger Terminal Sixteen, and from there to the Dwarma Sector."

"Well, Vall, I hate to bother you like this," Tortha Karf said, "but I wish you'd stop by Headquarters on your way to the rocketport. Something's come up—it may be a very nasty business—and I'd like to talk to you about it."

"Well, Chief, let me remind you that this vacation, which I've had to postpone four times already, has been overdue for four years," Vall said.

"Yes, Vall, I know. You've been working very hard, and you and Dalla are entitled to a little time together. I just want you to look into something, before you leave."

"It'll have to take some fast looking. Our rocket blasts off in two hours."

"It may take a little longer; if it does, you and Dalla can transpose to Police Terminal and take a rocket for Zarabar Equivalent, and transpose from there to Passenger Sixteen. It would save time if you brought Dalla with you to Headquarters."

"Dalla won't like this," Vall understated.

"No. I'm afraid not." Tortha Karf looked around apprehensively, as though estimating the damage an enraged Hadron Dalla could do to his office furnishings. "Well, try to get here as soon as you can."

* * * *

Thalvan Dras was holding forth, when Vall returned, on one of his favorite preoccupations.

"... Reason I'm taking such an especially active interest in this year's Arts Exhibitions; I've become disturbed at the extent to which so many of our artists have been content to derive their motifs, even their techniques, from outtime art." He was using his vocowriter, rather than his conversational, voice. "I yield to no one in my appreciation of outtime art—you all know how devotedly I collect objects of art from all over paratime—but our own artists should endeavor to express their artistic values in our own artistic idioms."

Vall bent over his wife's shoulder.

"We have to leave, right away," he whispered.

"But our rocket doesn't blast off for two hours—"

Thalvan Dras had stopped talking and was looking at them in annoyance.

"I have to go to Headquarters before we leave. It'll save time if you come along."

"Oh, no, Vall!" She looked at him in consternation. "Was that Tortha Karf, calling?" She replaced her plate on the table and got to her feet.

"I'm dreadfully sorry, Dras," he addressed their host. "I just had a call from Tortha Karf. A few minor details that must be cleared up, before I leave Home Time Line. If you'll accept our thanks for a wonderful luncheon—"

"Why, certainly, Vall. Brogoth, will you call—" He gave a slight chuckle. "I'm so used to having Brogoth Zaln at my elbow that I'd forgotten he wasn't here. Wait. I'll call one of the servants to have a car for you."

"Don't bother; we'll take an aircab," Vall told him.

"But you simply can't take a public cab!" The black-bearded nobleman was shocked at such an obscene idea. "I will have a car ready for you in a few minutes."

"Sorry, Dras; we have to hurry. We'll get a cab on the roof. Good-by, everybody; sorry to have to break away like this. See you all when we get back."

* * * *

Hadron Dalla watched dejectedly as the green crags and escarpments of the Paratime Building loomed above the city in front of them, and began slipping under the aircab. She felt like a prisoner recaptured at the moment when attempted escape was about to succeed.

"I knew it," she said. "I knew he'd find something. He's trying to break things up between us, the way he did twenty years ago.'"

Vall crushed out his cigarette and said nothing. That hadn't been true, and she knew it as well as he did. There had been many other factors involved in the disintegration of their previous marriage, most of them of her own contribution. But that had been twenty years ago, she told herself. This time it would be different, if only—

"Really, Vall, he's never liked me," she went on. "He's jealous of me, I think. You're to be his successor, when he retires, and he thinks I'm not a good influence—"

"Oh, rubbish, Dalla! The Chief has always liked you," Vall replied. "If he didn't, do you think he'd always be inviting us to that farm of his, on Fifth Level Sicily? It's just that this job of ours has no end; something's always turning up, outtime."

The music that the cab had been playing died away. "Paratime Building, just below," it said, in a light feminine voice. "Which landing stage, please?" Vall leaned forward and punched at the buttons in front of him. Something in the cab's electronic brain gave a rapid series of clicks as it shifted from the general Paratime Building beam to the beam of the Paratime Police landing stage, then it said, "Thank you." The building below seemed to rotate upward toward them as it settled down. Then the antigrav-field snapped off, the cab door popped open, and the cab said: "Good-by, now. Ride with me again, sometime."

They crossed the landing stage, entered the antigrav shaft, and floated downward; at the end of a hallway, below, Vall opened the door of Tortha Karf's office and ushered her through ahead of him.

Tortha Karf, inside the semicircle of his desk, was speaking into a recording phone as they approached. He shut off the machine and waved, a cigarette in his hand.

"Come on back and sit down," he invited. "Be with you in a moment." Then he switched on the phone again and went on talking—something about prompter evaluation and transmission of reports and less reliance on robot equipment. "Sign that up, my personal order, and see it's transmitted to everybody down to and including Sector Regional Subchief level," he finished, then hung up the phone and turned to them.

"Sorry about this," he said. "Sit down, if you please. Cigarettes?"

She shook her head and sat down in one of the chairs behind the desk; she started to relax and then caught herself and sat erect, her hands on her lap.

"This won't interfere with your vacation, Vall," Tortha Karf was saying. "I just need a little help before you transpose out."

"We have to catch the rocket for Zarabar in an hour and a half," Dalla reminded him.

"Don't worry about that; if you miss the commercial rocket, our police rockets can give it an hour's start and pass it before it gets to Zarabar," Tortha Karf said. Then he turned to Vall. "Here's what's happened," he said. "One of our field agents on detached duty as guard captain for Consolidated Outtime Foodstuffs on a fruit plantation in western North America, Third Level Esaron Sector, was looking over a lot of slaves who had been sold to the plantation by a local slave dealer. He heard them talking among themselves—in Kharanda."

Dalla caught the significance of that before Vall did. At first, she was puzzled; then, in spite of herself, she was horrified and angry. Tortha Karf was explaining to Vall just where and on what paratemporal sector Kharanda was spoken.

"No possibility that this agent, Skordran Kirv, could have been mistaken. He worked for a while on Kholghoor Sector, himself; knew the language by hypno-mech and by two years' use," Tortha Karf was saying. "So he ordered himself back on duty, had the slaves isolated and the slave dealers arrested, and then transposed to Police Terminal to report. The SecReg Subchief, old Vulthor Tharn, confirmed him in charge at this Esaron Sector plantation, and assigned him a couple of detectives and a psychist."

"When was this?" Vall asked.

"Yesterday. One-Five-Nine Day. About 1500 local time."

"Twenty-three hundred Dhergabar time," Vall commented.

"Yes. And I just found out about it. Came in in the late morning generalized report-digest; very inconspicuous item, no special urgency symbol or anything. Fortunately, one of the report editors spotted it and messaged Police Terminal for a copy of the original report."

"It's been a long time since we had anything like that," Vall said, studying the glowing tip of his cigarette, his face wearing the curiously withdrawn expression of a conscious memory recall. "Fifty years ago; the time that gang kidnaped some girls from Second Level Triplanetary Empire Sector and sold them into the harem of some Fourth Level Indo-Turanian sultan."

"Yes. That was your first independent case, Vall. That was when I began to think you'd really make a cop. One renegade First Level citizen and four or five ServSec Prole hoodlums, with a stolen fifty-foot conveyer. This looks like a rather more ambitious operation." Dalla got one of her own cigarettes out and lit it. Vall and Tortha Karf were talking cop talk about method of operation and possible size of the gang involved, and why the slaves had been shipped all the way from India to the west coast of North America.

"Always ready sale for slaves on the Esaron Sector," Vall was saying. "And so many small independent states, and different languages, that outtimers wouldn't be particularly conspicuous."

"And with this barbarian invasion going on on the Kholghoor Sector, slaves could be picked up cheaply," Tortha Karf added.

In spite of her determination to boycott the conversation, curiosity began to get the better of her. She had spent a year and a half on the Kholghoor Sector, investigating alleged psychic powers of the local priests. There'd been nothing to it—the prophecies weren't precognition, they were shrewd inferences, and the miracles weren't psychokinesis, they were sleight-of-hand. She found herself asking:

"What barbarian invasion's this?"

"Oh, Central Asian nomadic people, the Croutha," Tortha Karf told her. "They came down through Khyber Pass about three months ago, turned east, and hit the headwaters of the Ganges. Without punching a lot of buttons to find out exactly, I'd say they're halfway to the delta country by now. Leader seems to be a chieftain called Llamh Droogh the Red. A lot of paratime trading companies are yelling for permits to introduce firearms in the Kholghoor Sector to protect their holdings there."

She nodded. The Fourth Level Kholghoor Sector belonged to what was known as Indus-Ganges-Irriwady Basic Sector-Grouping—probability of civilization having developed late on the Indian subcontinent, with the rest of the world, including Europe, in Stone Age savagery or early Bronze Age barbarism. The Kharandas, the people among whom she had once done field-research work, had developed a pre-mechanical, animal-power, handcraft, edge-weapon culture. She could imagine the roads jammed with fugitives from the barbarian invaders, the conveyer hidden among the trees, the lurking slavers—

Watch it, Dalla! Don't let the old scoundrel play on your feelings!

* * * *

"Well, what do you want me to do, Chief?" Vall was asking.

"Well, I have to know just what this situation's likely to develop into, and I want to know why Vulthor Tharn's been sitting on this ever since Skordran Kirv reported it to him—"

"I can answer the second one now," Vall replied. "Vulthor Tharn is due to retire in a few years. He has a negatively good, undistinguished record. He's trying to play it safe."

Tortha Karf nodded. "That's what I thought. Look, Vall; suppose you and Dalla transpose from here to Police Terminal, and go to Novilan Equivalent, and give this a quick look-over and report to me, and then rocket to Zarabar Equivalent and go on with your trip to the Dwarma Sector. It may delay you eight or ten hours, but—"

"Closer twenty-four," Vall said. "I'd have to transpose to this plantation, on the Esaron Sector. How about it, Dalla? Would you want to do that?"

She hesitated for a moment, angry with him. He didn't want to refuse, and he was trying to make her do it for him.

"I know, it's a confounded imposition, Dalla," Tortha Karf told her. "But it's important that I get a prompt and full estimate of the situation. This may be something very serious. If it's an isolated incident, it can be handled in a routine manner, but I'm afraid it's not. It has all the marks of a large-scale operation, and if this is a matter of mass kidnapings from one sector and transpositions to another, you can see what a threat this is to the Paratime Secret."

"Moral considerations entirely aside," Vall said. "We don't need to discuss them; they're too obvious."

She nodded. For over twelve millennia, the people of her race and Vall's and Tortha Karf's had been existing as parasites on all the innumerable other worlds of alternate probability on the lateral dimension of time. Smart parasites never injure their hosts, and try never to reveal their existence.

"We could do that, couldn't we, Vall?" she asked, angry at herself now for giving in. "And if you want to question these slaves, I speak Kharanda, and I know how they think. And I'm a qualified and licensed narco-hypnotic technician."

"Well, that's splendid, Dalla!" Tortha Karf enthused. "Wait a moment; I'll message Police Terminal to have a rocket ready for you."

"I'll need a hypno-mech for Kharanda, myself," Vall said. "Dalla, do you know Acalan?" When she shook her head, he turned back to Tortha Karf. "Look; it's about a four-hour rocket hop to Novilan Equivalent. Say we have the hypno-mech machines installed in the rocket; Dalla and I can take our language lessons on the way, and be ready to go to work as soon as we land."

"Good idea," Tortha Karf approved. "I'll order that done, right away. Now—"

Oddly enough, she wasn't feeling so angry, now that she had committed herself and Vall. Come to think of it, she had never been on Police Terminal Time Line; very few people, outside the Paratime Police, ever had. And, she had always wanted to learn more about Vall's work, and participate in it with him. And if she'd made him refuse, it would have been something ugly between them all the time they would be on the Dwarma Sector. But this way—

* * * *

The big circular conveyer room was crowded, as it had been every minute of every day for the past ten thousand years. At the great circular desk in the center, departing or returning police officers were checking in or out with the flat-topped cylindrical robot clerks, or talking to human attendants. Some were in the regulation green uniform; others, like himself, were in civilian clothes; more were in outtime costumes from all over paratime. Fringed robes and cloth-of-gold sashes and conical caps from the Second Level Khiftan Sector; Fourth Level Proto-Aryan mail and helmets; the short tunics and kilts of Fourth Level Alexandrian-Roman Sector; the Zarkantha loincloth and felt cap and daggers; there were priestly vestments stiff with gold, and military uniforms; there were trousers and jackboots and bare legs; blasters, and swords, and pistols, and bows and quivers, and spears. And the place was loud with a babel of voices and the clatter of teleprinters.

Dalla was looking about her in surprised delight; for her, the vacation had already begun. He was glad; for a while, he had been afraid that she would be unhappy about it. He guided her through the crowd to the desk, spoke for a while to one of the human attendants, and found out which was their conveyer. It was a fixed-destination shuttler, operative only between Home Time Line and Police Terminal, from which most of the Paratime Police operations were routed. He put Dall in through the sliding door, followed, and closed it behind him, locking it. Then, before he closed the starting switch, he drew a pistollike weapon and checked it.

In theory, the Ghaldron-Hesthor paratemporal transposition field was uninfluenced by material objects outside it. In practice, however, such objects occasionally intruded, and sometimes they were alive and hostile. The last time he had been in this conveyer room, he had seen a quartet of returning officers emerge from a conveyer dome dragging a dead lion by the tail. The sigma-ray needler, which he carried, was the only weapon which could be used, under the circumstances. It had no effect whatever on any material structure and could be used inside an activated conveyer without deranging the conductor-mesh, as, say, a bullet or the vibration of an ultrasonic paralyzer would do, and it was instantly fatal to anything having a central nervous system. It was a good weapon to use outtime for that reason, also; even on the most civilized time-line, the most elaborate autopsy would reveal no specific cause of death.

"What's the Esaron Sector like?" Dalla asked, as the conveyer dome around them coruscated with shifting light and vanished.

"Third Level; probability of abortive attempt to colonize this planet from Mars about a hundred thousand years ago," he said. "A few survivors—a shipload or so—were left to shift for themselves while the parent civilization on Mars died out. They lost all vestiges of their original Martian culture, even memory of their extraterrestrial origin. About fifteen hundred to two thousand years ago, a reasonably high electrochemical civilization developed and they began working with nuclear energy and developed reaction-drive spaceships. But they'd concentrated so on the inorganic sciences, and so far neglected the bio-sciences, that when they launched their first ship for Venus they hadn't yet developed a germ theory of disease."

"What happened when they ran into the green-vomit fever?" Dalla asked.

"About what you could expect. The first—and only—ship to return brought it back to Terra. Of course, nobody knew what it was, and before the epidemic ended, it had almost depopulated this planet. Since the survivors knew nothing about germs, they blamed it on the anger of the gods—the old story of recourse to supernaturalism in the absence of a known explanation—and a fanatically anti-scientific cult got control. Of course, space travel was taboo; so was nuclear and even electric power. For some reason, steam power and gunpowder weren't offensive to the gods. They went back to a low-order steam-power, black-powder, culture, and haven't gotten beyond that to this day. The relatively civilized regions are on the east coast of Asia and the west coast of North America; civilized race more or less Caucasian. Political organization just barely above the tribal level—thousands of petty kingdoms and republics and principalities and feudal holdings and robbers' roosts. The principal industries are brigandage, piracy, slave-raiding, cattle-rustling and intercommunal warfare. They have a few ramshackle steam railways, and some steamboats on the rivers. We sell them coal and manufactured goods, mostly in exchange for foodstuffs and tobacco. Consolidated Outtime Foodstuffs has the sector franchise. That's one of the companies Thalvan Dras gets his money from."

They had run down through the civilized Second and Third Levels and were leaving the Fourth behind and entering the Fifth, existing in the probability of a world without human population. Once in a while, around them, they caught brief flashes of buildings and rocketports and spaceports and landing stages, as the conveyer took them through narrow paratime belts on which their own civilization had established outposts—Fifth Level Commercial, Fifth Level Passenger, Industrial Sector, Service Sector.

Finally the conveyer dome around them shimmered into visibility and materialized; when they emerged, there were policemen in green uniforms who entered to search the dome with drawn needlers to make sure they had picked up nothing dangerous on the way. The room outside was similar to the one they had left on Home Time Line, even to the shifting, noisy crowd in incongruously-mixed costumes.

* * * *

The rocketport was a ten minutes' trip by aircar from the conveyer head; when they boarded the stubby-winged strato-rocket, Vall saw that two of the passenger-seats had square metal cabinets bolted in place behind them and blue plastic helmets on swinging arms mounted above them.

"Everything's set up," the pilot told them. "Dr. Hadron, you sit on the left; that cabinet's loaded with language tape for Acalan. Yours is loaded with a tape of Kharanda; that's the Fourth Level Kholghoor language you wanted, Chief's Assistant. Shall I help you get fixed in your seats?"

"Yes, if you please. Here, Dalla, I'll fix that for you."

Dalla was already asleep when the pilot was adjusting his helmet and giving him his injection. He never felt the rocket tilt into firing position, and while he slept, the Kharands language, with all its vocabulary and grammar, became part of his subconscious knowledge, needing only the mental pronunciation of a trigger-symbol to bring it into consciousness. The pilot was already unfastening and raising his helmet when he opened his eyes. Dalla, beside him, was sipping a cup of spiced wine.

On the landing stage of the Sector-Regional Headquarters at Novilan Equivalent, four or five people were waiting for them. Vall recognized the subchief, Vulthor Tharn, who introduced another man, in riding boots and a white cloak, as Skordran Kirv. Vall clasped hands with him warmly.

"Good work, Agent Skordran. You got onto this promptly."

"I tried to, sir. Do you want the dope now? We have half an hour's flight to our spatial equivalent, and another half hour in transposition."

"Give it to me on the way," he said, and turned to Vulthor Tharn. "Our Esaron costumes ready?"

"Yes. Over there in the control tower. We have a temporary conveyer head set up about two hundred miles south of here, which will take you straight through to the plantation."

"Suppose you change now, Dalla," he said. "Subchief, I'd like a word with you privately."

He and Vulthor Tharn excused themselves and walked over to the edge of the landing stage. The SecReg Subchief was outwardly composed, but Vall sensed that he was worried and embarrassed.

"Now, what's been done since you got Agent Skordran's report?" Vall asked.

"Well, sir, it seems that this is more serious than we had anticipated. Field Agent Skordran, who will give you the particulars, says that there is every indication that a large and well-organized gang of paratemporal criminals, our own people, are at work. He says that he's found evidence of activities on Fourth Level Kholghoor that don't agree with any information we have about conditions on that sector."

"Beside transmitting Agent Skordran's report to Dhergabar through the robot report-system, what have you done about it?"

"I confirmed Agent Skordran in charge of the local investigation, and gave him two detectives and a psychist, sir. As soon as we could furnish hypno-mech indoctrination in Kharanda to other psychists, I sent them along. He now has four of them, and eight detectives. By that time, we had a conveyer head right at this Consolidated Outtime Foodstuffs plantation."

"Why didn't you just borrow psychists from SecReg for Kholghoor, Eastern India?" Vall asked. "Subchief Ranthar would have loaned you a few."

"Oh, I couldn't call on another SecReg for men without higher-echelon authorization. Especially not from another Sector Organization, even another Level Authority," Vulthor Tharn said. "Beside, it would have taken longer to bring them here than hypno-mech our own personnel."

He was right about the second point. Vall agreed mentally; however, his real reason was procedural.

"Did you alert Ranthar Jard to what was going on in his SecReg?" he asked.

"Gracious, no!" Vulthor Tharn was scandalized. "I have no authority to tell people of equal echelon in other Sector and Level organizations what to do. I put my report through regular channels; it wasn't my place to go outside my own jurisdiction."

And his report had crawled through channels for fourteen hours, Vall thought.

"Well, on my authority, and in the name of Chief Tortha, you message Ranthar Jard at once; send him every scrap of information you have on the subject, and forward additional information as it comes in to you. I doubt he'll find anything on any time-line that's being exploited by any legitimate paratimers. This gang probably work exclusively on unpenetrated time-lines; this business Skordran Kirv came across was a bad blunder on some underling's part." He saw Dalla emerge from the control tower in breeches and boots and a white cloak, buckling on a heavy revolver. "I'll go change, now; you get busy calling Ranthar Jard. I'll see you when I get back."

* * * *

"Are you taking over, Chief's Assistant?" Skordran Kirv asked, as the aircar lifted from the landing stage.

"Not at all. My wife and I are starting on our vacation, as soon as I find out what's been happening here, and report to Chief Tortha. Did your native troopers catch those slavers?"

"Yes, they got them yesterday afternoon; we've had them ever since. Do you want the whole thing just as it happened, Assistant Verkan, or just a condensation?"

"Give me what you think it indicates, remembering that you're probably trying to analyze a large situation from a very small sample."

"It's big, all right," Skordran Kirv said. "This gang can't number less than a hundred men, maybe several hundred. They must have at least two two-hundred-foot conveyers and several small ones, and bases on what sounds like some Fifth Level Time line, and at least one air freighter of around five thousand tons. They are operating on a number of Kholghoor and Esaron time lines."

Verkan Vall nodded. "I didn't think it was any petty larceny," he said.

"Wait till you hear the rest of it. On the Kholghoor Sector, this gang is known as the Wizard Traders; we've been using that as a convenience label. They pose as sorcerers—black robes and hood-masks covered with luminous symbols, voice-amplifiers, cold-light auras, energy-weapons, mechanical magic tricks, that sort of thing. They have all the Croutha scared witless. Their procedure is to establish camps in the forest near recently conquered Kharanda cities; then they appear to the Croutha, impress them with their magical powers, and trade manufactured goods for Kharanda captives. They mainly trade firearms, apparently some kind of flintlocks, and powder."

Then they were confining their operations to unpenetrated time lines; there had been no reports of firearms in the hands of the Croutha invaders.

"After they buy a batch of slaves," Skordran Kirv continued, "they transpose them to this presumably Fifth Level base, where they have concentration camps. The slaves we questioned had been airlifted to North America, where there's another concentration camp, and from there transposed to this Esaron Sector time line where I found them. They say that there were at least two to three thousand slaves in this North American concentration camp and that they are being transposed out in small batches and replaced by others airlifted in from India. This lot was sold to a Calera named Nebu-hin-Abenoz, the chieftain of a hill town, Careba, about fifty miles south-west of the plantation. There were two hundred and fifty in this batch; this Coru-hin-Irigod only bought the batch he sold at the plantation."

* * * *

The aircar lost speed and altitude; below, the countryside was dotted with conveyer heads, each spatially coexistent with some outtime police post or operation. There were a great many of them; the western coast of North America was a center of civilization on many paratemporal sectors, and while the conveyer heads of the commercial and passenger companies were scattered over hundreds of Fifth Level time lines, those of the Paratime Police were concentrated upon one. The anti-grav-car circled around a three-hundred-foot steel tower that supported a conveyer head spatially coexistent with one on a top floor of some outtime tall building, and let down in front of a low prefabricated steel shed. A man in police uniform came out to meet them. There was a fifty-foot conveyer dome inside, and a fifty-foot red-lined circle that marked the transposition point of an outtime conveyer. They all entered the dome, and the operator put on the transposition field.

"You haven't heard the worst of it yet." Skordran Kirv was saying. "On this time line, we have reason to think that the native, Nebu-hin-Abenoz, who bought the slaves, actually saw the slavers' conveyer. Maybe even saw it activated."

"If he did, we'll either have to capture him and give him a memory-obliteration, or kill him," Vall said. "What do you know about him?"

"Well, this Careba, the town he bosses, is a little walled town up in the hills. Everybody there is related to everybody else; this man we have, Coru-hin-Irigod, is the son of a sister of Nebu-hin-Abenoz's wife. They're all bandits and slavers and cattle rustlers and what have you. For the last ten years, Nebu-hin-Abenoz has been buying slaves from some secret source. Before the Kholghoor Sector people began coming in, they were mostly white, with a few brown people who might have been Polynesians. No Negroes—there's no black race on this sector, and I suppose the paratime slavers didn't want too many questions asked. Coru-hin-Irigod, under narco-hypnosis, said that they were all outland-ers, speaking strange languages."

"Ten years! And this is the first hint we've had of it," Vall said. "That's not a bright mark for any of us. I'll bet the slave population on some of these Esaron time lines is an anthropologist's nightmare."

"Why, if this has been going on for ten years, there must have been millions upon millions of people dragged from their own time lines into slavery!" Dalla said in a shocked voice.

"Ten years may not be all of it," Vall said. "This Nebu-hin-Abenoz looks like the only tangible lead we have, at present. How does he oper-ate?"

"About once every ten days, he'll take ten or fifteen men and go a day's ride—that may be as much as fifty miles; these Caleras have good horses and they're hard riders—into the hills. He'll take a big bag of money, all gold. After dark, when he has made camp, a couple of strangers in Calera dress will come in. He'll go off with them, and after about an hour, he'll come back with eight or ten of these strangers and a couple of hundred slaves, always chained in batches of ten. Nebu-hin-Abenoz pays for them, makes arrangements for the next meeting, and the next morning he and his party start marching the slaves to Careba. I might add that, until now, these slaves have been sold to the mines east of Careba; these are the first that have gotten into the coastal country."

"That's why this hasn't come to light before, then. The conveyer comes in every ten days, at about the same place?"

"Yes. I've been thinking of a way we might trap them," Skordran Kirv said. "I'll need more men, and equipment."

"Order them from Regional or General Reserve." Vall told him. "This thing's going to have overtop priority till it's cleared up."

He was mentally cursing Vulthor Tharn's procedure-bound timidity as the conveyer flickered and solidified around them and the overhead red light turned green.

* * * *

They emerged into the interior of a long shed, adobe-walled and thatch-roofed, with small barred windows set high above the earth floor. It was cool and shadowy, and the air was heavy with the fragrance of citrus fruits. There were bins along the walls, some partly full of oranges, and piles of wicker baskets. Another conveyer dome stood beside the one in which they had arrived; two men in white cloaks and riding boots sat on the edge of one of the bins, smoking and talking.

Skordran Kirv introduced them—Gathon Dard and Krador Arv, special detectives—and asked if anything new had come up. Krador Arv shook his head.

"We still have about forty to go," he said. "Nothing new in their stories; still the same two time lines."

"These people," Skordran Kirv explained, "were all peons on the estate of a Kharanda noble just above the big bend of the Ganges. The Croutha hit their master's estate about a ten-days ago, elapsed time. In telling about their capture, most of them say that their master's wife killed herself with a dagger after the Croutha killed her husband, but about one out of ten say that she was kidnaped by the Croutha. Two different time lines, of course. The ones who tell the suicide story saw no firearms among the Croutha; the ones who tell the kidnap story say that they all had some kind of muskets and pistols. We're making synthetic summaries of the two stories."

"We're having trouble with the locals about all these strangers coming in," Gathon Dard added. "They're getting curious."

"We'll have to take a chance on that," Vall said. "Are the interrogations still going on? Then let's have a look-in at them."

The big double doors at the end of the shed were barred on the inside. Krador Arv unlocked a small side door, letting Vall, Dalla and Gathon Dard out. In the yard outside, a gang of slaves were unloading a big wagon of oranges and packing them into hampers; they were guarded by a couple of native riflemen who seemed mostly concerned with keeping them away from the shed, and a man in a white cloak was watching the guards for the same purpose. He walked over and introduced himself to Vall.

"Golzan Doth, local alias Dosu Golan. I'm Consolidated Outtime Foodstuffs' manager here."

"Nasty business for you people," Vall sympathized. "If it's any consolation, it's a bigger headache for us."

"Have you any idea what's going to be done about these slaves?" Golzan Doth asked. "I have to remember that the Company has forty thousand Paratemporal Exchange Units invested in them. The top office was very specific in requesting information about that."

Vall shook his head. "That's over my echelon," he said. "Have to be decided by the Paratime Commission. I doubt if your company'll suffer. You bought them innocently, in conformity with local custom. Ever buy slaves from this Coru-hin-Irigod before?"

"I'm new, here. The man I'm replacing broke his neck when his horse put a foot in a gopher hole about two ten-days ago."

Beside him, Vall could see Dalla nod as though making a mental note. When she got back to Home Time Line, she'd put a crew of mediums to work trying to contact the discarnate former plantation manager; at Rhogom Institute, she had been working on the problem of return of a discarnate personality from outtime.

"A few times," Skordran Kirv said. "Nothing suspicious; all local stuff. We questioned Coru-hin-Irigod pretty closely on that point, and he says that this is the first time he ever brought a batch of Nebu-hin-Abenoz's outlanders this far west."

* * * *

The interrogations were being conducted inside the plantation house, in the secret central rooms where the paratimers lived. Skordran Kirv used a door-activator to slide open a hidden door.

"I suppose I don't have to warn either of you that any positive statement made in the hearing of a narco-hypnotized subject—" he began.

"... Has the effect of hypnotic suggestion—" Vall picked up after him.

"... And should be avoided unless such suggestion is intended," Dalla finished.

Skordran Kirv laughed, opening another, inner door, and stood aside. In what had been the paratimers' recreation room, most of the furniture had been shoved into the corners. Four small tables had been set up, widely spaced and with screens between; across each of them, with an electric recorder between, an almost naked Kharanda slave faced a Paratime Police psychist. At a long table at the far side of the room, four men and two girls were working over stacks of cards and two big charts.

"Phrakor Vuln," the man who was working on the charts introduced himself. "Synthesist." He introduced the others.

Vall made a point of the fact that Dalla was his wife, in case any of the cops began to get ideas, and mentioned that she spoke Kharanda, had spent some time on the Fourth Level Kholghoor, and was a qualified psychist.

"What have you got, so far?" he asked.

"Two different time lines, and two different gangs of Wizard Traders," Phrakor Vuln said. "We've established the latter from physical descriptions and because both batches were sold by the Croutha at equivalent periods of elapsed time."

Vall picked up one of the kidnap-story cards and glanced at it.

"I notice there's a fair verbal description of these firearms, and mention of electric whips," he said. "I'm curious about where they came from."

"Well, this is how we reconstructed them, Chief's Assistant," one of the girls said, handing him a couple of sheets of white drawing paper.

The sketches had been done with soft pencil; they bore repeated erasures and corrections. That of the whip showed a cylindrical handle, indicated as twelve inches in length and one in diameter, fitted with a thumb-switch.

"That's definitely Second Level Khiftan," Vall said, handing it back. "Made of braided copper or silver wire and powered with a little nuclear-conversion battery in the grip. They heat up to about two hundred centigrade; produce really painful burns."

"Why, that's beastly!" Dalla exclaimed.

"Anything on the Khiftan Sector is." Skordran Kirv looked at the four slaves at the tables. "We don't have a really bad case here, now. A few of these people were lash-burned horribly, though."

Vall was looking at the other sketches. One was a musket, with a wide butt and a band-fastened stock; the lock-mechanism, vaguely flintlock, had been dotted in tentatively. The other was a long pistol, similarly definite in outline and vague in mechanical detail; it was merely a knob-butted miniature of the musket.

"I've seen firearms like these; have a lot of them in my collection," he said, handing back the sketches. "Low-order mechanical or high-order pre-mechanical cultures. Fact is, things like those could have been made on the Kholghoor Sector, if the Kharandas had learned to combine sulfur, carbon and nitrates to make powder."

The interrogator at one of the tables had evidently heard all his subject could tell him. He rose, motioning the slave to stand.

"Now, go with that man," he said in Kharanda, motioning to one of the detectives in native guard uniform. "You will trust him; he is your friend and will not harm you. When you have left this room, you will forget everything that has happened here, except that you were kindly treated and that you were given wine to drink and your hurts were anointed. You will tell the others that we are their friends and that they have nothing to fear from us. And you will not try to remove the mark from the back of your left hand."

As the detective led the slave out a door at the other side of the room, the psychist came over to the long table, handing over a card and lighting a cigarette.

"Suicide story," he said to one of the girls, who took the card.

"Anything new?"

"Some minor details about the sale to the Caleras on this time line. I think we've about scraped bottom."

"You can't say that," Phrakor Vuln objected. "The very last one may give us something nobody else had noticed."

Another subject was sent out. The interrogator came over to the table.

"One of the kidnap-story crowd," he said. "This one was right beside that Croutha who took the shot at the wild pig or whatever it was on the way to the Wizard Traders' camp. Best description of the guns we've gotten so far. No question that they're flintlocks." He saw Verkan Vall. "Oh, hello, Assistant Verkan. What do you make of them? You're an authority on outtime weapons, I understand."

"I'd have to see them. These people simply don't think mechanically enough to give a good description. A lot of peoples make flintlock firearms."

He started running over, in his mind, the paratemporal areas in which gunpowder but not the percussion-cap was known. Expanding cultures, which had progressed as far as the former but not the latter. Static cultures, in which an accidental discovery of gunpowder had never been followed up by further research. Post-debacle cultures, in which a few stray bits of ancient knowledge had survived.

Another interrogator came over, and then the fourth. For a while they sat and talked and drank coffee, and then the next quartet of slaves, two men and two women, were brought in. One of the women had been badly blistered by the electric whips of the Wizard Traders; in spite of reassurances, all were visibly apprehensive.

"We will not harm you," one of the psychists told them. "Here; here is medicine for your hurts. At first, it will sting, as good medicines will, but soon it will take away all pain. And here is wine for you to drink."

A couple of detectives approached, making a great show of pouring wine and applying ointment; under cover of the medication, they jabbed each slave with a hypodermic needle, and then guided them to seats at the four tables. Vall and Dalla went over and stood behind one of the psychists, who had a small flashlight in his hand.

"Now, rest for a while," the psychist was saying. "Rest and let the good medicine do its work. You are tired and sleepy. Look at this magic light, which brings comfort to the troubled. Look at the light. Look ... at ... the ... light."

They moved to the next table.

"Did you have hand in the fighting?"

"No, lord. We were peasant folk, not fighting people. We had no weapons, nor weapon-skill. Those who fought were all killed; we held up empty hands, and were spared to be captives of the Croutha."

"What happened to your master, the Lord Ghromdour, and to his lady?"

"One of the Croutha threw a hatchet and killed our master, and then his lady drew a dagger and killed herself."

The psychist made a red mark on the card in front of him, and circled the number on the back of the slave's hand with red indelible crayon. Vall and Dalla went to the third table.

"They had the common weapons of the Croutha, lord, and they also had the weapons of the Wizard Traders. Of these, they carried the long weapons slung across their backs, and the short weapons thrust through their belts."

A blue mark on the card; a blue circle on the back of the slave's hand.

They listened to both versions of what had happened at the sack of the Lord Ghromdour's estate, and the march into the captured city of Jhirda, and the second march into the forest to the camp of the Wizard Traders.

"The servants of the Wizard Traders did not appear until after the Croutha had gone away; they wore different garb. They wore short jackets, and trousers, and short boots, and they carried small weapons on their belts—"

"They had whips of great cruelty that burned like fire; we were all lashed with these whips, as you may see, lord—"

"The Croutha had bound us two and two, with neck-yokes; these the servants of the Wizard Traders took off from us, and they chained us together by tens, with the chains we still wore when we came to this place—"

"They killed my child, my little Zhouzha!" the woman with the horribly blistered back was wailing. "They tore her out of my arms, and one of the servants of the Wizard Traders—may Khokhaat devour his soul forever!—dashed out her brains. And when I struggled to save her. I was thrown on the ground, and beaten with the fire-whips until I fainted. Then I was dragged into the forest, along with the others who were chained with me." She buried her head in her arms, sobbing bitterly.

Dalla stepped forward, taking the flashlight from the interrogator with one hand and lifting the woman's head with the other. She flashed the light quickly in the woman's eyes.

"You will grieve no more for your child," she said. "Already, you are forgetting what happened at the Wizard Traders' camp, and remembering only that your child is safe from harm. Soon you will remember her only as a dream of the child you hope to have, some day." She flashed the light again, then handed it back to the psychist. "Now, tell us what happened when you were taken into the forest; what did you see there?"

The psychist nodded approvingly, made a note on the card, and listened while the woman spoke. She had stopped sobbing, now, and her voice was clear and cheerful.

Vall went over to the long table.

"Those slaves were still chained with the Wizard Traders' chains when they were delivered here. Where are the chains?" he asked Skordran Kirv.

"In the permanent conveyer room," Skordran Kirv said. "You can look at them there; we didn't want to bring them in here, for fear these poor devils would think we were going to chain them again. They're very light, very strong; some kind of alloy steel. Files and power saws only polish them; it takes fifteen seconds to cut a link with an atomic torch. One long chain, and short lengths, fifteen inches long, staggered, every three feet, with a single hinge-shackle for the ankle. The shackles were riveted with soft wrought-iron rivets, evidently made with some sort of a power riveting-machine. We cut them easily with a cold chisel."

"They ought to be sent to Dhergabar Equivalent, Police Terminal, for study of material and workmanship. Now, you mentioned some scheme you had for capturing this conveyer that brings in the slaves for Nebu-hin-Abenoz. What have you in mind?"

"We still have Coru-hin-Irigod and all his gang, under hypno. I'd thought of giving them hypnotic conditioning, and sending them back to Careba with orders to put out some kind of signal the next time Nebu-hin-Abenoz starts out on a buying trip. We could have a couple of men posted in the hills overlooking Careba, and they could send a message-ball through to Police Terminal. Then, a party could be sent with a mobile conveyer to ambush Nebu-hin-Abenoz on the way, and wipe out his party. Our people could take their horses and clothing and go on to take the conveyer by surprise."

"I'd suggest one change. Instead of relying on visual signals by the hypno-conditioned Coru-hin-Irigod, send a couple of our men to Careba with midget radios."

Skordran Kirv nodded. "Sure. We can condition Coru-hin-Irigod to accept them as friends and vouch for them at Careba. Our boys can be traders and slave buyers. Careba's a market town; traders are always welcome. They can have firearms to sell—revolvers and repeating rifles. Any Calera'll buy any firearm that's better than the one he's carrying; they'll always buy revolvers and repeaters. We can get what we want from Commercial Four-Oh-Seven; we can get riding and pack horses here."

Vall nodded. "And the post overlooking or in radio range of Careba on this time line, and another on PolTerm. For the ambush of Nebu-hin-Abenoz's gang and the capture of the conveyer, use anything you want to—sleep-gas, paralyzers, energy-weapons, antigrav-equipment, anything. As far as regulations about using only equipment appropriate to local culture-levels, forget them entirely. But take that conveyer intact. You can locate the base time line from the settings of the instrument panel, and that's what we want most of all."

Dalla and the police psychist, having finished with and dismissed their subject, came over to the long table.

"... That poor creature," Dalla was saying. "What sort of fiends are they?"

"If that made you sick, remember we've been listening to things like that for the last eight hours. Some of the stories were even worse than that one."

"Well, I'd like to use a heat-gun on the whole lot of them, turned down to where it'd just fry them medium-rare," Dalla said. "And for whoever's back of this, take him to Second Level Khiftan and sell him to the priests of Fasif."

"Too bad you're not coming back from your vacation, instead of starting out. Chief's Assistant Verkan," Skordran Kirv said. "This is too big for me to handle alone, and I'd sooner work under you than anybody else Chief Tortha sends in."

"Vall!" Dalla cried in indignation. "You're not going to just report on this and then walk away from it, are you?"

"But, darling," Vall replied, in what he hoped was a convincing show of surprise. "You don't want our vacation postponed again, do you? If I get mixed up in this, there's no telling when I can get away, and by the time I'm free, something may come up at Rhogom Institute that you won't want to drop—"

"Vall, you know perfectly well that I wouldn't be happy for an instant on the Dwarma Sector, thinking about this—"

"All right, then; let's forget about the vacation. You want to stay on for a while and help me with this? It'll be a lot of hard work, but we'll be together."

"Yes, of course. I want to do something to smash those devils. Vall, if you'd heard some of the things they did to those poor people—"

"Well, I'll have to go back to PolTerm, as soon as I'm reasonably well filled in on this, and report to Tortha Karf and tell him I've taken charge. You can stay here and help with these interrogations; I'll be back in about ten hours. Then, we can go to Kholghoor East India SecReg HQ to talk to Ranthar Jard. We may be able to get something that'll help us on that end—"

"You may be able to have your vacation before too long, Dr. Hadron," Skordran Kirv told her. "Once we capture one of their conveyers, the instrument panel'll tell us what time line they're working from, and then we'll have them."

"There's an Indo-Turanian Sector parable about a snake charmer who thought he was picking up his snake and found that he had hold of an elephant's tail," Vall said. "That might be a good thing to bear in mind, till we find out just what we have picked up."

Coming down a hallway on the hundred and seventh floor of the Management wing of the Paratime Building, Yandar Yadd paused to admire, in the green mirror of the glassoid wall, the jaunty angle of his silver-feathered cap, the fit of his short jacket, and the way his weapon hung at his side. This last was not instantly recognizable as a weapon; it looked more like a portable radio, which indeed it was. It was, none the less, a potent weapon. One flick of his finger could connect that radio with one at Tri-Planet News Service, and within the hour anything he said into it would be heard by all Terra, Mars and Venus. In consequence, there existed around the Paratime Building a marked and understandable reluctance to antagonize Yandar Yadd.

He glanced at his watch. It was twenty minutes short of 1000, when he had an appointment with Baltan Vrath, the comptroller general. Glancing about, he saw that he was directly in front of the doorway of the Outtime Claims Bureau, and he strolled in, walking through the waiting room and into the claims-presentation office. At once, he stiffened like a bird dog at point.

Sphabron Larv, one of his young legmen, was in altercation across the counter-desk with Varkar Klav, the Deputy Claims Agent on duty at the time. Varkar was trying to be icily dignified; Sphabron Larv's black hair was in disarray and his face was suffused with anger. He was pounding with his fist on the plastic counter-top.

"You have to!" he was yelling in the older man's face. "That's a public document, and I have a right to see it. You want me to go into Tribunes' Court and get an order? If I do, there'll be a Question in Council about why I had to, before the day's out!"

"What's the matter, Larv?" Yandar Yadd asked lazily. "He trying to hold something out on you?"

Sphabron Larv turned; his eyes lit happily when he saw his boss, and then his anger returned.

"I want to see a copy of an indemnity claim that was filed this morning," he said. "Varkar, here, won't show it to me. What does he think this is, a Fourth Level dictatorship?"

"What kind of a claim, now?" Yandar Yadd addressed Larv, ignoring Varkar Klav.

"Consolidated Outtime Foodstuffs—one of the Thalvan Interests companies—just claimed forty thousand P.E.U. for a hundred slaves bought by one of their plantation managers on Third Level Esaron from a local slave dealer. The Paratime Police impounded the slaves for narco-hypnotic interrogation, and then transposed the lot of them to Police Terminal."

Yandar Yadd still held his affectation of sleepy indolence.

"Now why would the Paracops do that, I wonder? Slavery's an established local practice on Esaron Sector; our people have to buy slaves if they want to run a plantation."

"I know that." Sphabron Larv replied. "That's what I want to find out. There must be something wrong, either with the slaves, or the treatment our people were giving them, or the Paratime Police, and I want to find out which."

"To tell the truth, Larv, so do I." Yandar Yadd said. He turned to the man behind the counter. "Varkar, do we see that claim, or do I make a story out of your refusal to show it?" he asked.

"The Paratime Police asked me to keep this confidential," Varkar Klav said. "Publicity would seriously hamper an important police investigation."

Yandar Yadd made an impolite noise. "How do I know that all it would do would be to reveal police incompetence?" he retorted. "Look, Varkar; you and the Paratime Police and the Paratime Commission and the Home Time Line Management are all hired employees of the Home Time Line public. The public has a right to know what its employees are doing, and it's my business to see that they're informed. Now, for the last time—will you show us a copy of that claim?"

"Well, let me explain, off the record—" the official begged.

"Huh-uh! Huh-uh! I had that off-the-record gag worked on me when I was about Larv's age, fifty years ago. Anything I get, I put on the air or not at my own discretion."

"All right," Varkar Klav surrendered, pointing to a reading screen and twiddling a knob. "But when you read it, I hope you have enough discretion to keep quiet about it."

The screen lit, and Yandar Yadd automatically pressed a button for a photo-copy. The two newsmen stared for a moment, and then even Yandar Yadd's shell of drowsy negligence cracked and fell from him. His hand brushed the switch as he snatched the hand-phone from his belt.

"Marva!" he barked, before the girl at the news office could more than acknowledge. "Get this recorded for immediate telecast!... Ready? Beginning: The existence of a huge paratemporal slave trade came to light on the afternoon of One-Five-Nine Day, on a time line of the Third Level Esaron Sector, when Field Agent Skordran Kirv, Paratime Police, discovered, at an orange plantation of Consolidated Outtime Foodstuffs—"

* * * *

Salgath Trod sat alone in his private office, his half-finished lunch growing cold on the desk in front of him as he watched the teleview screen across the room, tuned to a pickup behind the Speaker's chair in the Executive Council Chamber ten stories below. The two thousand seats had been almost all empty at 1000, when Council had convened. Fifteen minutes later, the news had broken; now, at 1430, a good three quarters of the seats were occupied. He could see, in the aisles, the gold-plated robot pages gliding back and forth, receiving and delivering messages. One had just slid up to the seat of Councilman Hasthor Flan, and Hasthor was speaking urgently into the recorder mouthpiece. Another message for him, he supposed; he'd gotten at least a score such calls since the crisis had developed.

People were going to start wondering, he thought. This situation should have been perfect for his purposes; as leader of the Opposition he could easily make himself the next General Manager, if he exploited this scandal properly. He listened for a while to the Centrist-Management member who was speaking; he could rip that fellow's arguments to shreds in a hundred words—but he didn't dare. The Management was taking exactly the line Salgath Trod wanted the whole Council to take: treat this affair as an isolated and extraordinary occurrence, find a couple of convenient scapegoats, cobble up some explanation acceptable to the public, and forget it. He wondered what had happened to the imbecile who had transposed those Kholghoor Sector slaves onto an exploited time line. Ought to be shanghaied to the Khiftan Sector and sold to the priests of Fasif!

A buzzer sounded, and for an instant he thought it would be the message he had seen Hasthor Fan recording. Then he realized that it was the buzzer for the private door, which could only be operated by someone with a special identity sign. He pressed a button and unlocked the door.

The young man in the loose wrap-around tunic who entered was a stranger. At least, his face and his voice were strange, but voices could be mechanically altered, and a skilled cosmetician could render any face unrecognizable. He looked like a student, or a minor commercial executive, or an engineer, or something like that. Of course, his tunic bulged slightly under the left armpit, but even the most respectable tunics showed occasional weapon-bulges.

"Good afternoon, councilman," the newcomer said, sitting down across the desk from Salgath Trod. "I was just talking to ... somebody we both know."

Salgath Trod offered cigarettes, lighted his visitor's and then his own.

"What does Our Mutual Friend think about all this?" he asked, gesturing toward the screen.

"Our Mutual Friend isn't at all happy about it."

"You think, perhaps, that I'm bursting into wild huzzas?" Salgath Trod asked. "If I were to act as everybody expects me to, I'd be down there on the floor, now, clawing into the Management tooth and nail. All my adherents are wondering why I'm not. So are all my opponents, and before long one of them is going to guess the reason."

"Well, why not go down?" the stranger asked. "Our Mutual Friend thinks it would be an excellent idea. The leak couldn't be stopped, and it's gone so far already that the Management will never be able to play it down. So the next best thing is to try to exploit it."

Salgath Trod smiled mirthlessly. "So I am to get in front of it, and lead it in the right direction? Fine ... as long as I don't stumble over something. If I do, it'll go over me like a Fifth Level bison-herd."

"Don't worry about that," the stranger laughed reassuringly. "There are others on the floor who are also friends of Our Mutual Friend. Here: what you'd better do is attack the Paratime Police, especially Tortha Karf and Verkan Vall. Accuse them of negligence and incompetence, and, by implication, of collusion, and demand a special committee to investigate. And try to get a motion for a confidence vote passed. A motion to censure the Management, say—"

Salgath Trod nodded. "It would delay things, at least. And if Our Mutual Friend can keep properly covered, I might be able to overturn the Management." He looked at the screen again. "That old fool of a Nanthav is just getting started; it'll be an hour before I could get recognized. Plenty of time to get a speech together. Something short and vicious—"

"You'll have to be careful. It won't do, with your political record, to try to play down these stories of a gigantic criminal conspiracy. That's too close to the Management line. And at the same time, you want to avoid saying anything that would get Verkan Vall and Tortha Karf started off on any new lines of investigation."

Salgath Trod nodded. "Just depend on me; I'll handle it."

After the stranger had gone, he shut off the sound reception, relying on visual dumb-show to keep him informed of what was going on on the Council floor. He didn't like the situation. It was too easy to say the wrong thing. If only he knew more about the shadowy figures whose messengers used his private door—

* * * *

Coru-hin-Irigod held his aching head in both hands, as though he were afraid it would fall apart, and blinked in the sunlight from the window. Lord Safar, how much of that sweet brandy had he drunk, last night? He sat on the edge of the bed for a moment, trying to think. Then, suddenly apprehensive, he thrust his hand under his pillow. The heavy four-barreled pistols were there, all right, but—*The money!*

He rummaged frantically among the bedding, and among his clothes, piled on the floor, but the leather bag was nowhere to be found. Two thousand gold *obus*, the price of a hundred slaves. He snatched up one of the pistols, his headache forgotten. Then he laughed and tossed the pistol down again. Of course! He'd given the bag to the plantation manager, what was his outlandish name, Dosu Golan, to keep for him before the drinking bout had begun. It was safely waiting for him in the plantation strong box. Well, nothing like a good scare to make a man forget a brandy head, anyhow. And there was something else, something very nice—

Oh, yes, there it was, beside the bed. He picked up the beautiful gleaming repeater, pulled down the lever far enough to draw the cartridge halfway out of the chamber, and closed it again, lowering the hammer. Those two Jeseru traders from the North, what were their names? Ganadara and Atarazola. That was a stroke of luck, meeting them here. They'd given him this lovely rifle, and they were going to accompany him and his men back to Careba; they had a hundred such rifles, and two hundred six-shot revolvers, and they wanted to trade for slaves. The Lord Safar bless them both, wouldn't they be welcome at Careba!

He looked at the sunlight falling through the window on the still recumbent form of his companion, Faru-hin-Obaran. Outside, he could hear the sounds of the plantation coming to life—an ax thudding on wood, the clatter of pans from the kitchens. Crossing to Faru-hin-Obaran's bed, he grasped the sleeper by the ankle, tugging.

"Waken, Faru!" he shouted. "Get up and clear the fumes from your head! We start back to Careba today!"

Faru swore groggily and pushed himself into a sitting position, fumbling on the floor for his trousers.

"What day's this?" he asked.

"The day after we went to bed, ninny!" Then Coru-hin-Irigod wrinkled his brow. He could remember, clearly enough, the sale of the slaves, but after that—Oh, well, he'd been drinking; it would all come back to him, after a while.

* * * *

Verkan Vall rubbed his hand over his face wearily, started to light another cigarette, and threw it across the room in disgust. What he needed was a drink—a long drink of cool, tart white wine, laced with brandy—and then he needed to sleep.

"We're absolutely nowhere!" Ranthar Jard said. "Of course they're operating on time lines we've never penetrated. The fact that they're supplying the Croutha with guns proves that; there isn't a firearm on any of the time lines our people are legitimately exploiting. And there are only about three billion time lines on this belt of the Croutha invasion—"

"If we could think of a way to reduce it to some specific area of paratime—" one of Ranthar Jard's deputies began.

"That's precisely what we've been trying to do, Klav," Vall said. "We haven't done it."

Dalla, who had withdrawn from the discussion and was on a couch at the side of the room, surrounded by reports and abstracts and summaries, looked up.

"I took hours and hours of hypno-mech on Kholghoor Sector religions, before I went out on that wild-goose chase for psychokinesis and precognition data," she said. "About six or eight hundred years ago, there were religious wars and heresies and religious schisms all over the Kharanda country. No matter how uniform the Kholghoor Sector may be otherwise, there are dozens and dozens of small belts and sub-sectors of different religions or sects or god-cults."

"That's right," Ranthar Jard agreed, brightening. "We have hagiologists who know all that stuff; we'll have a couple of them interrogate those slaves. I don't know how much they can get out of them—lot of peasants, won't be up on the theological niceties—but a synthesis of what we get from the lot of them—"

"That's an idea," Vall agreed. "About the first idea we've had, here— Oh, how about politics, too? Check on who's the king, what the stories about the royal family are, that sort of thing."

Ranthar Jard looked at the map on the wall. "The Croutha have only gotten halfway to Nharkan, here. Say we transpose detectives in at night on some of these time lines we think are promising, and check up at the tax-collection offices on a big landowner north of Jhirda named Ghromdour? That might get us something."

"Well, I don't want you to think we're trying to get out of work, Chief's Assistant," one of the deputies said, "but is there any real necessity for our trying to locate the Wizard Trader time lines? If you can get them from the Esaron Sector, it'll be the same, won't it?"

"Marv, in this business you never depend on just one lead," Ranthar Jard told him. "And beside, when Skordran Kirv's gang hits the base of operations in North America, there's no guarantee that they may not have time to send off a radio warning to the crowd at the base here in India. We have to hit both places at once."

"Well, that, too," Vall said. "But the main thing is to get these Wizard Trader camps on the Kholghoor Sector cleaned out. How are you fixed for men and equipment, for a big raid, Jard?"

Ranthar Jard shrugged. "I can get about five hundred men with conveyers, including a couple of two-hundred-footers to carry airboats," he said.

"Not enough. Skordran Kirv has one complete armored brigade, one airborne infantry brigade, and an air cavalry regiment, with Ghaldron-Hesthor equipment for a simultaneous transposition," Vall said.

"Where in blazes did he get them all?" Ranthar Jard demanded.

"They're guard troops, from Service Sector and Industrial Sector. We'll get you the same sort of a force. I only hope we don't have another Prole insurrection while they're away—"

"Well, don't think I'm trying to argue policy with you," Ranthar Jard said, "but that could raise a dreadful stink on Home Time Line. Especially on top of this news-break about the slave trade."

"We'll have to take a chance on that," Vall said. "If you're worried about what the book says, forget it. We're throwing the book away, on this operation. Do you realize that this thing is a threat to the whole Paratime Civilization?"

"Of course I do," Ranthar Jard said. "I know the doctrine of Paratime Security as well as you or anybody else. The question is, does the public realize it?"

A buzzer sounded. Ranthar Jard pressed a switch on the intercom-box in front of him and said: "Ranthar here. Well?"

"Visiphone call, top urgency, just came in for Chief's Assistant Verkan, from Novilan Equivalent. Where can I put it through, sir?"

"Here; booth seven." Ranthar Jard pointed across the room, nodding to Vall. "In just a moment."

* * * *

Gathon Dard and Antrath Alv—temporary local aliases, Ganadara and Atarazola—sat relaxed in their saddles, swaying to the motion of their horses. They wore the rust-brown hooded cloaks of the northern Jeseru people, in sober contrast to the red and yellow and blue striped robes and sun-bonnets of the Caleras in whose company they rode. They carried short repeating carbines in saddle scabbards, and heavy revolvers and long knives on their belts, and each led six heavily-laden pack-horses.

Coru-hin-Irigod, riding beside Ganadara, pointed up the trail ahead.

"From up there," he said, speaking in Acalan, the lingua franca of the North American West Coast on that sector, "we can see across the valley to Careba. It will be an hour, as we ride, with the pack-horses. Then we will rest, and drink wine, and feast."

Ganadara nodded. "It was the guidance of our gods—and yours, Co-ru-hin-Irigod—that we met. Such slaves as you sold at the outlanders' plantation would bring a fine price in the North. The men are strong, and have the look of good field-workers; the women are comely and well-formed. Though I fear that my wife would little relish it did I bring home such handmaidens."

Coru-hin-Irigod laughed. "For your wife, I will give you one of our riding whips." He leaned to the side, slashing at a cactus with his quirt. "We in Careba have no trouble with our wives, about handmaidens or anything else."

"By Safar, if you doubt your welcome at Careba, wait till you show your wares," another Calera said. "Rifles and revolvers like those come to our country seldom, and then old and battered, sold or stolen many times before we see them. Rifles that fire seven times without taking butt from shoulder!" He invoked the name of the Great Lord Safar again.

The trail widened and leveled; they all came up abreast, with the pack-horses strung out behind, and sat looking across the valley to the adobe walls of the town that perched on the opposite ridge. After a while, riders began dismounting and checking and tightening saddle-girths; a couple of Caleras helped Ganadara and Atarazola inspect their pack-horses. When they remounted, Atarazola bowed his head, lifting his left sleeve to cover his mouth, and muttered into it at some length. The Caleras looked at him curiously, and Coru-hin-Irigod inquired of Ganadara what he did.

"He prays," Ganadara said. "He thanks our gods that we have lived to see your town, and asks that we be spared to bring many more trains of rifles and ammunition up this trail."

The slaver nodded understandingly. The Caleras were a pious people, too, who believed in keeping on friendly terms with the gods.

"May Safar's hand work with the hands of your gods for it," he said, making what, to a non-Calera, would have been an extremely ribald sign.

"The gods watch over us," Atarazola said, lifting his head. "They are near us even now; they have spoken words of comfort in my ear."

Ganadara nodded. The gods to whom his partner prayed were a couple of paratime policemen, crouching over a radio a mile or so down the ridge.

"My brother," he told Coru-hin-Irigod, "is much favored by our gods. Many people come to him to pray for them."

"Yes. So you told me, now that I think on it." That detail had been included in the pseudo-memories he had been given under hypnosis. "I serve Safar, as do all Caleras, but I have heard that the Jeserus' gods are good gods, dealing honestly with their servants."

* * * *

An hour later, under the walls of the town, Coru-hin-Irigod drew one of his pistols and fired all four barrels in rapid succession into the air, shouting, "Open! Open for Coru-hin-Irigod, and for the Jeseru traders, Ganadara and Atarazola, who are with him!"

A head, black-bearded and sun-bonneted, appeared between the brick merlons of the wall above the gate, shouted down a welcome, and then turned away to bawl orders. The gate slid aside, and, after the caravan had passed through, naked slaves pushed the massive thing shut again. Although they were familiar with the interior of the town, from photographs taken with boomerang-balls—automatic-return transposition spheres like message-balls—they looked around curiously. The central square was thronged—Caleras in striped robes, people from the south and east in baggy trousers and embroidered shirts, mountaineers in deerskins. A slave market was in progress, and some hundred-odd items of human merchandise were assembled in little groups, guarded by their owners and inspected by prospective buyers. They seemed to be all natives of that geographic and paratemporal area.

"Don't even look at those," Coru-hin-Irigod advised. "They are but culls; the market is almost over. We'll go to the house of Nebu-hin-Abenoz, where all the considerable men gather, and you will find those who will be able to trade slaves worthy of the goods you have with you. Meanwhile, let my people take your horses and packs to my house; you shall be my guests while you stay in Careba."

It was perfectly safe to trust Coru-hin-Irigod. He was a murderer and a brigand and a slaver, but he would never incur the scorn of men and the curse of the gods by dealing foully with a guest. The horses and packs were led away by his retainers; Ganadara and Atarazola pushed their horses after his and Faru-hin-Obaran's through the crowd.

The house of Nebu-hin-Abenoz, like every other building in Careba, was flat-roofed, adobe-walled and window-less except for narrow rifle-slits. The wide double-gate stood open, and five or six heavily armed Caleras lounged just inside. They greeted Coru and Faru by name, and the strangers by their assumed nationality. The four rode through, into what appeared to be the stables, turning their horses over to slaves, who took them away. There were between fifty and sixty other horses in the place.

Divesting themselves of their weapons in an anteroom at the head of a flight of steps, they passed under an arch and into a wide, shady patio, where thirty or forty men stood about or squatted on piles of cushions, smoking cheroots, drinking from silver cups, talking in a continuous ba-bel. Most of them were in Calera dress, though there were men of other communities and nations, in other garb. As they moved across the patio, Gathon Dard caught snatches of conversations about deals in slaves, and horse trades, about bandit raids and blood feuds, about women and horses and weapons.

An old man with a white beard and an unusually clean robe came over to intercept them.

"Ha, lord of my daughter, you're back at last. We had begun to fear for you," he said.

"Nothing to fear, father of my wife," Coru-hin-Irigod replied. "We sold the slaves for a good price, and tarried the night feasting in good company. Such good company that we brought some of it with us—Atarazola and Ganadara, men of the Jeseru; Cavu-hin-Avoran, whose daughter mothered my sons." He took his father-in-law by the sleeve and pulled him aside, motioning Gathon Dard and Antrath Alv to follow.

"They brought weapons; they want outland slaves, of the sort I took to sell in the Big Valley country," he whispered. "The weapons are re-peating rifles from across the ocean, and six-shot revolvers. They also have much ammunition."

"Oh, Safar bless you!" the white-beard cried, his eyes brightening. "Name your own price; satisfy yourselves that we have dealt fairly with you; go, and return often again! Come, lord of my daughter; let us make them known to Nebu-hin-Abenoz. But not a word about the kind of weapons you have, strangers, until we can speak privately. Say only that you have rifles to trade."

Gathon Dard nodded. Evidently there was some sort of power-struggle going on in Careba; Coru-hin-Irigod and his wife's father were of the party of Nebu-hin-Abenoz, and wanted the repeaters and six-shooters for themselves.

* * * *

Nebu-hin-Abenoz, swarthy, hook-nosed, with a square-cut graying beard, lounged in a low chair across the patio; near him four or five other Caleras sat or squatted or reclined, all smoking the rank black tobacco of the country and drinking wine or brandy. Their conversation ceased as Cavu-hin-Avoran and the others approached. The chief of Careba listened to the introduction, then heaved himself to his feet and clapped the newcomers on the shoulders.

"Good, good!" he said. "We know you Jeseru people; you're honest traders. You come this far into our mountains too seldom. We can trade with you. We need weapons. As for the sort of slaves you want, we have none too many now, but in eight days we will have plenty. If you stay with us that long—"

"Careba is a pleasant place to be," Ganadara said. "We can wait."

"What sort of weapons have you?" the chief asked.

"Pistols and rifles, lord of my father's sister," Coru-hin-Irigod answered for them. "The packs have been taken to my house, where our friends will stay. We can bring a few to show you, the hour after evening prayers."

Nebu-hin-Abenoz shot a keen glance at his brother-in-law's son and nodded. "Or, better, I will come to your house then; thus I can see the whole load. How will that be?"

"Better; I will be there, too," Cavu-hin-Avoran said, then turned to Gathon Dard and Antrath Alv. "You have been long on the road; come, let us drink cool wine, and then we will eat," he said. "Until this evening, Nebu-hin-Abenoz."

He led his son-in-law and the traders to one side, where several kegs stood on trestles with cups and flagons beside them. They filled a flagon, took a cup apiece, and went over to a pile of cushions at one side.

As they did, three men came pushing through the crowd toward Nebu-hin-Abenoz's seat. They wore a costume unfamiliar to Gathon Dard—little round caps with red and green streamers behind, and long, wide-sleeved white gowns—and one of them had gold rings in his ears.

"Nebu-hin-Abenoz?" one of them said, bowing. "We are three men of the Usasu cities. We have gold *obus* to spend; we seek a beautiful girl, to be first concubine to our king's son, who is now come to the estate of manhood."

Nebu-hin-Abenoz picked up the silver-mounted pipe he had laid aside, and re-lighted it, frowning.

"Men of the Usasu, you have a heavy responsibility," he said. "You have the responsibility for the future of your kingdom, for a boy's character is more shaped by his first concubine than by his teachers. How old is the boy?"

"Sixteen, Nebu-hin-Abenoz; the age of manhood among us."

"Then you want a girl older, but not much older. She should be versed in the arts of love, but innocent of heart. She should be wise, but teachable; gentle and loving, but with a will of her own—"

The three men in white gowns were fidgeting. Then, suddenly, like three marionettes on a single string, they put their right hands to their mouths and then plunged them into the left sleeves of their gowns, whipping out knives and then sprang as one upon Nebu-hin-Abenoz, slashing and stabbing.

Gathon Dard was on his feet at once; he hurled the wine flagon at the three murderers and leaped across the room. Antrath Alv went bounding after him, and by this time three or four of the group around Nebu-hin-Abenoz's chair had recovered their wits and jumped to their feet. One of the three assailants turned and slashed with his knife, almost disemboweling a Calera who had tried to grapple with him. Before he could free the blade, another Calera brought a brandy bottle down on his head. Gathon Dard sprang upon the back of a second assassin, hooking his left elbow under the fellow's chin and grabbing the wrist of his knife-hand with his right; the man struggled for an instant, then went limp and fell forward. The third of the trio of murderers was still slashing at the fallen chieftain when Antrath Alv chopped him along the side of the neck with the edge of his hand; he simply dropped and lay still.

Nebu-hin-Abenoz was dead. He had been slashed and cut and stabbed in twenty places; his throat had been cut at least three times, and he had almost been decapitated. The wounded Calera wasn't dead yet; however, even if he had been at the moment on the operating table of a First Level Home Time Line hospital, it was doubtful if he could have been saved, and under the circumstances, his life-expectancy could be measured in seconds. Some cushions were placed under his head, and women called to attend him, but he died before they arrived.

The three assassins were also dead. Except for a few cuts on the scalp of the one who had been felled with the bottle, there was not a mark on any of them. Cavu-hin-Avoran kicked one of them in the face and cursed.

"We killed the skunks too quickly!" he cried. "We should have overcome them alive, and then taken our time about dealing with them as they deserved." He went on to specify the nature of their deserts. "Such infamy!"

"Well, I'll swear I didn't think a little tap like I gave that one would kill him," the bottle-wielder excused himself. "Of course, I was thinking only of Nebu-hin-Abenoz, Safar receive him—"

Antrath Alv bent over the one he had hand-chopped.

"I didn't kill this one," he said. "The way I hit him, if I had, his neck would be broken, and it's not. See?" He twisted at the dead man's neck. "I think they took poison before they drew their knives."

"I saw all of them put their hands to their mouths!" a Calera exclaimed. "And look; see how their jaws are clenched." He picked up one of the knives and used it to pry the dead man's jaws apart, sniffing at his lips and looking into his mouth. "Look, his teeth and his tongue are discolored; there is a strange smell, too."

Antrath Alv sniffed, then turned to his partner. "Halatane," he whispered. Gathon Dard nodded. That was a First Level poison; paratimers often carried halatane capsules on the more barbaric time-lines, as a last insurance against torture.

"But, Holy Name of Safar, what manner of men were these?" Coru-hin-Irigod demanded. "There are those I would risk my life to kill, but I would not throw it away thus."

"They came knowing that we would kill them, and took the poison that they might die quickly and without pain," a Calera said.

"Or that your tortures would not wring from them the names and nation of those who sent them," an elderly man in the dress of a rancher from the southeast added. "If I were you, I would try to find out who these enemies are, and the sooner the better."

Gathon Dard was examining one of the knives—a folding knife with a broad single-edged blade, locked open with a spring; the handle was of tortoise shell, bolstered with brass.

"In all my travels," he said, "I never saw a knife of this workmanship before. Tell me, Coru-hin-Irigod, do you know from what country these outland slaves of Nebu-hin-Abenoz's come?"

"You think that might have something to do with it?" the Calera asked.

"It could. I think that these people might not have been born slaves, but people taken captive. Suppose, at some time, there had been sold to Nebu-hin-Abenoz, and sold elsewhere by him, one who was a person of consequence—the son of a king, or the priest of some god," Gathon Dard suggested.

"By Safar, yes! And now that nation, wherever it is, is at blood-feud with us," Cavu-hin-Avoran said. "This must be thought about; it is an ill thing to have unknown enemies."

"Look!" a Calera who had begun to strip the three dead men cried. "These are not of the Usasu cities, or any other people of this land. See, they are uncircumcised!"

"Many of the slaves whom Nebu-hin-Abenoz brought to Careba from the hills have been uncircumcised," Coru-hin-Irigod said. "Jeseru, I think you have your sights on the heart of it." He frowned. "Now, think you, will those who had this done be satisfied, or will they carry on their hatred against all of us?"

"A hard question," Antrath Alv said. "You Caleras do not serve our gods, but you are our friends. Suffer me to go apart and pray; I would take counsel with the gods, that they may aid us all in this."

Part 2

It was full daylight, but the sun was hidden; a thin rain fell on the landing around at Police Terminal Dhergabar Equivalent when Vall and Dalla left the rocket. Across the black lavalike pavement, they could see the bulky form of Tortha Karf, hunched under a long cloak, with his flat cap pulled down over his brow. He shook hands with Vall and kissed cheeks with Dalla when they joined him.

"Car's over here," he said, nodding toward the waiting vehicle. "Yesterday wasn't one of our better days, was it?"

"No. It wasn't." Vall agreed. They climbed into the car, and the driver lifted straight up to two thousand feet and turned, soaring down to land on the Chief's Headquarters Building, a mile away. "We're not completely stopped, sir. Ranthar Jard is working on a few ideas that may lead him to the Kholghoor time lines where the Wizard Traders are operating. If we can't get them through their output, we may nail them at the intake."

"Unless they've gotten the wind up and closed down all their operations," Tortha Karf said.

"I doubt if they've done that, Chief," Vall replied. "We don't know who these people are, of course, and it's hard to judge their reactions, but they're willing to take chances for big gains. I believe they think they're safe, now that they've closed out the compromised time line and killed the only witness against them."

"Well, what's Ranthar Jard doing?"

"Trying to locate the sub-sector and probability belt from what the slaves can tell him about their religious beliefs, about the local king, and the prince of Jhirda, and the noble families of the neighborhood," Vall said. "When he has it localized as closely as he can, he's going to start pelting the whole paratemporal area with photographic auto-return balls dropped from aircars on Police Terminal over the spatial equivalents of a couple of Croutha-conquered cities. As soon as he gets a photo that shows Croutha with firearms, he'll have a Wizard Trader time line."

"Sounds simple," the Chief said. The car landed, and he helped Dalla out. "I suppose both you and he know how many chances against one he has of finding anything." They went over to an antigrav-shaft and floated down to the floor on which Tortha Karf had a duplicate of the office in the Paratime Building on Home Time Line. "It's the only chance we have, though."

"There's one thing that bothers me," Dalla said, as they entered the office and went back behind the horseshoe-shaped desk. "I understand that the news about this didn't break on Home Time Line till the late morning of One-Six-One Day. Nebu-hin-Abenoz was murdered at about 1700 local time, which would be 0100 this morning Dhergabar time. That would give this gang fourteen hours to hear the news, transmit it to their base, and get these three men hypno-conditioned, disguised, transposed to this Esaron Sector time line, and into Careba." She shook her head. "That's pretty fast work."

Tortha Karf looked sidewise at Verkan Vall. "Your girl has the makings of a cop, Vall," he commented.

"She's been a big help, on Esaron and Kholghoor Sectors," Vall said.

"She wants to stay with it and help me; I'll be very glad to have her with me."

Tortha Karf nodded. He knew, too, that Dalla wouldn't want to have to go back to Home Time Line and wait the long investigation out.

"Of course; we can use all the help we can get. I think we can get a lot from Dalla. Fix her up with some kind of a title and police status—technical-expert, assistant, or something like that." He clasped hands, man-fashion, with her. "Glad to have you on the cops with us, Dalla," he said. Then he turned to Vall. "There was almost twenty-four hours between the time I heard about this and when this blasted Yandar Yadd got hold of the story. Of all the infernal, irresponsible—" He almost choked with indignation. "And it was another fourteen hours between the time Skordran sent in his report and I heard about it."

"Golzan Doth sent in a report to his company about the same time Skordran Kirv made his first report to his Sector-Regional Subchief." Vall mentioned.

"That might be it," Tortha Karf considered. "I wish there were another explanation, because that implies a very extensive intelligence network, which means a big organization. But I'm afraid that's it. I wish I could pull in everybody in Consolidated Outtime Foodstuffs who handled that report, and narco-hypnotize them. Of course, we can't do things like that on Home Time Line, and with the political situation what it is now—"

"Why, what's been happening, Chief?"

Tortha Karf swore with weary bitterness. "Salgath Trod's what's been happening. At first, after Yandar Yadd broke the story on the air, there was just a lot of unorganized Opposition sniping in Council; Salgath waited till the middle of the afternoon, when the Management members were beginning to rally, and took the floor. The Centrists and Right Moderates were trying the appeal-to-reason approach; that did as much good as trying to put out a Fifth Level forest fire with a hand-extinguisher. Finally. Salgath got a motion of censure against the Management recognized. That means a confidence vote in ten days. Salgath has a rabble of Leftists and dissident Centrists with him; I doubt if he can muster enough votes to overturn the Management, but it's going to make things rough for us."

"Which may be just the reason Salgath started this uproar," Vall suggested.

"That," Tortha Karf said, "is being considered; there is a discreet inquiry being made into Salgath Trod's associates, his sources of income, and so on. Nothing has turned up as yet, but we have hopes."

"I believe," Vall said, "that we have a better chance right on Home Time Line than outtime."

Tortha Karf looked up sharply. "So?" he asked.

Vall was stuffing tobacco into a pipe. "Yes. Chief. We have a big criminal organization—let's call it the Slave Trust, for a convenience-label. The people who run it aren't stupid. The fact that they've been shipping slaves to the Esaron Sector for ten years before we found out about it proves that. So does the speed with which they got rid of this Nebu-hin-Abenoz, right in front of a pair of our detectives. For that matter, so does the speed with which they moved in to exploit this Croutha invasion of Kholghoor Sector India.

"Well, I've studied illegal and subversive organizations all over paratime, and among the really successful ones, there are a few uniform principles. One is cellular organization—small groups, acting in isolation from one another, coöperating with other cells but ignorant of their composition. Another is the principle of no upward contact—leaders contacting their subordinates through contact-blocks and ignorant intermediaries. And another is a willingness to kill off anybody who looks like a potential betrayer or forced witness. The late Nebu-hin-Abenoz, for instance.

"I'll be willing to bet that if we pick up some of these Wizard Traders, say, or a gang that's selling slaves to some Nebu-hin-Abenoz personality on some other time line, and narco-hypnotize them, all they'll be able to do will be name a few immediate associates, and the group leader will know that he's contacted from time to time by some stranger with orders, and that he can make emergency contacts only through some blind accommodation-address. The men who are running this are right on Home Time Line, many of them in positions of prominence, and if we can catch one of them and narco-hyp him, we can start a chain-reaction of disclosures all through this Slave Trust."

"How are we going to get at these top men?" Tortha Karf wanted to know. "Advertise for them on telecast?"

"They'll leave traces; they won't be able to avoid it. I think, right now, that Salgath Trod is one of them. I think there are other prominent politicians, and business people. Look for irregularities and peculiarities in outtime currency-exchange transactions. For instance, to sections in Esaron Sector *obus*. Or big gold bullion transactions."

"Yes. And if they have any really elaborate outtime bases, they'll need equipment that can only be gotten on Home Time Line," Tortha Karf added. "Paratemporal conveyer parts, and field-conductor mesh. You can't just walk into a hardware store and buy that sort of thing."

Dalla leaned forward to drop her cigarette ash into a tray.

"Try looking into the Bureau of Psychological Hygiene," she suggested. "That's where you'll really strike it rich."

Vall and Tortha Karf both turned abruptly and looked at her for an instant.

"Go on," Tortha Karf encouraged. "This sounds interesting."

"The people back of this," Dalla said, "are definitely classifiable as criminals. They may never perform a criminal act themselves, but they give orders for and profit from such acts, and they must possess the motivation and psychology of criminals. We define people as criminals when they suffer from psychological aberrations of an antisocial character, usually paranoid—excessive egoism, disregard for the rights of others, inability to recognize the social necessity for mutual coöperation and confidence. On Home Time Line, we have universal psychological testing, for the purpose of detecting and eliminating such characteristics."

"It seems to have failed in this case," Tortha Karf began, then snapped his fingers. "Of course! How blasted silly can I get, when I'm not trying?"

"Yes, of course," Verkan Vall agreed. "Find out how these people missed being spotted by psychotesting; that'll lead us to *who* missed being tested adequately, and also who got into the Bureau of Psychological Hygiene who didn't belong there."

"I think you ought to give an investigation of the whole BuPsych-Hyg setup very high priority," Dalla said. "A psychotest is only as good as the people who give it, and if we have criminals administering these tests—"

"We have our friends on Executive Council," Tortha Karf said. "I'll see that that point is raised when Council re-convenes." He looked at the clock. "That'll be in three hours, by the way. If it doesn't accomplish another thing, it'll put Salgath Trod in the middle. He can't demand an investigation of the Paratime Police out of one side of his mouth and oppose an investigation of Psychological Hygiene out of the other. Now what else have we to talk about?"

"Those hundred slaves we got off the Esaron Sector," Vall said. "What are we going to do with them? And if we locate the time line the slavers have their bases on, we'll have hundreds, probably thousands, more."

"We can't sort them out and send them back to their own time lines, even if that would be desirable," Tortha Karf decided. "Why, settle them somewhere on the Service Sector. I know, the Paratime Transposition Code limits the Service Sector to natives of time lines below second-order barbarism, but the Paratime Transposition Code has been so badly battered by this business that a few more minor literal infractions here and there won't make any difference. Where are they now?"

"Police Terminal, Nharkan Equivalent."

"Better hold them there, for the time being. We may have to open a new ServSec time line to take care of all the slaves we find, if we can locate the outtime base line these people are using—Vall, this thing's too big to handle as a routine operation, along with our other work. You take charge of it. Set up your headquarters here, and help yourself to anything in the way of personnel and equipment you need. And bear in mind that this confidence vote is coming up in ten days—on the morning of One-Seven-Two Day. I'm not asking for any miracles, but if we don't get this thing cleared up by then, we're in for trouble."

"I realize that, sir. Dalla, you'd better go back to Home Time Line, with the Chief," he said. "There's nothing you can do to help me, here, at present. Get some rest, and then try to wangle an invitation for the two of us to dinner at Thalvan Dras' apartments this evening." He turned back to Tortha Karf. "Even if he never pays any attention to business, Dras still owns Consolidated Outtime Foodstuffs," he said. "He might be able to find out, or help us find out, how the story about those slaves leaked out of his company."

"Well, that won't take much doing," Dalla said. "If there's as much excitement on Home Time Line as I think, Dras would turn somersaults and jump through hoops to get us to one of his dinners, right now."

* * * *

Salgath Trod pushed the litter of papers and record-tape spools to one side impatiently.

"Well, what else did you expect?" he demanded. "This was the logical next move. BuPsychHyg is supposed to detect anybody who believes in looking out for his own interests first, and condition him into a pious law-abiding sucker. Well, the sacred Bureau of Sucker-Makers slipped up on a lot of us. It's a natural alibi for Tortha Karf."

"It's also a lot of grief for all of us," the young man in the wraparound tunic added. "I don't want my psychotests reviewed by some duty-struck bigot who can't be reasoned with, and neither do you."

"I'm getting something organized to counter that," Salgath Trod said. "I'm going to attack the whole scientific basis of psychotesting. There's Dr. Frasthor Klav; he's always contended that what are called criminal tendencies are the result of the individual's total environment, and that psychotesting and personality-analysis are valueless, because the total environment changes from day to day, even from hour to hour—"

"That won't do," the nameless young man who was the messenger of somebody equally nameless retorted. "Frasthor's a crackpot; no reputable psychologist or psychist gives his opinions a moment's consideration. And besides, we don't want to attack Psychological Hygiene. The people in it with whom we can do business are our safeguard; they've given all of us a clean bill of mental health, and we have papers to prove it. What we have to do is to make it appear that that incident on the Esaron Sector is all there is to this, and also involve the Paratime Police themselves. The slavers are all paracops. It isn't the fault of BuPsychHyg, because the Paratime Police have their own psychotesting staff. That's where the trouble is; the paracops haven't been adequately testing their own personnel."

"Now how are you going to do that?" Salgath Trod asked disdainfully.

"You'll take the floor, the first thing tomorrow, and utilize these new revelations about the Wizard Traders. You'll accuse the Paratime Police of being the Wizard Traders themselves. Why not? They have their own paratemporal transposition equipment shops on Police Terminal, they have facilities for manufacturing duplicates of any kind of outtime items, like the firearms, for instance, and they know which time lines on which sectors are being exploited by legitimate paratime traders and which aren't. What's to prevent a gang of unscrupulous paracops from moving in on a few unexploited Kholghoor time lines, buying captives from the Croutha, and shipping them to the Esaron Sector?"

"Then why would they let a thing like this get out?" Salgath Trod inquired.

"Somebody slipped up and moved a lot of slaves onto an exploited Esaron time line. Or, rather, Consolidated Outtime Foodstuffs established a plantation on a time line they were shipping slaves to. Parenthetically, that's what really did happen; the mistake our people made was in not closing out that time line as soon as Consolidated Foodstuffs moved in," the young man said.

"So, this Skordran Kirv, who is a dumb boy who doesn't know what the score is, found these slaves and blatted about it to this Golzan Doth, and Golzan reported it to his company, and it couldn't be hushed up, so now Tortha Karf is trying to scare the public with ghost stories about a gigantic paratemporal conspiracy, to get more appropriations and more power."

"How long do you think I'd get away with that?" Salgath Trod demanded. "I can only stretch parliamentary immunity so far. Sooner or later, I'd have to make formal charges to a special judicial committee, and that would mean narco-hypnosis, and then it would all come out."

"You'll have proof," the young man said. "We'll produce a couple of these Kharandas whom Verkan Vall didn't get hold of. Under narco-hypnosis, they'll testify that they saw a couple of Wizard Traders take their robes off. Under the robes were Paratime Police uniforms. Do you follow me?"

Salgath Trod made a noise of angry disgust.

"That's ridiculous! I suppose these Kharandas will be given what is deludedly known as memory obliteration, and a set of pseudo-memories; how long do you think that would last? About three ten-days. There is no such thing as memory obliteration; there's memory-suppression, and pseudo-memory overlay. You can't get behind that with any quickie narco-hypnosis in the back room of any police post, I'll admit that," he said. "But a skilled psychist can discover, inside of five minutes, when a narco-hypnotized subject is carrying a load of false memories, and in time, and not too much time, all that top layer of false memories and blockages can be peeled off. And then where would we be?"

"Now wait a minute, Councilman. This isn't just something I dreamed up," the visitor said. "This was decided upon at the top. At the very top."

"I don't care whose idea it was," Salgath Trod snapped. "The whole thing is idiotic, and I won't have anything to do with it."

The visitor's face froze. All the respect vanished from his manner and tone; his voice was like ice cakes grating together in a winter river.

"Look, Salgath; this is an Organization order," he said. "You don't refuse to obey Organization orders, and you don't quit the Organization. Now get smart, big boy; do what you're told to." He took a spool of record tape from his pocket and laid it on the desk. "Outline for your speech; put it in your own words, but follow it exactly." He stood watching Salgath Trod for a moment. "I won't bother telling you what'll happen to you if you don't," he added. "You can figure that out for yourself."

With that, he turned and went out the private door. For a while, Salgath Trod sat staring after him. Once he put his hand out toward the spool, then jerked it back as though the thing were radioactive. Once he looked at the clock; it was just 1600.

* * * *

The green aircar settled onto the landing stage; Verkan Vall, on the front seat beside the driver, opened the door.

"Want me to call for you later, Assistant Verkan?" the driver asked.

"No thank you, Drenth. My wife and I are going to a dinner-party, and we'll probably go night-clubbing afterward. Tomorrow morning, all the anti-Management commentators will be yakking about my carousing around when I ought to be battling the Slave Trust. No use advertising myself with an official car, and giving them a chance to add, 'at public expense.'"

"Well, have some fun while you can," the driver advised, reaching for the car-radio phone. "Want me to check you in here, sir?"

"Yes, if you will. Thank you. Drenth."

Kandagro, his human servant, admitted him to the apartment six floors down.

"Mistress Dalla is dressing," he said. "She asked me to tell you that you are invited to dinner, this evening, with Thalvan Dras at his apartment."

Vall nodded. "Ill talk to her about it now," he said. "Lay out my dress uniform: short jacket, boots and breeches, and needler."

"Yes, master: I'll go lay out your things and get your bath ready."

The servant turned and went into the alcove which gave access to the dressing rooms, turning right into Vall's. Vall followed him, turning left into his wife's.

"Oh, Dalla!" he called.

"In here!" her voice came out of her bathroom.

He passed through the dressing room, to find her stretched on a plastic-sheeted couch, while her maid, Rendarra, was rubbing her body vigorously with some pungent-smelling stuff about the consistency of machine-grease. Her face was masked in the stuff, and her hair was covered with an elastic cap. He had always suspected that beauty was the real feminine religion, from the willingness of its devotees to submit to martyrdom for it. She wiggled a hand at him in greeting.

"How did it go?" she asked.

"So-so. I organized myself a sort of miniature police force within a police force and I have liaison officers in every organization down to Sector Regional so that I can be informed promptly in case anything new turns up anywhere. What's been happening on Home Time Line? I picked up a news-summary at Paratime Police Headquarters; it seems that a lot more stuff has leaked out. Kholghoor Sector, Wizard Traders and all. How'd it happen?"

Dalla rolled over to allow Rendarra to rub the blue-green grease on her back.

"Consolidated Outtime Foodstuffs let a gang of reporters in, today. I think they're afraid somebody will accuse them of complicity, and they want to get their side of it before the public. All our crowd are off that Time line except a couple of detectives at the plantation."

"I know." He smiled; Dalla was thinking of the Paratime Police as "our crowd" now. "How about this dinner at Dras' place?"

"Oh, that was easy." She shifted position again. "I just called Dras up and told him that our vacation was off, and he invited us before I could begin hinting. What are you going to wear?"

"Short-jacket greens; I can carry a needler with that uniform, even wear it at the table. I don't think it's smart for me to run around unarmed, even on Home Time Line. Especially on Home Time Line," he amended. "When's this affair going to start, and how long will Rendarra take to get that goo off you?"

* * * *

Salgath Trod left his aircar at the top landing stage of his apartment building and sent it away to the hangars under robot control; he glanced about him as he went toward the antigrav shaft. There were a dozen vehicles in the air above; any of them might have followed him from the Paratime Building. He had no doubt that he had been under constant surveillance from the moment the nameless messenger had delivered the Organization's ultimatum. Until he delivered that speech, the next morning, or manifested an intention of refusing to do so, however, he would be safe. After that—

Alone in his office, he had reviewed the situation point by point, and then gone back and reviewed it again; the conclusion was inescapable. The Organization had ordered him to make an accusation which he himself knew to be false; that was the first premise. The conclusion was that he would be killed as soon as he had made it. That was the trouble with being mixed up with that kind of people—you were expendable, and sooner or later, they would decide that they would have to expend you. And what could you do?

To begin with, an accusation of criminal malfeasance made against a Management or Paratime Commission agency on the floor of Executive Council was tantamount to an accusation made in court; automatically, the accuser became a criminal prosecutor, and would have to repeat his accusation under narco-hypnosis. Then the whole story would come out, bit by bit, back to its beginning in that first illegal deal in Indo-Turanian opium, diverted from trade with the Khiftan Sector and sold on Second Level Luvarian Empire Sector, and the deals in radioactive poisons, and the slave trade. He would be able to name few names—the Organization kept its activities too well compartmented for that—but he could talk of things that had happened, and when, and where, and on what paratemporal areas.

No. The Organization wouldn't let that happen, and the only way it could be prevented would be by the death of Salgath Trod, as soon as he had made his speech. All the talk of providing him with corroborative evidence was silly; it had been intended to lead him more trustingly to the slaughter. They'd kill him, of course, in some way that would be calculated to substantiate the story he would no longer be able to repudiate. The killer, who would be promptly rayed dead by somebody else, would wear a Paratime Police uniform, or something like that. That was of no importance, however; by then, he'd be beyond caring.

One of his three ServSec Prole servants—the slim brown girl who was his housekeeper and hostess, and also his mistress—admitted him to the apartment. He kissed her perfunctorily and closed the door behind him.

"You're tired," she said. "Let me call Nindrandigro and have him bring you chilled wine; lie down and rest until dinner."

"No, no; I want brandy." He went to a cellaret and got out a decanter and goblet, pouring himself a drink. "How soon will dinner be ready?"

The brown girl squeezed a little golden globe that hung on a chain around her neck; a tiny voice, inside it, repeated: "Eighteen twenty-three ten, eighteen twenty-three eleven, eighteen twenty-three twelve—"

"In half an hour. It's still in the robo-chef," she told him.

He downed half the goblet-full, set it down, and went to a painting, a brutal scarlet and apple-green abstraction, that hung on the wall. Swinging it aside and revealing the safe behind it, he used his identity-sigil, took out a wad of Paratemporal Exchange Bank notes and gave them to the girl.

"Here, Zinganna; take these, and take Nindrandigro and Calilla out for the evening. Go where you can all have a good time, and don't come back till after midnight. There will be some business transacted here, and I want them out of this. Get them out of here as soon as you can; I'll see to the dinner myself. Spend all of that you want to."

The girl riffled through the wad of banknotes. "Why, *thank* you, Trod!" She threw her arms around his neck and kissed him enthusiastically. "I'll go tell them at once."

"And have a good time, Zinganna; have the best time you possibly can," he told her, embracing and kissing her. "Now, get out of here; I have to keep my mind on business."

When she had gone, he finished his drink and poured another. He drew and checked his needler. Then, after checking the window-shielding and activating the outside viewscreens, he lit a cheroot and sat down at the desk, his goblet and his needler in front of him, to wait until the servants were gone.

There was only one way out alive. He knew that, and yet he needed brandy, and a great deal of mental effort, to steel himself for it. Psycho-rehabilitation was a dreadful thing to face. There would be almost a year of unremitting agony, physical and mental, worse than a Khiftan torture rack. There would be the shame of having his innermost secrets poured out of him by the psychotherapists, and, at the end, there would emerge someone who would not be Salgath Trod, or anybody like Salgath Trod, and he would have to learn to know this stranger, and build a new life for him.

In one of the viewscreens, he saw the door to the service hallway open. Zinganna, in a black evening gown and a black velvet cloak, and Calilla, the housemaid, in what she believed to be a reasonable facsimile of fashionable First Level dress, and Nindrandigro, in one of his master's evening suits, emerged. Salgath Trod waited until they had gone down the hall to the antigrav shaft, and then he turned on the visiphone, checked the security, set it for sealed beam communication, and punched out a combination.

A girl in a green tunic looked out of the screen.

"Paratime Police," she said. "Office of Chief Tortha."

"I am Executive Councilman Salgath Trod," he told her. "I am, and for the past fifteen years have been, criminally involved with the organization responsible for the slave trade which recently came to light on Third Level Esaron. I give myself up unconditionally; I am willing to make full confession under narco-hypnosis, and will accept whatever disposition of my case is lawfully judged fit. You'll have to send an escort for me; I might start from my apartment alone, but I'd be killed before I got to your headquarters—"

The girl, who had begun to listen in the bored manner of public servants phone girls, was staring wide-eyed.

"Just a moment, Councilman Salgath; I'll put you through to Chief Tortha."

* * * *

The dinner lacked a half hour of being served; Thalvan Dras' guests loitered about the drawing room, sampling appetizers and chilled drinks and chatting in groups. It wasn't the artistic crowd usual at Thalvan Dras' dinners; most of the guests seemed to be business or political people. Thalvan Dras had gotten Vall and Dalla into the small group around him, along with pudgy, infantile-faced Brogoth Zaln, his confidential secretary, and Javrath Brend, his financial attorney.

"I don't see why they're making such a fuss about it," one of the Banking Cartel people was saying. "Causing a lot of public excitement all out of proportion to the importance of the affair. After all, those people were slaves on their own time line, and if anything, they're much better off on the Esaron Sector than they would be as captives of the Croutha. As far as that goes, what's the difference between that and the way we drag these Fourth Level Primitive Sector-Complex people off to Fifth Level Service Sector to work for us?"

"Oh, there's a big difference, Farn," Javrath Brend said. "We recruit those Fourth Level Primitives out of probability worlds of Stone Age savagery, and transpose them to our own Fifth Level time lines, practically outtime extensions of the Home Time Line. There's absolutely no question of the Paratime Secret being compromised."

"Beside, we need a certain amount of human labor, for tasks requiring original thought and decision that are beyond the ability of robots, and most of it is work our Citizens simply wouldn't perform," Thalvan Dras added.

"Well, from a moral standpoint, wouldn't these Esaron Sector people who buy the slaves justify slavery in the same terms?" a woman whom Vall had identified as a Left Moderate Council Member asked.

"There's still a big difference," Dalla told her. "The ServSec Proles aren't beaten or tortured or chained; we don't break up families or separate friends. When we recruit Fourth Level Primitives, we take whole tribes, and they come willingly. And—"

One of Thalvan Dras' black-liveried human servants, of the class under discussion, approached Vall.

"A visiphone call for your lordship," he whispered. "Chief Tortha Karf calling. If your lordship will come this way—"

In a screen-booth outside, Vall found Tortha Karf looking out of the screen; he was seated at his desk, fiddling with a gold multicolor pen.

"Oh, Vall; something interesting has just come up." He spoke in a voice of forced calmness. "I can't go into it now, but you'll want to hear about it. I'm sending a car for you. Better bring Dalla along; she'll want in on it, too."

"Right; we'll be on the top south-west landing stage in a few minutes."

Dalla was still heatedly repudiating any resemblance between the normal First Level methods of labor-recruitment and the activities of the Wizard Traders; she had just finished the story of the woman whose child had been brained when Vall rejoined the group.

"Dras, I'm awfully sorry," he said. "This is the second time in succession that Dalla and I have had to bolt away from here, but policemen are like doctors—always on call, and consequently unreliable guests. While you're feasting, think commiseratingly of Dalla and me; we'll probably be having a sandwich and a cup of coffee somewhere."

"I'm terribly sorry." Thalvan Dras replied. "We had all been looking forward—Well! Brogoth, have a car called for Vall and Dalla."

"Police car coming for us; it's probably on the landing stage now," Vall said. "Well, good-by, everybody. Coming, Dalla?"

* * * *

They had a few minutes to wait, under the marquee, before the green police aircar landed and came rolling across the rain-wet surface of the landing stage. Crossing to it and opening the rear door, he put Dalla in and climbed in after her, slamming the door. It was only then that he saw Tortha Karf hunched down in the rear seat. He motioned them to silence, and did not speak until the car was rising above the building.

"I wanted to fill you in on this, as soon as possible," he said. "Your hunch about Salgath Trod was good; just a few minutes before I called you, he called me. He says this slave trade is the work of something he calls the Organization; says he's been taking orders from them for years. His attack on the Management and motion for a censure-vote were dictated from Organization top echelon. Now he's convinced that they're going to force him to make false accusations against the Paratime Police and then kill him before he's compelled to repeat his charges under narco-hypnosis. So he's offered to surrender and trade information for protection."

"How much does he know?" Vall asked.

Tortha Karf shook his head. "Not as much as he claims to, I suppose; he wouldn't want to reduce his own trade-in value. But he's been involved in this thing for the last fifteen years, and with his political prominence, he'd know quite a lot."

"We can protect him from his own gang; can we protect him from psycho-rehabilitation?"

"No, and he knows it. He's willing to accept that. He seems to think that death at the hands of his own associates is the only other alternative. Probably right, too.”

The floodlighted green towers of the Paratime Building were wheeling under them as they circled down.

“Why would they sacrifice a valuable accomplice like Salgath Trod, in order to make a transparently false accusation against us?” Vall wondered.

“Ha, that’s our new rookie cop’s idea!” Tortha Karf chuckled, nodding toward Dalla. “We got Zortan Harn to introduce an urgent-business motion to appoint a committee to investigate BuPsychHyg, this morning. The motion passed, and this is the reaction to it. The Organization’s scared. Just as Dalla predicted, they don’t want us finding out how people with potentially criminal characteristics missed being spotted by psychotesting. Salgath Trod is being sacrificed to block or delay that.”

Vall nodded as the wheels bumped on the landing stage and the antigrav field went off. That was the sort of thing that happened when you started on a really fruitful line of investigation. They got out and hurried over under the marquee, the car lifting and moving off toward the hangars. This was the real break; no matter how this Organization might be compartmented, a man like Salgath Trod would know a great deal. He would name names, and the bearers of those names, arrested and narco-hypnotized, would name other names, in a perfect chain reaction of confessions and betrayals.

Another police car had landed just ahead of them, and three men were climbing out; two were in Paratime Police green, and the third, hand-cuffed, was in Service Sector Proletarian garb. At first, Vall though that Salgath Trod had been brought in disguised as a Prole prisoner, and then he saw that the prisoner was short and stocky, not at all like the slender and elegant politician. The two officers who had brought him in were talking to a lieutenant, Sothran Barth, outside the antigrav shaft kiosk. As Vall and Tortha Karf and Dalla walked over, the car which had brought them lifted out.

“Something that just came in from Industrial Twenty-four, Chief,” Lieutenant Sothran said in answer to Tortha Karf’s question. “May be for Assistant Verkan’s desk.”

“He’s a Prole named Yandragno, sir,” one of the policemen said. “Industrial Sector Constabulary grabbed him peddling Martian hellweed cigarettes to the girls in a textile mill at Kangabar Equivalent. Captain

Jamzar thinks he may have gotten them from somebody in the Organization."

* * * *

A little warning bell began ringing in the back of Verkan Vall's mind, but at first he could not consciously identify the cause of his suspicions. He looked the two policemen and their prisoner over carefully, but could see nothing visibly wrong with them. Then another car came in for a landing and rolled over under the marquee; the door opened, and a police officer got out, followed by an elegantly dressed civilian whom he recognized at once as Salgath Trod. A second policeman was emerging from the car when Vall suddenly realized what it was that had disturbed him.

It had been Salgath Trod, himself, less than half an hour ago, who had introduced the term, "the Organization," to the Paratime Police. At that time, if these people were what they claimed to be, they would have been in transposition from Industrial Twenty-four, on the Fifth Level. Immediately, he reached for his needler. He was clearing it of the holster when things began happening.

The handcuffs fell from the "prisoner's" wrists; he jerked a neutron-disruption blaster from under his jacket. Vall, his needler already drawn, rayed the fellow dead before he could aim it, then saw that the two pseudo-policemen had drawn their needlers and were aiming in the direction of Salgath Trod. There were no flashes or reports; only the spot of light that had winked on and off under Vall's rear sight had told him that his weapon had been activated. He saw it appear again as the sights centered on one of the "policemen." Then he saw the other imposter's needler aimed at himself. That was the last thing he expected ever to see, in that life; he tried to shift his own weapon, and time seemed frozen, with his arm barely moving. Then there was a white blur as Dalla's cloak moved in front of him, and the needler dropped from the fingers of the disguised murderer. Time went back to normal for him; he safetied his own weapon and dropped it, jumping forward.

He grabbed the fellow in the green uniform by the nose with his left hand, and punched him hard in the pit of the stomach with his right fist. The man's mouth flew open, and a green capsule, the size and shape of a small bean, flew out. Pushing Dalla aside before she would step on it, he kicked the murderer in the stomach, doubling him over, and chopped him on the base of the skull with the edge of his hand. The pseudo-policeman dropped senseless.

With a handful of handkerchief-tissue from his pocket, he picked up the disgorged capsule, wrapping it carefully after making sure that it was unbroken. Then he looked around. The other two assassins were dead. Tortha Karf, who had been looking at the man in Proletarian dress whom Vall had killed first, turned, looked in another direction, and then cursed. Vall followed his eyes, and cursed also. One of the two police-men who had gotten out of the aircar was dead, too, and so was the all-important witness, Salgath Trod—as dead as Nebu-hin-Abenoz, a hundred thousand parayears away.

* * * *

The whole thing had ended within thirty seconds; for about half as long, everybody waited, poised in a sort of action-vacuum, for some-thing else to happen. Dalla had dropped the shoulder-bag with which she had clubbed the prisoner's needler out of his hand, and caught up the fallen weapon. When she saw that the man was down and motion-less, she laid it aside and began picking up the glittering or silken tri-fles that had spilled from the burst bag. Vall retrieved his own weapon, glanced over it, and holstered it. Sothran Barth, the lieutenant in charge of the landing stage, was bawling orders, and men were coming out of the ready-room and piling into vehicles to pursue the aircar which had brought the assassins.

"Barth!" Vall called. "Have you a hypodermic and a sleep-drug am-poule? Well, give this boy a shot; he's only impact-stunned. Be careful of him; he's important." He glanced around the landing-stage. "Fact is, he's all we have to show for this business."

Then he stooped to help Dalla gather her things, picking up a few of them—a lighter, a tiny crystal perfume flask, miraculously unbroken, a face-powder box which had sprung open and spilled half its contents. He handed them to her, while Sothran Barth bent over the prisoner and gave him an injection, then went to the body of the other pseudo-police-man, forcing open his mouth. In his cheek, still unbroken, was a second capsule, which he added to the first. Tortha Karf was watching him.

"Same gang that killed that Carera slaver on Esaron Sector?" he asked. "Of course, exactly the same general procedure. Let's have a look at the other one."

The man in Proletarian dress must have had his capsule between his molars when he had been killed; it was broken, and there was a brownish discoloration and chemical odor in his mouth.

"Second time we've had a witness killed off under our noses," Tortha Karf said. "We're going to have to smarten up in a hurry."

"Here's one of us who doesn't have to, much," Vall said, nodding toward Dalla. "She knocked a needler out of one man's hand, and we took him alive. The Force owes her a new shoulder-bag: she spoiled that one using it for a club."

"Best shoulder-bag we can find you, Dalla," Tortha Karf promised. "You're promoted, herewith, to Special Chief's Assistant's Special Assistant—You know, this Organization murder-section is good; they could kill anybody. It won't be long before they assign a squad to us. Blast it, I don't want to have to go around bodyguarded like a Fourth Level dictator, but—"

A detective came out of the control room and approached.

"Screen call for you, sir," he told Tortha Karf. "One of the news services wants a comment on a story they've just picked up that we've illegally arrested Councilman Salgath and are holding him incommunicado and searching his apartment."

"That's the Organization," Vall said. "They don't know how their boys made out; they're hoping we'll tell them."

"No comment," Tortha Karf said. "Call the girl on my switchboard and tell her to answer any other news-service calls. We have nothing to say at this time, but there will be a public statement at ... at 2330," he decided after a glance at his watch. "That'll give us time to agree on a publicity line to adopt. Lieutenant Sothran! Take charge up here. Get all these bodies out of sight somewhere, including those of Councilman Salgath and Detective Malthor. Don't let anybody talk about this; put a blackout on the whole story. Vall, you and Dalla and ... oh, you, over there; take the prisoner down to my office. Sothran, any reports from any of the cars that were chasing that fake police car?"

Verkan Vall and Dalla were sitting behind Tortha Karf's desk; Vall was issuing orders over the intercom and talking to the detectives who had remained at Salgath Trod's apartment by visiscreen; Dalla was sorting over the things she had spilled when her bag had burst. They both looked up as Tortha Karf came in and joined them.

"The prisoner's still under the drug," the Chief said. "He'll be out for a couple of hours; the psych-techs want to let him come out of it naturally and sleep naturally for a while before they give him a hypno. He's not a ServSec Prole; uncircumcised, never had any syntho-enzyme shots or immunizations, and none of the longevity operations or grafts. Same thing for the two stiffs. And no identity records on any of the three."

"The men at Salgath's apartment say that his housekeeper and his two servants checked out through the house conveyer for ServSec One-Six-Five, at about 1830," Vall said. "There's a Prole entertainment center on that time line. I suppose Salgath gave them the evening off before he called you."

Tortha Karf nodded. "I suppose you ordered them picked up. The news services are going wild about this. I had to make a preliminary statement, to the effect that Salgath Trod was not arrested, came to Headquarters of his own volition, and is under no restraint whatever."

"Except, of course, a slight case of rigor mortis," Dalla added. "Did you mention that, Chief?"

"No, I didn't." Tortha Karf looked as though he had quinine in his mouth. "Vall, how in blazes are we going to handle this?"

"We ought to keep Salgath's death hushed up, as long as we can," Vall said. "The Organization doesn't know positively what happened here; that's why they're handing out tips to the news services. Let's try to make them believe he's still alive and talking."

"How can we do it?"

"There ought to be somebody on the Force close enough to Salgath Trod's anthropometric specifications that our cosmeticians could work him over into a passable impersonation. Our story is that Salgath is on PolTerm, undergoing narco-hypnosis. We will produce an audio-visual of him as soon as he is out of narco-hyp. That will give us time to fix up an impersonator; We'll need a lot of sound-recordings of Salgath Trod's voice, of course—"

"I'll take care of the Home Time Line end of it; as soon as we get you an impersonator, you go to work with him. Now, let's see whom we can depend on to help us with this. Lovranth Rolk, of course; Home Time Line section of the Paratime Code Enforcement Division. And—"

* * * *

Verkan Vall and Dalla and Tortha Karf and four or five others looked across the desk and to the end of the room as the telecast screen broke into a shifting light-pattern and then cleared. The face of the announcer appeared; a young woman.

"And now, we bring you the statement which Chief Tortha of the Paratime Police has promised for this time. This portion of the program was audio-visually recorded at Paratime Police Headquarters earlier this evening."

Tortha Karf's face appeared on the screen. His voice began an announcement of how Executive Councilman Salgath Trod had called him by visiphone, admitting to complicity in the recently-discovered paratemporal slave-trade.

"Here is a recording of Councilman Salgath's call to me from his apartment to my office at 1945 this evening."

The screen-image shattered into light-shards and rebuilt itself: Salgath Trod, at his desk in the library of his apartment, the brandy-goblet and the needler within reach, appeared. He began to speak: from time to time the voice of Tortha Karf interrupted, questioning or prompting him.

"You understand that this confession renders you liable to psycho-rehabilitation?" Tortha Karf asked.

Yes, Councilman Salgath understood that.

"And you agree to come voluntarily to Paratime Police Headquarters, and you will voluntarily undergo narco-hypnotic interrogation?"

Yes, Salgath Trod agreed to that.

"I am now terminating the playback of Councilman Salgath's call to me," Tortha Karf said, re-appearing on the screen. "At this point Councilman Salgath began making a statement about his criminal activities, which we have on record. Because he named a number of his criminal associates, whom we have no intention of warning, this portion of Councilman Salgath's call cannot at this time be made public. We have no intention of having any of these suspects escape, or of giving their associates an opportunity to murder them to prevent their furnishing us with additional information. Incidentally, there was an attempt, made on the landing stage of Paratime Police Headquarters, to murder Councilman Salgath, when he was brought here guarded by Paratime Police officers—"

He went on to give a colorful and, as far as possible, truthful, account of the attack by the two pseudo-policemen and their pseudo-prisoner. As he told it, however, all three had been killed before they could accomplish their purpose, one of them by Salgath Trod himself.

The image of Tortha Karf was replaced by a view of the three assassins lying on the landing stage. They all looked dead, even the one who wasn't; there was nothing to indicate that he was merely drugged. Then, one after another, their faces were shown in closeup, while Tortha Karf asked for close attention and memorization.

"We believe that these men were Fifth Level Proles; we think that they were under hypnotic influence or obeying posthypnotic commands when they made their suicidal attack. If any of you have ever seen any of these men before, it is your duty to inform the Paratime Police."

* * * *

That ended it. Tortha Karf pressed a button in front of him and the screen went dark. The spectators relaxed.

"Well! Nothing like being sincere with the public, is there?" Della commented. "I'll remember this the next time I tune in a Management public statement."

"In about five minutes," one of the bureau-chiefs, said, "all hell is going to break loose. I think the whole thing is crazy!"

"I hope you have somebody who can give a convincing impersonation," Lovranth Rolk said.

"Yes. A field agent named Kostran Galth," Tortha Karf said. "We ran the personal description cards for the whole Force through the machine; Kostran checked to within one-twentieth of one per cent; he's on Police Terminal, now, coming by rocket from Ravvanan Equivalent. We ought to have the whole thing ready for telecast by 1730 tomorrow."

"He can't learn to imitate Salgath's voice convincingly in that time, with all the work the cosmeticians'll have to be doing on him," Dalla said.

"Make up a tape of Salgath's own voice, out of that pile of recordings we got at his apartment, and what we can get out of the news file." Vall said. "We have phoneticists who can split syllables and splice them together. Kostran will deliver his speech in dumb-show, and we'll dub the sound in and telecast them as one. I've messaged PolTerm to get to work on that; they can start as soon as we have the speech written."

"The more it succeeds now, the worse the blow-up will be when we finally have to admit that Salgath was killed here tonight," the Chief Inter-officer Coördinator, Zostha Olv said. "We'd better have something to show the public to justify that."

"Yes, we had," Tortha Karf agreed. "Vall, how about the Kholghoor Sector operation. How far's Ranthar Jard gotten toward locating one of those Wizard Trader time lines?"

"Not very far," Vall admitted. "He has it pinned down to the sub-sector, but the belt seems to be one we haven't any information at all for. Never been any legitimate penetration by paratimers. He has his own hagiologists, and a couple borrowed from Outtime Religious Institute; they've gotten everything the slaves can give them on that. About the only thing to do is start random observation with boomerang-balls."

"Over about a hundred thousand time lines," Zostha Olv scoffed. He was an old man, even for his long-lived race; he had a thin nose and a narrow, bitter, mouth. "And what will he look for?"

"Croutha with guns." Tortha Karf told him, then turned to Vall. "Can't he narrow it more than that? What have his experts been getting out of those slaves?"

"That I don't know, to date." Vall looked at the clock. "I'll find out, though; I'll transpose to Police Terminal and call him up. And Skordran Kirv. No. Vulthor Tharn; it'd hurt the old fellow's feelings if I by-passed him and went to one of his subordinates. Half an hour each way, and at most another hour talking to Ranthar and Vulthor; there won't be anything doing here for two hours." He rose. "See you when I get back."

Dalla had turned on the telescreen again; after tuning out a dance orchestra and a comedy show, she got the image of an angry-faced man in evening clothes.

"... And I'm going to demand a full investigation, as soon as Council convenes tomorrow morning!" he was shouting. "This whole story is a preposterous insult to the integrity of the entire Executive Council, your elected representatives, and it shows the criminal lengths to which this would-be dictator, Tortha Karf, and his jackal Verkan Vall will go—"

"So long, jackal." Dalla called to him as he went out.

* * * *

He spent the half-hour transposition to Police Terminal sleeping.

Paratime-transpositions and rocket-flights seemed to be his only chance to get any sleep. He was still sleepy when he sat down in front of the radio telescreen behind his duplicate of Tortha Karf's desk and put through a call to Nharkan Equivalent. It was 0600 in India; the Sector Regional Deputy Subchief who was holding down Ranthar Jard's desk looked equally sleepy; he had a mug of coffee in front of him, and a brown-paper cigarette in his mouth.

"Oh, hello, Assistant Verkan. Want me to call Subchief Ranthar?"

"Is he sleeping? Then for mercy's sake don't. What's the present status of the investigation?"

"Well, we were dropping boomerang balls yesterday, while we had sun to mask the return-flashes. Nothing. The Croutha have taken the city of Sohram, just below the big bend of the river. Tomorrow, when we have sunlight, we're going to start boomerang-balling the central square. We may get something."

"The Wizard Traders'll be moving in near there, about now," Vall said. "The Croutha ought to have plenty of merchandise for them. Have you gotten anything more done on narrowing down the possible area?"

The deputy bit back a yawn and reached for his coffee mug.

"The experts have just about pumped these slaves empty," he said. "The local religion is a mess. Seems to have started out as a Great Mother cult; then it picked up a lot of gods borrowed from other peoples; then it turned into a dualistic monotheism; then it picked up a lot of minor gods and devils—new devils usually gods of the older pantheon. And we got a lot of gossip about the feudal wars and faction-fights among the nobility, and so on, all garbled, because these people are peasants who only knew what went on on the estate of their own lord."

"What did go on there?" Vall asked. "Ask them about recent improvements, new buildings, new fields cleared, new paddies flooded, that sort of thing. And pick out a few of the highest IQ's from both time lines, and have them locate this estate on a large-scale map, and draw plans showing the location of buildings, fields and other visible features. If you have to, teach them mapping and sketching by hypno-mech. And then drop about five hundred to a thousand boomerang balls, at regular intervals, over the whole paratemporal area. When you locate a time line that gives you a picture to correspond to their description, boomerang the main square in Sohram over the whole belt around it, to find Croutha with firearms."

The deputy looked at him for a moment then gulped more coffee.

"Can do, Assistant Verkan. I think I'll send somebody to wake up Subchief Ranthar, right now. Want to talk to him."

"Won't be necessary. You're recording this call, of course? Then play it back to him. And get cracking with the slaves; you want enough information out of them to enable you to start boomerang balling as soon as the sun's high enough."

* * * *

He broke off the connection and sent out for coffee for himself. Then he put through a call to Novilan Equivalent, in western North America.

It was 1530, there, when he got Vulthor Tharn on the screen.

"Good afternoon. Assistant Verkan. I suppose you're calling about the slave business. I've turned the entire matter over to Field Agent Skordran; gave him a temporary rank of Deputy Subchief. That's subject to your approval and Chief Tortha's, of course—"

"Make the appointment permanent," Vall said. "I'll have a confirmation along from Chief Tortha directly. And let me talk to him now, if you please. Subchief Vulthor."

"Yes, sir. Switching you over now." The screen went into a beautiful burst of abstract art, and cleared, after a while, with Skordran Kirv looking out of it.

"Hello, Deputy Skordran, and congratulations. What's come up since we had Nebu-hin-Abenoz cut out from under us?"

"We went in on that time line, that same night, with an airboat and made a recon in the hills back of Careba. Scared the fear of Safar into a party of Caleras while we were working at low altitude, by the way. We found the conveyer-head site: hundred-foot circle with all the grass and loose dirt transposed off it and a pole pen, very unsanitary where about two-three hundred slaves would be kept at a time. No indications of use in the last ten days. We did some pretty thorough boomeranging on that spatial equivalent over a couple of thousand time lines and found thirty more of them. I believe the slavers have closed out the whole Esaron Sector operation, at least temporarily."

That was what he'd been afraid of; he hoped they wouldn't do the same thing on the Kholghoor Sector.

"Let me have the designations of the time lines on which you found conveyer heads," he said.

"Just a moment, Chief's Assistant; I'll photoprint them to you. Set for reception?"

Vall opened a slide under the screen and saw that the photoprint film was in place, then closed it again, nodding. Skordran Kirv fed a sheet of paper into his screen cabinet and his arm moved forward out of the picture.

"On, sir," he said. He and Vall counted ten seconds together, and then Skordran Kirv said: "Through to you." Vall pressed a lever under his screen, and a rectangle of microcopy print popped out.

"That's about all I have, sir. Want me to keep my troops ready here, or shall I send them somewhere else?"

"Keep them ready, Kirv," Vall told him. "You may need them before long. Call you later."

He put the microcopy in an enlarger, and carried the enlarged print with him to the conveyer room. There was something odd about the list of time line designations. They were expressed numerically, in First Level notation; extremely short groups of symbols capable of exact expression of almost inconceivably enormous numbers. Vall had only a general-education smattering of mathematics—enough to qualify him for the chair of Higher Mathematics at any university on, say, the Fourth Level Europo-American Sector—and he could not identify the peculiarity, but he could recognize that there existed some sort of pattern. Shoving in the starting lever, he relaxed in one of the chairs, waiting for the transposition field to build up around him, and fell asleep before the mesh dome of the conveyer had vanished. He woke, the list of time line designations in his hand, when the conveyor rematerialized on Home Time Line. Putting it in his pocket, he hurried to an antigrav shaft and floated up to the floor on which Tortha Karf's office was.

* * * *

Tortha Karf was asleep in his chair; Dalla was eating a dinner that had been brought in to her—something better than the sandwich and mug of coffee Vall had mentioned to Thalvan Dras. Several of the bureau chiefs who had been there when he had gone out had left, and the psychist who had taken charge of the prisoner was there.

"I think he's coming out of the drug, now," he reported. "Still asleep, though. We want him to waken naturally before we start on him. They'll call me as soon as he shows signs of stirring."

"The Opposition's claiming, now, that we drugged and hypnotized Salgath into making that visiscreen confession," Dalla said. "Can you think of any way you could do that without making the subject incapable of lying?"

"Pseudo-memories," the psychist said. "It would take about three times as long as the time between Salgath Trod's departure from his apartment and the time of the telecast, though—"

"You know much higher math?" Vall asked the psychist.

"Well, enough to handle my job. Neuron-synapse inter-relations, memory-and-association patterns, that kind of thing, all have to be expressed mathematically."

Vall nodded and handed him the time-line designation list.

"See any kind of a pattern there?" he asked.

The psychist looked at the paper and blanked his face as he drew on hypnotically-acquired information.

"Yes. I'd say that all the numbers are related in some kind of a series to some other number. Simplified down to kindergarten level, say the difference between A and B is, maybe, one-decillionth of the difference between X and A, and the difference between B and C is one-decillionth of the difference between X and B, and so on—"

A voice came out of one of the communication boxes:

"Dr. Nentrov; the patient's out of the drug, and he's beginning to stir about."

"That's it," the psychist said. "I have to run." He handed the sheet back to Vall, took a last drink from his coffee cup, and bolted out of the room.

Dalla picked up the sheet of paper and looked at it. Vall told her what it was.

"If those time lines are in regular series, they relate to the base line of operations," she said. "Maybe you can have that worked out. I can see how it would be; a stated interval between the Esaron Sector lines, to simplify transposition control settings."

"That was what I was thinking. It's not quite as simple as Dr. Nentrov expressed it, but that could be the general idea. We might be able to work out the location of the base line from that. There seems to be a break in the number sequence in here; that would be the time line Skordran Kirv found those slaves on." He reached for the pipe he had left on the desk when he had gone to Police Terminal and began filling it.

A little later, a buzzer sounded and a light came on on one of the communication boxes. He flipped the switch and said, "Verkan Vall here." Sothran Barth's voice came cut of the box.

"They've just brought in Salgath Trod's servants. Picked them up as they came out of the house conveyer at the apartment building. I don't believe they know what's happened."

Vall flipped a switch and twiddled a dial; a viewscreen lit up, showing the landing stage. The police car had just landed: one detective had gotten out, and was helping the girl, Zinganna, who had been Salgath Trod's housekeeper and mistress, to descend. She was really beautiful. Vall thought: rather tall, slender, with dark eyes and a creamy light-brown skin. She wore a black cloak, and, under it, a black and silver evening gown. A single jewel twinkled in her black hair. She could have very easily passed for a woman of his own race.

The housemaid and the butler were a couple of entirely different articles. Both were about four or five generations from Fourth Level Primitive savagery. The maid, in garishly cheap finery, was big-boned and heavy-bodied, with red-brown hair; she looked like a member of one of the northern European reindeer-herding peoples who had barely managed to progress as far as the bow and arrow. The butler was probably a mixture of half a dozen primitive races; he was wearing one of his late master's evening suits, a bright mellow-pink, which was distinctly unflattering to his complexion.

The sound-pickup was too far away to give him what they were saying, but the butler and maid were waving their arms and protesting vehemently. One of the detectives took the woman by the arm; she jerked it loose and aimed a backhand slap at him. He blocked it on his forearm. Immediately, the girl in black turned and said something to her, and she subsided. Vall said, into the box:

"Barth, have the girl in the black cloak brought down to Number Four Interview Room. Put the other two in separate detention cubicles; we'll talk to them later." He broke the connection and got to his feet. "Come on, Dalla. I want you to help me with the girl."

"Just try and stop me," Dalla told him. "Any interviews you have with that little item, I want to sit in on."

* * * *

The Proletarian girl, still guarded by a detective, had already been placed in the interview room. The detective nodded to Vall, tried to suppress a grin when he saw Dalla behind him, and went out. Vall saw his wife and the prisoner seated, and produced his cigarette case, handing it around.

"You're Zinganna; you're of the household of Councilman Salgath Trod, aren't you?" he asked.

"Housekeeper and hostess," the girl replied. "I am also his mistress."

Vall nodded, smiling. "Which confirms my long-standing respect for Councilman Salgath's exquisite taste."

"Why, thank you," she said. "But I doubt if I was brought here to receive compliments. Or was I?"

"No, I'm afraid not. Have you heard the newscasts of the past few hours concerning Councilman Salgath?"

She straightened in her seat, looking at him seriously.

"No. I and Nindrandigro and Calilla spent the evening on ServSec One-Six-Five. Councilman Salgath told me that he had some business and wanted them out of the apartment, and wanted me to keep an eye on them. We didn't hear any news at all." She hesitated. "Has anything ... serious ... happened?"

Vall studied her for a moment, then glanced at Dalla. There existed between himself and his wife a sort of vague, semitelepathic, rapport; they had never been able to transmit definite and exact thoughts, but they could clearly prehend one another's feelings and emotions. He was conscious, now, of Dalla's sympathy for the Proletarian girl.

"Zinganna, I'm going to tell you something that is being kept from the public," he said. "By doing so, I will make it necessary for us to detain you, at least for a few days. I hope you will forgive me, but I think you would forgive me less if I didn't tell you."

"Something's happened to him," she said, her eyes widening and her body tensing.

"Yes, Zinganna. At about 2010, this evening," he said, "Councilman Salgath was murdered."

"Oh!" She leaned back in the chair, closing her eyes. "He's dead?" Then, again, statement instead of question: "He's dead!"

For a long moment, she lay back in the chair, as though trying to reorient her mind to the fact of Salgath Trod's death, while Vall and Dalla sat watching her. Then she stirred, opened her eyes, looked at the cigarette in her fingers as though she had never seen it before, and leaned forward to stuff it into an ash receiver.

"Who did it?" she asked, the Stone Age savage who had been her ancestor not ten generations ago peeping out of her eyes.

"The men who actually used the needlers are dead," Vall told her. "I killed a couple of them myself. We still have to find the men who planned it. I'd hoped you'd want to help us do that, Zinganna."

He side-glanced to Dalla again; she nodded. The relationship between Zinganna and Salgath Trod hadn't been purely business with her; there had been some real affection. He told her what had happened, and when he reached the point at which Salgath Trod had called Tortha Karf to confess complicity in the slave trade, her lips tightened and she nodded.

"I was afraid it was something like that," she said. "For the last few days, well, ever since the news about the slave trade got out, he's been worried about something. I've always thought somebody had some kind of a hold over him. Different times in the past, he's done things so far against his own political best interests that I've had to believe he was being forced into them. Well, this time they tried to force him too far. What then?"

Vall continued the story. "So we're keeping this hushed up, for a while. The way we're letting it out, Salgath Trod is still alive, on Police Terminal, talking under narco-hypnosis."

She smiled savagely. "And they'll get frightened, and frightened men do foolish things," she finished. She hadn't been a politician's mistress for nothing. "What can I do to help?"

"Tell us everything you can," he said. "Maybe we can be able to take such actions as we would have taken if Salgath Trod had lived to talk to us."

"Yes, of course." She got another cigarette from the case Vall had laid on the table. "I think, though, that you'd better give me a narco-hypnosis. You want to be able to depend on what I'm going to tell you, and I want to be able to remember things exactly."

Vall nodded approvingly and turned to Dalla.

"Can you handle this, yourself?" he asked. "There's an audio-visual recorder on now; here's everything you need." He opened the drawers in the table to show her the narco-hypnotic equipment. "And the phone has a whisper mouthpiece; you can call out without worrying about your message getting into Zinganna's subconscious. Well, I'll see you when you're through; you bring Zinganna to Police Terminal; I'll probably be there."

He went out, closing the door behind him, and went down the hall, meeting the officer who had taken charge of the butler and housemaid.

"We're having trouble with them, sir," he said. "Hostile. Yelling about their rights, and demanding to see a representative of Proletarian Protective League."

Vall mentioned the Proletarian Protective League with unflattering vulgarity.

"If they don't coöperate, drag them out and inject them and question them anyhow," he said.

The detective-lieutenant looked worried. "We've been taking a pretty high hand with them as it is," he protested. "It's safer to kill a Citizen than bloody a Prole's nose; they have all sorts of laws to protect them."

"There are all sorts of laws to protect the Paratime Secret," Vall replied. "And I think there are one or two laws against murdering members of the Executive Council. In case P.P.L. makes any trouble, they aren't here; they have faithfully joined their beloved master in his refuge on PolTerm. But one or both of them work for the Organization."

"You're sure of that?"

"The Organization is too thorough not to have had a spy in Salgath's household. It wasn't Zinganna, because she's volunteered to talk to us under narco-hyp. So who does that leave?"

"Well, that's different; that makes them suspects." The lieutenant seemed relieved. "We'll pump that pair out right away."

When he got back to Tortha Karf's office, the Chief was awake, and doodling on his notepad with his multicolor pen. Vall looked at the pad and winced; the Chief was doodling bugs again—red ants with black legs, and blue-and-green beetles. Then he saw that the psychist, Nentrov Dard, was drinking straight 150-proof palm-rum.

"Well, tell me the worst," he said.

"Our boy's memory-obliterated," Nentrov Dard said, draining his glass and filling it again. "And he's plastered with pseudo-memories a foot thick. It'll be five or six ten-days before we can get all that stuff peeled off and get him unblocked. I put him to sleep and had him transposed to Police Terminal. I'm going there, myself, tomorrow morning, after I've had some sleep, and get to work on him. If you're hoping to get anything useful out of him in time to head off this Council crisis that's building up, just forget it."

"And that leaves us right back with our old friends, the Wizard Traders," Tortha Karf added. "And if they've decided to suspend activities on the Kholghoor Sector, too—" He began drawing a big blue and black spider in the middle of the pad.

Nentrov Dard crushed out his cigar, drank his rum, and got to his feet.

"Well, good night, Chief; Vall. If you decide to wake me up before 1000, send somebody you want to get rid of in a hurry." He walked around the deck and out the side door.

"I hope they don't," Vall said to Tortha Karf. "Really, though, I doubt if they do. This is their chance to pick up a lot of slaves cheaply; the Croutha are too busy to bother haggling. I'm going through to PolTerm, now; when Dalla and Zinganna get through, tell them to join me there."

* * * *

On Police Terminal, he found Kostran Galth, the agent who had been selected to impersonate Salgath Trod. After calling Zulthran Torv, the mathematician in charge of the Computer Office and giving him the Esaron time-line designations and Nentrov Dard's ideas about them, he spent about an hour briefing Kostran Galth on the role he was to play. Finally, he undressed and went to bed on a couch in the rest room behind the office.

It was noon when he woke. After showering, shaving and dressing hastily, he went out to the desk for breakfast, which arrived while he was putting a call through to Ranthar Jard, at Nharkan Equivalent.

"Your idea paid off, Chief's Assistant," the Kholghoor SecReg Subchief told him. "The slaves gave us a lot of physical description data on the estate, and told us about new fields that had been cleared, and a dam this Lord Ghromdour was building to flood some new rice-paddies. We located a belt of about five parayears where these improvements had been made: we started boomeranging the whole belt, time line by time line. So far, we have ten or fifteen pictures of the main square at Sohram showing Croutha with firearms, and pictures of Wizard Trader camps and conveyer heads on the same time lines. Here, let me show you; this is from an airboat over the forest outside the equivalent of Sohram."

There was no jungle visible when the view changed; nothing but clusters of steel towers and platforms and buildings that marked conveyer heads, and a large rectangle of red-and-white antigrav-buoys moored to warn air traffic out of the area being boomeranged. The pickup seemed to be pointed downward from the bow of an airboat circling at about ten thousand feet.

"Balls ready to go," a voice called, and then repeated a string of time-line designations. "Estimated return, 1820, give or take four minutes."

"Varth," Ranthar Jard said, evidently out of the boat's radio. "Your telecast is being beamed on Dhergabar Equivalent; Chief's Assistant Verkan is watching. When do you estimate your next return?"

"Any moment, now, sir; we're holding this drop till they rematerialize."

Vall watched unblinkingly, his fork poised halfway to his mouth. Suddenly, about a thousand feet below the eye of the pickup, there was a series of blue flashes, and, an instant later, a blossoming of red-and-white parachutes, ejected from the photo-reconnaissance balls that had returned from the Kholghoor Sector.

"All right; drop away," the boat captain called. There was a gush, from underneath, of eight-inch spheres, their conductor-mesh twinkling golden-bright in the sunlight. They dropped in a tight cluster for a thousand or so feet and then flashed and vanished. From the ground, six or eight aircars rose to meet the descending parachutes and catch them.

The screen went cubist for a moment, and then Ranthar Jard's swarthy, wide-jawed face looked out of it again. He took his pipe from his mouth.

"We'll probably get a positive out of the batch you just saw coming in," he said. "We get one out of about every two drops."

"Message a list of the time-line designations you've gotten so far to Zulthran Torv, at Computer Office here," Vall said. "He's working on the Esaron Sector dope; we think a pattern can be established. I'll be seeing you in about five hours; I'm rocketing out of here as soon as I get a few more things cleared up here."

Zulthran Torv, normally cautious to the degree of pessimism, was jubilant when Vall called him.

"We have something, Vall," he said. "It is, roughly, what Dr. Nentrov suggested—each of the intervals between the designations is a very minute but very exact fraction of the difference between lesser designation and the base-line designation."

"You have the base-line designation?" Vall demanded.

"Oh, yes. That's what I was telling you. We worked that out from the designations you gave me." He recited it. "All the designations you gave me are—"

Vall wasn't listening to him. He frowned in puzzlement.

"That's not a Fifth Level designation," he said. "That's First Level!"

"That's correct. First Level Abzar Sector."

"Now why in blazes didn't anybody think of that before?" he marveled, and as he did, he knew the answer. Nobody ever thought of the Abzar sector.

Twelve millennia ago, the world of the First Level had been exhausted; having used up the resources of their home planet, Mars, a hundred thousand years before, the descendants of the population that had migrated across space had repeated on the third planet the devastation of the fourth. The ancestors of Verkan Vall's people had discovered the principle of paratime transposition and had begun to exploit an infinity of worlds on other lines of probability. The people of the First Level Dwarma Sector, reduced by sheer starvation to a tiny handful, had abandoned their cities and renounced their technologies and created for themselves a farm-and-village culture without progress or change or curiosity or struggle or ambition, and a way of life in which every day was like every other day that had been or that would come.

The Abzar people had done neither. They had wasted their resources to the last, fighting bitterly over the ultimate crumbs, with fission bombs, and with muskets, and with swords, and with spears and clubs, and finally they had died out, leaving a planet of almost uniform desert dotted with vast empty cities which even twelve thousand years had hardly begun to obliterate.

So nobody on the Paratime Sector went to the Abzar Sector. There was nothing there—except a hiding-place.

"Well, message that to Subchief Ranthar Jard, Kholghoor Sector at Nharkan Equivalent, and to Subchief Vulthor, Esaron Sector, Novilan Equivalent," Vall said. "And be sure to mark what you send Vulthor, 'Immediate attention Deputy Subchief Skordran.'"

That reminded him of something; as soon as he was through with

Zulthran, he got out an order in the name of Tortha Karf authorizing Skordran Kirv's promotion on a permanent basis and messaged it out. Something was going to have to be done with Vulthor Tharn, too. A promotion of course—say Deputy Bureau Chief. Hypno-Mech Tape Library at Dhergabar Home Time Line; there Vulthor's passion for procedure and his caution would be assets instead of liabilities. He called Vlasthor Arph, the Chief's Deputy assigned to him as adjutant.

"I want more troops from ServSec and IndSec," he said. "Go over the TO's and see what can be spared from where; don't strip any time line, but get a force of the order of about three divisions. And locate all the big antigrav-equipped ship transposition docks on Commercial and Passenger Sectors, and a list of freighters and passenger ships that can be commandeered in a hurry. We think we've spotted the time line the Organization's using as a base. As soon as we raid a couple of places near Nharkan and Novilan Equivalents, we're going to move in for a planet-wide cleanup."

"I get it, Chief's Assistant. I do everything I can to get ready for a big move, without letting anything leak out. After you strike the first blow, there won't be any security problem, and the lid will be off. In the meantime, I make up a general plan, and alert all our own people. Right?"

"Right. And for your information, the base isn't Fifth Level; it's First Level Abzar." He gave the designation.

Vlasthor Arph chuckled. "Well, think of that! I'd even forgotten there was an Abzar Sector. Shall I tell the reporters that?"

"Fangs of Fasif, no!" Vall fairly howled. Then, curiously: "What reporters? How'd they get onto PolTerm?"

"About fifty or sixty news-service people Chief Tortha sent down here, this morning, with orders to prevent them from filing any stories from here but to let them cover the raids, when they come off. We were instructed to furnish them weapons and audio-visual equipment and vocowriters and anything else they needed, and—"

Vall grinned. "That was one I'd never thought of," he admitted. "The old fox is still the old fox. No, tell them nothing; we'll just take them along and show them. Oh, and where are Dr. Hadron Dalla and that girl of Salgath Trod's?"

"They're sleeping, now. Rest Room Eighteen."

* * * *

Dalla and Zinganna were asleep on a big mound of silk cushions in one corner, their glossy black heads close together and Zinganna's brown arm around Dalla's white shoulder. Their faces were calmly beautiful in repose, and they smiled slightly, as though they were wandering through a happy dream. For a little while, Vall stood looking at them, then he began whistling softly. On the third or fourth bar, Dalla woke and sat up, waking Zinganna, and blinked at him perplexedly.

"What time is it?" she asked.

"About 1245," he told her.

"Ohhh! We just got to sleep," she said. "We're both bushed!"

"You had a hard time. Feel all right after your narco-hyp, Zinganna?"

"It wasn't so bad, and I had a nice sleep. And Dalla ... Dr. Hadron, I mean—"

"Dalla," Vall's wife corrected. "Remember what I told you?"

"Dalla, then," Zinganna smiled. "Dalla gave me some hypno-treatment, too. I don't feel so badly about Trod, any more."

"Well, look, Zinganna. We're going to have a man impersonate Councilman Salgath on a telecast. The cosmeticians are making him over now. Would you find it too painful to meet him, and talk to him?"

"No, I wouldn't mind. I can criticize the impersonation; remember, I knew Trod very well. You know, I was his hostess, too. I met many of the people with whom he was associated, and they know me. Would things look more convincing if I appeared on the telecast with your man?"

"It certainly would; it would be a great help!" he told her enthusiastically. "Maybe you girls ought to get up, now. The telecast isn't till 1930, but there's a lot to be done getting ready."

Dalla yawned. "What I get, trying to be a cop," she said, then caught the other girl's hands and rose, pulling her up. "Come on, Zinna; we have to get to work!"

* * * *

Vall rose from behind the reading-screen in Ranthar Jard's office, stretching his arms over his head. For almost an hour, he had sat there pushing buttons and twiddling selector and magnification-adjustment knobs, looking at the pictures the Kholghoor-Nharkan cops had taken with auto-return balls dropped over the spatial equivalent of Sohram.

One set of pictures, taken at two thousand feet, showed the central square of the city. The effects of the Croutha sack were plainly visible; so were the captives herded together under guard like cattle. By increasing magnification, he looked at groups of the barbarian conquerors, big men with blond or reddish-brown hair, in loose shirts and baggy trousers and rough cowhide buskins. Many of them wore bowl-shaped helmets, some had shirts of ring-mail, all of them carried long straight swords with cross-hilts, and about half of them had pistols thrust through their belts or muskets slung from their shoulders.

The other set of pictures showed the Wizard Trader camps and conveyer heads. In each case, a wide oval had been burned out in the jungle, probably with heavy-duty heat guns. The camps were surrounded with stout wire-mesh fence: in each there were a number of metal prefab-huts, and an inner fenced slave-pen. A trail had been cut from each to a similarly cleared circle farther back in the forest, and in the centers of one or two of these circles he saw the actual conveyer domes. There was a great deal of activity in all of them, and he screwed the magnification-adjustment to the limit to scrutinize each human figure in turn. A few of the men, he was sure, were First Level Citizens; more were either Proles or outtimers. Quite a few of them were of a dark, heavy-featured, black-bearded type.

"Some of these fellows look like Second Level Khiftans," he said. "Rush an individual picture of each one, maximum magnification consistent with clarity, to Dhergabar Equivalent to be transposed to Home Time Line. You get all the dope from Zulthran Torv?"

"Yes; Abzar Sector," Ranthar Jard said. "I'd never have thought of that. Wonder why they used that series system, though. I'd have tried to spot my operations as completely at random as possible."

"Only thing they could have done," Vall said. "When we get hold of one of their conveyers, we're going to find the control panel's just a mess of arbitrary symbols, and there'll be something like a computer-machine built into the control cabinet, to select the right time line whenever a dial's set or a button pushed, and the only way that could be done would be by establishing some kind of a numerical series. And we were trustingly expecting to locate their base from one of their conveyers! Why, if we give all those people in the pictures narco-hyps, we won't learn the base-line designation; none of them will know it. They just go where the conveyers take them."

"Well, we're all set now," Ranthar Jard said. "I have a plan of attack worked out; subject to your approval, I'm ready to start implementing it now." He glanced at his watch. "The Salgath telecast is over, on Home Time Line, and in a little while, a transcript will be on this time line. Want to watch it here, sir?"

* * * *

The telecast screen in the living room of Tortha Karf's town apartment was still on; in it, a girl with bright red hair danced slowly to soft music against a background of shifting color. The four men who sat in a semicircle facing it sipped their drinks and watched idly.

"Ought to be getting some sort of public reaction soon," Tortha Karf said, glancing at his watch.

"Well, I'll have to admit, it was done convincingly," Zostha Olv, the Chief Interoffice Coördinator, admitted grudgingly. "I'd have believed it, if I hadn't known the real facts."

"Shooting it against the background of those wide windows was smart," Lovranth Rolk said. "Every schoolchild would recognize that view of the rocketport as being on Police Terminal. And including that girl Zinganna; that was a real masterpiece!"

"I've met her, a few times," Elbraz Vark, the Political Liaison Assistant, said. "Isn't she lovely!"

"Good actress, too," Tortha Karf said. "It's not easy to impersonate yourself."

"Well, Kostran Galth did a fine job of acting, too," Lovranth Rolk said. "That was done to perfection—the distinguished politician, supported by his loyal mistress, bravely facing the disgraceful end of his public career."

"You know, I believe I could get that girl a booking with one of the big theatrical companies. Now that Salgath's dead, she'll need somebody to look after her."

"What sharp, furry ears you have, Mr. Elbraz!" Zostha Olv grunted.

The music stopped as though cut off with a knife, and the slim girl with the red hair vanished in a shatter of many colors. When the screen cleared, one of the announcers was looking out of it.

"We interrupt the program for an important newscast of a sensational development in the Salgath affair," he said. "Your next speaker will be

Yandar Yadd—"

"I thought you'd managed to get that blabbermouth transposed to PolTerm," Zostha said.

"He wouldn't go." Tortha Karf replied. "Said it was just a trick to get him off Home Time Line during the Council crisis."

Yandar Yadd had appeared on the screen as the pickup swung about.

"... Recording ostensibly made by Councilman Salgath on Police Terminal Time Line, and telecast on Home Time Line an hour ago. Well, I don't know who he was, but I now have positive proof that he definitely was not Salgath Trod!"

"We're sunk!" Zostha Olv grunted. "He'd never make a statement like that unless he could prove it."

"... Something suspicious about the whole thing, from the beginning," the newsman was saying. "So I checked. If you recall, the actor impersonating Salgath gestured rather freely with his hands, in imitation of a well-known mannerism of the real Salgath Trod; at one point, the ball of his right thumb was presented directly to the pickup. Here's a still of that scene."

He stepped aside, revealing a viewscreen behind him; when he pressed a button, the screen lighted; on it was a stationary picture of Kostran Galth as Salgath Trod, his right hand raised in front of him.

"Now watch this. I'm going to step up the magnification, slowly, so that you can be sure there's no substitution. Camera a little closer, Trath!"

The screen in the background seemed to advance, until it filled the entire screen. Yandar Yadd was still talking, out of the picture; a metal-tipped pointer came into the picture, touching the right thumb, which grew larger and larger until it was the only thing visible.

"Now here," Yandar Yadd's voice continued. "Any of you who are familiar with the ancient science of dactyloscopy will recognize this thumb as having the ridge-pattern known as a 'twin loop.' Even with the high degree of magnification possible with the microgrid screen, we can't bring out the individual ridges, but the pattern is unmistakable. I ask you to memorize that image, while I show you another right thumb print, this time a certified photo-copy of the thumb print of the real Salgath Trod." The magnification was reduced a little, a card was moved into the picture, and it was stepped up again. "See, this thumb print is of the type known as a 'tented arch.' Observe the difference."

"That does it!" Zostha Olv cried. "Karf, for the first and last time, let me remind you that I opposed this lunacy from the beginning. Now, what are we going to do next?"

"I suggest that we get to Headquarters as soon as we can," Tortha Karf said. "If we wait too long, we may not be able to get in."

Yandar Yadd was back on the screen, denouncing Tortha Karf passionately. Tortha went over and snapped it off.

"I suggest we transpose to PolTerm," Lovranth Rolk said. "It won't be so easy for them to serve a summons on us there."

"You can go to PolTerm if you want to," Tortha Karf retorted. "I'm going to stay here and fight back, and if they try to serve me with a summons, they'd better send a robot for a process server."

"Fight back!" Zostha Olv echoed. "You can't fight the Council and the whole Management! They'll tear you into inch bits!"

"I can hold them off till Vall's able to raid those Abzar Sector bases," Tortha Karf said. He thought for a moment. "Maybe this is all for the best, after all. If it distracts the Organization's attention—"

* * * *

"I wish we could have made a boomerang-ball reconnaissance," Ranthar Jard was saying, watching one of the viewscreens, in which a film, taken from an airboat transposed to an adjoining Abzar sector time line, was being shown. The boat had circled over the Ganges, a mere trickle between wide, deeply cut banks, and was crossing a gullied plain, sparsely grown with thornbush. "The base ought to be about there, but we have no idea what sort of changes this gang has made."

"Well, we couldn't: we didn't dare take the chance of it being spotted. This has to be a complete surprise. It'll be about like the other place, the one the slaves described. There won't be any permanent buildings. This operation only started a few months ago, with the Croutha invasion; it may go on for four or five months, till the Croutha have all their surplus captives sold off. That country," he added, gesturing at the screen, "will be flooded out when the rains come. See how it's suffered from flood-erosion. There won't be a thing there that can't be knocked down and transposed out in a day or so."

"I wish you'd let me go along," Ranthar Jard worried.

"We can't do that, either," Vall said. "Somebody's got to be in charge here, and you know your own people better than I do. Beside, this won't be the last operation like this. Next time, I'll have to stay on Police Terminal and command from a desk; I want first-hand experience with the outtime end of the job, and this is the only way I can get it."

He watched the four police-girls who were working at the big terrain board showing the area of the Police Terminal time line around them. They had covered the miniature buildings and platforms and towers with a fine mesh, at a scale-equivalent of fifty feet; each intersection marked the location of a three-foot conveyer ball, loaded with a sleep-gas bomb and rigged with an automatic detonator which would explode it and release the gas as soon as it rematerialized on the Abzar Sector. Higher, on stiff wires that raised them to what represented three thousand feet, were the disks that stood for ten hundred-foot conveyers; they would carry squads of Paratime Police in aircars and thirty-foot air boats. There was a ring of big two-hundred-foot conveyers a mile out; they would carry the armor and the airborne infantry and the little two-man scooters of the air-cavalry, from the Service and Industrial Sectors. Directly over the spatial equivalent of the Kholghoor Sector Wizard Traders' conveyers was the single disk of Verkan Vall's command conveyer, at a represented five thousand feet, and in a half-mile circle around it were the five news service conveyers.

"Where's the ship-conveyer?" he asked.

"Actually it's on antigrav about five miles north of here," one of the girls said. "Representationally, about where Subchief Ranthar's standing."

Another girl added a few more bits to the network that represented the sleep-gas bombs and stepped back, taking off her earphones.

"Everything's in place, now, Assistant Verkan," she told him.

"Good. I'm going aboard, now," he said. "You can have it, Jard."

He shook hands with Ranthar Jard, who moved to the switch which would activate all the conveyers simultaneously, and accepted the good wishes of the girls at the terrain board. Then he walked to the mesh-covered dome of the hundred-foot conveyer, with the five news service conveyers surrounding it in as regular a circle as the buildings and towers of the regular conveyer heads would permit. The members of his own detail, smoking and chatting outside, saw him and started moving inside; so did the news people. A public-address speaker began yelping, in a hundred voices all over the area, warning those who were going with the conveyers to get aboard. He went in through a door, between two aircars, and on to the central control-desks, going up to a visiscreen over which somebody had crayoned "Novilan EQ." It gave him a view, over the shoulder of a man in the uniform of a field agent third class, of the interior of a conveyer like his own.

* * * *

"Hello, Assistant Verkan," a voice came out of the speaker under the screen, as the man moved his lips. "Deputy Skordran! Here's Chief's Assistant Verkan, now!"

Skordran Kirv moved in front of the screen as the operator got up from his stool.

"Hello, Vall; we're all set to move out as soon as you give the word," he said. "We're all in position on antigrav."

"That's smart work. We've just finished our gas-bomb net," Vall said. "Going on antigrav now," he added, as he felt the dome lift. "I hope you won't be too disappointed if you draw a blank on your end."

"We realize that they've closed out the whole Esaron Sector," Skordran Kirv, eight thousand odd miles away, replied. "We're taking in a couple of ships; we're going to make a survey all up the coast. There are a lot of other sectors where slaves can be sold in this area."

In the outside viewscreen, tuned to a slowly rotating pickup on the top of a tower spatially equivalent with a room in a tall building on Second Level Triplanetary Empire Sector, he could see his own conveyer rising vertically, with the news conveyers following, and the troop conveyers, several miles away, coming into position. Finally, they were all placed; he reported the fact to Skordran Kirv and then picked up a hand-phone.

"Everybody ready for transposition?" he called. "On my count. Thirty seconds ... Twenty seconds ... Fifteen seconds ... Five seconds ... Four seconds ... Three seconds ... Two seconds ... One second, *out!*"

All the screens went gray. The inside of the dome passed into another space-time continuum, even into another kind of space-time. The transposition would take half an hour; that seemed to be the time needed to build up and collapse the transposition field, regardless of the para-temporal distance covered. The dome above and around them vanished; the bare, tower-forested, building-dotted world of Police Terminal vanished, too, into the uniform green of the uninhabited Fifth Level. A planet could take pretty good care of itself, he thought, if people would only leave it alone. Then he began to see the fields and villages of Fourth Level. Cities appeared and vanished, growing higher and vaster as they went across the more civilized Third Level. One was under air attack—there was almost never a paratemporal transposition which did not run through some scene of battle.

He unbuckled his belt and took off his boots and tunic; all around him, the others were doing the same. Sleep-gas didn't have to be breathed; it could enter the nervous system by any orifice or lesion, even a pore or a scratch. A spacesuit was the only protection. One of the detectives helped him on with his metal and plastic armor; before sealing his gauntlets, he reciprocated the assistance, then checked the needler and blaster and the long batonlike ultrasonic paralyzer on his belt and made sure that the radio and sound-phones in his helmet were working. He hoped that the frantic efforts to gather several thousand spacesuits onto Police Terminal from the Industrial and Commercial and Interplanetary Sectors hadn't started rumors which had gotten to the ears of some of the Organization's ubiquitous agents.

* * * *

The country below was already turning to the parched browns and yellows of the Abzar Sector. There was not another of the conveyers in sight, but electronic and mechanical lag in the individual controls and even the distance-difference between them and the central radio control would have prevented them from going into transposition at the same fractional microsecond. The recon-details began piling into their cars. Then the red light overhead winked to green, and the dome flickered and solidified into cold, inert metal. The screens lighted up again, and Vall could see Skordran Kirv, across Asia and the Pacific, getting into his helmet. A dot of light in the center of the underview screen widened as the mesh under the conveyer irised open around the pickup.

Below, the Organization base—big rectangles of fenced slave pens, with metal barracks inside; the huge circle of the Kholghoor Sector conveyer-head building, and a smaller structure that must house conveyers to other Abzar Sector time lines; the work-shops and living quarters and hangars and warehouses and docks—was wreathed in white-green mist.

The ring of conveyers at three thousand feet were opening and spewing out aircars and airboats, farther away, the greater ring of heavy conveyers were unloading armored and shielded combat-craft. An aircar which must have been above the reach of the gas was streaking away toward the west, with three police cars after it. As he watched, the air around it fairly sizzled blue with the rays of neutron disruption blasters, and then it blew apart. The three police cars turned and came back more slowly. The three-thousand-ton passenger ship which had been hastily fitted with armament was circling about; the great dock conveyer which had brought it was gone, transposed back to Police Terminal to pick up another ship.

He recorded a message announcing the arrival of the task-force, pulled out the tape and sealed it in a capsule, and put the capsule in a mesh message ball, attaching it to a couple of wires and flipping a switch. The ball flashed and vanished, leaving the wires cleanly sheared off. When it got back to Police Terminal, half an hour later, it would rematerialize, eject a parachute, and turn on a whistle to call attention to itself. Then he sealed on his helmet, climbed into an aircar, and turned on his helmet-radio to speak to the driver. The car lifted a few inches, floated out an open port, and dived downward.

He landed at the big conveyer-head building. There were spaces for fifty conveyers around it, and all but eight of them were in place. One must have arrived since the gas bombs burst; it was crammed with senseless Kharanda slaves. A couple of Paratime Police officers were towing a tank of sleep-gas around on an antigrav-lifter, maintaining the proper concentration in case any more came in. At the smaller conveyer building, there were no conveyers, only a number of red-lined fifty-foot circles around a central two-hundred-foot circle. The Organization personnel there had been dragged outside, and a group of paracops were sealing it up, installing robot watchmen, and preparing to flood it with gas. At the slave pens, a string of two-hundred-foot conveyers, having unloaded soldiers and fighting-gear, were coming in to take on unconscious slaves for transposition to Police Terminal. Aircars and airboats were bringing in gassed slavers; they were being shackled and dumped into the slave barracks; as soon as the gas cleared and they could be brought back to consciousness, they would be narco-hypnotized and questioned.

He had finished a tour of the warehouses, looking at the kegs of gunpowder and the casks of brandy, the piles of pig lead, the stacks of cases containing muskets. These must have all come from some low-order handcraft time line. Then there were swords and hatchets and knives that had been made on Industrial Sector—the Organization must be getting them through some legitimate trading company—and mirrors and perfumes and synthetic fiber textiles and cheap jewelry, of similar provenance. It looked as though this stuff had been brought in by ship from somewhere else on this time line; the warehouses were too far from the conveyers and right beside the ship dock—

There was a tremendous explosion somewhere. Vall and the men with him ran outside, looking about, the sound-phones of their helmets giving them no idea of the source of the sound. One of the policemen pointed, and Vall's eyes followed his arm. The ship that had been transposed in in the big conveyer was falling, blown in half; as he looked, both sections hit the ground several miles away. A strange ship, a freighter, was coming in fast, and as he watched, a blue spark winked from her bow as a heavy-duty blaster was activated. There was another explosion, overhead; they all ran for shelter as Vall's command-conveyer disintegrated into falling scrap-metal. At once, all the other conveyers which were on antigrav began flashing and vanishing. That was the right, the only, thing to do, he knew. But it was leaving him and his men isolated and under attack.

* * * *

"So that was it," Dalgroth Sorn, the Paratime Commissioner for Security said, relieved when Tortha Karf had finished.

"Yes, and I'll repeat it under narco-hyp, too," Tortha Karf added.

"Oh, don't talk that way, Karf," Dalgroth Sorn scolded. He was at least a century Tortha Karf's senior; he had the face of an elderly and sore-toothed lion. "You wanted to keep this prisoner under wraps till you could mind-pump him, and you wanted the Organization to think Salgath was alive and talking. I approve both. But—"

He gestured to the viewscreen across the room, tuned to a pickup back of the Speaker's chair in the Council Chamber. Tortha Karf turned a knob to bring the sound volume up.

"Well. I'm raising this point," a member from the Management seats in the center was saying, "because these earlier charges of illegal arrest and illegal detention are part and parcel with the charges growing out of the telecast last evening."

"Well, that telecast was a fake; that's been established," somebody on the left heckled.

"Councilman Salgath's confession on the evening of One-Six-Two Day wasn't a fake, the Management supporter, Nanthav Skov, retorted.

"Well, then why was it necessary to fake the second one?"

A light began winking on the big panel in front of the Speaker, Asthar Varn.

"I recognize Councilman Hasthor Flan," Asthar said.

"I believe I can construct a theory that will explain that," Hasthor Flan said. "I suggest that when the Paratime Police were questioning Councilman Salgath under narco-hypnosis, he made statements incriminating either the Paratime Police as a whole or some member of the Paratime Police whom Tortha Karf had to protect—say somebody like Assistant Verkan. So they just killed him, and made up this impostor—"

Tortha Karf began, alphabetically, to blaspheme every god he had ever heard of. He had only gotten as far as a Fourth Level deity named Allah when a red light began flashing in front of Asthar Varn, and the voice of a page-robot, amplified, roared:

"Point of special urgency! Point of special urgency! It has been requested that the news telecast screen be activated at once, with playback to 1107. An important bulletin has just come in from Nagorabar, Home Time Line, on the Indian subcontinent—"

"You can stop swearing, now, Karf," Dalgroth Sorn grinned. "I think this is it."

* * * *

Kostran Galth sat on the edge of the couch, with one arm around Zinganna's waist; on the other side of him, Hadron Dalla lay at full length, her elbows propped and her chin in her hands. The screen in front of them showed a fading sunset, although it was only a little past noon at Dhergabar Equivalent. A dark ship was coming slowly in against the red sky; in the center of a wire-fenced compound a hundred-foot conveyer hung on antigrav twenty feet from the ground, and beyond, a long metal prefab-shed was spilling light from open doors and windows.

"That crowd that was just taken in won't be finished for a couple of hours," a voice was saying. "I don't know how much they'll be able to tell; the psychists say they're all telling about the same stories. What those stories are, of course, I'm not able to repeat. After the trouble caused by a certain news commentator who shall be nameless—he's not connected with this news service, I'm happy to say—we're all leaning over backward to keep from breaking Paratime Police security.

"One thing; shortly after the arrival of the second ship from Police Terminal—and believe me, that ship came in just in the nick of time!—the dead Abzar city which the criminals were using as their main base for this time line, and from which they launched the air attack against us, was located, and now word has come in that it is entirely in the hands of the Paratime Police. Personally, I doubt if a great deal of information has been gotten from any prisoners taken there. The lengths to which this Organization went to keep their own people in ignorance is simply unbelievable."

A man appeared for a moment in the lighted doorway of the shed, then stepped outside.

"Look!" Dalla cried. "There's Vall!"

"There's Assistant Verkan, now," the commentator agreed. "Chief's Assistant, would you mind saying a few words, here? I know you're a busy man, sir, but you are also the public hero of Home Time Line, and everybody will be glad if you say something to them—"

* * * *

Tortha Karf sealed the door of the apartment behind them, then activated one of the robot servants and sent it gliding out of the room for drinks. Verkan Vall took off his belt and holster and laid them aside, then dropped into a deep chair with a sigh of relief. Dalla advanced to the middle of the room and stood looking about in surprised delight.

"Didn't expect this, from the mess outside?" Vall asked. "You know, you really are on the paracops, now. Nobody off the Force knows about this hideout of the Chief's."

"You'd better find a place like this, too," Tortha Karf advised. "From now on, you'll have about as much privacy at that apartment in Turquoise Towers as you'd enjoy on the stage of Dhergabar Opera House."

"Just what is my new position?" Vall asked, hunting his cigarette case out of his tunic. "Duplicate Chief of Paratime Police?"

The robot came back with three tall glasses and a refrigerated decanter on its top. It stopped in front of Tortha Karf and slewed around on its treads; he filled a glass and sent it to the chair where Dalla had seated herself; when she got a drink, she sent it to Vall. Vall sent if back to Tortha Karf, who turned it off.

"No; you have the modifier in the wrong place. You're Chief of Duplicate Paratime Police. You take the setup you have now, and expand it; continue the present lines of investigation, and be ready to exploit anything new that comes up. You won't bother with any of this routine flying-saucer-scare stuff; just handle the Organization business. That'll keep you busy for a long time, I'm afraid."

"I notice you slammed down on the first Council member who began shouting about how you'd wiped out the Great Paratemporal Crime-Ring," Vall said.

"Yes. It isn't wiped out, and it won't be wiped out for a long time. I shall be unspeakably delighted if, when I turn my job over to you, you have it wiped out. And even then, there'll be a loose end to pick up every now and then till you retire."

"We have Council and the Management with us, now," Vall said. "This was the first secret session of Executive Council in over two thousand years. And I thought I'd drop dead when they passed that motion to submit themselves to narco-hypnosis."

"A few Councilmen are going to drop dead before they can be narco-hypped," Dalla prophesied over the rim of her glass.

"A few have already. I have a list of about a dozen of them who have had fatal accidents or committed suicide, or just died or vanished since the news of your raid broke. Four of them I saw, in the screen, jump up and run out as soon as the news came in, on One-Six-Five Day. And a lot of other people; our friend Yandar Yadd's dropped out of sight, for one. You heard what we got out of those servants of Salgath Trod's?"

"I didn't," Dalla said. "What?"

"Both spies for the Organization. They reported to a woman named Farilla, who ran a fortune-telling parlor in the Prole district. Her occult powers didn't warn her before we sent a squad of plain-clothes men for her. That was an entirely illegal arrest, by the way, but it netted us a list of about three hundred prominent political, business and social persons whose servants have been reporting to her. She thought she was working for a telecast gossipist."

"That's why we have a new butler, darling," Vall interrupted. "Kandagro was reporting on us."

"Who did she pass the reports on to?" Dalla asked.

Tortha Karf beamed. "She thinks more like a cop every time I talk to her," he told Vall. "You better appoint her your Special Assistant. Why, about 1800 every day, some Prole would come in, give the recognition sign, and get the day's accumulation. We only got one of them, a fourteen-year-old girl. We're having some trouble getting her deconditioned to a point where she can be hypnotized into talking; by the time we do, they'll have everything closed out, I suppose. What's the latest from Abzar Sector? I missed the last report in the rush to get to this Council session."

"All stalled. We're still boomeranging the sector, but it's about five billion time-lines deep, and the pattern for the Kholghoor and Esaron Sectors doesn't seem to apply. I think they have a lot of these Abzar time lines close together, and they get from one to another via some terminal on Fifth Level."

Tortha Karf nodded. It was impossible to make a transposition of less than ten parayears—a hundred thousand time lines. It was impossible that the field could build and collapse that soon.

"We also think that this Abzar time line was only used for the Croutha-Wizard Trader operation. Nothing we found there was more than a couple of months old; nothing since the last rainy season in India, for instance. Everything was cleaned out on Skordran Kirv's end."

"Tell him to try the Mississippi, Missouri and Ohio Valleys," Tortha Karf said. "A lot of those slaves are sure to have been sold to Second Level Khiftan Sector."

"Well, it looks as though our vacation's out the window for a long time," Dalla said resignedly.

"Why don't you and Vall go to my farm, on Fifth Level Sicily," Tortha Karf suggested. "I own the whole island, on that time line, and you can always be reached in a hurry if anything comes up."

"We could have as much fun there as on the Dwarma Sector," Dalla said. "Chief, could we take a couple of friends along?"

"Well, who?"

"Zinganna and Kostran Galth," she replied. "They've gotten interested in one another; they're talking about a tentative marriage."

"It'll have to be mighty tentative," Vall said. "Kostran Galth can't marry a Prole."

"She won't be a Prole very long. I'm going to adopt her as my sister."

Tortha Karf looked at her sharply. "You sure you know what you're doing, Dalla?" he asked.

"Of course I'm sure. I know that girl better than she knows herself. I narco-hypped her, remember. Zinna's the kind of a sister I've always wished I'd had."

"Well, that's all right then. But about this marriage. She was in love with Salgath Trod," Tortha Karf said. "Now, she's identifying Agent Kostran with him—"

"She was in love with the kind of man Salgath could have been if he hadn't gotten into this Organization filth," Dalla replied. "Galth is that kind of a man. They'll get along all right."

"Well, she'll qualify on IQ and general psych rating for Citizenship. I'll say that. And she's the kind of girl I like to see my boys take up with. Like you, Dalla. Yes, of course; take them along with you. Sicily's big enough that two couples won't get in each others' way."

A phone-robot, its slender metal stem topped by a metal globe, slid into the room on its ball-rollers, moving falteringly, like a blind man. It could sense Tortha Karf's electro-encephalic wave-patterns, but it was having trouble locating the source. They all sat motionless, waiting; finally it came over to Tortha Karf's chair and stopped. He unhooked the phone and held a lengthy whispered conversation with somebody before replacing it.

"Now, there," he explained to Dalla. "That's a sample of why we have to set up this duplicate organization. Revolution just broke out at Ftanna, on Third Level Tsorshay Sector; a lot of our people, mostly tourists and students, are cut off from their conveyers by street fighting. Going to be a pretty bloody business getting them out." He finished his drink and got to his feet. "Sit still; I just have to make a few screen-calls. Send the robot for something to eat, Vall. I'll be right back."

www.ingramcontent.com/pod-product-compliance
Lightning Source LLC
Chambersburg PA
CBHW050410260626
47156CB00003B/944